A Book A Day Presents:

Color Theory

Love knows no boundaries

A Book A Day Presents: Color Theory Foreword

Reading books has always been my escape. The journey I took when the world seemed to be closing in on me.

Ed Lofton, my grandfather, taught me as a child that words without action are meaningless, but action without words is confusing. Or in layman's terms, put your money where your mouth is.

Has something ever awakened you in the middle of the night? Where you pop up in the midst of sheets, pillows, Kindles, phones, iPads, and crumbs along with whatever other items seem to find their way into your bed? Your mind is all sleepy stupor but an idea has just popped in your drowsy psyche, from nowhere, seemingly for no reason. Well yeah, that happened to me about a year ago and-*A Book A Day Presents: Color Theory* was born. Perhaps, I should give a little background first to explain how that idea even found its way into my innermost thought process at zero-dark thirty in the morning.

Growing up in the racial divide of the South in the 60s and 70s, I had two things going for me. My love of reading and a big mouth (the big mouth part doesn't pay off until later, just stick with me here). Also, being the only Black child in an all-white school in Arkansas in the 60s, using that big mouth was not going to be to my advantage. I suffered enough disparity without adding my words of wisdom to the list of disadvantages piled before me. So silently I read. And read and read until 58 years later…

My reading had become more than an escape to entertain a disenfranchised Black girl in the South. It was now a passion, my therapy, and as necessary to me as the air we breathe. And that mouth, it just got louder and louder. But this time they were not the ramblings of a child, but the voice of a woman who has survived and gone through hell to be who she is today. Strong. Determined. Fierce. Loyal. Honest. Truthful.

That earlier me was raised by my grandparents. They were sharecroppers who had little money or material things, but gave me the best moral compass in which to live this life.

"To whom much is given, much is expected," Margaret Lofton, my grandmother, would say to me on a daily basis, along with others such as, "As long as you can read, you can do anything." "Nothing beats a failure but a try." "You aren't any better than anyone, but no one is better than you."

Her words and wisdom resonate with me every single day of my life.

My grandparents were realistic in the battles they told me I would face in this world: That my Blackness would not always seem beautiful to everyone. That I would be hated and mistreated because of it. That the color of my skin would overrule the content of my character.

So, now we are back to that mouth. The mouth that learned to shout to the world, "My Black is
Beautiful." The mouth that speaks out against racism, systemic and otherwise. The mouth that cries out, "don't murder my sons, daughters, nieces, nephews, or anyone whose skin-compares to the darkness of my hue." The mouth that screams for equality. The mouth that will never be quiet as long as my skin is seen as a weapon, and a possible reason for death.

But I still wasn't ready to put the action behind the words. Though I had traveled the world as a military spouse or lived in one of the most diverse cities in the country. Though my daughter is biracial. Though my "kids" are a rainbow coalition. Though I learned to successfully navigate myself in a world that still didn't totally accept me. I still hadn't had the rude awakening like I did a year ago in the middle of the night.

It all started when my sons bought me a Kindle. This little reading apparatus prevented me from carrying around four or five books at a time. I suddenly had thousands, no millions of words at my fingertip at any given point and time. That Kindle led to a community I affectionately call Bookverse.

A community of "my" people. A community of people who understands my needs for words. A community of people where the color of my skin was irrelevant.

And that's where I discovered another depth to my voice. That voice has the ability to tell authors what works and doesn't work in their stories. That voice teaches white authors how to write Black characters. That voice could be open and honest about who I am as a Black woman, how I feel about the racism in this country and more importantly, how it affects me.

But my grandfather's words were always coming back to me—words without action, action without words.

And then in the middle of the night a year ago, during my mind's slumber I got the wake-up call. Like a force to be reckoned with! It said, "Take what you love and mix in who you are." Reading and a Black woman. Make that your action.

And so, in finding another layer to my voice, I was off on a mission to find authors who would walk this road with me. That could also see the vision of my actions. And they answered the call. From every corner of the US and countries outside our boundaries. They brought stories with realism no matter how painful, with truth no matter how ugly, with honesty no matter how brutal, and with unconditional love no matter how hard. And always, always an HEA.

A Book A Day Presents: Color Theory. The marriage of voice and action. The coming together of diversity and love.

Coming from a family of educators, with both my son and daughter-in-law in the educational field, I could think of no better project, no greater venture that providing assistance to the college education of Black students.
A Book A Day is teaming with a local organization in my hometown of San Antonio to provide scholarships to Black students that wish to expand their education beyond high school. Having the means to help prepare students of today for the world tomorrow fills my heart with unbiased joy.

Readers and Bookverse Community, the English language does not possess enough words to thank you for your love, support, stepping up, and dedication to this project. My eyes are filled with tears of thankfulness and my heart overflows with gratitude.

Much Love. Be Blessed

17 Exclusive ALL-NEW romance stories by bestselling authors about couples who defy convention and follow their hearts.

These stories are all brand new and only available in this box set!

Love is blind, but it's never easy. *A Book a Day Presents: Color Theory* is a collection of stories about love that is determined not by the color of one's skin, but by the connection of two hearts. They face challenges, but together they not only overcome—but soar. These couples know the color of one's skin can't determine who a person loves. Love is so much more.

This amazing anthology will only be available for a short time, and all the proceeds will go to the education of students of color.

A.M. KusiFight With Me
A new adult, second chance, BMWF story taking place in Boston, MA. She works in HR for the company he's been hired to consult as the diversity expert. A second chance romance.

Anne WelchOnly Owen
WMBF Sometimes, things aren't as they seem. When Deja and Owen discover this, can they find a way to heal their broken hearts and make the life together they always should have had?

Arden AoideThrough A Glass Darkly
Orion hunts for lost and hidden stars through the farthest reaches of space and time. Then the Universe offers him the heart of the most beautiful one.

Blair Babylon Ten Most Eligible Lords

"The Right Honorable Christopher "Kit" Somerset, the Viscount Greenwood, is perhaps the most elusive aristocrat on our list of the Ten Most Eligible Lords in England. He's dodged titled ladies, well-endowed heiresses, and coffee baristas for years. Highly enjoyable for an evening, but don't expect to become Lady Greenwood." Because his heart has always belonged to Simone

Carmen Cook   Coming to Sapphire Creek

Deanna Chase works hard. As a single mom, she takes her responsibilities seriously...except that one night she escaped reality in the strong arms of a stranger. Sebastian Dunn is out of the Army and ready to settle down into a quiet life in a small town. But he has one more mission to run. To find out if the sparks he felt all those years ago were just a one time thing, or if he can convince Deanna to take a chance on love.

CA Miconi Majoring in Love

A coming of age love story set in a southern university in 1975.

Danielle Pearl Saving Us

Remy Goodman has spent months looking forward to her summer before college, but when her plans are destroyed before graduation, she is at an absolute loss. Her goal is to make it through these few months under the radar, but Jacob Canon is the new head lifeguard at work—and her boss— and he's about to complicate everything.

Eden Butler Love Jones

Set in New Orleans, ten years ago. Once high school sweethearts reunite to see if the spark between them is still flickering. (Spoiler: It. So. Is.)

Elizabeth Marx You've Got the Love

Romance author Flannery Flame wrote the bestselling memoir *You've Got the Love,* but she lost it all in an accident that stole her reasons to live. Ex-football player Rand Collins has taken the knee for a principal before, leaving his reputation decimated. The second Rand touches Flame she sets him on fire, but he wonders if he should pass on this lost cause or if she's a Hail Mary play.

Janet A. Mota My Love, My Life, You
A best friends to lovers romance. They have been best friends for years with underlying feelings for each other. They decide to throw caution to the wind and try out a relationship.

Kenna Rey Queen of the Dark
 Retired Special Forces agent, Nadia, is not as retired as she claims. She owns a fashion house, Queen of the Dark, by day, and at night, she and a team of women work for a top-secret government agency. But a secret from her boyfriend, Claud, changes every hesitation she has dreamed up.

Lori Ryan Sienna Sentinel
Lori Ryan brings heart-stopping suspense and heart-warming romance with this story set in her upcoming HALO Security series. Bodyguard Boon Montgomery hasn't seen his childhood friend, Sienna Evans, in more than a decade, but that doesn't mean he ever stopped thinking of her. And it sure doesn't mean he's not going to do all he can to keep her safe now she's in the crosshairs of a bigot who looks ready to take his anger at the world out on Sienna.

M. Jane Colette Pacing
When his stepfather asks Akin for dating advice, Akin sets him up with the hot redhead at the bar… only to fall for her, hard, himself. (Hijinks ensue. Hot but also funny.)

Piper Rayne Tropical Hat Trick
Set at a tropical resort, NHL teammates are down there for one of their fellow players' weddings, and a vacation fling with a girl turns into so much more.

Shannon Bruno In the Light

WFBM romance and mystery set in New York City during the World's Fair in 1939. Iris finds herself embroiled in the mystery her ailing boss was trying to solve; but being this close to handsome (and distracting) Oscar Davies he becomes a force she can't ignore- even when their lives are in danger.

Sierra Hill Above the Rim
In this college sports romance, Tra'Von Matthews is a sophomore leading scorer on his basketball team. The game changes for him the night he meets Olivia Peterson after a wardrobe malfunction has her stuck in his bathroom at a frat party. Olivia soon learns not all superheroes wear costumes. Some are simply heroes through their actions to protect those they love.

Willow Aster Peace
Brienne serves as the queen's guard and has always put her own desires last. She prefers it that way—it's easier and safer. But when she meets Silas, love turns her life upside down and she discovers she enjoys the trouble. (WFBM)

A Book A Day Presents: Color Theory Acknowledgments

When I set out to produce this anthology I had no idea what I was doing. I knew where I wanted to go, but getting there was going to be the issue, or so I thought. Pushing through Covid and 2020 with determination and fortitude, people stepped up and showed me.

Authors have always been my rock stars! Your ability to take twenty-six letters and some punctuation to create worlds, families, and characters that stay with me a lifetime astounds me. The idea that the seventeen of you chose to create those worlds and characters in A Book A Day Presents: Color Theory renders me speechless but beyond grateful. Thank you is not enough, but perhaps the five stars I give each of you will display my gratitude.

Ruth A.Cardello, you are my sounding board, my voice of reason, and the person who can talk me off the edge. Without you there is no A Book A Day. There is no Renita in Bookverse. My love for you flows like the River Jordan. Thank you for always being there, believing in me and encouraging me even through the rough days.

Chelle Bliss, my babygirl, what can I say about us? You encourage me, cuss me, and make me want to choke you. But you make me a better and more patient person, and I love you for it. Thank you for telling me I could do this even when I doubted myself. I hope I make you proud.

My editing partner, my sidekick, and the bossiest person I know. Curtis Evans, you are the reason I stay on track. Thanks for always being that thorn in my side. The one that makes me do what I need, when I need. You make me work harder, better, and help to keep me organized. You're simply the best.

Karen Lawson, my book sister. Friend is not a strong enough word to define us. We are certainly proof that opposites attract. You are my confidant and I think you are the best copy/line editor around. Thank you for always squeezing my words in. Even at the last minute.

Danielle Sanchez and Wildfire Marketing, thank you so much for donating your PR services.
For spreading the word and listening to me whine. This project would have fallen flat without you telling me I could do it.

Regina Wamba, girl that cover! It's all that, but so are you! Thank you for working tirelessly with me. Especially since I had no clue who or what I was doing. Your donation of this cover set it off!

Yolanda Harrison McGee, thank you for doing a proof on the stories. I love you hard and I am so glad Bookverse brought us together.

To my sons, Lamontre and Brandon, you are my reasons. You have given each day a purpose and a meaning. My inspiration has always been sealed in the idea of making you proud. To my daughter, Holly, my body may not have birthed you, but my love for you runs as deep as it does for your brothers. You are as just as much mine as they are.

To everyone who helped me in every capacity. Whether it was questions you answered, consistently telling me I could do this, or just that whisper of encouragement, thank you, thank you, thank you.

Bookverse, what can I say? You are my solace, my safe haven, and there are not enough words to say thank you for always rallying around me. Much love!

Dedication

Ed and Margaret Lofton, Granddaddy and Grandmama, this book is dedicated to you. Though you are no longer on this earth, I am who I am because you were who you were. Thank you for giving me the foundation in which to grow and build. Your light still shines bright in my every move. I love you with all I have and all I am. I hope when you look down on me, your heart fills with pride, because when I look up at you my heart fills with thanks.

Table of Contents

FIGHT WITH ME

A.M. Kusi

Published by A. M. Kusi 2021
amkusinovels@gmail.com
Visit our website at www.amkusi.com
Editor: Anna Bishop of CREATING ink
Sensitivity Edit: Renita McKinney of A Book A Day
Proofreader: Judy's Proofreading

Chapter 1

Cory

Cory Stone flipped through his files, double checking everything he needed to go over in this meeting. If he could get August Healthcare as a client, his income would be set for the next year at least. Stability was something he'd never take for granted. Being able to make the workplace—and by default, the world—a little better, was the icing on the cake. *Everything I put on the line five months ago is riding on this deal.*

"Mr. Stone?" a blond woman asked as she entered the waiting room.

He tucked the folder into the briefcase and stood. "Yes?"

"The board is ready to see you now." She motioned to the frosted-glass door in the corner of the room. He straightened his shoulders and twisted the knob before pushing the door open.

Here goes everything.

Seven sets of eyes turned towards him as he entered.

"Hello."

"You must be Mr. Stone. Thank you so much for meeting with us today." The greying man at the end of the table said, standing and offering his hand to shake.

"Yes, sir, I am." Cory returned the gesture.

"I'm Rick Langdon, CEO of this fine company." He motioned to the others. "Take a seat and I'll introduce everyone around the table."

Cory sat, pulling out his files.

1

A.M. Kusi

"This is our Diversity and Inclusion Officer, Jamal Lee. He's the reason you're here today." Jamal, the only Black man in the room besides Cory, nodded with a smile. It was nice to put a face to the e-mails he'd exchanged back and forth for the last couple weeks.

"Our Head of Marketing, Tom Bradford. Next to him is the Director of Healthcare Services, Jack Huxley. Then, our CFO, Brad Russo," Mr. Langdon introduced the men.

Cory nodded to each of them, trying to remember their names.

"Director of Mobile Health Services is Stanley Smith, and next to him is our Director of Women's Healthcare Initiative, Joanne Rice."

One Black man, five white men, and one woman. It was his job to keep track of these details; that was why he was here, after all.

"Where is your Head of Human Resources?" Cory asked. This was the person he'd work with more closely than all the others to enact change.

"She is running a little late—" Joanna explained as the door burst open.

The woman entering had a stack of papers in front of her, but the moment she spoke, the blood in Cory's veins froze.

"So sorry I'm late. The copy machine was on the fritz again, and I wanted to have all the information we needed." She set the mound of paperwork in the only empty spot at the table, next to him, before looking up. The quick intake of air had everyone's attention on her. Something he knew she hated.

"Here she is. Mr. Stone, this is Brittany Morse, our new Director of HR." Mr. Langdon said as if Cory's whole world hadn't been shaken off its axis.

Brittany Morse. His ex-girlfriend of six months. The only woman he'd ever loved. The one who'd broken his heart. Cory's lungs squeezed painfully. Conflicting emotions splintered through him.

"Cory? I—I mean, Mister Stone. It's . . . nice to see you." She bit her bottom lip, a tell that she was nervous. The shock melted in his body, morphing to anger. Had she planned this?

No. Mr. Lee had been the one to reach out to him. And, based on his last conversation with Brittany, she'd be the last person to call a consultant for diversity and inclusion to the company she worked for.

Her sweet scent drifted over him, triggering countless memories of being tangled around her, tasting her flesh, breathing her in. He fisted his hand under the table and grit his teeth. "Miss Morse."

She blinked and looked away, her shoulders dropping with the action. His heart raced as the CEO handed the conversation off to Jamal. Cory tried to pay attention and not think of the beautiful woman next to him who he knew so intimately. Her auburn hair was shorter than it used to be, cut above her shoulders. Her golden-brown eyes focused intently on the man speaking, like Cory's should be. But the frantic pulsing in her throat told him she was just as affected by this reunion as he was.

"I'm excited to hear what your initial assessment of the company is, Mr. Stone," Jamal finished.

Cory's gaze snapped back to the man he hadn't been paying attention to. Hot anger burned his flesh. Brittany had always been a distraction; that was probably why he'd ignored the signs for so long. *Until I couldn't.*

"I'm happy to be here. First, let me start by telling you a little bit about who I am and what I do for companies such as yours. As a Diversity and Inclusivity Consultant, I'll be working closely with you, the board, to ensure that any change needed happens from the top down. Because when a board tracks performance, its corporation gets in line." Cory stood, needing space from Brittany so he could think straight.

"I will work with your departments to develop and execute strategies to help meet *your* company goals and foster a relationship of equal employment opportunities. I'll help you stay aware of relevant legislation in regards to this topic, and aid you in creating a channel to source a variety of candidates of women and minorities qualified for job openings."

Mr. Langdon nodded before Cory continued explaining why functional integration was so important and the roles he'd play within the company.

"Now, from the documents I was sent by Mr. Lee, and my own observations in this very boardroom, I can see you need some improvement if you want to transform your company to be one of inclusion."

Mr. Langdon's brows drew together. "How so? I looked at the records and it says twenty percent of our staff is a minority and women."

Cory pulled out a sheet of paper from his file and passed it over to the CEO. "Yes, but those employees are all in lower-level positions, such as janitorial staff, assistants, and secretaries."

The CEO's blue eyes searched the faces around him. "But Mr. Lee here is a Bla—an African American. And we have Mrs. Rice and Miss Morse as women in leadership positions."

Cory sat back down, turning to face the man. "Yes, you have a Black man in the role of Director of Diversity and Inclusion, and a woman as Head of Women's Services. Both are stereotypically positions where you have to include the person affected by the policies. I commend you for taking those steps; not all companies do. But we are not here for you to meet a certain quota."

"We aren't?" Mr. Langdon asked.

Cory shook his head. "We're here to strategize how to make this company grow by utilizing a diverse culture that promotes inclusivity. By joining the unique strengths that everyone can bring to the table."

"I don't think we've had anyone apply for higher positions that were qualified. Are you saying I should give up a position to someone less qualified simply because they are African American or a woman?" Mr. Langdon asked.

"We have," Brittany said, her voice wavering.

Everyone's attention darted to her. She bit her lip. Her hand trembled as she raised it to flick through the pages in front of her. If they were still dating, this was when he'd do something to draw the attention away from her, knowing her social anxiety was piquing. But he wasn't her boyfriend anymore.

"What do you mean, Miss Morse?" Cory asked.

She swallowed and shifted in her seat before going through the color-coded stack of paperwork in front of her. She stood, passing out a copy to everyone and then sat. "I've gone through the applications and hiring decisions for the last year. As you can see, in the red tabs, there were several candidates who applied with equal or greater qualifications than their white male counterparts. But only two were hired, and that was Mister Lee and myself."

"But it says here there were six doctors hired, half were women and four out of six were non-white," Mr. Langdon pointed out.

Brittany's face flushed red. "Those were in the last four months after we enacted some changes in the HR department."

Since she started working here. "You hired those people?" Cory asked her.

Her gaze flicked to his. "Yes."

His stomach flipped and knotted. Was this her trying to prove something to him? Was this her way of redeeming the choices that had made them break up in the first place? Well, it was too late.

"It seems I have a lot to consider," Mr. Langdon said.

"I've compiled a list of some basic changes and strategies you and your board can start implementing in the company to ensure a fair chance is given for inclusion if you choose to hire my services and bring me on board." Cory handed the man the laminated document he'd stayed up all night perfecting.

Mr. Langdon stood and shook his hand.

Brittany turned to him, her full lips parting as if she wanted to say something.

"Mr. Stone, could I run a few questions by you?" Jamal asked.

Cory turned his attention to the man. "Of course."

He peeked over Jamal's shoulder. The disappointment and uncertainty in Brittany's expression shifted into one of resignation. She picked up the stack of paperwork that was left in front of her and headed towards the main offices. The younger blond man, Tom Bradford, opened the door for her. She smiled at him but it didn't reach her eyes. He placed his hand on her lower back, guiding her out the door and out of Cory's life once again. Jealousy slicked up his spine. He had no right to her anymore. But that didn't matter to his shattered heart. He'd just been beginning to pick up the pieces, throwing himself into his work. And now here she was, front and center in his life. If he got this contract he'd have to work with her the most. And his fucking heart couldn't take it.

Chapter 2

Brittany

Brittany shut the door to her office with her foot, closing off the prying eyes of any of her coworkers. She set down the stack of paperwork on her otherwise organized desk and lifted her trembling hands to her flushed face. *Holy shit. It was him.* She blinked away the tears that stung the back of her eyes. After six months of no contact, he was the last person she'd expected to run into today. She closed her eyes, taking a steadying breath. Flashes of their last argument spun her up. The betrayal etched across the dark ridges of his expression. The hurt in his eyes. Her stomach rolled. She'd do anything to make peace with him. She'd tried for a solid six weeks, but he'd ghosted her. Never given her a chance. *Did he ever really love me? If he could just walk out the door and never even respond to my phone calls or messages?*

She'd just wanted to apologize. She'd taken it upon herself to understand what he'd been so upset about that night. She regretted her ignorance. Guilt had weighed her shoulders down. But he'd just snapped, never giving her the chance to communicate.

Brittany turned to grab her bottle of water on her desk and froze. All six feet of the man she still loved walked through her doorway and stood in front of her. His button up shirt strained across the width of his broad shoulders, taut with tension. His dark eyes were devoid of all emotion but one—anger.

He tucked a stray loc behind his ear. "What the hell was that?"

A.M. Kusi

Chapter 3

Cory

"W-what do you mean?" Brittany stammered.

Cory stepped forward, the stack of books on the shelf catching his eye. *So You Want to Talk About Race, How To Be An Antiracist* and several other similar titles focusing on racism in the workplace adorned her shelf.

He shook his head. Nothing was adding up. He motioned to the books. "You read a couple books and now you're woke? You think this changes what happened?"

She took a tentative step towards him, her hand reaching out and then dropping to her side, like she thought better of it. "No, Cory. That's not what I think. I've done a lot of learning since . . . everything happened. I'm just trying to educate myself so I won't . . . hurt anyone else the way I hurt you."

The sincerity that flashed in her watery brown eyes was like a bolt of lightning to his system. His instinct was to reach out and wipe the tears away before they could fall. To comfort her. Everything was swirling in his head. Confusion between what he was seeing and what he knew about her. Attraction that only seemed fueled by distance. Hope that this was real. And shame for how he'd left things between them.

Her breathing came faster—too quick. She turned away from him, facing the window and the view of the city down below. Her hand settled on her chest. He shook his head, lowering his eyes. *Fuck.* The scene during the meeting mixed with their reunion must have been too much for her, triggering Brittany's anxiety.

He searched her desk. "Where is your bag?"

"D-desk drawer, left side."

He opened the cabinet, finding the black leather bag he'd gotten her for Christmas. His heart lurched as unwelcome memories of happier times flooded through his mind. Cory opened it, finding the glass bottle he needed and brought it over to her.

"Open your mouth." He unscrewed the cap and brought the dropper to her tongue.

"The whole thing?" he asked.

She gave a slight nod. The herbal scent of the CBD oil grew pungent as he emptied it into her mouth. He put it away and then, on instinct, pulled her against his chest. Her body trembled, and her breathing was still too erratic.

Worry tangled in his gut. He lifted her hand in his, and started slow dancing like he used to do to help calm her. Back and forth. Palm against palm, his fingers intertwined with hers. The contact of her skin against his sent a jolt of awareness and longing clamoring through him. Even though his mind told him to run, he held her so that she could get through her anxiety attack.

Several minutes later, her breath evened out. Her head lifted from his chest. "Thank you."

She licked her lips, drawing his attention to them. God, he wanted to taste her once more. To steal one last kiss before their worlds separated again. They were so different, and yet so much the same. He knew her body better than he knew his own. A mixture of arousal and hope gleamed in her eyes as he squeezed her tighter, holding on to what they shared just a little bit longer. A cord cinched tight, drawing him to her as if whatever they had between them was inescapable. She shivered. Her hot breath whispered across his lips, digging into his soul and taking root. Her scent was both drugging and damning. He tucked a stray strand of hair behind her ear.

"Can we talk over dinner?" she asked.

A cold jolt of reality shot through him. He couldn't risk the heartbreak. It almost broke him to walk away from her once. If he had to do it again, it would destroy him. They were too different. They came from opposite worlds, and nothing made that clearer than the conflicting color of her fair skin against his dark brown. Something would happen again, and it would tear them apart eventually.

No. He needed to push her away for good this time.

"So you think we can just pick up the pieces where we left off because you've read a few books?"

Hurt reflected in her eyes. "That's not—"

He dropped his arms to his side and stepped away. "It doesn't matter. This can't be fixed. If I see you again here, pretend we were never together. We'll keep it strictly professional."

"I'm sorry, Cory—"

"The damage has already been done."

Chapter 4

Cory

The next two weeks went by in a blur. A dark shadow seemed to follow him around. He got the job with August Healthcare. But he'd been too harsh with Brittany. His anger had won out. He pulled out his phone, searching her name on social media. *Out of curiosity.* It was perfectly normal to check out your ex's social media profile if it was set to public. He settled into the chair to wait for his friends. Low hanging lights gave the restaurant a warm glow. Outside men and women hurried along on their commute home from work. Several couples walked past hand in hand, on their way to spend the evening together no doubt. *Will I ever have that?* He focused his attention back on his cell and scrolled through Brittany's posts. She'd been sharing almost completely about the current events taking place. She was pushing for police reform, Black Lives Matter, and similar posts admitting her own bias.

Is this because of me? Or because this is what's popular to talk about right now?

He clicked on the comments for one post. Her uncle had responded, *All lives matter!*

He laughed when he read her response.

Brittany: *They will once Black lives (and other minorities) do.*

Pete: *What about blue lives?*

Brittany: *There is no such thing as a blue life. But if you have no problem saying 'blue lives matter,' and 'all lives matter,' then the real issue you have is the word Black. What do you think that means?*

Cory exited out of the app and set his phone on the table. *Maybe she is getting it.*

"Did you order without me?" a familiar voice said, and Cory looked up from the square wooden table. Dre slid into the seat across from him. Another man slipped in beside him.

"Hey, Dre." Cory reached out and fist-bumped his cousin. "Mikel." He repeated the gesture for his other cousin.

"How are you doing?" Andre asked.

"Pretty good. How's family life treating you two?"

Andre smiled. "The best."

"How is Mia doing with the pregnancy?"

The waitress interrupted, taking their drink and meal order. When she left, Andre answered, "Mia's enjoying the second trimester now that she can hold food down. She and Remy are shopping for baby items. Taking full advantage of this trip to the city."

Mikel chuckled. "And my kids are with their grandparents and probably getting spoiled rotten."

Cory laughed. "I'm sure Aunty Tilda and Uncle Matt are enjoying it just as much as them."

A familiar figure walked across the room on the other side of the restaurant led by one of the waitresses. *Brittany.* She looked better than she had the other day, and that was saying something. Hair he wanted to tangle his fingers in, a body he yearned to touch...She walked over to a table with a man he didn't recognize. The man pulled out her chair for her before sitting across from her. *Fuck. She was on a date.*

His fists clenched and he ground his teeth together.

Andre's head swiveled around to look over his shoulder, recognition flashing in his eyes when he faced him again. "Isn't that Brittany?"

Cory focused back on his hands. "Yup."

The waitress delivered their drinks. "It will be a few more minutes for your meals."

"Thanks," Mikel said, before taking a sip of his cola.

Cory grabbed the beer he'd ordered and drained half of

it.

"What happened between you two?" Andre asked, sitting forward.

"Yeah, you guys seemed so good together," Mikel added.

Cory shook his head and sighed. He ran a hand over his face. He hadn't told anyone about that night, but if anyone would understand it would be these two. "We went to dinner with her friends. One of them made an ignorant comment. They kept asking me shit like if I liked watermelon. And when the waitress came to take our order, one guy thought he'd be funny and order me fried chicken. It went downhill from there. One girl reached out to touch my dreads. And then I heard one of the others ask Brittany about my dick size, and if the rumors really are true."

"What the fuck?" Mikel asked.

"What did Brittany say?" Andre asked.

"She laughed about the chicken joke." *Though it was her nervous laughter.* "She defended the personal space invader by saying the girl was just curious. And then she brushed off the sexual comments saying that was too personal."

Andre and Mikel both shook their heads.

"Did you talk to her about it after?" Andre asked.

Cory took another gulp of beer, eyeing Brittany over his cousin's shoulder. Jealousy lit him up. "Sort of."

"What the hell does that mean?" Mikel asked.

"I had a lot going on at the time, you know. I was just passed over for that promotion I'd worked my ass off for. The police killings were all over the media, and all I could think about was how fucking frustrating it was that I had to fear for my life constantly and these idiots were laughing about the stereotypes that have been pushed on us. They don't even see how they are part of the problem. Having my own girlfriend not stand up and say something, but also defend them, made me see red. I yelled at her and called her a racist and stormed out of her apartment."

His buddies stayed silent with wide eyes, as if they needed a minute to take it all in.

"That was a shitty thing for her to do," Mikel said.

"Yup." Cory drained the rest of his beer.

"But you acted like an asshole too." Mikel added.

Cory coughed, choking on his drink. "What? You're taking her side?"

Mikel shook his head. "I'm just saying you both screwed up. I know better than most about what challenges an interracial couple face. I'm white, my wife is Black, and our children are brown. We have the world telling us we're different, that we shouldn't mix. Both with their stares or side-eyes when we go out in public, and sometimes verbally. We face more adversity than a couple who stays within their race, which is why communication is paramount."

"He's right, bro," Andre agreed. "Mia and I sucked at communicating in the beginning, but we had to set our egos aside and be willing to sit in the uncomfortableness. We had to both learn to listen to each other and try to see where the other was coming from. Not that we had to agree, but empathize. Understanding each other helped us to educate one another about our different cultures and histories."

"It's hard for us white people to fully grasp the extent of how much racism affects other races. We don't see it because it doesn't affect us. We've been taught this is normal. Not that this is an excuse. I'm just trying to explain that accepting that most of what we've been taught is a lie is terrifying." Mikel took a sip of his drink and shook his head before continuing, "I won't ever fully grasp what it is to be Black, and face what you, my wife, Dre, or my brown kids will face. But by being with Remy I get a sneak peek into the microaggressions, the prejudice, fear, and other challenges you face on a daily basis. I'm ashamed to admit I didn't see a lot of it until Remy pointed it out to me, or Dre. Especially when it comes to running our construction business." Mikel motioned to Andre.

The waitress dropped off their food, but Cory wasn't hungry anymore.

Andre took a drink and motioned behind himself. "If Brittany really loves you, she'd be willing to listen, and educate herself on the true history that so many don't know because it isn't taught. And the way that woman looked at you when you brought her to Shattered Cove? Man, I thought she'd propose to you before you could get the chance." He chuckled.

She has been learning. She's been educating herself. Without him in her life, she'd been putting in the hard work.

Why could he give his clients such grace, but not the woman he loved?

"She's gonna have to unlearn a whole lot of shit that's been ingrained in her. If you wanna be with a white woman, as long as she is putting in the work, you gotta be more compassionate and patient with her."

Brittany laughed, presumably at something her date had said. Her whole face lit up. A pang of guilt flitted through him. He'd treated her horribly in his anger. Though he'd had every right to be upset, he should have handled it better.

Another man approached her table—Brittany's brother. The man across from Brittany stood, giving her brother, Paul, a kiss on the mouth. Cory's shoulders relaxed. Brittany was out to dinner with her brother and *his* boyfriend. *Not a date.*

But someday soon, someone would come and win her heart. Cory needed to make a choice. Was the love he and Brittany shared worth fighting for? Could they forgive each other for the hurt they'd each caused? Could they face the challenges of being an interracial couple and make it work? Were they doomed to fail from the beginning?

His chest squeezed tight as she laughed again at something her brother said. The space between their tables seeming far more distant than the length of a restaurant. They had so much to overcome to make this work.

Maybe was it too late for them after all.

Chapter 5

Brittany

Brittany shuffled the paperwork around on her desk. She had everything color-coded and arranged in the most logical order in anticipation of Cory's arrival. Today was his first day consulting with August Healthcare, and of course, she'd run into him this morning when he'd needed some documents from her department.

She ran a hand through her reddish-brown curls, taking a deep breath. She lifted her water bottle and took a sip. The familiar herbing taste of her CBD oil calmed her. She'd at least had the forethought to take it in advance, as today promised to be stressful. She didn't need another embarrassing moment like the one previously. *I don't need his pity.* That was all those brief moments of kindness he'd shown her were—sympathy-driven, as a man like him was meant to do. She'd hurt him so badly, and yet he'd still taken care of her when she'd broken down in front of him.

Knock. Knock.

Damn. He was here.

She inhaled a shaky breath, steeling herself. Begging her body not to spark alive and betray her.

Brittany opened the door, trying not to let her eyes linger too long on the other half of her heart she still hadn't gotten back.

The corner of his mouth turned up, like it did when he was nervous. He stepped into her office, holding out one of the cardboard coffee containers to her.

"I bought you a caramel latte—decaf, of course."

Her favorite. *A peace offering?* She accepted the gift with a smile. "Thank you." She motioned to the empty seat across her desk. "Please make yourself comfortable. I have out all the documentation I thought you'd need."

Brittany went around to her side of the desk and took a seat opposite him. She sipped the coffee, enjoying the sweet and earthy notes blending together. Setting her cup down, she refocused her attention on him. His gaze locked onto her desk. She turned, finding what had caught his attention. Her copy of *A People's History of the United States* was on the side table where she'd left it yesterday after her lunch break.

"Sorry." She grabbed the book, and tucked it into a drawer, out of sight. Heat rose to her cheeks, no doubt leaving a rosy blush—the curse of her fair-skinned ancestors.

"You don't have to be sorry," he said.

Her gaze snapped to his.

"I was wrong to go off on you about the books. How hypocritical is it for me to be a Diversity and Inclusion Consultant, helping companies educate themselves and change policies, if I get mad at you for doing the same thing? It's good, and I'm sorry I allowed what happened in the past to cloud my judgment of now."

Brittany blinked, stunned. This was her chance to apologize and at least make the peace between them that she'd wanted.

"Cory, I need to—"

"Well, well, what do we have here? I didn't know you'd be in today," Tom said as he walked into her still open door.

Cory turned and nodded. "First day."

Tom's gaze swept between her and Cory. She grit her teeth. He was always finding a way to just *drop in* or touch her—a gentle brush of the shoulders in the hall, or a lingering hand on her back as she exited a room. It made her skin crawl.

"Brittany, *honey*, why don't you go get us a couple

coffees and let the men handle the hard lifting? I'm sure Mr. Stone here would rather have someone a little more knowledgeable about the company and policies to work with," Tom said, walking over to her chair like he expected her to get up and obey him.

Anger burned her skin. He'd made passing comments before, but Tom had never been so bold about his harassment. *Must be because I turned down his request for a date—for the second time.*

"Actually, I think I can handle my job. That's why they chose me to be head of this department, after all. If we need something regarding marketing, you can be sure we'll let you know." Her stomach churned and her neck burned under his stupefied stare, but she kept her voice even. "Oh, please close the door on your way out. We don't need any more disturbances. Thanks." She waved him away dismissively.

Tom turned to Cory, as if asking for backup. Cory smirked, a glint of mischief in his eyes. "I can see we have a lot to work on when it comes to appropriate behavior in the workplace relating to sexism. You can be sure we'll be talking soon, Mr. Bradford."

Tom nodded, his face flushing as he turned to leave.

"Oh, you know there is one thing you could get together for me," Cory said, halting Tom's exit.

"What's that?" Tom asked warily.

"I'd like the details on every sales campaign and market research activity you've undertaken since you started working here."

"But that's seven years' worth," Tom protested.

"Then it's a good thing you can handle the heavy lifting." Cory chuckled.

"Sure thing." Tom's shoulders straightened before he walked out of the room, and the door snicked softly closed as he left.

"Is he always such a dick?" Cory asked, breaking the silence.

She laughed. "Only when his pride has been hurt."

20

Cory's brows creased with concern.

"I can handle him."

He chuckled. "Did you see the look on his face when you told him to close the door behind him?"

She laughed. "What about you? Seven years of data?"

"Should keep him busy for a while and out of your hair." Cory's voice was light, but the meaning punched her in the gut.

He'd protected her. He had always been her advocate. He'd stood by her side while she'd fought her own battles and backed her up when needed. *And when he needed me most, I wasn't there for him.* Thick shame weighed heavily, sinking down over her like lead weights.

"Okay, now that the fun is over, let's get to work," Cory directed, picking up the binder she'd prepared. "I knew you'd have everything organized. You always were type A."

"Unlike you—a fly-by-the-seat-of-your-pants kind of guy." She smiled. The memory of their trip to Peru came to mind. The only thing planned about the adventure was their departure and the return date. She'd left the rest up to him and discovered the man hadn't planned a damn thing. But it had turned out to be the best experience of her life. They'd talked to locals, finding beautiful sights off the beaten path that other tourists didn't know about. They'd stayed in the community and enjoyed their delectable foods. She'd gotten to see the Aztec ruins and drink tea with a shaman.

Her eyes met his, memories flitting between them like he was thinking about the same thing. They'd shared so many good moments. And all it had taken was one night to break them apart. Maybe he was better off without her. She wasn't perfect, and she was sure to mess up again. But every day she learned more. It was overwhelming at times. She'd get sucked into a feeling of hopelessness. What could one person do, after all? The system seemed too big to overcome. If she and Cory couldn't even work it out, what hope was there for an entire country? Or the entire world? But then she'd see the videos on social media, of people out there protesting, the change happening in cities all over the United

States. People like her sharing how wrong they'd been, or how blind they were. Every single day, more and more people were waking up to the injustice of racism and prejudice and ignorance that plagued the nation. It gave her hope.

"Cory?"

"Yeah?"

"Can we . . . I'd really like to clear the air." She swallowed.

He took a deep breath, shaking his head. "No."

Her stomach sank. Rejection squeezed her chest tight.

"Not here," he said.

Does that mean somewhere else? Later?

He'd turned down dinner. Had he changed his mind?

She needed to clear the air, sure, but she couldn't deny that little spark of hope that flamed to life in her chest. What if there was a chance he wanted more? That this thing between them wasn't over? She couldn't push it now—that was clear. But she could wait. For him, she'd wait as long as he needed.

Chapter 6

Brittany

Brittany curled up on the couch, glass of wine in hand. It had been a long week. She'd worked with Cory until Wednesday, and then he'd gone on to different departments. She'd seen him in passing today, talking to a woman in the café downstairs she didn't recognize. She'd been laughing, her hand on his arm—she was obviously smitten with him. *Maybe he's seeing her.* Pain sliced through her chest. It had been six months since he'd walked out that very door she stared at. Since then she'd had one date, and she hadn't even been able to enjoy her dinner. It had felt wrong. The man she had wanted to see across from her had shut her out of his life.

Bzzzzz. Bzzzzz.

Her intercom buzzed. Who could that be?

She sipped her wine as she pressed the button. "Yes?"

"It's Cory. Can I come up?" His voice came through the static.

Her stomach leapt into her throat. Nerves swirled inside her stomach. She couldn't speak. She pressed the other button, holding it a good five seconds so he could enter the building.

She gulped down the rest of her wine and darted to the bathroom to check her appearance. She'd changed into sleep shorts and an off-the-shoulder T-shirt. Brittany ran her fingers through her hair quickly. *Do I have time to put on a bra?*

Knock. Knock.

"Guess not." It wasn't like he hadn't seen her naked

before anyway.

She ran to the door, stumbling over a blanket that had fallen off the couch. "Damn it!"

At least he hadn't seen her clumsy-ass fall.

She made it to the door, taking a deep breath to steady herself before she opened it.

Cory stood there with his hands in his pocket, a sign he might be as nervous as she was.

"Come on in." She motioned inside.

He entered, and she shut the door behind him. His gaze traveled around the room. The last time they were both standing here was the night they fought and he walked out.

"Can I get you anything to drink? I still have that IPA you like."

"Sure." He nodded.

"Make yourself comfortable." She filled her glass with more red wine and grabbed the beer that had tormented her in her fridge for six months. She hadn't been able to get rid of it, clinging onto what little she had left of him. *I'm pathetic. He's probably just coming here to hear my apology and then leave again—but for good this time.*

She turned in her small kitchen, looking over to the open living room in the tiny apartment. Gulping down half her glass, she readied herself. This was her chance. She'd put it all on the table.

Brittany carried their drinks around the couch and handed him his before she took a seat next to him.

They sat in silence for a moment, sipping their alcohol as if they both needed the extra liquid courage.

"This is weird." She laughed nervously, speaking her thoughts aloud. She cringed. *And I just made it worse.*

He set down his beer on the coffee table and turned to face her. His gaze was serious, intent, and filled with pain. "How'd we get here?"

Her eyes flicked down and then back to him. She

placed her glass next to his. "Because I messed up."

He shook his head. "And then I made it worse by shutting you out . . .We were good together, weren't we?"

A flicker of hope brought a flutter to her chest. "I thought so."

"Can we talk about that night?"

She nodded.

"I'd like to explain why I felt . . . the way I felt." He shifted in his seat, seemingly uncomfortable. It had never been easy for him to talk about feelings. It was part of the reason she'd felt so lost at times in their relationship.

"I'm listening."

He ran his hands down his thighs to his knees. "I'd had a really bad day at work. I'd been passed over a promotion that I'd worked my ass off for again. My boss told me I didn't have the right *look* for the company, and the new position would require a lot of face time with the board."

Her heart sunk. "Because of your dreads?"

He nodded. "He stared at my hair as he said it."

"I'm sorry." She wanted to reach out and touch his arm, hold his hand, do something to encourage him. But she held back, she wouldn't risk disrupting this fragile moment.

"Then everything going on in the news, and yet another white woman calling the cops on a Black man for doing absolutely nothing. I was already on edge." He sighed.

"At dinner, all those people saying that shit grated on my nerves. But your reaction—or inaction—it just—it felt like you'd betrayed me. Like when I needed to lean on you, know you had my back, I wasn't even safe with the woman I loved."

Tears sprung to her eyes, falling down her cheeks. "Cory, I'm so sorry. I know those words are not enough. I know what I did hurt you in the worst way. You're right. I should have said something sooner."

"Yes, but *I* know your anxiety is heightened in social situations. Maybe I expected too much."

She shook her head. "No. That's no excuse. At least we could have got up and left."

"After we got back here, I was totally shut down. I saw you as the enemy," Cory admitted.

"I get it. I really was trying to understand. But then you just walked out the door. And you wouldn't answer my calls or texts. I came to your apartment a couple times, but you weren't there."

He nodded. "I took the coward's way out. But I felt justified because of how bad you'd hurt me."

She wiped her tears with her T-shirt. "I've done a lot of reading and learning since you left. I really thought that if I was in a relationship with a Black man, there was no way I could be racist. So, when you called me that, I just—I just got defensive. I thought you were calling me a bad person . . . Now I know how wrong I was. I'm working hard at unlearning my bias, and trying to be antiracist. I understand that there is no neutral ground, especially if I'm in a relationship with a Black man."

"I see that. And I'm proud of you." His gaze flashed with sincerity. "I'm sorry for walking out and ghosting you like that. You deserved better."

His eyes swirled with sincere emotion. She offered him a tentative smile.

"So, where do we go from here?" she asked, her voice shaking.

He turned his attention to his hands and then back to her. "I tried to forget you. To fall out of love with you."

Brittany focused on the tan rug on floor. Her chest squeezed tight, emotion burning the back of her eyes. Pain lanced her heart as she prepared for his final rejection.

A strong hand lifted her chin towards him, forcing her eyes back to his. Cory's touch burned her. Her belly stirred, yearning for more.

"But I couldn't." His voice was coarse like gravel.

He still loves me?

"Am I too late? Have we screwed this up beyond

repair?" Cory asked, vulnerability reflected in his dark eyes.

She shook her head. "No. You're not too late."

Relief flitted through his expression. Wow! Was this really happening? Her joy clouded over with uncertainty. She couldn't lose him over something like this again, and she knew things would be hard—because she would always be learning. But it couldn't be like last time. "We need to make some changes this time. We have to communicate better. Be honest with each other. I need you to be open and share your emotions, even the most difficult ones. Don't let this all build inside you until it erupts onto me."

He nodded. "And you have to keep learning. Keep listening."

"I promise I will."

"If we hang out with your friends again—"

"Half of them are blocked. The other half, like me, are on a path of learning after I had conversations with each of them."

His eyed widened slightly in surprise before a smile lit his face.

"I'm willing to cut people who are hurtful out of my life in order to be a safe person for you."

His forehead dropped to hers. "I promise to be the man you deserve."

"And I promise to be the woman who fights with you."

Soft lips slid against hers, sending a rush of liquid heat thrumming from her womb and traveling to every live nerve ending. Her skin heated, flushed, buzzing with awareness and delicious anticipation. It had been six long months since she'd been kissed like this. Like she was life and death and everything in between.

She wrapped her arms around his neck, pulling him closer. His strong hands grabbed her hips, lifting her and planting her on his lap. He deepened the kiss, swiping his tongue inside her mouth.

She moaned, tasting him. She raked her teeth across his bottom lip, sucking onto it. His grip on her ass tightened. Fingers dug into her skin, no doubt leaving a mark.

Empowered by his desire, she ground herself against his hard cock.

His hand moved to her belly, slipping underneath the loose fabric. He cupped her heavy, sensitive breast. Cory skimmed his thumb over her nipple, already painfully hard with her arousal. She gasped.

"Is this too much?" he asked, panting.

She shook her head. "No. I want you. So much."

He lifted her shirt over her head, tossing it on the floor, baring her from the waist up. His eyes darkened before he slipped his hot mouth over the bud of her breast, sucking. She hissed, grinding against him. Raking her fingernails over his shoulders. Needing more. Craving him. She pulled his shirt off, interrupting the pleasured torture.

"Take it all off," she commanded, getting off his lap. She slipped off her sleep pants, leaving her completely naked. Cory stood, his muscles highlighted in the low light and shadows of her living room from the setting sun. He slipped his boxers off along with his pants. This beautiful man stood before her, bare and breathtaking. She slipped her palm over his hard pec, leaning down to lick his nipple.

He groaned, his hand threading into her hair, tugging her in place. She sucked, raking her teeth across his dark bud as her hand dropped to his hard cock, pumping from tip to root. He sucked in a gasp. Strong fingers wrapped around her wrist, forcing her hand away.

"Not gonna last if you touch me, baby. It's been too long," he said, his voice gruff.

She looked up at him, hoping she didn't have to voice the question.

"Nobody since you." He kissed her forehead as she melted against him.

"Me either."

"So we don't need to use a condom?" he asked.

She nodded. "I have an IUD now."

"Bend over," he commanded.

She did as he said in the small space between the couch and the coffee table.

He knelt behind her and pressed her thighs apart.

"Oh fuck." She gasped as he licked up her slit.

"I'm gonna make you come on my mouth, and you're gonna take it like a good girl, aren't you?"

"Yes!"

He inserted two fingers inside her core, stretching her as he hit that sensitive spot. Pressure built. His hot tongue licked her clit. His thick five o'clock shadow scratched against her thighs, sending a tingling sensation prickling over her skin that burned icy hot.

"Oh god!" she cried as he fucked her with his fingers and tongue in tandem.

"Pinch those nipples for me, baby," he said.

She obeyed. Pleasure tugged her in all directions as she neared the peak.

He licked and swirled and sucked her clit, driving her closer and closer to the edge. Dark spots covered her vision.

"You taste so fucking good. Sweetest pussy I've ever eaten." He hummed, sending her over the edge of the cliff.

She spasmed. Her orgasm rocketed through her. "Cory!"

Her climax only fueled her want. Her pussy ached for him to fill her up. To become one with him after their long separation.

"I need you inside me," she breathed, wild with want, insatiable with need. "Now."

Chapter 7

Cory

Cory lapped at the wet essence that dripped down Brittany's leg. Her knees wobbled, too weak to hold her anymore as she came down from her orgasm. Intoxicated by her taste, he breathed her in.

He stood, reaching out for her hand and helping her to her feet. She wobbled. He pulled her against his body, steadying her.

"I don't think I have bones anymore." She smiled drunkenly. Her expression was relaxed, but her eyes sparked with hunger for more.

"Well it's a good thing I've got one you can have." He smirked.

She smacked his chest playfully. "Sit down."

He settled onto the couch before she climbed over him. He lined himself up at her entrance, sliding over her swollen clit.

She sucked in a breath, her lips parting. He wrapped his hand around her neck and slammed his mouth against hers. They joined, as he drove his cock deep inside her. Their moans and groans mixed into an erotic chorus.

"So hot and tight, baby."

"Just for you," she panted.

"I missed you," he confessed.

"Me too."

He sat back, relaxing against the couch as she rode him. His hands dug into her hips, picking her up and crashing her back down onto his aching cock. Her tits bounced. Her skin glistened with a thin sheen of sweat in the disappearing sun. Oranges and reds glowed across her bare skin like a painting. She was the most beautiful woman he'd ever laid eyes on. A masterpiece.

"You feel so good."

"Yes!" she cried out, another orgasm taking hold as her sex tightened and pulsed around him. She was a gorgeous sight to behold. Her hair, wild and free. Brown amber eyes almost black in the rapture of desire.

"That's it, baby. Take it," he said, his spine tingling at the base, pleasure gathering. His impending release was on the horizon.

"Look at me. I want to see when you come," she said.

His gaze met hers. She writhed with urgency, needy and desperate as she gripped his shoulders and drove down on him. Rocking them together in a sensual dance.

"I love you. Cory!" Her forehead creased as she cried out.

His own release came barreling forward. Pleasure electrified every synapse. He roared as they came, tangled together. He squeezed his arms around her, holding on as euphoria washed over him like warm wave. His seed spilled inside her.

There was no other sound than their bated breaths. Heart against heart. Skin against skin. He kissed her, soft and slow. For the first time in six months, he felt whole.

"I love you too."

This time would be different. They'd face whatever came at them and come out stronger. Because from now on, they would fight together as a unit. Together, they'd be unstoppable.

A.M. Kusi

The End

Other Books by A. M. Kusi

Find out more about Mikel and Remy's story in:
A Fallen Star
 (Book 1 in The Shattered Cove Series)

Or Andre and Mia's story in:
 Glass Secrets
(Book 2 in The Shattered Cove Series)

Defying Gravity
(Book 3 in The Shattered Cove Series)

About A. M. Kusi

A. M. Kusi is the pen name of a wife-and-husband team, Ash and Marcus Kusi. We enjoy writing romance novels that are inspired by our experiences as an interracial/multicultural couple.

Our novels are about strong women and the sexy heroes they fall in love with, are emotionally satisfying, and always have a happy ending.

Happy reading!

Ash and Marcus

ONLY OWEN

By
Anne Welch

Chapter One

"Deja Marie Garrett, I'd better see you next weekend. You have not been home in over a year!" her mom yelled through the phone.

"Mom, it's a high school reunion. Who goes to those anyway? Besides, I am behind on orders at work and I need to catch up."

Deja knew she should make more time to visit her mother, but the thought of going to her hometown did not appeal to her at all. She'd left that place behind ten years ago and hadn't looked back, except for the few times she had popped in to visit her mom. Guilt hit Deja as she padded around her sprawling apartment in the middle of downtown Atlanta. The cosmetic company that she had started after graduating from college had taken off. She was on her way to being a millionaire before she hit thirty.

"Honey, please. I would love to see you," her mom pleaded.

"Okay, Mom. I will come."

"I can't wait to see you. Love you."

"I love you too, Mom."

While Deja was proud of her success, often times she was lonely. She didn't date much, but there was always a special male friend to satisfy her carnal needs. She'd been in love once—head over heels for the quarterback of her high school football team, Owen Walsh. They were going to run away after high school and get married. She loved him with everything in her until he broke her heart. Deja vowed never to let anyone get that close to her again. Before she could change her mind, she went to her closet and pulled out a suitcase. An old shoe box on the top shelf caught her attention.

Crossing her legs under her she sat on the bed and opened the lid, memories came flooding back. Deja and Owen, in the back of his truck watching the stars after prom, sitting in the stands cheering him on as he threw another touchdown. He would find her in the crowd and place his hand over his heart. Making love the first time in a tent by the lake, Owen never pushed her. She had been the one to initiate it, on her seventeenth birthday. The first time was a little awkward. But as time went on, their fire was all consuming. They couldn't get enough of each other.

Owen was over six feet tall, with blonde hair and blue eyes. And he came from money. His dad ran everything in their small town. He looked down on everyone around him, especially a poor black girl from the wrong side of town. With Owen, none of that mattered. He wasn't ashamed of their love and never hid his feelings for her. After they ran off and got married, he wanted to play professional football, and Deja was going to build her cosmetic empire. They wanted a house full of children and had even picked out names. Then it all fell apart in the blink of eye.

Deja slammed the lid back on the shoe box when she saw that check and put it away. That was why she didn't want to go to this damn reunion. Who was she kidding? Part of her always wondered what it would be like to show them who was she was now, a beautiful, strong, successful woman. She called her assistant and had her clear her schedule for a few days. After the guilt trip her mom had laid on her earlier, she would spend an extra few days with her. Once her bags were packed, she ate a light dinner and went to bed. It was a four-hour drive to her mom's, and she wanted to get an early start.

***

"A caramel Frappuccino with a shot of expresso please." Deja placed her order.

Five am was too early to be out driving. Normally, she didn't indulge in these many calories. She preferred to eat healthy. But today, her sweet tooth won. She took a sip of the sweet nectar and exhaled. She made great time and arrived at her mother's house before nine. The scent of bacon reached her before she opened the door. Deja smiled to herself. Every morning, her mom had to have her bacon and coffee.

"Mom, I'm here."

"Deja? I am in the kitchen."

She walked down the hallway to the kitchen, and the photographs on the wall caught her attention. One was of her and Owen, dressed for the senior prom. He wore a black tux with a royal blue bow tie and cummerbund to match her sequined, off the shoulder dress. *Two dumb kids without a clue*, she mumbled to herself. Her mom came around the counter and pulled her into a bear hug. It felt so good to be in her mother's arms again. Deja chastised herself for staying away so long.

"Beautiful as ever, but you are a little skinny. Here, sit down and eat."

"Well, you look great, Mom," Deja replied before eating a strip of the tasty meat.

Deja cleaned up the dishes and helped her mom with a few things around the house. Her mom did look good, but there was a sadness in her eyes. She would get to the bottom of that before she went back to Atlanta. Her phone rang and she excused herself to deal with a few business issues. Voices in the den caught her attention, and when she came out of her old bedroom, there was a lady sitting on the couch across from her mom.

"Deja, so glad you could join us. You remember Sydney, don't you?"

"Sydney Anderson? Is that you?"

"Deja! You look great. Of course, you were the prettiest

girl at our school."

After a hug, they talked for hours, catching up on each other's lives. Sydney was a divorced mom of four year old twin girls. They were the cutest things Deja had ever seen. Sydney looked the same; her dark hair was longer, and she wore glasses that highlighted her dark brown eyes. They were best friends from kindergarten until graduation but had lost touch after they both went off to college. Oh, how she'd missed her friend. Deja felt bad for not keeping in touch. After things ended with Owen, she'd thrown herself into college and her company.

"Have you seen Owen yet?" Sydney asked her.

"No. I haven't seen or talked to him in ten years."

"Come on, Deja, don't tell me you haven't looked him up on Facebook or googled him."

"I did once and heard he was playing football in Florida."

"He did play professional football for a few years, but after his injury he was cut from the team. He's back in town now, coaching the high school football team."

Deja had to admit she wanted to know more, but she refused to show it. Her heart was behind a wall of concrete and it would stay there.

"High school football. Really." She snubbed her nose at that.

"Yes. He's never been married, either. But all the single moms chase him around." Sydney laughed.

A pang of jealousy roared up in Deja. It caught her off guard. This man had broken her heart, so why did she care who chased him? Besides, it wasn't like she'd sat around like a maiden, pining for him all these years. Maybe coming back was a mistake. She didn't need this complication in her life.

"We should go together tomorrow night," Sydney interrupted her thoughts.

"Yes, we should."

"Great. I will text you later. I need to go pick up the

girls from my mom's."

Deja walked her friend to the door and gave her a hug. She went searching for her mom and found her sitting on the back porch having a glass of tea. Fall was in the air and the leaves were turning orange and yellow. Deja sat in the rocking chair beside her mom soaking up the quiet. Her life was so busy, it was nice just to relax. Her mom still lived the same house Deja had grown up in. Deja had tried several times to buy or build her a new one, but she always turned her down. Thankfully, she had let her make some improvements.

"Did you have a nice visit with Sydney?" her mom asked.

"I did. It was great to catch up with her."

"It was a shame what that ex-husband of hers done."

"What do you mean, Mom?"

"He cheated on her while she was pregnant with those babies. He left her to raise those precious girls by herself. Never even visits them."

"What an asshole," Deja commented.

"Watch your mouth."

"Yes, ma'am."

Her mom stood. "Come on; let's go make supper. You know my show comes on tonight, and I don't want to miss it."

Deja followed her mom inside, hoping to stop her mind from racing. She couldn't help but wonder what it would be like to see Owen again.

Chapter Two

"Dammit, Johnny, you are supposed to catch the ball," Owen yelled. "All right, go hit the showers, boys."

Frustrated wasn't the word to describe how he was feeling. If they didn't turn this season around and start winning games, he would be fired. This is not how he imaged his life would go. Two years ago, he was a starting quarterback, playing in the NFL, and now he was coaching high school football at his alma mater. Don't get him wrong, he did love this job, but sometimes it just got to him.

"Coach Walsh, I'm sorry," Johnny said to him.

"Here." Owen threw a football to him. "Carry this around with you at all times. Even when you go to bed."

"Yes, sir."

Owen took a seat behind his desk and began to go over the playbooks for the next day, before he remembered his high school reunion was tomorrow night. There would be no practice. He shut down his laptop and left the office. When he walked down the hall outside the gym, the glass case caught his eye. Inside, was the football championship trophy from his senior year and a picture of him hugging Deja after the game. He'd heard a rumor that she would be at the reunion. No one had owned him like she had. Owen had loved her from the first day he laid eyes on her.

At first, she wouldn't give him the time of day. But he pursued her until she gave in and agreed to go to the ninth-grade dance with him. He was so nervous on their first date. Owen was great on the football field but had two left feet when it came to dancing. Deja didn't mind him stepping on her toes, though. They were inseparable after that date. They lost their virginity together and were planning to marry after high school. All he wanted was to take her away from this small town and be happy—away from his father.

His father, Victor Walsh, owned nearly their entire town. He came from old money and had a problem with his son dating out of his class. Deja's family didn't have money, but that never bothered Owen. He didn't give a shit about money. He loved Deja. She was the one person he trusted with his heart, which was why, when she broke it, he learned never to let anyone near it again. That didn't mean he couldn't have a little fun. He'd gone through his fair share of women during his six-year NFL career. When it was over, he was alone and lost.

Years had passed since he'd spoken to his father. His mom died when he was young, and he had no siblings. When he thought he'd hit rock bottom, his cell phone rang, and his old coach said he was retiring and wanted him to take his place. Owen's first instinct was to decline the offer. But since there was nothing left for him, he took the job. Turns out, it was the best decision he'd made in a long time. Coaching this team became the most important thing to him. He had some money left from his NFL days and built a house outside of town. It was a modest, three thousand square foot farmhouse, with a wraparound porch.

He had fifty acres of land for his horses, dogs, and cats. There was a big red barn, complete with a hayloft, and last summer he'd put in an inground pool with a jacuzzi. Owen loved his little piece of paradise. It was a lot different than the huge condo on the beach he'd owned when he lived in Florida. At first, Owen missed playing football, but not anymore. He really loved coaching. It gave him a purpose. He was happy, and no one would mess that up again. Not even the only woman he'd ever loved.

ONLY OWEN

***

Owen finished mucking the horse's stalls, put down fresh hay, and fed the animals. He thought about going for a run but decided against it. His knee had been giving him a fit. He went inside, put on a pot of coffee, and iced his knee. He'd had three surgeries to put his knee back together. Even though it had ended his career, he was glad he could still run. After swallowing some ibuprofen, he took a hot shower. Deja had filled his dreams last night. When they were together before, they were just kids. He wondered what it would feel like to be inside her again. Owen woke up with his hand on his dick, wishing it was Deja's mouth instead.

The connection between them had always been electric. The hair on his arms stood on end when she touched him. When they came together, the fire couldn't be contained. But when it ended, a part of him shut down. He no longer felt complete. Deja owned his heart. Owen quickly turned on the cold water. He hand wasn't going to satisfy him again. Only Deja would. He just had to convince her.

***

"Sydney, your eyes are beautiful. This eyeshadow will highlight the brown in them but also match your dress," Deja told her friend.

They spent the day at Deja's mom's house, getting ready for the reunion later that night. Deja had a new line of eye products she was releasing later that year, so she was testing them on herself and Sydney.

"I look so beautiful, Deja," Sydney replied, looking in the mirror.

"You *are* beautiful, Syd."

Sydney was shorter than Deja and had more curves. Her black hair was shoulder length and curly. The gold knee length dress highlighted her warm brown skin.

44

"Scratch that; you are not hot! That asshole ex of yours doesn't know what he's missing," Deja said, smiling.

"You are right about that. Who knows, maybe we will both get lucky tonight?" Sydney said, laughing.

Deja gave herself one last mirror check. Her dress was a deep red and hugged her like a second skin. Sleeveless, with a low neck, it showed a hint of her large breasts. She wore her red strapped heels that met the hem of her long gown. Deja's long black hair flowed straight down her back with a few curls on the ends. She finished her outfit with a few bracelets and long diamond earrings.

"Damn, Deja. Owen is going to swallow his tongue when he sees you."

"I'm not wearing this for him," Deja argued.

As much as she denied it, a big part of her wore this dress knowing he would see her. Deja wanted him to see what he'd been missing the last ten years. She wondered if Owen would bring a date tonight or if he would be solo. It didn't matter. If she wanted him, she would have him. Then she would break his heart like he did hers. No one except her mom knew what had happened. It had taught her a hard lesson, but one she needed to learn. Deja shook those thoughts from her mind. Tonight, was about reconnecting with old friends.

"Keep telling yourself you didn't wear that dress for him," Sydney said.

Deja slid her cell phone into her little red clutch purse. "Let's go, Syd."

A long, black stretch limo was waiting for them in the driveway. Deja smiled at the expression on her friend's face.

"You got a fucking limo! Deja?"

During the entire limo ride to the school, Sydney played with all the buttons like a little child. Deja smiled at the happiness on her friend's face. Then the guilt for not being here for Sydney hit her in the gut. She would work on being a better friend. She had to. The limo pulled up in front of the school gym, and Sydney was the first one out of the car. The theme for this year's reunion was Hollywood premiere. Deja stepped onto the red carpet lined with lighted stars and followed it into the gym.

They stopped in front of the paparazzi area and took photos before entering the gym. It was beautifully decorated, with flowing silver and gold fabric and twinkling lights. Each table had an array of red and white roses, in an Oscar shaped vase. The transformation from the old gym she remembered was amazing. She and Syd spoke to several people as they made their way to their assigned table. Deja scanned the space, looking for Owen, but she hadn't seen him yet. They stopped at the bar and both decided to try the Cosmopolitan.

Deja took a drink of the delicious cocktail and felt an electric sensation down to her toes. At first, she thought it was the drink until she turned her head and *there he was*. Owen was standing across the room. Immediately, her heart began to pound, and she squeezed her legs shut. He was dressed in a dark gray suit, with a bright blue tie that matched his bright blue eyes. His blond hair was a shade darker now, and it matched his five o'clock shadow. Damn, how he filled that suit out. The jacket hugged his broad shoulders and narrow waist. His thighs were nearly bursting through the seams of his pants. Clearly, this man stayed in shape. Deja's mouth watered at what was under those clothes.

"Deja, you are drooling." Sydney elbowed her.

Oh shit, was she in trouble now.

Chapter Three

Owen made his way around the gym, catching up with old friends. He felt Deja's eyes on him. He wanted to pick her up over his shoulder and carry her out of this room like a damn caveman. She was wearing that red dress. Her breasts were so much fuller, and her hips had just the right amount of flair. She was wearing her hair longer, and a once shy teen was now a confident, sexy, beautiful woman. Deja owned the room. Owen took his time working his way over to her table.

"Looking beautiful, Deja," he said as he came up behind her.

She cleared her throat and looked up at him. "Thank you, Owen."

He made small talk with her and the others at the table. But all he could think about was getting Deja to himself. The pull between them was as strong as it ever was. His body ached to claim her.

"Dance with me," he said as their song began playing in the background.

Turns out, the DJ was a fan of his NFL days, so he'd arranged for him to play *Just the Way You Are* by Bruno Mars. Deja slid her small hand in his larger one and let him lead her to the dance floor. Owen pulled her close and wrapped his arms around her waist. Deja linked her arms around his neck and laid her head on his chest. Everyone around them disappeared. The world stopped. It was perfect. She nestled closer to him, and he couldn't help it when his dick hardened.

Owen was glad he had a jacket on to cover him. The song ended too soon. He didn't want to let her go.

Slowly, she raised her head and looked at him. "The song's over, Owen."

He felt a tap on his shoulder. "Coach, can you help us a minute?" Michelle, one of the teachers and former classmate, asked him.

"Go ahead; I need a drink anyway," Deja replied, walking away.

Son of a bitch. He needed time alone with her. He just had to make it happen.

***

Back at the table, Deja downed her drink while trying to stop her hands from shaking. Being in Owen's arms again, was pure fire. The heat between them had not faded at all. She'd often heard stories about true soulmates, mostly from her mom. She had told Deja she would never and could never love another man the way she'd loved Deja's father. Their marriage had its shares of ups and downs, but they had stood together through it all. When her dad passed away, Deja had thought her mom would die too. She was so confused. Her intentions were to let Owen see what he'd missed out on all these years, not to realize she still had feelings for him.

"Girl, are you okay? That dance. Holy shit," Sydney chided.

"I need another drink," Deja said.

"Here, drink this." Sydney put a shot glass in front of her.

Deja downed the liquid and followed it up with another. She wasn't much of a drinker and she felt that last shot. She kept scanning the room for Owen but didn't see him. Sydney pulled her onto the dance floor, and they danced to every fast song that came on. Deja was having a great time but wondered where Owen was. By the fifth song, she had to have another drink.

"Come with me," Owen said, coming up behind her.

Before she could answer, he took her hand and led her down a long hallway. It was dark, and she couldn't see where she was going, but Owen had a firm grip around his waist, leading her so she wouldn't fall. They walked past the boys' locker room, through a door at the end of the hall. She realized it was his office. He unlocked the door, and when they were inside, he pushed her up against it and took her lips in a fiery kiss. Owen didn't ask permission as he pushed his tongue inside of her mouth. He took what he wanted, and she let him.

She could feel the heat from his fingers on every inch of skin he touched. He drove his knee in between her legs. She could feel the heat building between her thighs. He ran his hands up her dress and moved her panties aside then replaced his knee with his fingers while his thumb worked her clit. He sucked her bottom lip when he broke the kiss. Deja could feel the warmth rising up in her belly and she began to shake.

"Come for me, Deja," Owen whispered as he nipped her ear.

Deja felt a wave of energy overtake her as she began to shake. When her orgasm hit, her release was so intense, she nearly fell. Owen picked her up and sat on his worn leather couch with her in his lap. He tucked her head under his chin and just held her.

"Come home with me tonight, Deja? I need to be with you. And not in some smelly office," Owen asked her.

She knew this was probably not the best idea, but she agreed to go. Maybe it was the alcohol or the nostalgia of tonight. She texted Sydney to let her know they were leaving, and they headed out. Deja wanted to be with Owen. It may be just one night, but that would have to do. Owen held her hand for the entire ride to his house. He lived a few miles out of town, but it seemed to take forever to get there. The heat between them was building. Before long, it would explode.

Deja let Owen lead her inside his house. He quickly shut the door behind them and kissed her. He delved, deep stroking his tongue over hers, exploring every inch of her mouth. Deja reached for his jacket, sliding it off until it hit the floor. She felt him moving her backwards toward another room, never breaking the kiss. Oh, how this man could kiss. Deja stopped when she felt the bed behind her. Owen helped her remove his tie and his shirt. She broke the kiss long enough to take him in. This man was beautiful. Deja kissed her way down his muscular chest.

She lifted her arms as Owen pulled her dress over her head. Her breath hitched as he took one nipple into his mouth. "You are the most beautiful woman I've ever seen."

She reached for his zipper and freed his cock. It was so much bigger than she remembered. His thick member reached past his belly button. She wanted to taste him, but Owen stopped her.

"Not right now, baby. I won't last. And when I come, I want to be inside you."

Owen ripped her underwear off and laid her back on the bed. He made quick work of removing the rest of his clothes until he was completely naked. Deja drank him in as he stood over her like a Greek god. There wasn't an ounce of flab on him, from his broad shoulders, past his six pack, to the V-shape of his hips. Deja got wetter just looking at him. She rubbed her nipples into tight peaks. When Owen couldn't take any more, he pulled her to the end of the bed and lined his cock up with her waiting heat.

"I've waited so long."

"Me too," she replied, breathless.

Deja grabbed the sheets when Owen slid his cock into her. He paused for a minute to allow her to adjust to him before he began pounding into her. She wrapped her legs around him, her ankles pressing into his tight ass pulling him deeper. Her hands grabbed his shoulders as he moved over her. Owen kissed her again, syncing his tongue with the rhythm of their lovemaking. He reached between them and rubbed her clit.

"Come with me, Deja."

Her eyes rolled back in her head when her orgasm hit. Owen pounded once, then twice more, before letting out a scream when his own release came. He collapsed on top of her, breathing heavily in her ear. Still joined, he rolled them over until Deja was lying on his chest. Owen rubbed circles up and down her back. When she shivered, he covered them with a blanket and held her closer to him.

"I've missed you so much, Deja."

"I've missed you too, Owen," she replied, kissing his chest.

"We have a lot to talk about. But sleep now. I am not done with you," Owen said to her as she drifted off.

Chapter Four

The smell of bacon woke Deja up the next morning. She reached out for Owen, but he wasn't next to her. Last night had been amazing, and she was sore in all the right places. That man knew what he was doing. Owen had taken her several times during the night. The first time was fast and furious. The others, he took his time with her, worshiping her body from head to toe. Deja had taken her time savoring him as well. Her stomach growled, forcing her out of bed. She pulled one of Owen's t-shirts over her head and followed the smell to the kitchen. He was standing in front of the stove in nothing but a pair of boxer briefs. Deja stood for a minute admiring the view.

"Something smells good," she finally said.

"Morning, beautiful. I hope you're hungry," Owen replied as he planted a kiss on her lips.

He pulled her chair out as she sat at his kitchen table. He placed a plate of bacon, eggs, and fruit in front of her, with a cup of hot coffee. Deja savored every bite while taking in his home. The house was masculine but warm and inviting. It was him. She loved living in the city, but country living appealed to her too.

"Do you want to meet my horses?" Owen asked her after breakfast.

"I'd like that."

He gave her a pair of his sweatpants and muck boots. Deja was glad they had a drawstring so they would stay up. Owen dressed in a pair of worn jeans and an old t-shirt. After Deja sent a quick text to her mom and Sydney, he led her out to the huge red barn.

"Deja, this is Chewy and Yoda," he said, stopping in front of the two large brown horses.

"I forgot how much you love Star Wars." She smiled. "Okay, I understand Chewy because he is brown and furry, but Yoda?"

"Look at those ears."

They both laughed. Poor Yoda did have huge ears. Deja helped Owen feed and water the horses before they headed back to the house. Once there, he helped her remove her boots and they took a seat on the porch swing.

"How long are you in town?" Owen asked, linking his hand with hers.

"I have to be back in Atlanta by Monday."

"I don't want this to end, Deja."

Her heart began to beat a little faster. A huge part of her hoped he would say those words to her. But the part of her heart that he'd broken couldn't go through that pain again. She wouldn't regret last night, but she knew they had no future.

"Owen, we tried before, and you know what happened," Deja replied, letting his hand go.

He turned to face her. "We were so young then. I'm willing to try again if you are."

"It's not that simple, Owen. You don't understand what it felt like," Deja said, standing.

"You're right. I didn't know what that was like, but I understood why," Owen said, rising to stand in front of her.

"Understood what?" Deja felt her blood heating. "Why you stood by and let your father try to pay me off? Because I wasn't good enough for his rich, white son?"

When Deja looked at Owen, the expression on his face made her step back. He looked like she had just slapped him.

"I don't know which was worse, that you let him offer me the money, or that you thought I would actually take it." She was so angry, she wouldn't let him say anything. "I knew this was a mistake."

"What money, Deja?" Owen asked, blocking her way inside.

The look in his eyes said everything. *Was it possible? Did he not know? But he said he understood why. So he had to know.*

"The ten thousand dollars your father offered me to break up with you."

Owen's face was pale, and he took a step back from her.

"You said you understood why?"

"Why you had to leave. You had a full ride to Emory University, and I was headed to Florida," Owen replied, leaning against the front porch railing.

"A few weeks after graduation, your father came to see me. He told me you were too young to settle down, that it would ruin your future playing football. And I knew how much you loved football, Owen," Deja said.

"I didn't love anything more than you, Deja."

She felt the tears well up. Oh God! She had been so wrong about Owen.

"Your father handed me an envelope, and inside, was the check. He convinced me you knew about it, and I believed him." She wiped at the tears rolling down her cheek. "I tried to call you that night, Owen, to talk, and the next day I had to leave for school. But I never cashed the damn thing."

"I can't believe that son of a bitch. I didn't know anything. I would have strangled him, Deja. Didn't you know how much I loved you? That I would have given up everything for you?"

She could only nod her head. Owen walked past her and took a seat on his front steps. Deja saw the pain in his eyes. She hated that she had put it there.

"Did you know I came by your house that morning, to drive you to Emory? When I got there, your mom said you had already left, and she gave me your letter."

Owen paused, looking at his feet. "You made it clear, you never wanted to see me again. It hurt, but I

54

gave you some space. I thought after some time, I would reach out to you. But I never did."

Deja sat beside him, their knees resting against each other. "I am so sorry, Owen."

"Me too, Dej," He said with a sad smile.

"What now?" she asked, holding her breath.

Was this it? Deja knew she'd hurt him. All the pain and anger she'd felt toward him for ten years melted away and was replaced by guilt. From the first time Deja met Owen, she truly thought they would be together forever. A second chance with him was the reason she'd showed up for this damn reunion. Now it could end before it was able to begin again.

"I think we both need some space right now," Owen replied, standing.

Unable to speak, Deja could only nod her head. Owen kissed the top of her head and she watched him walk toward the barn. She texted Sydney to pick her up and went inside to gather her things.

***

Owen saddled up Chewy and took a long ride. He couldn't believe what his father had done. He'd never had a great relationship with him, but to do what he did was unthinkable. It shouldn't surprise Owen. His father had mapped out his life since he was born. But Owen never wanted to be like him. He was a terrible person and even worse father. He always thought because he had money, others were beneath him. Since Owen had moved back to town, his father had reached out a few times. They'd gone to lunch a couple of times. He was trying to build their relationship. His father was the only family he had. But after this, there was no hope of that ever happening.

After a while, Owen looked up and he had ridden to his old home where his father still lived. He tied Chewy up to the front porch and gave him some water. The front door was unlocked, so he went in.

"Dad!" he yelled.

"Owen, is that you?"

His father was showing his seventy years. He could barely stand without using a cane. And he had to be on oxygen. The years of smoking had finally taken their toll.

"How did the reunion go, son?"

"I saw Deja. Remember her?" Owen asked, the anger welling up inside him.

His father's face went pale, and he had to sit back down in his chair.

"How could you?" Owen asked the frail man. "I loved her, Dad."

"I am sorry, son. That is one of my biggest regrets. I thought I knew what was best for you. I am so sorry. I know I made so many mistakes with you."

Owen was taken aback by his father's admission. Not once in his entire life, did he ever hear Victor Walsh admit he'd made a mistake.

"I know I was not the father you wanted or needed. I wish more than anything, I could go back and fix my mistakes, but I can't."

His father began to cough, and his home nurse came in the room. She put a breathing mask on him to help.

"I am sorry, but Mr. Walsh needs to rest."

Owen gave his father one last look before he headed to the door. He heard his father call out, "I am sorry."

Chapter Five

Two weeks later, Deja was sitting in her office overlooking downtown Atlanta, staring at her phone. After Sydney had picked her up from Owen's, she'd packed her bag and went back to Atlanta. Her friend thought she was crazy for leaving, and her mom had asked her to stay, but she couldn't. Deja hoped Owen would call or maybe text her, but she hadn't heard a word. In all honesty, she knew she should be the one calling him but, no, she ran instead. She knew she needed to get her ass back there and apologize to Owen. She was still in love with him. The minute she touched him, her heart mended. These two weeks without him had been hell.

"Deja?" Her office phone beeped.

"Yes."

"There is a Mr. Walsh here to see you. He doesn't have an appointment," her assistant continued.

Deja's heart began to beat faster. He was here. Owen had come to see her.

"That's okay; send him in."

She stood up and straightened her skirt. A knock sounded at the door, and she hurriedly opened it.

"Miss Garrett? By the look on your face, I was not the Walsh you were expecting?"

"No, you weren't. Why are you here?" Deja said, trying to keep her composure.

The last person she thought she would ever see in her office was Victor Walsh, the man responsible for the heartache between and Owen and her. He looked nothing like she remembered. He had to be in his seventies now. He walked with a cane and was using oxygen.

"I won't take up much of your time. Would you mind if I sit?"

Deja nodded her head, and he sat in one of the chairs facing her desk. Needing space between them, she returned to her seat. Having a barrier between them made her feel better.

"I came here to tell you how sorry I am for what I did." He paused to cough. "I could try to blame it on the way I was raised or say that's how it was in a small southern town, but there was no excuse. I was wrong."

Deja was in complete shock. For once in her life, she was speechless.

"Do you believe people can change? I have spent the last ten years working on becoming a better person. My biggest regret is that I hurt my son and you."

She watched him pull out a handkerchief and wipe his eyes. "Believe it or not, I love my son and I want him to be happy. You make him happy, Deja. Please don't give up on Owen. I know that because of me, you have lost ten years. I can never make up for that. But I would like to try if you will let me."

He reached for his cane and stood up. "Thank you for listening to me."

"I do believe people can change, Mr. Walsh. Forgiveness, however, takes time. I love your son and I always have, since the first moment I met him. And if he will let me, I want to spend the rest of my life with him."

"That sounds like a start then. By the way, Owen has been away at a football training camp, but I hear he will be back in town on Saturday."

After Mr. Walsh left, Deja asked her secretary to clear her calendar. She had her man to win back.

***

Bang! Owen threw his gear in the back of his truck. He had just gotten back from a two-week training camp with ten of his starting football players. An old buddy of his who played in Tennessee had arranged it. It was a great learning experience for the boys, and they had a good time. Owen, on the other hand, had been miserable the entire trip. All he could think about was Deja. He knew she'd gone back to Atlanta right after their night together. After the conversation with his father, he could see her side. They were both young, and they both made mistakes. They were older now, and he wanted to be with her.

So, why did she leave without a word? Would she run every time they had a fight? Maybe she didn't think they would work. It was dark when he arrived at home. All he wanted, was a hot shower and his bed. A buddy of his had been tending to the animals while he was away, so he knew they were good until the morning. Owen dropped his bag inside the door, not bothering to put it away. He took a hot shower, letting the water massage his tired muscles. He pulled on a pair of old gym shorts and grabbed a beer from the fridge and an ice pack for his knee. He was about to sit on his leather couch when a knock sounded at the door. He walked over to see who was there.

"Deja?"

Owen was surprised but excited to see her standing there.

"May I come in?" she asked him.

He ushered her in and shut the door behind her.

"I had to see you," she began before he could say another word. "We can make this work, Owen. I can't lose you again. I know I hurt you but—"

"Shhh." Owen placed his index finger gently across her mouth. "We both screwed up, Deja. I don't want to lose you again, either." He replaced his finger with his lips. Owen meant to give her a gentle kiss but broke it before things got to heated. Tonight, he needed to show her without words how much she meant to him.

Deja wrapped her arms around him, and they just held

each other for a while. Owen led her to the bedroom. He needed to show her how much she meant to him. Slowly, he undressed her, worshiping every inch of her body. He slowly suckled one breast while massaging the other. Owen made his way down her stomach, circling her belly button with his tongue. When he reached the juncture of her thighs, he dropped to his knees and licked and probed until Deja came. While she was still shaking, he quickly removed his shorts and moved over her.

He positioned his erection at her entrance, waiting. Deja pulled his head down and kissed him. While their tongues did their own mating dance, he slowly slid into her. He moved in and out, slowly at first. Their hands linked together as Owen sped up his rhythm. It didn't take long until they both climaxed. He gave Deja another kiss and rolled off her, pulling her to his side.

"I love you, Deja."

"I love you too, Owen."

***

The next morning, Owen left Deja sleeping in his warm bed while he took care of the animals. Last night had been amazing, but waking up with her in his arms felt right. He knew they had things to talk about and work out, and they would. He was anxious to get back to Deja, so he made quick work of doing his daily chores. When he left the barn, he saw her sitting on the porch swing, wrapped up in a blanket. He ran up the steps and joined her. He gave her a quick kiss, and she snuggled closer to him.

"Morning," Deja said with a big smile on her face.

"How long can you stay?" he asked.

"How long do you want me to stay?"

"Forever."

Deja sat up and turned to face him. Owen's stomach dropped, waiting for her answer.

She put a hand on each side of his face. "I want forever with you too. There is something I need to tell you, though. I had a visit from your dad."

"My father? What did he say to you?" Owen felt anger rising in him.

"He apologized and admitted he had been so wrong and asked for my forgiveness."

He stood up, not knowing how to process what she'd told him. Deja reached for his hand and pulled him back down beside her.

"I believed him, Owen. I think he truly regrets what he's done and what it cost us all."

"I don't know how to handle that. You think someone like him can really change?"

"I do, and we will handle it together. I know we still have a lot to talk about and work through, and we will," Deja replied, pulling Owen into her embrace.

"Together. I like the sound of that."

Epilogue

Deja linked her arm with her mom's as she walked down the aisle toward her future husband. Owen was dressed in a form fitting, black tux that hugged every inch of his fine physique. She was wearing the wedding dress her mom had worn when she married Deja's dad. The church was filled with family and friends, and Sydney was her maid-of-honor. Owen's father was sitting on the front row. Deja had encouraged Owen to work on having a relationship with his dad. While Deja wasn't his dad's biggest fan, she did believe he had changed.

Owen and Deja split their time between the farm and her condo in Atlanta. She couldn't be happier. She loved this man with all her heart, and he loved her the same. Her heartbeat sped up when she reached him at the altar. He held her small hands in his larger ones as they said their vows. When the preacher said, 'kiss your bride', he laid one on her in front of everyone. Finally, they were husband and wife. Deja knew the past may rear its ugly head from time to time, but they would take it head-on together.

At the reception, they had their first dance with their song playing in the background. Owen whispered the lyrics in her ear, "Girl, you're amazing just the way you are."

Deja gave him a soft kiss on the lips. "Do you want your wedding gift now?" she asked him.

Owen looked down at her with one eyebrow

cocked. "Right here in front of everyone, Deja? Kinky."

She laughed at him. "No, that's for later. The surprise I'm talking about is that I'm pregnant."

A stunned Owen placed his hand on her belly. "Seriously?"

Deja nodded her head. Tears welled up in both their eyes.

"I didn't think I could love you any more, but I was wrong." He pulled her into his embrace and circled the dance floor with her. "I love you, Deja Marie Garrett Walsh. You have made me the happiest man in the world."

"I love you too, Owen."

About the Author

Anne grew up in a very small town in South Carolina, where, as a kid, she always loved to read books, make people laugh, and write songs. After having success in her home state, she decided to pursue dreams of becoming a writer and moved to Nashville, TN. When she's not writing, you can find her reading or searching for a husband. She loves spending time with her friends, nieces, nephews, and her two fur babies. She enjoys making people laugh, so if you would like, please feel free to follow her on Twitter @merri_aw or on Facebook.com/itsanannething. You can visit her website at http://www.annewelchauthor.com. She loves hearing from her readers.

Also by Anne Welch

It's An Anne Thing
It's An Anne Thing Two
Burning Fury
Burning Rage
Carolina Hope
Carolina Longing
Carolina Faith (coming soon)
Catching Chase
Sweet Betrayal

THROUGH A GLASS DARKLY

Arden Aoide

1

Marfa, Texas
Elevation: 4,685 feet
Satellites: 2,666

Solana watched the little boy for a while before stepping a little closer. She was eleven, and he looked younger than her, but most of the boys in her grade looked younger. He was flat on his back on a picnic table looking through binoculars at the night sky. It was especially dark out, but she could also see his thick glasses and unkempt blond hair.

It was the annual Perseid meteor shower, and he was clearly interested in something else. It was the New Moon, so he couldn't be looking at that.

"What are you trying to see with those?" Solana's knees knocked against the bench.

He didn't look at her. "Looking for the Horsehead Nebula. My dad got me these binoculars for my birthday, and he said I might be able to see it with them. Usually we have to have a telescope."

"Can I see?" She climbed up and sat on the table, but he wasn't budging. "Please?"

The boy looked her way briefly before he refocused. "Sorry, one second. I think I see a dark spot. Trying to see if it has the right shape."

She waited patiently for a second because it was clear he was fine with her presence. She was used to the dumb boys back at her school, but so far, he was harder to work out. Solana hadn't seen someone around her age so preoccupied unless it was a different sort of glass screen.

"Okay. I think I have it." He scooted over about four inches, but he was skinny enough for her to make room for herself. She followed his finger upward as he pointed toward Orion.

"You see those three bright stars—"

"Orion's Belt."

That earned her another glance, but he kept talking and pointing. "The left star, Alnitak. If you look just directly under it, you can see a bit of bright fuzziness, which is part of the nebula. To see the horse head, move very very very slowly to the right." He held out his binoculars and stayed facing her as she took them from him. Their knuckles brushed as he showed her how to adjust them for her face.

It took her a while to get a handle on Orion's Belt, and that was after she got lost around Bellatrix. "Okay. I'm at the belt. I'm pretty sure I have the correct star." She moved the binoculars a hair lower. "Oh! It looks cloudy. Is that it?"

"That's part of it. If you find it faster than I did, I'm going to be mad."

She laughed and lost her place. "Shit!"

And surprisingly, she got a laugh out of him.

"Okay, okay. Back on track. I've got this." She found the star, and the haziness, and she carefully and patiently scanned to the right. "I do see a spot. It's not very horsey, though. It's like someone cut something out of the clouds."

"Keep very still. I'm going to make them a little stronger." His fingers brushed her forehead, and the binoculars still knocked off course, but only back to Alnitak. It took a few minutes of silence, until her breath caught. "That's a horse. You can actually see the shape of its head."

"Really? You can tell it's a horse?"

She looked over at him. "I thought you saw it."

"I did see it, but only when I found it. I didn't try to look closer at it." The implication that he let her see it up close first made her stomach flutter. She didn't much like that.

"Here, look." Solana handed them back, and he eagerly took them.

They were quiet. A few minutes passed, and she was trying to see the cloudiness of the nebula with the naked eye. She could catch something, possibly the star's reflection, but mostly the sky just looked so dark in certain areas, that it highlighted the others.

"This is the coolest thing. It's dark enough to see the horse. I can't believe it. I thought my dad was exaggerating." His voice had a tinge of awe that made him sound like he was rarely in awe of anything. He turned his head back toward her, and she realized she was staring at him. "What's your name? Is your family here for the Perseid's too?"

Solana rolled to her side and leaned on her elbow. He was staring right back at her. She was used to such questions online, so she was initially cautious, but there wasn't a chance she'd see him again. "Mmhm. I'm Solana. We live in Waco. My dad teaches Cosmology at Baylor." She knew better than to share that last part, but all her classmates knew. She held his eyes, insanely curious about him. "What's your name?"

"Ryan. I'm named after him." He pointed back toward Orion in the sky, then offered her his hand to shake. She took it. It was gritty from the desert, but not sweaty. Even in the summer, the nights were mild in some parts of west Texas.

"We're on our way to the McDonald Observatory tomorrow. My dad works on the big telescopes. He just got finished with one in San Antonio."

"No wonder those binoculars are so good."

He nodded and looked back up at the sky. "'Sol' means 'sun'. Did your parents do that on purpose? Like mine did?"

"Yep. Mom wanted something pretty, and Dad wanted something from the stars."

"For me, Mom wanted a normal boy's name, and Dad

wanted Orion. Solana is very pretty. S-O-L-A-N-A. Is that how you spell it, or—?"

"You got it the first time. Thanks. I like it. I think it's cool you're named after Orion. So...what do you hunt?" She kicked at his shoe.

Ryan laughed. "Everything. Once I thought I found a UFO, but it was just a satellite. Dad says you have to account for all the satellites to really study what's beyond them."

Solana didn't know anything about satellites, but it made sense. She knew they served a purpose, but she could see how they could interfere with study.

"I'm going to discover something one day," he said, as he checked his watch and sat up.

She sat up as well. She was inclined to believe him. "What will you name it?"

"I've never thought about that. I should have a name ready."

"That would be smart."

He looked at his watch again. "Mom wants me in by midnight. It was really fun hanging out with you." He held out his hand again, and she took it automatically. But he had rendered her speechless.

Her parents didn't give her a time, but they'd probably come looking for her soon. They were in the hot tub behind their cabin, and it was their anniversary, so she was going to leave them alone.

She wanted to ask if she would see him in the morning, but she was paralyzed with sudden shyness. She cleared her throat. "Thanks for showing me the nebula. It was very cool."

He was standing now, and he looked up at Orion. He was dorky and cute. And a little shorter than her. "It *is* very cool." He waved as he walked backward. "It was nice meeting you."

She waved back. "You, too." Solana watched him walk away before shaking her head and smiling. There was no point developing a crush on a random little white boy in west Texas she'd never see again. She hopped off the table and stopped when she heard her name.

"Solana!" Ryan was a little out of breath as he ran back toward her.

"Yes?" She didn't need to run to be out of breath. Apparently. She inhaled deeply and exhaled.

"That's a good name for a star, right?" He smiled with teeth before running off again.

2

15 years later, Chile
Elevation: 8,645 feet
Satellites: 5,774

Ryan loved the desert. Ryan especially loved a desert with the ocean a dune buggy trip away.

He'd landed in Antofagasta, Chile, and rented a Jeep. He would need to return it within a week, but depending on how often he drove back to Antofagasta, he thought of leasing something a little longer. The trip to the European Southern Observatory at Cerro Paranol would take two hours from the airport, and they were expecting some snow flurries. Ryan wanted to get to the ESO Hotel before dark. He'd never been, so he wanted to see everything. On his way out of Antofagasta, he made sure his gas tank was full, and bought some snacks for the road.

ESO Hotel was exclusive. It wasn't for the general public. It was for people who worked at the observatory, and for scientists to come further study there. Ryan was an astrophysicist who was currently studying Orbital Debris. His assignment was Ceres for the foreseeable future, but there was always something going on with Orion that he monitored. Ceres evolved into a dwarf planet from an asteroid, and it was recently discovered that she held saltwater. With her being so close to Earth, it was quite an amazing find. ESO was a great place to search for more data because she'd moved to the Southern Hemisphere. Or rather Earth's dance with her was going to be best viewed at ESO for a good while.

From what he understood, Paranol was like a tiny hi-tech village in the middle of the Atacama Desert. All the creature comforts of home were provided, and he'd flown in from Germany, where he had been accepted into the Fellowship Program, and was approved for Chile after his three years were up in Garching. It was while studying there that he found several deep space objects. He chased shadows and logged coordinates for things he couldn't find with a telescope. They would eclipse other known objects, but anytime he'd get the math in order and could predict an exact location, almost always, a satellite would block his view. It took far longer to locate and study the Orion Nebula of newborn stars. Ryan spent most of his research dodging useless private satellites, and it would be difficult to enact legislation the entire planet could agree on.

One of the things he liked to discuss with his father was making satellites more efficient, so they could detect anything that might impact the planet. Anyone who worked in Cosmology was starting to get worried. But he didn't want to dwell on apocalyptic asteroid impacts. He wasn't dramatic. Just don't ask his mother.

He liked to follow his parents, so they could be on the same hemisphere at least. Continent and country were even better. But soon, they would be at Paranol with him.

His parents were in Santiago for a telescope there, but would be meeting him in the next year. His dad was coming to help with the Very Large Telescope atop of Paranol. It was going to be the largest in the world. There was so much work to be done, and his parents loved the area so much, they might stay, and retire there. His mom wrote articles about Galápagos Islands for various media, so being close to that also helped their decision. She went back to college when he was in high school.

Ryan hoped he liked it, and from the drive, with peeks of the ocean, and the desert mountains, he felt as close to a religious experience as he imaged was possible.

The closer he got to ESO, the more his soul settled.

He pulled onto the road leading to the compound, and laid out in front of him was a view of the ocean, and a skyline of observatories. As he turned the corner into the valley, he could see everything else. Sun-bleached warehouses were abundant, but he couldn't see the hotel yet. He passed through the gate, and found a spot to park up front. There was a passageway and a dome, but no obvious building. There was an arrow pointing toward the tunnel labeled 'La Residencia', so he knew he was in the right place. He didn't have much luggage. He had enough to live. He had a phone, laptop, and his binoculars along with his clothes. ESO provided a better computer, and all the paper and pencils he'd require. He didn't think of material things often. All the things he truly desired were quite literally out of his reach.

He wanted to see as far away as possible. He wanted to see how far back in time he could truly travel. There were remnants of the Big Bang, and he wanted to experience that knowledge with his own eyes. It was amazing what a massive piece of reflective glass could show him about his own planet.

Ryan realized the hotel was tucked into the side of a hill, and this was the normal way to enter. After about a hundred meters through the tunnel, he found what was under the dome: An atrium with a pool, abundant seating, and a cafeteria. There weren't many people around. There were a few seated in the cafeteria, and a handful of people getting to where they needed to go pretty quickly. No one acknowledged him, and that was his preference. He worked fine with others, but he was exhausted and could barely remember social niceties unless he was awake and doing his best.

Ryan wasn't a deliberate ass, and thankfully he came off as too optimistic and cheerful for anyone to think he was awful when he was cranky. He just misplaced how to be social in the back of his brain when tired. He knew that was normal for a lot of people, but since he tried especially hard when he was awake, he was already putting in the effort.

He made his way to the front desk, and since he was expected, he was given his key, and a folder with all the information he needed. Martin was friendly enough, and appreciated he was tired.

"How do people handle transportation around here?"

He laughed. "Usually last minute with much frustration."

"So, if I were to go back to town in a week or two to return my car, leasing one would make things more convenient here?"

Martin nodded. "If you are making a trip to town, expect folks to invite themselves along. It's usually people going stir crazy because we can easily get deliveries here."

"I can't imagine getting restless here, but I know how tedious it can be to work on the same thing and it delivers nothing for years."

"There is a lot of that here."

As Martin began warning about the incoming snow, he read the business card stapled to the inside of the folder he was given.

Solana Williams
Human Resources Director

3

Solana flew from Santiago, where she was visiting her parents, to Antofagasta, and there she hitched a ride on the last seat of a helicopter to get back to ESO. She was going to pay a taxi another exorbitant amount, or see if anyone had been spending the weekend in town before they got snowed in. It wouldn't be much snow, but enough that it was probably best to stay put. They were supposed to have flurries every night for the next week, but it would be melted by noon.

Thankfully, she made it before the helicopter left. There was a prominent scientist on his way out tonight, and she was going to take advantage of his means of travel.

She'd been in a helicopter several times since she'd been to Chile. Solana had been the Human Resources Director for ESO in Santiago, but since they were building the Very Large Telescope, they needed a full time director.

It had been her chance to be independent. She had lived with her parents, and while it was easy, she was itching to see what it felt like to truly be on her own.

Her mom had been a doctor of oncology in the states, but since her dad made good money at the university in Santiago, they invested well, and the cost of living was inexpensive, her mom wanted to get back in the lab. She stayed very busy, and she never sat still, unless she was in front of a microscope.

THROUGH A GLASS DARKLY

Solana knew she could never escape the sciences, but she could do something she liked anyway.

They weren't happy at first when she left, but they were proud of her. Solana hadn't wanted to disappoint them or her older brother when she dropped her science major for business. She liked the tangibility of an office. She would always be passionate about the stars, but she wasn't like Orion, the Hunter.

She took classes for Human Resources and Industrial Relations, but the thing that set her apart for ESO was knowing what the scientists were talking about, so she could commiserate disappointments, and celebrate discoveries.

Solana found people to be naturally condescending, but not at ESO. They had to be smart to get in the gate. They had to have a hunger to face infinity. She made a point early on to remember names, to ask about their latest projects, and to keep up with the conversations. She earned respect quickly. She didn't waste time letting others form opinions about her abilities.

Some days she felt like the honorary mayor to a small village of super-nerds. Herding them was her superpower, and not many had the temperament to be corralled by just anybody when on the brink of a new discovery. But she considered herself a nerd, too. She could explain the logic of an inconvenience or a machine upgrade, instead of brushing them off from ignorance.

Solana was respected. She commanded it.

Sometimes she felt she was insulating herself from the real world, but what was more real than the work being done by scientists?

It was just so isolating.

Her brother tells her every time they talk, that she's welcome to come back to Houston. They'd lived a lot of places, and Houston was where they lived when her brother started medical school. He stayed when they left for Puerto Rico, but he flies down with his girlfriend at Christmas and for a week to escape the Texas summer.

Solana was relieved helicopters were too loud to

converse in, so she watched the ocean as the sun began to set. It didn't feel like snow was coming, but the temperature hadn't dropped yet.

The helicopter touched down, and she's ushered out efficiently, and given her bag. She rolled her suitcase toward the tunnel, and since it was on her way, she would stop by the desk, get her mail, and check any non-vital messages before she went to her room.

As the dome came into view, she stopped to pull out her phone, then began to walk while texting to let her parents know she was back and safe. "Hello," she called to Martin and another man as she walked into the front desk area. She pressed 'Send' before putting her phone away and smiling up at Martin.

"Solana! How was your trip?"

"It was great. Did you manage without me?"

"Barely," Martin said, but her attention snapped toward the other man.

She frowned as he walked toward her as if in a trance. He was well over six feet, and he needed some supper. It was a little uncomfortable and awkward, but she wasn't scared. He had zero social graces. "Is there something I can help you with?"

"I named a star after you," he blurted.

Something shook loose in her mind. It shot to her heart. "Excuse me?" *It couldn't be.*

He smiled and it was everything she had forgotten. A mess of blond hair and much more stylish glasses. "That's not exactly right. A globular cluster. It's...a lot of stars named after you."

"Orion," she breathed, and his face lit up. "You grew...up. Literally. I can't believe you're here."

"Just got here. I never thought I'd see you again. You don't have social media."

She shook her head. Social media was too much drama and gossip. "I didn't know your last name, so I figured Marfa was it."

"I thought so, too."

She wanted to change the subject. She was getting too flustered.

"You're here for Betelgeuse? That's what we're all buzzing about here."

He inclined his head. "That and the salt on Ceres. I'm after the debris. Orion is a mess. I'm pretty familiar with the area."

Solana laughed. "Yeah, I remember." She looked down at the ground before she spoke again. "Horsehead Nebula was the first thing I looked at when I got the job here."

"I haven't seen it here, yet. I was just going to take a peek through my binoculars later. You can join me if you'd like."

Oh, she'd like. Solana looked toward Martin, who was leaning on the desk with chin in hand, smiling. She glared quickly before smiling back at Ryan. "I need to touch base with Martin, then I can show you around if you're up for it. Unless you're jet-lagged."

And so he yawned. Of course. He chuckled. "I slept some, but didn't really rest. I left Germany...I don't know the date here, but I spent half a day in Mexico City at the airport trying not to miss my flight by not falling asleep."

"Then I'll show you around tomorrow. We'll have to coordinate. You'll be up nights, I'm assuming."

Ryan nodded. "I'd really like to...visit some more with you. Tonight."

"Dinner?" Solana nearly interrupted. "Cafeteria?"

"That sounds great. But I need to shower. Should I come back here when I'm done?"

"Please. Martin can show you to my office. It's through there." She pointed behind him.

But he wouldn't take his eyes from her. He moved his body down, and she realized he was going to hug her, so she tried to relax and reciprocate. It was too quick for her to feel anything but chaos, but she knew how to plaster on a smile. For him, it wasn't hard. "Go. Before you fall asleep." She half expected him to once he got to his room.

Once he left, she held her hand up at Martin. "We met

when we were kids, and that's all I'm saying about it right now."

Martin sighed heavily. "Fine. Maybe I'll get more out of him later."

"Let him settle in first, at least."

"Don't let it be said I can't compromise."

"And I appreciate it. Now catch me up. Tell me about your week."

Martin turned and grabbed her mail before giving her ten straight minutes of non-stop observatory gossip. Solana was so glad to be home.

4

In all his fantasies, she had grown with him. How boring his fantasies had been. She eclipsed everything in his view.

And now he was awake, even if his body was rebelling.

She was so much shorter than he imagined, but he always overestimated the height of people. He wasn't sure at first it was her, but there was something in the lilt of her voice that transported him. Girls hadn't ever paid him any mind, but she had been interested and interesting. She was kind and smart. And though it had been dark, she was the prettiest thing he'd ever seen, earthly or cosmic.

As a woman, she was indescribably perfect. And he didn't want to fuck it up by being too weird. As he was teaching himself to breathe again, he nearly missed his room.

The key card worked effortlessly, even with the slight tremor in his hand. His nerves were making themselves known.

His room was small and efficient, a little less lived in than Germany, and it had that trendy minimalist flair he was growing to love. His bedroom at his parents was a bridge between his childhood to the adulthood he found himself experiencing just then. He liked it.

And Solana was there. But why couldn't he breathe properly? He wasn't asthmatic. He put his duffel on the bench at the end of the bed, and pulled out something neat and clean. He had a decent sweater on top, so he would look like he was trying. Because he was. He might need to order some nicer clothes.

Ryan just ignored most of the silent rules guys followed to impress a girl. He was smart and was gainfully employed in a career he was passionate about, so he could narrow down his looks and his behavior as needing a keen eye. His eye was not so accommodating, and he nearly called his mother. But he remembered the only times Solana had ever seen him, he was untidy. If he tried too hard, he might lose track of the conversation.

He quickly showered, and rushed through drying and dressing, and kept his breathing steady. A headache was forming. He had never in his life been as nervous as he was then, and this was just dinner.

Once he was ready, he grabbed his binoculars and made his way back to the front desk. There were quite a few people in the cafeteria now, and he dodged several with trays, and he pulled his mind inward, and concentrated on his racing heart. Martin was on the phone, but pointed toward the hall. He mouthed something Ryan didn't catch, but he could figure it out.

The hall wasn't very long, and he peeked into the only open door. When he saw Solana, he knocked to catch her attention.

She was sitting behind a glass desk, and she waved him in with a smile. "Get settled in okay?"

He nodded. "Is there somewhere more quiet we can eat? The cafeteria had a lot more people there. They seemed ready to socialize." He looked very anxious, and Solana appeared initially confused, then defensive. She stared at him, but her expression stilled and she settled on inquisitive.

Ryan didn't want to mess up. "We can if it's important. I'm just not going to remember anyone if I meet them tonight. I don't want to be rude." He didn't know why it was difficult to talk. "I'll be ready to take on people after sleep."

"It's not important. I was just momentarily worried thinking you didn't work well with others," she laughed, and relaxed a bit. Though she still clearly was questioning his reasoning. "There are some more secluded tables that—"

Ryan cleared his throat, and his head began to pound. He was clearly not well. He couldn't figure out how to vocalize it.

"Jesus, are you all right?" She stood and walked around to him. She made him sit down. She touched his head.

"I don't know. I think I'm just hungry. Tired." He was inhaling deeply. It couldn't be just her that was making him light-headed. He closed his eyes.

She pressed something over his face. "Breathe. We're so dumb. I should've seen it before. I was just so shocked to see you."

It took him a few seconds before he opened his eyes. Then he laughed. "This is so embarrassing."

"It's normal. Breathe. No laughing. No talking. Breathe."

He wanted to talk, but closed his eyes again and breathed in the canister of oxygen. He let her have a moment of silence. "Do you get altitude sickness?"

"I used to. Whenever I go see my parents in Santiago, I have some oxygen when I get back. I don't know if I still need it, but as you can feel, it's something you want to avoid. I have Tylenol if you have a headache. It's from my mom for this purpose, so it's got a little Codeine in it. We can get some prescribed for you if this becomes a habit." She took the mask off him. "Hopefully this will prevent any migraine that might try to break through. It does mine. My head will still hurt a little tomorrow, but it could be so much worse without these."

"Looks like I'm going to sleep well." Ryan could now tell the difference between being out of breath because of altitude, and just sitting next to her again. She was sitting close with her knees touching his.

"I want you to get something in your stomach, then we'll take our medicine, then we'll get you to bed."

"I want to hang out more, but I'm not going to argue."

He was deliriously pleased she wasn't ditching him for dinner.

"I like that you're not arguing when you know I'm right."

"It doesn't seem like an efficient way to spend an evening. Arguing. Especially if you're right."

"You are wise beyond your years, Mr.——. I don't even know your last name."

Ryan smiled. "Smith."

"Mr. Smith. That sounds like a name that has its shit together." She squeezed his knees with her hands before standing up.

He laughed, then coughed. She slapped him on the back. "There's a small semi-private lounge across from the front desk right before the cafeteria. It has a small sofa and coffee table. You're going to sit in there and I'm going to get food."

He opened his mouth to argue, then he remembered he wouldn't. She looked at him knowingly. He was slightly embarrassed. This wasn't how he wanted the night to go.

Once he got to his feet, she turned off the light, and led them toward dinner. He made sure his binoculars' strap wasn't choking him. It was amazing what a little oxygen could do.

"Do you like soup? I was thinking soup and sandwiches." Solana steered him with a hand on his forearm.

"I'll eat anything you bring me."

"I believe it. But, where do you put it?" She knocked him with her elbow.

He blushed. "If my mom hasn't figured that out, I'm not going to bother."

5

"You left your phone, so I programmed my number. I didn't take yours, though. I thought through the appropriateness after the fact." As soon as Solana put their shared tray down, he spoke, and he looked so much better that she almost didn't understand him. "But I'm not sorry."

She grabbed her phone, and gave him a long-suffering look. She opened up her texting app, and selected him. She changed 'Ryan' to 'Orion, the Hunter'. Because no one was safe in her phone. She would need to sneak a picture later.

Solana: You're lucky I like you.

She arranged their plates while he checked his phone, and when she saw his blush, she realized it might've been a little too flirtatious. He didn't text back, and she should've been relieved he didn't.

"So your parents. Your dad is teaching in Santiago now? Or is he retired?" He spoke quickly, before taking a bite of a chicken salad sandwich. "What's the soup?"

"Uh, yeah. Dad's been there for several years. They love it." She motioned toward the soup with her spoon. "Vegetable. But good." She gave him the Tylenol.

He smiled in thanks and took his medicine. "What does your mom do?"

"She works in cancer research."

"Wow. Cool. Did you rebel early against the sciences?"

She laughed. He was asking questions like he needed to

know. "Halfway through college. I wanted more control than the sciences could give me." She watched him inhale his soup. She was going to need to request a higher food budget. "Your dad worked on telescopes, right?"

"Mmhm. They're in Santiago, too. They'll be coming to stay here when they need him. Within the next year."

"That thing is so big I can barely comprehend it. Does your mom work, or do the mom thing?"

"She started back to school when I was in high school. She studies the Galápagos now, and goes a couple times a year. She writes articles for different newspapers and magazines."

Solana was impressed. "How cool is that?"

Ryan nodded, then looked up at her. "Wait a minute. I saw your business card stapled to the inside of the folder. Your name is Williams. Is your father Professor Michael Williams?"

"Oh, my God! Yes! Do you know him?" If she could've just made an effort to find this boy. It might not've been as difficult as she thought.

"Just by name and correspondence. I've never had him as a teacher. I was referred to him about something or another when I was in Puerto Rico, but by the time I needed an answer, he was already transferred out. Oh! It had something to do with a book on meteorology he recommended. El Niño stuff. I eventually e-mailed him about it. I can't believe I missed you guys by less than a few months. Don't tell me you ever lived in Germany."

"No. I don't think my dad ever looked for work there. My mom maybe, but they would have to agree, and they never mentioned it."

Solana was too shy to ask about her star. She would Google it. She wanted to call her dad and ask if he'd known, but she didn't think he really kept up with the random names of space objects, unless it was an unprecedented find.

86

If she were more sentimental, she would've looked for the name 'Ryan' on any space discoveries, and she could kick herself for not doing it. Solana could've found him years ago.

"You stay here. I'm going to take this back up since people don't normally eat in here."

When she looked over at him, he was staring back at her, like he was up to something, so she was just going to let him do his thing. She made a point to pocket her phone. After she picked up the tray, and left, she heard her text alert go off, and she smiled.

She returned their dishes and tray, then pulled her phone out of her pocket.

The text was nonsensical at first glance, but then she realized he was reminding her. She was sure she was looking at coordinates to the star cluster that was named for her. She was still amazed he named it for her. Solana never doubted that boy in the desert when he said he was going to find a star.

That boy who was now currently asleep when she walked back into the lounge. She put her hand on his shoulder and shook. "Let's get you to bed."

He blinked up at her. "No, no. I'm just resting my eyes. We need to go see—"

"The snow is coming down, so there may not be visibility for hours. We might get lucky tomorrow night. I want to see my star cluster, too."

"I want to spend more time with you." He stood and grabbed his binoculars.

"We will tomorrow. I have to be up early, so I need to get to bed."

"Oh shit. I didn't mean—"

"If I didn't want to be up with you right now, I wouldn't be. Now, come on. I'm walking you back to your room."

"I can walk you to yours."

"Tomorrow. It's your first night here, so you get turn down service."

"Is that a normal service?"

"Nope."

Ryan offered his arm to her this time, and since she took it the last time, it was easy to keep at it.

He led her down the hall to his room, and brought her inside. She made a point to pull his bedding down, then walked back toward him with her arms out. Ryan had no problem getting wrapped in her, but as their height difference became more noticeable, he lifted her, and that shocked a laugh out of her.

His arms were fixed around her waist, and his face nuzzled her neck. He didn't seem to be aware of what he was doing, and when his mouth brushed innocently against her throat, she gave him full access as she moaned.

Ryan clearly wasn't expecting that. He turned and pressed her to his door as his mouth sought hers. After a few insane seconds, they found a rhythm, and their bodies molded together.

His mouth went back to her neck. "I've been looking at your neck all fucking night. I didn't even know I had a thing for necks."

Solana's stomach flipped and it was too much. She needed to *think*.

"Stop. Stop, please."

He did so. Rapidly. He nearly dropped her. "I'm sorry! Sometimes I don't know when to shut up." He placed her down slowly and backed up.

She shook her head, and smoothed down her pixie cut. "No. It's not that. This is just a lot to take in and I have to think about my position here."

"Neither of us are subordinate to the other. We work in two different fields."

"HR handles a lot. And I'm the boss." She didn't handle behavioral issues among the scientists when they came up, though, so she knew she was deflecting. She would see the paperwork, but it wasn't her call. She handled all areas of ESO permanent staffing, and questions and accommodations of the temporary scientists.

Solana hated the look on his face. It was hard for her to admit to herself that she felt so strongly for Ryan, and quickly.

He sat down. "I just found you again. My only option is to find somewhere else where it wouldn't be a conflict for you."

Solana cringed. He would leave just to be with her, and she realized he wasn't capable of playing. "God, no. I'm sorry. I'm overwhelmed. I'm not...I don't know. This is just too much for me right now."

"I'm sorry. I'm terrible at reading signs. I thought—"

"You didn't read anything wrong. I got lost in you." She put her hand on his shoulder so he would look at her again. "We just need to take a step back."

"If you feel like that's best." He shrugged the shoulder her hand was on, so she removed it. "We'll be working opposite schedules, so..." He frowned. It didn't seem like he wanted to hear how that sentence ended out loud. He wouldn't look at her. "I...need to get to sleep."

Solana resisted kissing him again. "If you have any questions, or need anything, call or text me. Anytime. Okay?"

He nodded, but he was looking past her. God, she hurt him, and she hated herself for it. She nearly asked him if he thought his parents would be fine if his girlfriend was Black, but that would lead to hours of conversation she didn't know she was ready to have. That's what it came down to. If Solana pursued a relationship with Ryan, she knew it would be permanent. He was it.

She would need to get her thoughts in order because she would have to be honest with him. He deserved that.

Solana had a secret worry he would remain angry and insulted if she explained they needed to talk about race and the things they may deal with. Or worse, that he's proud to be colorblind.

She took one last look at him before she left, and met his eyes before he looked down at his hands.

ARDEN AOIDE

6

Ryan managed to fall asleep quickly, but Solana's rejection hit him hard the next morning. He'd slept for fourteen hours, and he didn't feel well-rested. He dressed and found the very small market attached to the hotel. He bought stuff for sandwiches, some doughnuts, milk, and soda. He wanted to stay in his room until dark. Then he might go exploring.

The snow had already melted out his window, but the forecast called for more snow that night, so he couldn't really work. He was familiar with the observatories, and he had the folder of information.

He tried not to think of Solana, but it wasn't easy. He'd imagined their reunion a thousand times. He thought of their first kiss so many times, and he never imagined he'd have so little control. The smell of her, and the feel of her skin beneath his face, the taste of her, the feel of her against his mouth...

Ryan sat heavily on his bed. He was still very tired, and he didn't know if it was because he was hurt or exhausted or a little of both. He'd eat, then sleep a little more. He needed to get his schedule together anyway.

Solana grabbed herself a quick dinner, then went to her room. After she ate, she had a long bath, and put on her most comfortable two-piece pajamas and the massive flannel robe she stole from her dad.

She was feeling sorry for herself, and checked her phone

every half hour to see if Ryan texted. She felt a little negligent that she didn't check on him, but she had to get her head straight first.

Solana wasn't afraid for her job, or even her standing within the company. It wasn't uncommon for relationships to form out here in the middle of nowhere especially when most programs lasted for years.

She wanted to protect him from any looks they may get because he was so ignorantly innocent. She didn't know if she was ready for him to actually ignore the looks because he truly didn't see them. She needed a man who was aware of things like that if they were going to be serious.

She felt paranoid and she was letting every single uncomfortable racial memory come to the surface, and she tried to picture his face in all of those. For some, it was easy, but others it was difficult. She'd never seen him in a position where he lost his cool. Even last night, he seemed to make a point to respect her wishes, even though he vehemently disagreed.

He was far too kind for the world, but to be with her, and to possibly give her children, he would need to tap into mean.

Her parents wouldn't care, and her brother might raise an eyebrow, but Ryan would smile, and be exceedingly polite. She could picture Ryan and her father connecting over their work.

It was tempting to think of their secluded little life at ESO, and romanticize everything else. Because she knew he would want to keep her safe and happy right here. And it would be the easiest thing she'd ever do. But it wouldn't be right. Did she think he could handle it?

Yeah. She thought he could. But if he couldn't, it was better they find out now.

She pulled out her phone. He could easily brush her off and she wouldn't blame him if he wanted to keep his distance.

Solana: Where are you right now?

He answered immediately. The relief she felt was immense.

Orion, the Hunter: On the roof.

It took her a moment to understand what he meant.

Solana: Of the hotel?

Orion, the Hunter: Yes. Visibility is poor, so I'm waiting for the snow.

Solana: The temp is dropping.

Orion, the Hunter: I'm fully winterized.

Solana rolled her eyes, but her cheeks hurt from smiling. She didn't text back. She wanted him. So, she was going to have him. Even if she had to trudge up to the damn roof.

She put on her gloves, cap, and boots. Her robe was plenty warm.

7

Ryan was trying very hard not to feel anxious. He didn't understand her, but he wanted to spend time with her regardless.

He had a long nap, and woke up surprisingly refreshed. The snow hadn't started, so he thought he would go out and wait for it.

He assumed she would keep her distance, so it was bittersweet that she was seeking him out.

The temperature had dropped noticeably. A surprise inch or two of snow was expected, and whenever he lived in warmer climates, the excitement in the air for snow was addicting. He found a secluded spot no one had considered.

He had a thick blanket beneath him that he had found in some communal camping gear. There was room enough for Solana to fit, so he shifted over. The ground through the blanket was warm, so he was almost overdressed.

Nerves started to eat at him, so he rested his binoculars against his face. He got lost in the cold weight, and he didn't hear her footsteps.

"Where are your glasses?"

He removed the binoculars and squinted at her. "Back in my room. These were created for my eyes. But they also function normally."

Solana sat for a moment before she lay down. "That's actually quite cool. Do you still have your old ones?"

He was still squinting at her. "I do. They're back with my parents."

Solana smoothed his brows with her gloved fingers so he would relax his face. It was hard for him to do. "Stop. Relax." She was frowning.

"Why do you look at me as if I've done something wrong?" He didn't want to sound accusatory.

"Was I?"

"Yeah. Like you were a little disappointed in me." He also didn't want to sound pathetic, but he was whining a little.

"I didn't mean to do that at all. I never look happy when I've got a lot on my mind. I don't even need to be stressed."

He couldn't clearly make out much of anything without his glasses, but he felt her hand eventually curl itself into his palm, and he realized what she was doing. She wanted to be with him. She made a decision. He was thankful he had the instincts not to show his frustration, because he'd rather feel anger than hurt, but being angry at her felt almost disloyal. "Yeah?"

"Yeah," she whispered.

The quick surge of adrenaline had his mouth moving before his brain. "Sometimes I hack into and disable abandoned private satellites and watch them fall out of the sky and burn up in the atmosphere. Out of spite. Because I would have found your star cluster a full fucking year earlier if I had access to more than just the shadows of it."

She was silent for a moment. "That is the most criminally wholesome thing ever, and I didn't hear it."

Her fingers entwined with his, and he didn't understand anything about the universe at all. Hormones and emotions were *insane.*

He put his binoculars down. "Do you want to wait for the snow with me?"

"You don't need to track any stardust tonight?...Or destroy any satellites?"

"Nope. Busy tonight." He moved closer to her and

pressed his cheek to the top of her head. He rubbed his face on her knit cap. "Before you ask, it's a very clean hack, and I don't mess with Space X or NASA, or anyone who has a team I suspect could track me. Just people too dumb to learn proper Astronomy who want something to orbit them."

She pressed her face against his arm and he could feel her laughing. Solana cleared her throat. "Once the snow starts, I'm taking you to my room." She smiled as she heard him inhale. "I'm tired, but I still want to spend some time with you before I go to sleep."

"What if someone—?"

"I don't care." She met his eyes close enough for him to see. "Do you care?"

Ryan shook his head rapidly. "Of course not. What are we—" He looked back up to the sky. "What do you want to do?" He asked carefully.

"Make out like teenagers where it's warm."

He exhaled. "You're asking for a bad time. I didn't make out with anyone until I was twenty."

"Last night was very nice." He was thankful for the humor in her voice.

"Yeah, I should be doing groundbreaking work tonight, but all I can think about is last night," he admitted.

"You shouldn't've said 'groundbreaking work'. Kissing was just fine. I might have expectations now."

His breath shook as she pulled up the sleeve of his shirt to kiss his wrist. "I might know what I'm doing. Might. Just...manage your expectations the first week or two. I'd have to be an idiot not to eventually figure out how...best we fit."

Her grin against his wrist made him shudder. "You find deep space objects. You've seen billions of years just through a piece of glass. You know all the dips and curves of the universe even occluded. You'd have me memorized in ten minutes."

The snow started to fall, but he ignored it as he

turned to his side. Ryan looked like she smacked him. *Ten minutes?* "And yet, I look at Orion every night it's visible. I look for the Horsehead Nebula because it's ours. And I look at Solana11 every night. Because I was eleven when this started. All before I even started on the satellites. If I memorize it, I come back for it forever. It's mine."

"Then it can't be said that this is too fast," she murmured.

He shook his head emphatically. "I've been pining for you since puberty. Too fast is laughable."

"That's what I wanted to hear," she said, then slowly slotted her nose next to his. When he closed his eyes, she kissed him.

It was a surprise for both of them when he rolled them over and spread her knees. He thought they fit naturally, instinctively together, and he never felt the chill in the air once their mouths and hips were aligned.

8

Snow was especially cold if one was making out and didn't notice it for a while.

Ryan had been covered in it.

She held his hand when they came in. And she led him to her room. She wanted him to fall into her, on her bed, and never leave.

"I'm sorry for being so cautious, but not explaining why," she said between kisses. "I just want you to be ready for things you might face."

He pulled back to look at her. It seemed like a light turned on. "I never want to be dismissive, but some things are off my radar. You might need to slap sense into me sometimes." He sat on her bed and held her hands in front of him. Their faces were closer together when he sat.

"I need you to develop your radar then."

He nodded. He bent his head down so he could pull her gloves off properly. Then he kissed both hands. "Whatever you need. Truly. And not because of this. Even if you only wanted to be friends, and you needed me to help you or protect you, I'd do whatever was needed."

"Hopefully it won't be just me you'd want to help or protect if needed," she whispered. "Understand?"

He kissed her mouth once before pulling away, and he nodded again while keeping eye contact. "I get it." Another nod, and his mouth met hers again, and he didn't let up.

They needed to talk. Really talk. But she hadn't learned her lesson from the previous kiss. She wanted to keep her head. She appreciated he was still choosing his words carefully. He might think she's overreacting, because he truly didn't know. But he was good. And that meant everything to her.

Solana believed in him. So she would let him have her, foolishly, but it felt exhilarating to trust this man.

She attempted to pull off his shirt, but he quickly did most of the work. It gave him the courage to stand and remove her robe and nightshirt. He backed up again after and sat on her bed once she was in her bra. When he eventually made eye contact again, she reached back and unclipped it.

Her breasts were large and heavy, and she wasn't sure if Ryan was going to look her in the eye at all while she was apparently edible. His eyes were hungry and she had to step closer to see what that meant.

Ryan held her waist tentatively, and she rested her arms on his shoulders as he mouthed at her breasts, grazing her nipples more often than not. She hugged his head loosely.

His fingers followed her waistband, and after a moment, managed to untie it. Once he had her pants down, she stepped out of them, and went to climb on the bed. She wasn't expecting to be pinned to her front while Ryan pressed his mouth, tongue, and teeth to the entire back of her neck.

Solana pressed back against him as he began to subtly thrust forward. He pulled back. "I don't have any condoms. Shit."

She turned over and he clearly forgot what he was talking about. "I'm on birth control."

"So, we're good?"

"Hopefully."

"The pressure. Yikes," he breathed before spreading her out like he had her on the roof.

"No pressure," she whispered against his mouth. He stood suddenly to take care of the rest of his clothes, and he didn't bother being shy. He was down again with his mouth at her breasts while he slipped his fingers into the band of her panties to remove them.

Once they were dangling from her foot, his head moved between her legs, and if she had known the evening was going to go so well, she would've been more reluctant to leave his room the previous night.

It was clear he was aiming to please her, but he seemed to get distracted on his own, if his fingers and mouth were any indication. Usually Solana had to be in the right state of mind to have an orgasm, but Ryan was tapping into a part of her pleasure that she was finally ready to let loose. She trusted him, so she sang her pleasure to the room.

That spurred him further, and while she was coming down, he was sliding carefully into her. She was going to tell him he didn't have to be so sweet, but she realized he had no choice. It was slow out of his necessity, so she took advantage of his kiss. She was surprised she felt the need to come again. Solana wanted him to watch. She knew he would once she moved her hand down.

He did. He watched her in awe, and when she moaned and squeezed him, he didn't have a choice but to finish roughly.

It was perfect.

Ryan fell down beside her, and he pulled her against him. This was going to be more trouble than she thought, because she didn't want to spend a night away from him. She sighed, and pressed her cheek to his chest. He grabbed her hand and entwined their fingers. They saw for the first time how beautiful they looked together.

"Are you coherent? We need to talk, but I don't want you to freak out. It's hard to talk about this out of context."

"You're not talking about blatant racism, right? It's the small insidious stuff I may not normally notice?"

So, he dived in. Good. He wasn't ignorant. "Right.

100

It's the microaggressions that you could easily overlook by taking the high road. Sometimes you can, but sometimes you absolutely cannot." She took a deep breath because she could potentially freak him out. "I can't pursue a serious indefinite relationship with a white man until he thinks about our potential children. His Black children."

"Ah," he said, but he tightened his hold on her, so she exhaled.

"I can handle my own shit, but to be in my life as my partner, I would need you to understand things you don't normally think about, and most of the time, I'll still want to handle it. You ready to run, yet?"

"Not unless you're lying about being on the pill."

"Ryan." She slapped his arm.

"I understand. Kids are a little abstract right now, but yeah, when I think of our kids, they look like you. You have to know I'd protect them."

"I do. I just want you to be armed with information you wouldn't normally have. People are going to disappoint you. You're probably going to disappoint me. I just need you to always listen."

He seemed to be making the effort for the conversation without getting defensive. "Are you disappointed often?"

"Not lately. ESO has been great. And I can read people's intentions. If I go elsewhere, there's always something. Most of the time you can ignore it, but sometimes you can't. I just need you ready and aware. You'll know by my behavior if I feel safe. Or you'll learn quickly."

"I don't want to ask you to be patient with me, but if you think I'm not getting it, you'll tell me?"

"Of course," she swallowed. "Would your parents mind?"

He laughed. "My parents found out about you the night we met. They know about the stars."

"They know I'm Black?"

"I'm assuming. They told me they had coffee with your parents outside in the mornings. Dad just knew your dad's name was Michael."

"Another damn thing! If I would've told my parents about you, they might've had your parent's names."

"The universe finally had enough and threw us together."

"I guess we better listen." She felt mischievous. She stroked a hand down his stomach until he inhaled sharply. "Tell me about your first time." The lamp was low, but she could see his blush, and yeah, she wanted to keep him.

"Why don't we keep talking about our children instead," he suggested hopefully.

She bit the side of his abs playfully. "Tell me." She felt his chest rise and fall.

"I don't know if this is a beneficial subject change. But since you're asking for the ugly truth. It was terrifying until I was nearly done. It sounds awful, but I knew nothing going in. It was over so fast."

"What?" She couldn't keep the laughter out of her voice.

"I mean, I knew where I was supposed to put my penis, but that was about it."

She screamed a laugh, and he was momentarily alarmed. It was the most sound he'd ever heard her make. He wanted her to keep making it.

"I learned about the clitoris just Googling one day."

She put the pillow over her face and screamed into it, and he tickled her on her ribs. "I don't want to brag, but I think I did a decent enough job with yours."

Solana moved the pillow from her face, and climbed on top of him. "Good thing you Googled."

She could see how he closed up a bit, and she leaned down and rested her body against his. She kissed his perfectly smooth chin. She didn't think he was capable of growing facial hair. He opened his mouth, closed it, then opened it again. "So, it was okay? I haven't done anything with anyone since that first time."

She was usually fond of his natural confidence, but

this was also endearing. Usually she wouldn't tolerate it, but she knew he wasn't asking for his ego. He really wanted her pleased. "I've had a couple boyfriends. Nothing that lasted more than a few months. Nothing I look back on with particular fondness." She kissed his chin again. Then down his neck until he laughed. "I didn't fake any of that, Ryan. This was...exactly what every woman should experience. And I've never experienced anything like you."

He put his arms around her to hug her tight. "Am I supposed to smile at that?"

"Oh, now you're trying to get a boost."

"I didn't know it would feel so nice. No wonder men always think they can be president. I'm ready to run right now." Ryan was rambling and Solana was captivated. "I wonder if all the men who ran for president had perfect sex and great compliments the night before they decided to run."

Solana shuddered. "Have you seen some of our presidents?"

Ryan cringed. "You might need to distract me so I'll stop talking." He beamed with pride. He was learning to flirt so good.

She shifted her hips, and he moved his hands to grip them hard. "You're...we're. This." He couldn't find the words. It was too much being inside her. "Us."

Solana worked her hips down. She nodded. "Just us. Only ever us."

"Oh," he breathed with wonder. Then Solana came completely undone.

KIT SOMERSET, VISCOUNT GREENWOOD: MOST LIKELY TO REMAIN ON THE LIST

Ten Most Eligible Lords List

Blair Babylon

0 Prologue

Ten Most Eligible Lords List

The London Weekly Chat, Gossip Column

The Right Honorable Christopher "Kit" Somerset, the Viscount Greenwood, is perhaps the most elusive aristocrat on our list of the Ten Most Eligible Lords in England, as he seems to be the most upright and responsible one of the dirty bunch. He is incessantly working at his family's trust. Doesn't he know that posh people hire commoners to manage boring twaddle like that?

During the Social Season, one can often find this green-eyed, natural ash-blond, buff hottie at the usual smart haunts, especially the sporting events like the Badminton Horse Trials and Wimbledon. Always impeccably dressed in a fashionable suit or debonair formalwear, Kit Somerset cuts a dashing figure in the boardroom and at parties.

Underneath his smart sartorial choices, however, Kit has a rock-hard body that should be criminal to cover up, the broadest of shoulders, and a truly spectacular arse, so you may enjoy the view when he's coming and going. When this reporter put Kit Somerset to the ultimate test, those smart fashion choices were indicative of an attention to detail and dedication to craft that left this reporter weak in the knees just remembering our encounter for weeks afterward, which was how long I was sore from this enormous member of the House of Lords.

In his wake, Kit Somerset leaves a trail of broken hearts, including several of our noblest English roses plucked and discarded on the garden path of his massive country estate, Greenwood Manor. If you find yourself talking to this naughty lord at the high-society parties he frequents, be aware that we've named Kit Somerset "Most Likely to Remain on the Most Eligible Lords List."

Highly enjoyable for an evening, but don't expect to become Lady Greenwood.

1

NYE in NYC

Christopher "Kit" Somerset, Viscount Greenwood caught a flight from London to New York City and crashed his cousin's New Year's Eve party at fifteen minutes before midnight. A friend had texted him a wild rumor, and he had to know whether it was true.

A dense crowd packed the voluminous drawing room of the Fifth Avenue penthouse. Enormous window panes, four stories high, overlooked the twinkling lights of Manhattan, and the cold night sky mirrored the glitter with stars. Much of the crowd was of the smart set like Kit and his cousin Maud St Leger, but Maud had many friends from the wealthy and powerful elite who were in attendance that night.

Kit found Maud in the center of a knot of people over by the piano, sipping brandy and talking to the heir to the defunct throne of Greece and a tech billionaire who made her money patenting medical devices that reduced damage from strokes and spinal injuries. He called over the din, "Maud, cousin! And Nikolaos and Ebony! How are you?"

"Oh, here's one of our Most Eligible Lords," Maud smirked.

"Maud, please," Kit said, refusing to shrink from her teasing. Four months before, a sordid tabloid article had ranked Kit and nine of his friends and peers as "England's Most Eligible Lords" and described their lordships in excruciating detail for readers. They'd brought it on themselves for even speaking to that reporter, not to mention other indiscretions that had occurred.

Maud kissed Kit on the cheek and called a waiter over to make sure he was supplied with champagne. "Kit, darling, Ebony is releasing a new product in a few months and assures us that her stock is a strong buy. Other than that, I didn't understand a word she's said. Ebbs, dearest, could you back up and take a run at that again?"

Ebony flipped her long braids behind her shoulder. Her scarlet and ivory manicure flashed against her midnight skin and hair. "It's okay. I know you won't get it this time, either. Let's just say that I'm going to keep a million people from dying next year from a heart attack."

Nikolaos laughed. "Next time, lead with saving a million lives." Nikolaos was in marketing and gave everyone promotion advice, whether they needed it or not.

Maud turned back to Kit. "I'm so glad to see you. I thought you were going to stay in London for New Year's Eve this year."

Kit grinned at his cousin. "I heard Simone Maina is going to be here."

Maud kept smiling at him, but her eyebrows flinched toward the middle of her forehead as far as her latest Botox injections would allow. "She's over by the fireplace, but I should warn you that Cordelia Cochrane is upstairs at the bar."

He shrugged. "Cordy and I broke up three months ago."

"Yes, Aunt Hildy isn't pleased about that and is telling anyone who will listen about how Cordy is 'perfect for the family.'"

"Mummy is never pleased about anything I do. I heard Simone got a divorce," Kit said.

"Yes, it was final three weeks ago."

Kit smirked. "So, it's *final.*"

Maud lifted one eyebrow a quarter of an inch.

KIT SOMERSET, VISCOUNT GREENWOOD: MOST LIKELY TO REMAIN ON THE LIST

"When your father is a government minister and your uncle is a judge, divorces tend to happen quickly. You aren't going to pick her up and dump that poor woman, *too,* are you? She's been through quite a lot."

"Me? Never." Kit squeezed Maud's arm and wedged himself between two people, starting to make his way over to the fireplace.

She yelled after him, "I say, Kit, you should know—"

But Kit was already wedging himself between groups of people and skirting the edges of clusters, drawing closer to Simone Maina.

[***]

Simone Maina sat near the fireplace in a cluster of her friends from the elite Swiss boarding school Le Rosey, where she'd spent most of her childhood. The fire warmed one side of her face, which was a lovely relief because the thermostat of Maud's New York penthouse evidently had been set to Ice Station Zebra. Simone wasn't sure what the actual number was, but it was at least ten degrees lower than in Mauritius, where she had left just days before. The New York climate was always a rude shock after home.

Her friends with whom she was sitting all looked relieved and happy when she announced that she had finally divorced her now ex-husband.

One of her best friends from school, Emi Abebe, was sitting beside Simone but on the floor, her very long legs folded up, and she was resting her elbows on them. They'd been friends ever since they'd arrived at the Swiss boarding school and discovered that Emi was from Ethiopia and Simone, from Mauritius. They were practically neighbors in a school predominated by Western Europeans, Russians, and Chinese students.

Simone had been playing with Emi's ears and the long line of her neck, careful not to nudge her short Afro that fitted as tightly to her head as a skullcap. The penthouse was a little darker over near the fireplace, and in the dim, flickering light from the flames, the dark bronze skin of Simone's finger was almost indistinguishable from Emi's dark gray-brown tones.

Emi flapped her long-fingered hand at her ear where Simone was bugging her. "Will you stop?"

Simone tugged on Emi's drooping earlobe. *"Ayo,* probably not."

Aamir rolled his eyes and bent down to talk to Emi. "She has not changed since we were three. She did the same thing to me the whole time we were kids, even before we went away to boarding school."

Aamir's parents had been friends with Simone's back on Mauritius as they were all variously employed in the government or tourism industry, and both couples owned racehorses. The four of them had hatched their plan to send their children to the most expensive boarding school in the world so they could "make contacts."

Simone couldn't say that it had worked, but then again, she'd married the French billionaire Estebe Fournier whom she'd met there right after she'd graduated from college. So, that was a contact.

Now, newly divorced and with all the complications that usually stemmed from a marriage break-up plus one, Simone was trying to put her life back together.

She was going to need these elite Le Rosey contacts.

The party bubbled around them, a rambunctious rabble of talking with long-time friends with whom she hadn't been able to have a real conversation for years because that's what happens when one is suffering through a bad marriage. Flames danced in the fireplace as she projected her voice to talk over the string quartet and three hundred people who were all carrying on extended conversations, discussions, and debates from the last time that they'd all seen each other at one of the huge parties Maud threw every few months in New York.

A sexy, male baritone voice called over the music and chatter, "Simone! *Simone Maina!"*

She turned, pushing herself around with her hands to see who was hollering her name across the penthouse.

Aamir half-stood to get a better look, too.

A lot of people in the crowd were tall, so it took a second for the white man calling her name to come into view. He was ridiculously tall, well over six feet, and his ash-blond hair had a distinct wave to it. Between his English-pale skin and black-tie tuxedo, his bright blue eyes were startling as the only pop of vibrant color about him. He had a square, hard jaw and cheekbones that hinted at a little Viking blood in his ancestry, though Simone knew Christopher Somerset was too much of an Englishman to ever admit it.

Simone pushed herself to her feet, her sleek baby bump leading the way as she leveraged herself off the sofa. "Kit? *Kit Somerset?"*

Kit Somerset pushed his way through the crowd with one hand holding a champagne flute, obviously trying not to spill it. He had been handsome in high school, his strong jaw and cheekbones evident even when everyone had the softness of adolescence on their faces and bodies. In the intervening decade and a half, that childhood chub had burned away, leaving a tall, rock-hard man with broad shoulders, a slim waist, and long legs. He was a trim English nobleman, his body lean and muscular without resembling a steroid-abusing lunkhead, and the only word to describe Kit Somerset in a fashionable tuxedo was *debonair.*

Kit finally managed to swim through the crush and reach where she was standing. She looked up to his eyes, and he beamed as he looked down at her.

His gaze traveled down her deep sapphire blue dress, and she saw the moment her mid-term pregnancy registered in his eyes. He blinked rapidly twice as his eyebrows twitched upward.

Well, everybody seemed to have heard about her divorce, but few people seemed to be talking about the fact she was knocked up, too.

And then she saw something interesting: Kit had an instant to think about her baby bump as he inspected her, one of his eyebrows lowered for just a moment as he considered whatever he was thinking about, and then his shoulders twitched.

He raised his gaze from Simone's tummy and met her eyes, and he smiled. "I heard you divorced Estebe."

That was an odd way to lead into a conversation. "Hello to you, too, Kit. Yes, it's been a long time since I've seen you. I've been fine, spending a lot of time with my parents and cousins in Mauritius lately. How's your life been? And can't we address all the other small talk before we start talking about the fact that my life just ripped apart?"

Kit stood in front of her and drained his glass of champagne, smiling down at her with a heat she hadn't seen in his eyes in years. "Can we talk somewhere?"

Simone glanced back at Emi, Aamir, and the rest of the old school friends whom she had been catching up with.

Every single one of them was watching Simone and Kit with their eyebrows raised and chins slightly turned, wearing various expressions of surprise and a bit of dismay that he was immediately pulling her away for a private chat.

She said, "Um, okay, but I should come right back to talk with these people in a few minutes. It's not polite to just go off—"

Emi snorted and waved her long fingers at Simone like banners waving in a breeze. "Go. We'll be here."

Kit took her hand as if Emi's consent was sufficient, his strong fingers warm and comforting in hers. He led her over by the windows that overlooked the skyline of New York City. The dark rectangle in the middle of the thousands of points of light was Central Park.

As Simone followed him, the tails of his tuxedo jacket fluttered as he strode, and all she could think of was that the reporter who had seduced all ten of the Most Eligible Lords in the interest of journalism had been absolutely right about Kit Somerset's arse. It was spectacular.

Simone couldn't stop thinking about the rest of that woman's reportage, either. "Kit? What are you doing?"

He turned toward her once they reached the wall but didn't let go of her fingers. Their joined hands and arms hung in the air between them like a bridge. "Are you okay?"

"Well, of course, I'm okay." Simone gestured to the designer gown she wore, the last alterations made just the day before to make sure it fit her growing pregnancy perfectly. "Don't I look okay?"

Kit looked at her with a sultry glance, and one side of his mouth turned up in a smile. "You look fantastic. I heard about what happened in Monte Carlo."

A month before, when Simone's husband had turned from a garden-variety asshole to outright abusive and tried to really hurt her, she'd managed to get away from him when they were at the Monte Carlo casino in Monaco. An old Le Rosey friend of hers who'd happened to be there helped her escape from Estebe. A few hours later, she'd been on a plane back to Mauritius and her family.

Which meant, of course, the Le Rosey "rose-vine" (because gossip "grapevines" are for commoners) had carried the news about that daring escape and quick yacht ride to Genoa to most of her friends from boarding school. "I'm okay now."

Kit leaned back against the wall behind him and, still holding onto her fingers, tugged her closer. "I'm sorry that happened. I threatened to punch Estebe in the face when he stole you away from me in high school, and that threat is still good if I ever see him again."

"I don't like to think about violence. It's not funny

anymore."

Kit shook his head, his pale blond hair swaying where it fell over his forehead. "Sorry. I didn't think."

"But he'd better never set foot on the continent of Africa again. My father put out a warrant for his arrest, and most of the other countries in Africa will extradite him to Mauritius to stand trial."

Kit's amused grin was just as sunny as she remembered from high school. He used her fingers to tug her a little closer to him, so that her feet were on either side of one of his.

She continued, "And my father put liens on a bunch of his property in Asia and Africa, rather than going after him for alimony. I've already got the money from what would have been a divorce settlement. Deutsche Bank, the preferred bank for the Russian mafia and money launderers, informed Estebe that he had loans to repay to them."

Kit laughed aloud at this, and his eyes sparkled with glee.

Simone asked him, "Aren't you dating Cordelia Cochrane? She's around here somewhere. I saw her talking to Maud earlier."

"We broke up three months ago."

Oh. "I didn't hear about that."

His pull on her hand was just a little more insistent. "I was rather hoping you had, and that's why you were here."

She stepped a little closer to him, and his knee caught on the long skirt of her dress. "Estebe kept me away from people, so I didn't hear much news."

On the other side of the huge room, three furniture groupings away, somebody yelled, "Two minutes!"

Kit's hand rested on her hip. "Here we are, both of us available for the first time in years, at midnight on New Year's Eve."

Simone glanced at the clock on the wall above the fireplace. Both its hands pointed upward, near the

114

twelve. "I guess it is midnight already."

"When I heard you were in New York for Maud's party, I hopped on a plane. I got here just in time."

Simone looked back at him, thinking that he was probably kidding her, but he was looking directly into her eyes. "High school was a long time ago."

"A lifetime ago. When I broke up with Cordelia, that group of boys that I used to hang around with in school—"

Simone remembered them. The five guys were all British aristocracy. By the time they'd graduated upper school, each one of them was hotter than the last. She said, "Yeah, you guys were all in that magazine, *The London Weekly Chat.*"

Kit laughed, and his chortle was easy and unaffected as if he didn't mind that he'd been *so* thoroughly described for everyone to read.

Unable to resist taunting him just a bit, Simone continued, "So, how does it feel to headline 'The Ten Most Eligible Lords List'?"

He said, "Unfortunately, it's taken on quite a life of its own. As with everything, it will pass, but someday I do plan to torment my future teenage sons by having the article enlarged, framed, and displayed above the mantle for all to see."

Simone cracked up. Kit was never mean.

"Anyway, after that last fight with Cordelia when she threw a drink in my face at the Goodwood Revival, those four sods came up to Greenwood Manor for a week and sat me down for a postmortem. Evidently, the last three times Cordelia and I parted ways distressed them. They wanted me to either go back to her with a proposal of marriage or give her up for good, but this waffling back and forth was 'unseemly and quite common.'"

Simone laughed. "I can hear Orlando saying that."

Over on the other side of the room, the crowd yelled, "One minute!"

Kit said, "Tristan has been studying psychology and counseling and believes he may now rival Freud and Jung with his keen insight. After some dream analysis, word association, and reading of my tea leaves—"

"You're *kidding.*"

"I am not. Tristan is earnest about his studies. Anyway, Tristan endeavored to persuade me that I have never gotten over *you,* and I must put this matter to rest in my own mind or I shall never be fully committed to another relationship."

Simone raised an eyebrow at him. "Are you serious?"

"Deadly."

"He's gone round the twist."

"Most assuredly, but he may not be wrong."

Simone couldn't quite tell whether Kit was kidding her or whether he was just trying to get her into bed. "Back at school, some of those guys were pretty wild. You didn't make a list of all the girls from school and bet on who could sleep with the most of them in a year or something, did you?"

The honest shock in Kit's widened eyes and his pause before he spoke convinced her. "We did go too far when we were back in school sometimes, but we're all thirty years old now, give or take. We don't indulge in such games. Tristan is studying in all seriousness to be a counselor, and I am responsible for running my family's trust and the businesses thereof. I'm responsible for the property of the trust and the employment of several thousand people. I don't have the time or interest for childish games."

"Then why are you here? People don't just hop on planes to see high-school crushes."

"I did. I wanted to see you tonight and discover where this might lead us."

Simone ran her fingers up the fine wool of Kit's tuxedo sleeves to his shoulders. "I just got out of an awful marriage, one that had been bad for several years and then got much worse. I'm not looking for a relationship right now." She ran her hand over the smooth swell of her tummy where a baby was growing. "I have other priorities, and I'm not interested in anything else."

Kit might've looked a little sad for a second, but his smile didn't waver. He settled his other hand on her waist on the other side. "I got on a plane and raced here to kiss you at midnight because, for the first time in almost half of our lifetimes, we both can. Just a kiss at midnight for old time's sake?"

Over on the other side of the room, people started counting down from ten.

The chant spread across the couches, past the curving staircase to the upper floor, through the dining room area arranged with buffet tables, and beyond two more couch groupings to the fireplace and the corner where she and Kit stood.

Simone trailed her hands from Kit's shoulders to behind his neck and interlaced her fingers there. "Just one kiss, for old time's sake."

He guided her in by his grip on her waist.

Even with being so early in her second trimester, Simone wasn't he used to the additional bulk of her tummy. She overbalanced and toppled, her hands splaying against his chest. "Oh! I'm sorry."

"I'm not." Kit kissed her, wrapping his arms around her back and dragging her to him.

His soft lips on hers were magic, a sweet brush and a nibble that implored her to open her lips. She did, and he deepened the kiss, stroking her tongue with his and sucking on her lower lip gently.

His large hands spread across her, one drifting down to the small of her back and the other wrapping around her shoulders.

Kit was wearing a posh sandalwood and citrus cologne. The faint whiff of it was clean and refined and very masculine.

The thought came to her that she wanted to be surrounded by that scent.

He was a much better kisser now than when they had been fifteen.

So was she, Simone hoped.

She was practically lying on his chest and abdomen where she had fallen against him. The warmth from his heavy pectorals and rippled lumps of his abdominal muscles seeped through the thin silk of his shirt under his tuxedo jacket.

The rest of the crowd was cheering, and Simone faintly heard their whoops through her heartbeat pounding in her ears.

She couldn't stop kissing him. Kit started to lift his head away at some point, and she reached up to the back of his neck and pulled him back down to her.

Simone hadn't been kissed like this in years. The passion in her marriage had atrophied and fallen away years before, and she'd become accustomed to its absence. She'd tried to rekindle things, like everyone tries to. Looking back after the divorce, the problem hadn't been with her. The problem had been that Estebe was screwing every employee or random woman who'd seemed amenable, and knowing Estebe, probably some who weren't.

But kissing Kit felt like the fire and rushing blood in her veins when they had been sixteen together, and every kiss had been new and different and special.

Kissing Kit felt like a second chance to begin her life again.

The penthouse in the New York City high-rise spun around her, and she felt the wall against her back. Kit was still kissing her, but he'd whirled them around.

She held on with her arms around his neck.

Finally, Kit broke it off, but his forehead still pressed against hers. "Come back to my hotel with me."

"I said I'm not looking for anything right now. I just

got divorced a few weeks ago."

"I'll take whatever you can give. I'll understand. I won't push. Just for tonight, come be with me."

Later, Simone would blame her decision on horny pregnancy hormones, needing to be comforted, and wondering what she had missed when she'd chosen Estebe a decade before. "Okay."

She hadn't been drinking, of course, and yet their quick escape from Maud's party, the cab ride back to his hotel a few blocks away, and the elevator ride up to his suite near the top of the Four Seasons Hotel New York felt like a whirlwind. In what seemed to be seconds, he was kissing her again as she walked backward into his hotel room, and he slammed the door behind them.

Simone was in a mad rush, struggling with the zipper down the back of her gown so pathetically that Kit spun her around in his hands and unzipped her silk dress, his lips chasing the zipper's head down her spine.

He was on his knees when she turned around, his hands slipping over her hips. She tried to catch her dress as it fell, but Kit tugged the silk down and over her body with just a flick of his fingers as he stood.

His blue eyes were narrowed, drunk with desire, as he crowded her backward toward the bed. "One last chance. If you want me to back off, let it be now."

"Don't you *dare* stop. But do you have a condom?"

"Absolutely."

Not that she could get pregnant again, but Kit wasn't a saint. The tabloid article had pointed *that* out in no uncertain terms.

He fumbled with his shirt and his clothes, yanking off his tuxedo pants. Simone was quite sure she heard fabric rip at some point. She clambered onto the bed backward, and he followed her, already stripped down to his boxers.

Kit was a grown man, not the skinny teenager Simone remembered experimenting with a decade before. Now, when his broad chest expanded as he breathed, muscle covered his ribs and torso like braided ropes. A thin sheen of dark gold, masculine hair softened the hard planes of his musculature.

Simone grabbed for the sheets because insecurity about her newly curvy body rose in her mind, but Kit yanked them away. "I have been waiting to look at you for more than a decade. Don't deny me."

"But I'm—" Her fingers spread over the soft swell of her tummy.

"You're beautiful." He kissed her sternum, and Simone lay back on the bed. "You said that we only have tonight. Let me remember it."

The firmness of his body covered her as his lips and hands traced her curves and blossoming body on the sheets.

He grabbed the condom from the dresser and sat back on his heels, his long legs folded underneath him.

Simone opened her eyes for a moment. "Oh, my God."

"I can hold back. I won't hurt you. I can do it," he told her, sliding his hands up her legs to her hips. "Wait, with the baby, is it okay? Do I need to know anything?"

"It's fine," she whispered, holding his face in her hands. His skin was so smooth under her palms. He must have shaved for the party. He'd certainly showered, and the scent of his cologne drifted in the air every time she breathed. "I'm fine. All the same."

"God, you are so beautiful," he murmured against her shoulder, his voice hoarse in his throat.

He held back until she was squirming with desire for him, and then pressed inside her gently, kissing her forehead, cheeks, and jaw as he entered her. He moved slowly, his hard flesh silken on her soft skin.

Simone felt like she couldn't open her eyes most of the time because she was overwhelmed by his touch and him kissing her on her lips, her throat, and lower. Still, one of the few glimpses that she managed during their lovemaking was the pale skin of his hand with his fingers splayed on her dark thigh and the bright white of the sheets below them.

The fire of their passion roared through her like a memory of the intensity of their teenage years had deepened into something mature and real, and her body pulsed like she hadn't felt for years. Ecstasy sped up her spine, and her head floated in a blinding light.

Kit's arms tightened around her as he gasped, his muscles clenching.

A few hours later in the darkness, Simone couldn't sleep.

Kit kissed her shoulder. "I know we said it was just tonight, but can we stay in touch? Emails or phone calls, maybe texts?"

"Yes. I'd like that."

Morning sunlight touched the bed, and she lay with Kit's arm and strong leg wrapped around her. She asked, "Are you over me now?"

". . . No," he whispered.

"What are you going to do?"

"Give you time."

2 Texts

Kit: Where are you?

Simone: Sitting on the beach near my father's home. The water is turquoise, and the alabaster sand is warm under my toes. You haven't been to Mauritius since that one summer break in upper school when a few of your fancy friends and some of my girlfriends came for a visit because you wanted to see it.

Kit: The beaches were incredible. The water was as clear as glass, and so was the air. It was cooler than I thought it would be because it was winter there. I hadn't thought of it being the southern hemisphere.

Simone: It's autumn now. Autumn is my favorite time in Mauritius. Everything is ripe.

Kit: Right. It's springtime up here in England. The gardens are blooming at the manor house. We're getting some dust from a sandstorm, somewhere, and the sunsets are beautiful.

Simone: We're so far off the eastern coast of Africa that we don't get much pollution, if any. It's as pristine as it gets. That was a good summer break, that year when you came.

Kit: I loved it. Your father was upset French wasn't my first language. I think he suspected we were dating.

Simone: That was one of the few things he liked about Estebe, that French was his first language. Everything else, not so much.

Kit: How are you feeling?

Simone: Well enough. Bulky. The baby will be here in a month or less.

Kit: Do you know the gender?

Simone: Opted not to. I love surprises!

Kit: Are you working or just waiting upon the arrival?

Simone: I've been working for my uncle, the judge. It's been quite an education. I always thought I would go to medical school because I like science, but he says I should go to law school.

Kit: You didn't continue on, earlier?

Simone: When I married Estebe, he didn't want me living away from him for school. He just wanted somebody to have fun with, I thought. Actually, I don't know what he wanted. He certainly didn't want a family.

Kit: Is your father sorry you got divorced?

Simone: Just about the thought of it. He wasn't sad to see the backside of Estebe.

Kit: Are you sorry you got divorced?

Simone: Never. I would never stay with a man who tried to choke me. Men like that turn out to be murderers.

Kit: How would your father feel *now* about you dating somebody whose first language was English?

Simone: Why? You have anybody in mind?

Kit: Maybe.

3

August

Kit Somerset texted, emailed, and video-chatted with Simone for long months, until she finally mentioned that she would be moving in August to New York to attend Columbia Law School.

The week before her classes would be starting, his cousin Maud had planned another of her opulent parties at her Fifth Avenue penthouse. Maud was involved with politics, somehow, and Kit suspected these parties were something closer akin to networking opportunities than merely an excuse for drink and revelry.

The day before, Kit texted Simone and asked if she was going to Maud's little soirée. Simone texted back that she was planning to, so Kit hopped on another plane from London to New York to surprise her.

She did like surprises.

Kit flew in that morning, checked into his hotel, refreshed himself, and headed over to Maud's party at a fashionable hour, which is to say after ten-thirty at night. Considering his responsibilities to his family's trust in the United Kingdom, it hadn't been reasonable for him to book an earlier flight.

When he arrived, Kit grabbed a plate from the buffet and piled on hors d'oeuvres from the strolling waiters because he was famished. The airplane food had been less than palatable even in first class, and he hadn't been at The Plaza long enough to order room service. Soon, he had a plate full of carbohydrate-rich pastries and doughy treats.

However, he was having problems finding Simone in the extensive crowd where everyone was half-sloshed and laughing uproariously about nothing in particular.

Kit was stuffing appetizers into his mouth and was washing them down with red wine when he noticed Simone over by the piano, standing with his cousin Maud and Cordelia Cochrane, Kit's ex-girlfriend with whom he'd broken up nearly a year before. Maud had changed her hair to a dark auburn-black, but Cordelia was the honey-and-cream English rose she'd been groomed to be since childhood.

In the intervening seven and a half months, Simone had let her natural Afro grow out into a diaphanous halo around her slim face and was even more beautiful than Kit remembered. When he'd last seen her on New Year's Eve, she'd been curvy with her growing pregnancy, and her face had been chubby and youthful like when they had been in high school together.

Now, even seeing her across the room like this, he was reminded what a beautiful, stunning woman she'd become. Seeing her as a slim, sexy woman wearing a form-fitting dress that nipped in at her waist, the image of her in his mind changed to include this vision of sensual womanhood. Her rich, bronze skin glowed against the pale gold dress she'd chosen, and the gold discs looped around her neck and hanging from her ears made her seem bedecked in precious metals.

Beside Simone, Kit's cousin Maud looked overdressed and plastic, and Cordelia was a ghost wearing a black dress that she'd chosen out of fear for what people would think if she tried too hard to be fashionable.

All three women were staring directly at him, and none of them were smiling.

The puff pastry in his mouth turned to ash on his tongue.
[***]

Simone Maina steeled herself to absolutely rebuff any advance Kit Somerset made as she watched him stalk across the room toward her.

Simone had met Maud St Leger, Kit's cousin, a few years ago in Paris at a charity event. They'd hit it off because they had both attended several weddings of mutual friends and noticed each other but never actually made a connection. They'd been texting one another for years and hanging out at events when they saw each other.

Cordelia Cochrane was a friend of Maud's whom Simone had briefly met a few times at one of Maud's parties.

Maud St Leger whispered near Simone's ear, "I talked to his mother last week. She assured me that he and Cordelia have been seeing each other for months."

Cordelia nodded. "We attended the Badminton Horse Trials together in May. We had a lovely time. Springtime in England is beautiful. The roses are in bloom. Roses come in red, pinks, peaches, and ivory colors, and we have many other flowers, too, in England."

"Yes, I know," Simone said, trying to keep the sarcasm out of her voice. Roses thrived in Mauritius—there was a city named "Beau Bassin-Rose Hill"—and she'd experienced an English spring. In upper school, Simone had once visited Kit at his family's historical manor house during spring break. Several of Kit's aristocratic buddies had come for the entire break, and a few of Simone's friends had tagged along, too. While Simone did appreciate the pale, pretty colors of an English spring, she much preferred the lush tropical climate of Mauritius.

Cordelia told Simone, "Kit and I had dinner together twice in the past few weeks."

A few dinners didn't necessarily make a relationship. Simone had shared dinner with her uncle probably ten times in the previous month to discuss law school.

But eating meals with an ex regularly was suspicious.

Simone had learned many of the signs of cheating from her ex-husband, and the ones for impending violence, too.

"Thank you for informing me of the situation," Simone said to the two of them and walked away, moving through the crowd to meet Kit over by the staircase.

As Simone approached, Kit hastily set down his plate and wineglass on a credenza and held out both arms toward her. "Surprise!"

"Indeed, this is a surprise. I didn't know you were going to be in New York."

"When you said you were going to come to Maud's party, I wouldn't have missed it for the world. You look amazing. How is Zyaad?"

At the sound of her baby's name, Simone couldn't help herself and grinned. "He's doing so well. My Auntie Yashna came with me to New York to take care of him while I'm at class and studying, so she has him tonight. He's growing faster than I thought a baby would. I can't believe he's already rolling over."

Kit was smiling, too. "He'll be walking soon. My sister's daughter pulled up and started taking steps at eight months. Once they start walking, they have their hands free, and you never have a moment's peace ever again. If he starts to pull up before his time, trip him."

Simone couldn't help but laugh at that. It seemed like pretty helpful parenting advice.

He said, "I hope I can meet Zyaad sometime. Those pictures of him are adorable. He looks just like you."

Kit was acting like he had some sort of a relationship with Simone when they didn't, not if his mother and his cousin thought that he was still dating that white English girl over there and they were going out to eat regularly. "Maybe."

"So, Columbia Law School?" he asked. "Do you want

to be a lawyer or a judge like your uncle?"

"I haven't decided. The road to both of those is through law school, so I figured I might as well start there."

"Did you ever consider the bar course in London instead of an American law school?"

She looked up into his blue eyes, his lying blue eyes. "Why would I ever want to live in London, *Kit?*"

He blinked, his eyelids briefly shuttering his eyes. "I was hoping, at some point, I might see more of you."

"I don't think that's a good idea."

Kit's face smoothed, his expression becoming almost nonexistent but with a slight smile that might have been a trace of amusement or boredom. His comment sounded almost offhand when he said, "I thought our texting had been going quite well."

"Texting is just texting. Obviously, we're just friends."

Kit picked up his wineglass and gazed over the party. The crowd of people were dressed in glittering formal gowns and black tuxedos, chatting with each other in the penthouse high above the sparkling city of Manhattan. "Have you met someone?"

"No. Zyaad has been keeping me busy. I understand that's common."

"If I said something misguided, I apologize for it."

"No, you've been a perfect gentleman," she said through her teeth. Not a good *man.* Good *men* don't cheat, and she was *not* going to make that mistake again.

But his gentlemanly manners had been above reproach.

Kit said, still speaking to the air above the heads of the crowd, "I rather thought last New Year's Eve was memorable. Or at least it was to me."

"It was memorable," she mumbled.

Kit's smile curved sardonically. "That sounds ominous."

Simone decided she was taking this too hard. Kit

had never said anything was serious between them. She'd just thought it was. "I didn't mean it like that. It was very memorable."

"Oh, thank heavens. One wouldn't want to get the reputation for leaving a lady less than pleased with an encounter. Gossip among Le Rosey alumni is virulent. I might never get a bit of how's-your-father again."

Simone snort-laughed a little and looked off over the crowd.

"And if word had gotten around, Lord only knows what that tabloid would have printed in an update."

She chuckled.

Kit had always been good at making her laugh, even when she should have been pissed off at him.

He said, "I can stay in New York for a few days this weekend. What do you say we take Zyaad to Central Park for a perambulation?"

Just because she was laughing didn't mean that she was going to get involved with a cheater. "I'm not sure that's a good idea."

"I think it's a splendid idea. I think it's enough of a splendid idea for both of us."

"I'm getting ready to start classes soon. There's a lot to be done ahead of time."

"Come on, I'll only be here for a few days. I want to meet this chubby baby of yours."

"I'm really sorry, Kit, but I'm just too busy."

"I shall have nothing to do in New York. I shall be bereft of entertainment and in absolute misery."

"I'm sure you'll find something to do. Besides, you have Cordelia to keep you company."

"I shall wander the streets at twilight, morose and—*wait.* What did you say?"

"Cordelia Cochrane. Look, I'm not mad." She was. "I imagine it was fun to flirt with me on the side, and sexy video calls are entertaining. Maud told me that you're dating

Cordelia Cochrane again, and then Cordelia told me that you two are going to the social season events and dining together."

"I wish someone had told *me* I was dating her. I would've broken up with her *yet again.*"

"Maud said that your mother told her you were still dating Cordelia."

"My *mother?* Oh, hell." Kit pulled his phone from the pocket of his trousers and tapped the screen a few times.

He turned the phone around to show Simone. The screen read *Mummy.*

Oh, no. "Kit, you don't have to—"

He pressed his phone to his cheek. "Hello, Mummy? Have you been telling people again that I am still dating Cordelia Cochrane?" He paused. "We broke up nearly a year ago. I do wish you would stop telling people that and getting the poor girl's hopes up. It's patently unkind." He tapped the phone, and the screen went black. Of Simone, he asked, "Are we clear?"

"You didn't have to do that."

"Oh, I absolutely did. What's more, I need to do this." He took Simone's hand in his and led her back over to where Maud was standing with Cordelia.

Cordelia looked Simone up and down and put her nose in the air.

Kit told Cordelia, "Cordy, this must stop. We broke up nearly a year ago. This manipulation is unseemly." To Maud, he said, "You know better than to listen to my mother."

Maud's eyes had grown twice their size, and her eyebrows had nearly lifted. "You and Cordelia aren't an item?"

"Not at all."

Maud turned to Cordelia. "You said the two of you were dating, that you'd been going to supper twice a week."

Kit told Simone, his eyes serious, "Cordelia's

father and I have some mutual and pressing business goals. Meetings are often liquid lunches or over supper. Cordelia has been present at some of these meetings, but there are usually at least four other people with us. I haven't even been seated next to her at any of them. They were not *dates.*"

Simone asked, "And the Badminton Horse Trials?" The Badminton Horse Trials was an important event on the London social calendar, where the aristocrats, royals, and a few of the selected uber-wealthy mingled.

Kit lowered one eyebrow. "I attended Badminton with Lysander and Orlando. Cordy latched onto us and followed us around because we were too polite to shake her off. I thought she was after Lysander, actually." He turned back to Maud and Cordelia. "Tell them what happened, Cordy."

Simone glanced at Cordelia, who was staring into her highball glass, her eyes wet with tears. "I mean, we met there. I drove over with Mummy and Daddy, but I saw you and joined your party. We had a nice time."

"You were crawling all over Lys."

A tear fell down her cheek, taking some of her mascara with it. "I was trying to make you jealous. I thought we were back together, afterward."

He sighed. "We weren't *together.* I rescued Lysander from you because you were on the verge of sexually assaulting him, and he didn't know how to handle it. Oh, Cordy. I'm sorry, but we need to acknowledge this is over and has been for many months."

Cordelia sniffed, and more tears streaked down her face. She turned and left them, mincing away in her high-heeled pumps.

Maud winced. "I'm sorry, Simone. All clues pointed to a problem, and I wanted to let you know before you got involved if he was cheating. I'll send someone to deal with Cordelia." She walked away, sliding her finger over her phone as she texted.

Kit sighed again. "So, that's over."

"I'm surprised you didn't run after Cordelia when she started crying."

Kit pressed his lips together for a moment before he muttered, "I've done quite enough of *that* for one lifetime."

Oh. "I'm sorry I believed them."

Kit shrugged. "There was significant evidence and eyewitnesses, and you are training to be a lawyer or a judge."

She let herself smile. "A lot of it was hearsay, though."

Kit clapped his hands together, indicating a change of subject. "So, about that trip to Central Park with Zyaad? Would Saturday morning be amenable?"

Simone smiled at him. "Yes, Saturday morning would be amenable."

4

More Texting

Simone started law school that fall and had a thousand questions for her uncle every day. Indeed, she texted with her uncle nearly as often as she texted, video-chatted, emailed, and sent pictures to Kit.

Kit wrote, *I miss you.*

Simone wrote about her classes and about how Zyaad was growing larger every day and that he was scooting, almost crawling.

Finally, she texted back, *I miss you, too.*

Kit flew to New York for a quick visit before Halloween. He played with Zyaad so much that Simone began to get jealous. When she finally put the cranky baby down for a nap, Kit confessed, "I've always liked kids and puppies. I've been told I am 'a sucker' for them."

While they stretched out in recliners, her with her laptop and him with his, working on their respective things that needed to be done that day, Kit mentioned, "So, how about it, then? I can't move to the Colonies—"

"You're English. Don't say 'colonies.'"

"Too soon?"

"It'll always be too soon."

"Oh, right. Anyhow, I can't move to *the States* because the family business is headquartered in London."

"So, what are we going to do?"

"I know it would mean you would lose a year of schooling, and I'm sorry about that, but would you consider doing the bar course in London? I've got friends who are barristers. There is one chap I know who went to Le Rosey with us. His wife is a pit bull barrister in London. You could discuss admissions or particulars with her. You might know him—Arthur Finch-Hatten?"

"I remember him. One of his friends, Maxence Grimaldi, helped me get away from Estebe."

"That's right. The Le Rosey gossip chain mentioned that. I could make some inquiries, perhaps look into some recommendations, so you would be admitted to the bar course."

Simone sighed, not wanting to tell him but knowing that she must. "I don't want to live in London my whole life. It's dreary."

Kit frowned. "It would be difficult to conduct the family business from anywhere that we don't have significant investments. However, my family has been investing in hotels for the last few decades, and we were considering investing in some underutilized areas. I'm still gobsmacked by what I remember from when I went there to visit you in Mauritius when we were teenagers."

"So, come visit me in Mauritius when I go home for winter break. Maybe you can scout some hotel venues."

Kit stared at his computer screen and finally nodded again. "Perhaps."

***

Kit did arrive in Mauritius a week before Christmas during a sweltering summer heatwave. Simone didn't find it so very different, though the temperatures were a few degrees higher than usual. At least Kit had traveled there before the monsoon season started in January. He put on a brave face and a stiff upper lip, but he drank a lot of water and showered four times a day.

A few properties seemed appropriate for the development of a high-end luxury hotel like the several that were already on Mauritius. Kit met with Simone's father, who was a minister in the national government, to discuss possible transactions.

Unfortunately, her father seemed altogether unimpressed by Kit's offers.

Afterward, Simone cornered her father. "I know his offer for the beachfront property north of Pointe aux Piments was far better than the previous offer, and you were seriously considering that one. Kit has the cash to do the deal upfront. He doesn't need financing like that other group."

Her father frowned at her. "Mauritius doesn't need any more foreign-owned hotels, and his French is atrocious."

She scowled at her father. "It is *not.* The whole point of that overpriced boarding school was that everybody who goes there speaks at least five languages like a native. French is one of Kit's. I *know* his French is impeccable."

"But his *first* language is not French," her father sniffed. "And besides, he doesn't speak Creole."

Kit returned to London the day before Christmas, and Simone made no move to stop him.

He texted her, *Have you considered the bar course in London for next year?*

She didn't reply for over a day. Then she finally answered, *My father thinks I should read law in the US.*

Which was true.

But it wasn't an answer.

Simone stewed over what she should do for several days before she made her decision.

5

Greenwood Manor

A week after Kit Somerset returned to Great Britain, he spread his arms wide as he welcomed the first party guests into his family home, Greenwood Manor. "I'm so glad you could come! When Maud said she wasn't going to give a New Year's Eve party this year, I saw my opportunity to throw a bash in England, as is proper."

His four best friends from his days at boarding school strode inside the enormous front doors, arriving early to settle into their roles as co-hosts and to sample the liquor before the other guests arrived and drank it all.

The additional staff Kit had retained for the party had already arranged the hors d'oeuvres and drinks on long buffet tables in the formal dining room. Other waitstaff were loitering about the catering kitchen and front rooms and holding large trays, ready to circulate with drinks and food among the guests when they arrived.

The four gentlemen dressed in white ties and tails were plundering the long buffet tables, each insisting that they had not eaten in a week and must decimate the hors d'oeuvres or else they would die.

Lord Lysander Harley, Earl Mortimer—a lanky, green-eyed, pale-blond man who was the younger brother of four sisters who had dressed him like a doll most of his life and so had the most lazy, unfortunate

136

fashion sense when one of them was not around to instruct him—stuffed shrimp into his mouth so quickly that two tails wiggled outside of his lips like he had pink-crustacean fangs.

Luckily, his sister Lily must have told him which tuxedo and cufflinks to wear that night, as his clothes were perfectly in the midpoint of acceptable men's formalwear.

Kit had known Lys so long that he could discern which sister had dressed him that day.

And anyone could tell when none of his sisters had intervened.

While his friends, who had promised to help out with hosting duties, continued to destroy the buffet, much to the consternation of the staff who began to replenish the serving dishes, Kit heard the first of the real guests begin to traipse up the stone steps to the front door and went to welcome them.

His friends, extended family, and business associates arrived steadily for several hours, filling the house with camaraderie, laughter, and all the best gossip. As usual, much of the gossip was about Kit and the other noblemen and minor royals who had found themselves to be the subjects of the Most Eligible Lords List, a conflagration of poor taste that showed no signs of dimming after an entire year. Kit was resigned to be the "spectacular butt" of every joke for the foreseeable future.

If Kit had found a way to marry Simone Maina, he might have lived down that vile reputation a little sooner, but evidently, marriage had not been in the stars for them.

He was still carrying in his pocket the engagement ring he'd had crafted. The central sapphire had come from India over a century before and been set in a platinum ring his grandmother had worn. This fresh incarnation of the jewel was set in shiny gold and surrounded by a cluster of diamonds, and it had traveled to Mauritius and back with him.

The islands had seemed like an extension of Simone

when he had been there, like he was surrounded by her beauty and grace wherever he'd gone.

If they couldn't agree on a continent on which to be together and raise a family, a proposal had made no sense and felt like a prelude to further heartbreak for both of them.

Maybe this time, Kit would get over Simone Maina and be able to move on.

But he probably wouldn't as long as he carried that ill-fated engagement ring in his pocket with him everywhere he went.

Tomorrow, he would leave it in a drawer. He promised himself that.

Tomorrow.

Shouts and peals of laughter rang from the Italian marble and antique plasterwork of the entry hall and entertaining rooms of the Georgian manor house. Everyone seemed to be having a good time, Kit saw as he stood on one of the curved staircases that flanked the large foyer. He was so absorbed with checking on every minute detail and making sure no one was standing in a corner alone that he nearly missed when a new group arrived.

A chilly gust of wind ruffled the short hair on the back of Kit's head and crept down his collar, drawing his attention to the great doors that some staff were just closing.

Simone Maina stood in the entrance hall.

One of his house staff was helping her out of her long coat and taking her gloves. She gently fluffed her hair with her fingers, perfecting the illusion of a dark halo around her face.

Kit inhaled a steadying breath because her presence didn't mean anything had changed about their intractable situation.

Nevertheless, Kit charged down the stairs to shoo away his servant, who would surely make a mess of things and was not appropriately stowing her coat. He draped her outerwear over his arm and smiled at Simone, not letting on that anything might be breaking inside his heart.

Simone beamed at him, a joyous smile radiating happiness. "Surprise!"

"I can't believe you made it," he said, smiling gently.

"I got on a plane yesterday morning. Is there someplace we can talk, just for a minute?"

"Of course. Yes, of course, Simone." He stepped back and gestured toward a door that led to a small antechamber off the main room. As they walked, he said, "I'm so glad you could make it. I didn't expect you."

"Why? You didn't ask Cordelia to be your date, did you?"

He laughed, even though he was cringing inside. "My mother insisted that Cordy be invited and made the phone call herself, but I did not ask her to be my date. I don't think she's here yet." He closed the door behind them.

The room around them had been repurposed as a coat room. The house had been designed for throwing large parties back in the days when traveling by horse-drawn carriage meant that parties lasted days or weeks. Clothes rods with hangers lined the walls, and extra rolling racks in the center of the room had been brought in for the overflow. The scents of damp cashmere and musty furs filled the quiet room.

Simone's dark eyes were wide, and she looked hesitant. "Now, I don't know what to say."

"I'm not dating her. We really did break up just about a year ago. She's certainly not here as my date. As a matter of fact, my co-hosts of record are Lysander, Orlando, Tristan, and Rafe, as usual."

"I guess that does make a difference."

They hadn't parted on bad terms in Mauritius, but just with a realization that there were no easy decisions for them. Kit ran the back of his hand and his knuckles up her silky arm to her bare shoulder. "Makes a difference for what, love?"

He felt her shiver under his hand. When she looked up at him, her gaze had softened, and her full lips had fallen the slightest bit apart.

He knew that look, and it was an invitation.

Kit crashed against her, driving her backward between the coats and against the wall. Her arms had clasped around his neck, but now she was fumbling with the buttons on his shirt. He shrugged the tuxedo jacket off his arms and tossed it to the floor behind him.

Simone grabbed handfuls of his shirt, her lips on his throat, and yanked the fabric, trying to strip his clothes off of him. Kit heartily approved and fumbled around under his cummerbund, rolling it into a tight band around his waist, to unlatch the hooks on his trousers' waistband.

Something small and metallic fell to the stone floor with a sharp *ping.*

He kissed her neck and shoulder, nipping her fragrant skin there. Her soft whimper nearly drove him wild. Under her dress, the scents of gardenias and roses lingered on her skin, a lush and fragrant trace of Mauritius he associated with beauty and femininity.

He ran his hand up her bare leg and realized she wasn't wearing stockings.

Or panties.

She was wearing a strapless dress, and a quick pull of the zipper down her spine left the hot pink satin puddled on the floor. Her dark bronze high-heeled pumps matched her slim ankles and calves as if the sexy shoes were just another part of her sexy legs.

Everything about her body was a smooth, elegant curve, and running his hand over the dips and swells of her breasts and hips ignited a dark fire deep within his soul.

The burnished bronzes and dark amber of her skin gave way to plum nipples, and he remembered the dark pink between her legs looked like the petals of a black-red rose. He stroked there with one fingertip rolling between her folds on her clit, then he slid his finger inside her until she moaned his name.

He groaned deep in his throat and grabbed himself, angling his erection to find the center of her.

Her back arched as he pressed into her, and her fluttering breath feathered his shoulder and trickled from his collar down his back.

In moments, he was pumping into her hard, and she was pressing her forehead against his shoulder while she made those little cries that drove him wild every time. When she threw her head back and gasped, her fingernails biting at the shirt over his shoulders, Kit let himself go. A moment of tension, and then the blinding bliss of his orgasm took him, and his balls pumped into her body.

After a moment of struggling to breathe and collect his mind, Simone whispered in Kit's ear, "Did you lock the door?"

Behind him, gears clicked.

Kit dragged coats on hangers over them while he pulled himself from her and twisted to stand flat against the wall, stuffing his dick back in his pants as he moved.

Beside him, Simone had already retrieved her dress from around her feet and was holding the bustier top over her breasts and her other hand over her mouth. Her eyes were huge and mischievous, and it was obvious that she was desperately trying not to laugh out loud.

A bright glimmer beside Kit's shoe caught his attention.

The engagement ring bearing the historically important sapphire and several carats' worth of white diamonds was lying on the floor between them. Simone would be sure to see it if she looked down.

Kit stared straight ahead and prayed that whoever was out there wouldn't notice them, that Simone wouldn't see the priceless engagement ring glittering on the floor between them, and that he wouldn't get his balls stuck in his fly that he was trying to zip up.

He held his breath.

Simone glanced at him out of the corners of her eyes. The mirth in her eyes was absolutely hysterical, and Kit nearly burst out laughing, too.

Luckily, he was British, so he refrained.

The last thing his reputation needed was to be caught *in flagrante delicto* in the coat closet with a guest at a party at his estate, especially this early in the evening. The gossip pages and the Le Rosey grapevine would go crazy if one of the Most Eligible Lords was discovered in such a compromising situation.

Kit's entire body broke out in a cold sweat.

After a moment of both of them breathing shallowly through their noses and trying not to crack up, the servant hanging up another guest's coat left the room and closed the door behind them.

Kit expelled the last of his air and leaned over, bracing himself on his knees as he laughed.

Beside him, Simone slithered down the wall, laughing helplessly.

Before her hand touched the floor, Kit swiped the ring out from under her palm just before she would have felt it.

Kit tucked the engagement ring in his pocket. "Let's get out of here before someone else comes in."

"Fine. Zip me up."

Fifteen minutes later, they were slow dancing to a string quartet in the grand ballroom at Greenwood Manor. Three enormous crystal chandeliers hung from the ceiling and threw sparkling light over the fifty or so other guests who were dancing. Red velvet covered the chandeliers chains and electric cords that led from the top of the confections to the ceiling far above. This room had been meant as a throne room, built in the anticipation that the Somerset family might someday rule the United Kingdom and was evidence of their continuing disappointment in that arena.

Simone was somehow entirely unruffled by their impromptu shag in the coat room, whereas Kit felt that he must be a mess. A quick check in one of the bathrooms had assured him that this did not appear to be the case, but he still felt like he must be rumpled.

The blissful smile on Simone's bright pink lips, done in lipstick that matched the satin of her gown and that Kit had found on his neck when he had been repairing the damage in the bathroom, seemed to him to be a dead giveaway that they had shared a moment.

She said, "I still don't want to live in England all my life."

Kit pulled her closer and wrapped his arm more firmly around her lithe waist. "We don't have to discuss this right now. Let's just enjoy tonight."

Simone said, "I should like to start a negotiation."

Kit looked down at her, intrigued. "You certainly sound like a barrister."

"About being a barrister rather than attending an American law school, the legal system in Mauritius is more similar to British courts than it is to American ones. No matter what my father thinks, it seems logical that a bar course in London would be more relevant."

Kit, ever the Devil's advocate when he should just shut up, asked, "Where did your uncle go to law school?"

"Cambridge."

"I think we may be onto something." He didn't allow himself to become too excited, though.

"And after that, it occurred to me that for part of the year, you could live in Mauritius to keep an eye on your holdings there."

"I wasn't aware I had any holdings in Mauritius."

"I convinced my father to accept your offer for that land you wanted to purchase to develop a luxury resort."

Kit was sensing a theme to this conversation. "Excellent. I'm delighted. I certainly enjoyed Mauritius while I was there, and owning a property would be an excellent excuse to stay for extended periods of time."

"And I was thinking about having a dual law practice in London and in Mauritius. As technology becomes more prevalent, it will be increasingly easier to coordinate such endeavors as that."

Kit stopped dancing and looked down at her. Her eyes were practically sparkling with stars of excitement that she had figured this situation out. He said, "Technology is making it easier to organize remote business operations. I think I could indeed spend part of the year in Mauritius, overseeing holdings there, and part of the year in London. It would seem to me that we should not spend too much of the summer in Mauritius, however. I nearly died of heatstroke several times."

Simone nodded. "It would be a shame to miss Christmas and New Year's in London."

"And spending part of England's ghastly summer in the cool winter in Mauritius would be an acceptable solution."

Simone rested both of her hands around his neck and smiled up at him. "So, we figured everything out."

"Almost everything." Kit gently disengaged her arms from around his neck and stepped back with one leg.

Around them, gasps rippled through the crowd in a wave.

Everyone turned to watch the host of the party, the Viscount Greenwood and the nobleman voted Most Likely to Remain on the Most Eligible Lords List, hold up a ring in his fingers and ask, "Simone Maina, would you do me the absolute honor of marrying me and becoming Lady Greenwood?"

[***]

As Kit had slowly slid one toe behind him and his eyes never left hers, Simone had realized he was making

144

his way down to one knee with surely the intention of proposing.

For the split-second he stood with one toe behind him, Simone could have stopped him, but she didn't.

If she hadn't wanted to spend the rest of her life with him, she wouldn't have figured out how to do it.

He proposed, his deep voice echoing in the hushed ballroom.

The light from the chandeliers floating above them glittered off the blue sapphire and white diamonds of the ring he held in his fingers, which was quite a surprise.

Simone said, *"Yes."*

Kit's smile widened. He slid the sapphire engagement ring onto her left hand and swept her up into his arms, kissing her soundly.

Over by one of the doors, a soprano gasp and sob echoed, but the rest of the room cheered.

A flood of people—many of them lifelong friends from boarding school—rushed forward to congratulate them. Emi was there, wrapping her wiry arms around Simone and hugging her tightly.

The usual suspects came forward and pounded Kit's shoulders, Lysander chief among them.

In the chaos, a woman's creaky voice announced over the din, *"Wait just a bloody minute!"*

Kit squeezed his eyes tightly closed and muttered, *"Bollocks."*

Kit's mother, Lady Hildy Somerset, emerged from the crowd and demanded, "You're getting married?"

"Yes," Kit said, his voice more resolute than Simone had ever heard it.

Uh-oh. Simone hadn't thought about Kit's family much.

His mother asked, her voice rising with each word, "Really? You two are getting married?"

"Yes, Mummy," Kit said. "I know you thought Cordy was a good fit for our family—"

But Hildy Somerset, matriarch of the Somerset family and the Dowager Viscountess Greenwood, had already launched herself through the air, latched onto Simone, and was hugging her tightly around her neck.

Simone patted the woman's bony back. "Um, *hi?*"

"Mummy!" Kit exclaimed. "Please, keep it British!"

"Oh, thank God, *thank God,*" Lady Hildy sobbed. "After that horrible article came out in that gossip rag, I thought Kit was *ruined.* I thought no decent woman would ever marry him, even *Cordy* no matter how much I tried, and the estate and viscount title would have to be turned over to my late husband's horrible cousin Algernon. It's *entailed,* you know. People don't think estates are *entailed* these days, but this one is. I've always hated telling Kit that he must marry and carry on the line because it's such a stupid, old-fashioned thing, but for the love of God, Algernon is such a twatwaffle!"

The End

MAJORING IN LOVE

By:
CA Miconi

Prologue

Chicago, Illinois
Present Day
Salynda

I've been at Lake Shore North Hospital every day for two weeks now. It won't be long before Mama's suffering is over and she goes to be with the Lord. And with my father, who passed away before I was born. It brings me some peace sitting here, watching Mama while she sleeps. She must be free of pain right now and thinking about happier days, because she has a sweet smile on her face…

Chapter One – Linda

Georgia State University
Fall 1975

I'm so excited about what the future will bring for me! Chicago is all I've known in my eighteen years. Some people call my city the capital of Black America. I'm from the south side, the Black Belt, in a neighborhood called Roseland. We have everything we need right here in our little corner of the city: Jackie Robinson Park, Holy Angel Catholic Church, and Gwendolyn Brooks College Prep High School. We even have our own beach on Lake Michigan off of Twelfth Street. Well, technically it's more off of Thirteenth Street, but some superstitious folks decided it was better to call it Twelfth Street beach.

I graduated from all-black Brooks College Prep with honors and received academic scholarship offers from several colleges. I was most intrigued by the offer from Georgia State University. Georgia State recently expanded their presence in downtown Atlanta, and is making an effort to increase its minority student population, as the first Black students were admitted only thirteen years ago. My grandparents left Georgia for Chicago in search of jobs in the early 1930s, so my roots are firmly planted down south. Perhaps this is what's pulling me in that direction.

MAJORING IN LOVE

My daddy planned our long drive, loading down the car with everything I would need for my dorm room. Even though the Civil Rights Act of 1964 technically eliminated the need for the Green Book, old habits die hard with my parents. Daddy still keeps a copy in the glove compartment of the car, just in case he needs to know safe places for us to stop for hotels and restaurants. Mama packed snacks and drinks so we can eat on the road when we get hungry, and we only pull into the rest areas along Interstate 65 to use the bathroom as we travel through Indiana, Kentucky, Tennessee, and finally Georgia. We broke the trip up into two days to make the driving easier for Daddy, and to allow us to arrive on campus early enough to unpack and get me settled into my dorm room. For the entire trip, my parents continue to lecture me about being careful as a Black person living "alone" in the South. They gave up on trying to talk me out of going to school in Atlanta months ago, once they realized I was determined to forge my own path into adulthood.

I can barely contain my excitement as we pull up in front of my dormitory building. Staff are on hand to check me in and direct us where to go. My parents are shocked to see the building integrated, not only mixing whites and blacks as roommates, but the same building houses males and females on different floors. I think it's great; my parents aren't as enthusiastic. I assure them they have nothing to worry about on both accounts, and honestly can't wait for them to leave! I love my parents, but I'm so ready for the independence that comes along with being in college. Mama and Daddy plan to visit some cousins in a nearby county, spending the night with them before they head back home.

When we enter the dorm, my roommate and her parents are already inside, setting up her part of the room. They don't act surprised to see Black folks walking in, but I just assumed, and I'm sure my parents did too, that I'd be assigned a Black roommate. Introductions are made quickly, and they seem nice enough. Mary Constance is from Macon, about two hours away from Atlanta. Her father is in the military, and he related to us that he requested his daughter be assigned to the integrated dormitory. In his words, the two races work together and fight side-by-side for our country, so he sees no reason for his daughter's university experience to be segregated. He wants her to live in the real world as she prepares for adulthood. It should be a learning experience for us both, as we couldn't be more different in looks, upbringing, and where we're from.

The next day, I've finished picking up my books and class lists, so I decide to stroll along the quad checking out some of the organizations represented at the club fair, sponsored by the Greek Life Council. One of the first tables I see is the Black Student Alliance. A guy calls out to me and motions me over.

"Welcome. Are you a freshman?"

"Yes. How can you tell?" I smile as I respond, hoping I don't sound too juvenile.

"Well, you look a little lost. But don't worry, I can help point you in the right direction. What are you interested in and what's your major?" Before I can answer, he hands me a list of organizations. "Here's a list of the Black clubs and the Divine Nine."

"The Divine Nine?"

"The nine traditionally Black Greek-Lettered Organizations. They function as service organizations and can be a great way to meet people and volunteer in service to others. By the way, I'm André." He extends a hand toward me.

I shake it briefly, then respond. "I'm Linda. And

pre-law is my intended major."

"Nice to meet you, Linda. You should definitely check out NBLSA."

"What's that?" I ask as I scan the list.

"The National Black Law Students Association. They have a table around here somewhere. I can help you find it."

I see a look of interest in his eyes. He's cute enough with his wire-rimmed glasses, short *fro*, and attempt at a mustache, but I don't feel any sort of attraction. I haven't seen any other Black guys around campus yet, but classes haven't even started, so I'm sure I'll be meeting more people who look like me soon enough.

"Thank you, André, but I'm sure I can find it on my own. Plus, I'm supposed to be meeting my roommate in a few minutes," I fib, hoping God doesn't strike me dead before my first college class. Before he can try to change my mind, I wave goodbye, and move down the sidewalk looking for the NBLSA table.

Just as I contemplate giving up my search, I notice Mary Constance walking toward me. I've started calling her MC already, because her first and middle names take too long to say! I asked her if she had a nickname or something else she goes by, and she looked at me like I was crazy. That's just how they name people in the south, she said. You get two names, and they're typically family names at that. I'm kinda surprised she's alone right now. Even though we both just got here, I figured with her pretty looks and cheerleader-like peppy personality, she'd already have an admiring crowd surrounding her. Before I can speak to her, she calls out to me.

"Linda! Hey!"

"Hey girl! What are you up to?"

"I picked up my schedule and books and thought I'd check out what was happening out here."

"Me too! I just talked to a guy at the Black Student Alliance table and he gave me a list of clubs on campus."

MC flips her blonde hair over her shoulder. She looks stunning in a paisley mini dress and chunky platform heels. It didn't take me long to figure out that she always dresses to impress, even if it's just to get a snack at the dining hall. "My mother says pledging a sorority is the best way to meet friends and sisters for life. Will you check out the sorority tables with me?"

I shrug. "Sure."

I'm not as outgoing as MC appears to be, so I'm content to walk along with her, as she smiles and says "hello" to everyone we pass. We happen upon the Greek row of tables and there's excitement in the air. Some clubs have music playing and others have members singing or performing precision routines with stomping of feet and clapping of hands. It appears that the Black Greeks are doing the step routines, while the White Greeks are singing or playing songs on the radio. I'm struck right away by the segregation of these groups. It seems races don't mix in the Greeks; they are either black or white, just as they are either male or female.

My roommate grabs my arm and makes a beeline for the first fraternity table she sees, Alpha Tau Omega. As soon as we reach the table, I see why. There are several guys manning this table, but one stands out. He is the finest white boy I have ever seen. Not that I've been around that many. He's dressed differently from the other guys he's standing with. He's sporting a short haircut and a preppy look, with pressed khaki pants and a shirt with the collar turned up, like he just stepped out of a college recruiting brochure. He has light brown hair the color of sand and piercing blue eyes. Although I'm at a total loss for words, MC steps up and turns on the charm.

"Hey! I'm Mary Constance, and this is my roommate, Linda."

"Nice to meet you, ladies. My name's Sanford, but my friends call me Sandy." Sandy, like a beach, I think to myself. He continues. "Are you girls thinking about pledging? All of the sororities are represented here today."

I still can't think of anything to say, so I let MC do the talking. "We're freshmen, so we're still checking everything out. Is there one you recommend?"

"I'm sure they all have something to offer, but our sister sorority is Delta Zeta, over there." He points to a table nearby with members that look just like MC.

"Thanks, Sandy, we'll keep it in mind." MC gives him such a beaming smile, it's practically blinding in its intensity.

His smile is equally bright. "Why don't you girls stop by the frat house tonight? We're holding our fall mixer and it's an open party—you don't have to be Greek to attend."

"Why thank you, Sandy, we'd love to come, wouldn't we Linda?" She not so subtly elbows me in the side.

That's my cue to speak up I suppose, so I make my best attempt at a smile, aiming it in Sandy's direction as well. "Sure, why not?"

Sandy's gorgeous blue eyes look directly into mine. Or

155

is it my imagination? "I look forward to seeing you girls later."

Chapter Two - Sandy

Sandy had arrived back at school a few days ago to begin his sophomore year. After a boring summer back in Green Springs working at the family business, his father's commercial real estate firm, he was ready to get back in the swing of college and city life at the "concrete campus," also known as Georgia State, labeled such since the school is spread out in multiple buildings in the heart of downtown Atlanta.

Since he was a second-year member of his fraternity, he was expected to pull duty at their table at the Greek Life fair, as well as to man the kegs and keep freshmen from doing stupid shit at the frat's fall mixer that night. A tradition that always occurred on the first weekend back on campus, one of the benefits of hosting the party was the guys could get a first look at all the incoming freshman hotties.

He'd been at the table for a few hours, handing out brochures and chatting with prospective pledges when two girls approached. The more outgoing one, Mary Constance, he thought she said her name was, looked like every girl he had gone to high school with. Long blonde hair, dressed to perfection. Although she was doing all the talking, his attention was drawn to her quiet friend, Linda. He wouldn't forget that name. She was different, in a good way. The polar opposite of the blonde in looks. Her thick long hair framed her face in loose curls, and was a gorgeous jet-black color, sleek and shiny. Her shy smile lit up her face, causing her tawny-brown skin tone and hazel eyes to glow like a million flecks of gold in the sun.

Sandy felt a burning need to get to know this girl better. He extended an invite to the mixer, and held his breath waiting for a response. The blonde answered right away, but he was far more interested in what Linda was going to say. Chicks traveled in pairs, didn't they? Soon after, he heard a soft "sure, why not?"

She just made his day.

Chapter Three - Linda

MC is super excited about the fraternity mixer tonight. I promised I'd go with her, so we're in our room trying to figure out what to wear. She's sorting through the dresses in her closet, while I think it's probably a more casual affair, if it's anything like house parties back home. We finally compromise, settling on our baddest bell-bottom jeans, platform sandals, and cute blouses that we tie up at the waist, showing a hint of skin—her idea, not mine. Since we're wearing jeans, we don't need purses. We can stow our campus ID, lip gloss, dorm key, and a little cash in our front pockets, so we don't have any lines messing up the look of our asses—my idea, not hers!

As we walk along the main drive of campus toward fraternity row, I take in all of the activity. Groups of students are heading to or from the dining hall, library, and other dorms. Many, like us, appear to be heading for parties. We get a fair amount of attention from guys as we walk along. Some shoot us admiring glances, while the more outspoken ones whistle or yell catcalls. MC seems shocked by it, but I've seen and heard much worse on the streets of Chicago. Doesn't mean I like it, though. I thought college boys would be more mature, I say to myself, shaking my head in disappointment, but not letting it spoil my good mood.

We approach a large house with a sign on the lawn designating it as the Alpha Tau Omega fraternity. Looks like we're in the right place. MC grabs my hand and practically races for the front door. "Come on, we're about to attend our first college party!"

I'm not as excited about this as she is, since I have a feeling I'll be the only Black person in the place. As we step into the front room, I quickly scan the crowd and see I'm right. I'm not used to being around so many white folks. Might as well get accustomed to it, I suppose, since the campus is majority white. I affix a smile to my face and put my best foot forward.

Chapter Four - Sandy

While pulling security duty at the kegs, Sandy kept glancing at the front door every time it opened, hoping to see the two girls that had come by the table earlier. Specifically, the curvy, dark, and quiet one. There was something about her that definitely grabbed his interest. He had dated occasionally during his freshman year, and made some good friends, but hadn't really connected physically or emotionally with anyone special. Maybe now was the time.

Before too long, the girls he'd been hoping to see walked through the door. He spotted the blonde first, leading the way. Following her was Linda, and his mouth instantly went dry. She looked hot, with a capital H-O-T! He took it all in from afar. Her legs, encased in jeans that were tight around the waist and down the leg, then flared wide at the bottom, appeared to go on for days. She was wearing shoes with a chunky heel that added a couple of inches to her height, but she still looked far short of his six-foot-two-inches. He noted the exposure of a little bit of her golden-brown stomach below the blouse she had tied at the waist. Her hair was pulled back by a scarf that matched the material of her shirt, allowing him to see every feature of that gorgeous face, including her dazzling smile.

It didn't take long for some of his frat brothers to spy fresh meat, and they zeroed in on Mary Constance. She was immediately surrounded and swept up in conversation. Linda was standing by herself, looking a little lonely, but still smiling. That was his cue, so he put on his best game face and strolled over to her. He had to practically shout at her as he struggled to be heard over the loud music. "Hey, Linda! Glad you could make it."

She gave him a look that he interpreted as grateful. "Hi. Thanks for inviting us."

"Looks like your friend is already having a good time." He glanced toward the group of guys surrounding Mary Constance.

Linda looked their way as well, and what she said next surprised him. "I'm sure MC would love for you to cut in."

"MC?"

"That's what I call her since Mary Constance is such a mouthful. I guess I'm not used to southern names."

He wanted her to know that he wasn't interested in Mary Constance or MC or whatever the hell else she went by, so he moved in closer and looked directly into her eyes. "I don't want to join that conversation. I'd rather talk to you." *Shit*, he hoped he didn't scare her off.

She responded with a sweet smile. "What would you like to talk about?"

"Whatever you'd like to talk about." He put the ball back in her court.

She volleyed right back. "Well, maybe you can explain these names to me. I take it you're from the south, since you sound like most of the people down here."

"Yeah, you guessed right, and we southerners do have some strange names," he chuckled. "People ask me all the time why I have a last name for my first name and a first name for my last."

"What's your last name?"

"Patrick."

She giggled. "You're right. Seems backward. But I like the name Sanford. Is it okay if I call you that?"

Ah! She remembered my first name! And she can call me anything she likes, just so she calls. "Well, Sanford is a family name somewhere in a previous generation and Patrick is actually an Irish surname. No one else calls me Sanford. Except for my father when I'm in trouble."

"I'm not everyone else. I like to be different," she said saucily.

Right on, pretty girl. He continued the conversation aloud. "I'm from a small town in Mississippi near Tupelo. Where are you from? You definitely do *not* have a southern accent."

"I'm from the Windy City—Chicago."

He leaned in closer. She may have thought it was due to the noise, but he was drawn to her scent. She smelled a little spicy, seductive. *Bet she's wearing that Musk perfume.* "Cool. I've always wanted to visit there."

"And you should. It's a great city. We've got the world's biggest Ferris wheel, some nice beaches, and the best food anyone could ask for!"

"I'm all about the food! But for now, how 'bout some beer or punch?" He held out his hand, and to his surprise, she took it. It was so soft, and her thumb stroked the inside of his palm. He wondered if that was deliberate or by accident. He also wondered if the rest of her skin was just as soft as he led her through the crowd and toward the drinks.

She gestured toward the big barrel next to the kegs. "What is that?"

"I take it you've never had grain punch? It's a staple at frat parties. It's made with grain alcohol, fresh fruit, fruit punch, and who knows what else, and it's normally mixed up in a large trash can or barrel. I'll warn you, it can pack a mean punch, if you'll pardon the pun. It really sneaks up on you if you aren't careful."

She grinned. "I'd like to try it. I'm not much of a beer drinker."

He picked up the ladle and poured a plastic cup about halfway full. "Let's see how you do with this. I've got keg duty, so would you mind hangin' out here with me?"

"Sure. I've got nothing better to do at the moment," she teased.

They stood in silence for a few moments as he wracked his brain, trying to think of something witty to say. He wasn't usually at a loss for words, but this girl had him tongue-tied.

Linda looked around, taking in her surroundings, when she suddenly grabbed his arm. "Oh my goodness! Shouldn't you stop him?" She pointed toward the big fireplace in the front room of the old mansion that served as the frat house, just as a kid he didn't recognize took a dive off the mantel into a crowd of people who caught him and let out a cheer.

He laughed off her concern. "Don't worry, we won't let anyone get hurt. If he falls on the floor or breaks something, we'll take him over to the student clinic to get patched up. There's actually a line of people waiting to do the same thing." He paused. "Don't look now, but isn't that your roommate over there waiting her turn?"

Linda practically threw her punch at him and took off for the other side of the room. Abandoning the kegs without a second thought, he rushed over to assist Linda as she grabbed her friend by the arm and tried to pull her out of the line. "MC, are you crazy? Tell me you are not about to try this! You'll break your neck!"

Mary Constance giggled, bobbing back and forth between Linda and the line of people in a kind of push and pull game. It was obvious to Sandy she couldn't hold her alcohol. And none of the frat brothers seemed concerned about her safety. He'd take that up with them later.

"Aww, Linda, I'm just tryin' to have some fun! Don't be such a party pooper!"

Linda turned to him. "I need to get her back to the dorm."

"Hang on. You can't do that by yourself. I'll take you."

"Don't you need to stay here?"

"No. Someone can cover for me. It's more important we get her home safely. We'll take my car. It's too far for her to walk like this. Meet me out front and I'll pick y'all up."

"Okay." She touched his arm. "Thank you."

Sandy gave her a wink and headed for his room to retrieve his car keys.

Chapter Five - Linda

Fifteen minutes later, we pull up in front of the dorm. MC and I are in the back seat of Sanford's Gran Torino, since it was much easier for me to get in the car first and pull her in with me. As soon as Sanford shut the car door, she promptly passed out on my lap.

He cuts the engine, and comes around to the rear passenger door to open it for us. "I'll take her. Then you can get out and we can walk her in together."

MC doesn't even open her eyes, but seems to know she's on the move. Fortunately, Sanford takes the bulk of her weight on his side, and depends on me to open the doors and lead the way to our room. I'm grateful there's an elevator, since we stay on the fifth floor.

When we get into the room, I strip back the bedspread on MC's bed so we can cover her after Sanford lays her on it. I reach down and remove her shoes, then tuck her in fully clothed. Her eyes haven't opened since we brought her in from the car, and she quickly turns on her side and emits some soft snores.

"Thank you so much for helping me and MC. Not the way I thought I would spend my first weekend at college!"

"No thanks needed. I'm glad I could help."

An awkward silence descends. I'm not sure what the protocol is for having boys in the dorm room, or for showing my appreciation. Is he just being gentlemanly? Or is he interested? "Umm, would you like me to walk you out? You know, in case you get caught on the girls' floor, I could explain."

"Sure, I'd like that."

He takes a step closer to me. Then another, closing the distance and invading my personal space. Suddenly, the room seems so small. And warm. I feel like my face is shiny from sweat; I'm praying he doesn't notice. The smell of his cologne draws me in like a moth to a flame. I'd know that scent anywhere, since I'd spent countless hours sniffing it at the perfume counter at Bloomingdales. *Jovan Musk for Men*. He reaches out and tips my chin up so I'm looking straight into those sea blue eyes. I feel like I'm drowning in them. My heart races and I unconsciously wet my lips. His eyes go there, followed by his own lips. My eyes drift close as I melt into the contact. Too soon, he breaks the connection. My eyes open and I see something in his. Desire? Longing? Regret? I can't tell. My mind is racing through a range of emotions, including confusion. I don't want to like him. I shouldn't like him. He's *white*. I need to remember why I'm here. And it certainly is not to start something that can never be. What would my parents think?

Sanford steps back. "I guess I better get going. They'll need me back at the house to clean up from the party."

"Yes. I'm sure they do." Neither of us move. I hold my breath, uncertain about what to do next. The silence is broken by a loud snort of a snore coming from MC. We both burst out laughing, and the weird moment passes.

He grabs my hand. "C'mon, you promised to walk me out, remember?"

I laugh again, nervously. "Oh! Yes, sorry!" I retrieve my key from where I set it down when we came in and put it back in my pocket using my other hand, reluctant to break the bond with Sanford.

He guides us toward the door and grasps the doorknob. Before opening it, he turns toward me. "Can I see you again?"

"I'm sure you'll see me around campus."

"That's not what I mean. I want to *see* you. Get to know you. Hang out."

Wow! Back home, hanging out has a very distinct meaning—having sex. I wonder if it means the same thing to him. "You do?"

"Yes."

My heart flutters with excitement. I'm hoping he knows what hanging out means. Because I am definitely up for *hanging out* with him. My body tingles at the thought. I'm ready to explore my sexuality far from my parents' prying eyes. This could be fun. No strings attached. It's not like we would be a couple. We're still holding hands and I make no attempt to withdraw mine from his.

The words come out with no further hesitation. "Yes. I'd like that."

Chapter Six - Sandy

Sandy returned to the frat house as the party was winding down. His frat brother and roommate from last year, Jamie, greeted him as he entered through the back door.

"Hey, where'd you go?"

"I had to help a drunk freshman girl get back to the dorm before she killed herself jumping off the mantel."

"Holy shit, good thing you were keeping an eye on that. We could have gotten into a heap of trouble if a girl got hurt here. Mantel diving is supposed to be for pledges only."

"You better believe it. The guys in charge of house monitoring should have been doin' their job. I'll be talkin' to Skip about it."

"Speaking of talking, I saw you *talking* to that Black girl." He lifted his eyebrow in question although it was a statement.

Sandy went on the defensive. "Yeah, so what?"

"So, we don't usually see Blacks at our parties."

He wasn't sure why he felt compelled to justify

MAJORING IN LOVE

anything to his friend, and he wished he would stop with the twenty questions. "She came with her roommate. Who was the one about to jump off the fuckin' fireplace, by the way. What's the big deal?"

"So, you were just trying to keep the frat out of trouble."

"Yes. No." Sandy ran his hand through his hair out of frustration. "I wasn't *tryin'* to do anything. Is there a point to this conversation?" His temper was starting to boil, but he wasn't sure why.

Jamie gave him that *yeah, right* look. "I didn't know that was your *thing*, is all."

"What are you talkin' about?"

He slapped Sandy on the back. "Hey, makes no difference to me who or what turns you on, brother. And I don't blame you for wanting a piece of that."

Sandy now knew why he was feeling angry toward his friend. He wasn't just trying to get in Linda's pants. Sure, she was hot, but there was more to it than that. He had a real interest in getting to know her. The physical attraction was an added bonus. He needed to walk away from his friend before he did or said something he might later regret.

171

Chapter Seven - Linda

It's the morning after the frat party. I've already been to the dining hall for breakfast, and I brought back something for MC. Not sure she's up to eating anything, but I brought it back anyway.

I tiptoe into the room and quietly shut the door behind me. She's awake, sitting on the edge of the bed with her head in her hands. I approach her tentatively.

"Hey. How are you feeling?"

My head hurts somethin' awful."

"I brought you something to eat."

"I'm not hungry."

"How about some aspirin for your headache?"

"That I'll take."

I retrieve the aspirin bottle from my toiletry drawer and go next door to the bathroom to get her some water. When I hand it over, she gives me an appreciative look and whispers, "thank you."

After swallowing the two pills and giving me back the cup, she gingerly lies back down on the bed, but turns to her side so she can see me as she speaks.

"How did I get home last night? I don't remember much."

"Well, you were about to do something stupid. Do you remember that?"

"Ummmm, no. I remember drinking that spiked fruit punch and talking to some cute guys. That's about it."

"MC! You could have been hurt. What if I hadn't been there with you, it's no telling what would have happened."

She actually looks contrite as she says, "I promise I'll be more careful. I don't like this hangover and I definitely don't like not remembering how I got back to the dorm. Thank you for looking after me."

My heart warms as I think of our hero from last night. "Sanford, I mean Sandy, helped me get you back here. I don't think I could have done it alone."

"Sandy? That cute frat boy who invited us to the party?"

I can't help but smile when I respond. "Yes, that cute frat boy."

Even though she's not feeling one hundred percent, MC doesn't miss a thing. "I don't think *I* was talking to him last night. That means you were. Okay, roomie, give me the skinny!"

Do I want to share what I'm feeling with her? Or do I want to keep it all to myself? Am I really only interested in hanging out, or do I want more? I decide I'm not ready to discuss it with anyone, so I downplay it. "I'm sure he was just being nice. And thank goodness he was talking to me when he noticed you about to jump off the fireplace!"

"What?"

"You were going to jump off the fireplace mantel into a crowd of people."

MC groans as if her head is still hurting. "Oh, my. Remind me never to drink that spiked punch again!"

Chapter Eight - Sandy

Sandy couldn't seem to get a certain girl from Chicago out of his head. The dark-haired beauty had invaded his dreams every night since the party. He didn't know her class schedule or her phone number, and he didn't want to be so obvious as to go to her dorm looking for her, so he decided to eat in the dining hall during all three meal times, hoping to run into her.

After a few days of suffering through the bland food in the student cafeteria, lady luck finally rewarded him. He spotted Linda entering the seating area with her food tray during the dinner hour. But crap, she wasn't alone. She sat down with a group of about five people, both girls and guys.

Is she hangin' out with someone already? Did I miss my chance? Shit! What do I do now?

Sandy lingered over his food, while surreptitiously keeping an eye on Linda. He didn't want her to think he was a stalker, but he didn't want to blow a chance to talk to her, either. One thing his father always taught him—when opportunity knocks, you better be ready to open the door. It sure had worked for his dad in business, so it should work for him too, right?

After about twenty minutes, from the corner of his eye, he saw Linda rise from her seat, say goodbye to the group, and head toward the area where trays and trash were disposed of. He casually got up and walked over to the same area with his tray, timing it so that when she turned around, he'd be right in front of her.

Showtime! "Hey Linda. How are ya?"

Her hazel eyes sparkled as she noticed him standing in front of her. "Oh! Hi, Sanford!"

"How are your classes goin'?"

"Great! I'm enjoying everything so far."

He was so mesmerized by her beauty that he stood there gazing at her like an idiot, making no move to bus his tray. He quickly came to his senses when she spoke again.

"Well, uh, nice to see you, and thanks again for helping out with MC the other night."

He mentally kicked himself for almost screwing things up. "My pleasure. Hey, can I walk you back to your dorm?"

"I'm actually on my way to the library."

Even better. "Can I walk with you there?"

"Sure. If you like."

Sandy hurried to discard his trash and set his tray on the conveyor belt, then turned back to Linda. "Shall we?"

As they strolled along, they talked about their classes and majors, their families, and their interests and hobbies. Sandy had a plan for asking her out, so he set it in motion.

"How do you like Atlanta?"

Linda responded, "I like it very much so far, but I must admit I haven't seen much of the city beyond campus."

Perfect. "Well, we must remedy that. I know the best spot in the city for catchin' a view of Atlanta's downtown skyline."

"Oh, really? Where is it?"

"It's about a twenty-minute drive from campus, but believe me it's well worth the trip. It's also best to go at sunset. How 'bout I take you there tomorrow?"

Linda stopped in her tracks. "Are you asking me out?"

He couldn't gauge how she felt about his question, as her tone and her expression were neutral. Was she interested? Grossed out? Curious? Had she forgotten that he said he wanted to get to know her better? He wanted to leave her with no doubt that he liked her and was definitely asking her out.

"Yes. Linda, will you go out with me?"

He steeled himself for her answer, hoping he wouldn't have to run back to the frat house to lick his wounds.

She looked up at him with the sweetest expression he'd ever seen. "Yes, Sanford, I will go out with you."

Chapter Nine - Linda

I have butterflies in my stomach as I get ready for my date with Sanford. Even though he asked me out, is it really a date, or is he just being nice about showing me the city? Self-doubt creeps in. I'm sure I'm not his type. Why do I care if I'm just looking to *hang out*? Why would he be interested in a Black girl? What would his family say if they knew? What would *my* parents say? Despite the worries, I'm excited at the same time. He's so cute, and nice too, and an awesome kisser.

Fortunately, MC went home for the weekend, because I'm not sure I want her to know I'm going out with him. We get along great, but would she really feel the same way about me if she knew I was seeing Sanford? Or would she feel like I was encroaching on white girls' territory? Since this could be a one-time thing, I feel like it's better that she's not here.

Sanford said he would pick me up at 5:30 so that we could get to the bridge in time for sunset. I take one last look in the mirror before heading out the door and downstairs. Even though it's late September, it's still warm during the day, but gets chilly after the sun goes down. Since we're going to be outdoors, I opt for corduroy Levi's, a plaid shirt, and a light sweater draped around my shoulders. I've got leather Wallabees on my feet since I assume we'll be doing some walking. I love the milder weather here. Back home in Chicago people are already wearing winter parkas!

True to his word, Sanford pulls up at 5:30 p.m. sharp in his Gran Torino that looks exactly like the one on the TV show *Starsky & Hutch*, red with a white stripe on the side. Before I reach the passenger door, he hops out and comes around to open it for me. Such a gentleman. I blush for no reason. "Thank you."

Sanford looks so good in jeans and a flannel shirt. And the inside of his car has the scent I already associate with him: *Musk for Men*. As he drives us through the city toward the Jackson Street bridge, he serves as my tour guide, pointing out places of interest, including the boyhood home of Martin Luther King, Jr.; Ebenezer Baptist Church; the Fox Theatre; the state capitol building, and the governor's mansion.

When we get about two blocks away from Jackson Street, Sanford finds a place to park and we set out on foot for the bridge. As we walk along the busy street at rush hour, I notice a few glances our way, but nothing overt or rude. The sun is still a bright orange blaze in the sky as we approach the bridge, which is actually an overpass atop Freedom Parkway, a four-lane highway running right through the middle of the city. Sanford takes my hand and leads me to the midway point of the bridge, right above the median between the two lanes dividing each direction of the freeway.

"Welcome to the best kept secret in Atlanta."

"Wow! You can see the entire downtown landscape from here."

"Just wait. We've come at the best part of the day. We're gonna watch the sunset, and then when it's dark, the lights will be spectacular."

As we sit and get as comfortable as we can on the concrete sidewalk, the sun starts sinking quickly, reflecting off of the buildings and projecting rays of colorful warm hues in brown, orange, yellow, and pink. Surprisingly, no one else is around to view this visual work of art. Sitting with our backs leaning against the concrete wall taking in the scene before us, Sanford pulls me closer to him and drapes his arm around my shoulders.

Within a few moments, the sun disappears completely. The scene changes to another spectacular one. A cacophony of colors explodes against the dark sky. The multicolored buildings stand united in salute and two solid stripes of light shine for miles ahead on the freeway—white streaks representing the headlights glowing toward us and red tail lights moving away from us. As I take it all in, I can think of only one word to describe it. "Beautiful." I turn to look at Sanford. He's not looking ahead at the lights, but is gazing at me instead as he responds.

"Yes."

Although we have a front row seat to the busiest view in the city, we are in our own little world.

Chapter Ten - Sandy

Sandy was feeling pretty confident about the date given Linda's reaction to the view from the bridge. He regretted not bringing a camera, not so much to take pictures of the skyline, but it would have been an opportunity to snap some images of Linda. Next on his agenda was wooing her with some great food.

"How about some authentic southern cookin' from the best place in Atlanta?"

"Authentic southern cooking, huh?"

"Yes. Big Daddy's Southern Cuisine is the best!"

"Now that you mention it, I *am* hungry. Sounds great!"

Big Daddy's was probably the most integrated place in all of Atlanta. Blacks and whites alike came from all over the greater metropolitan area to get their soul food fix. After his first time eating there, Sandy had decided that Big Daddy's was better than anything his grannie made, and her cooking was to die for. After perusing the menu, Linda opted for the meatloaf dinner, while Sandy decided to have fried catfish since it was Friday. He was thrilled to introduce Linda to sweet tea and the best peach cobbler around.

When they arrived back at the dorm, he was pleasantly surprised when she invited him up to her room. "Will your roommate mind if I come in?"

Her response made Sandy feel like he had just hit the jackpot. "MC went home for the weekend."

Chapter Eleven - Linda

I know I'm playing with fire inviting Sanford to my room, but I've had such a good time with him, and I'm not ready for the night to end. I'm a little nervous anticipating what might happen in here, and I hope he doesn't notice my hand shaking as I insert my room key into the lock. Once inside, I glance around the room, reminding myself that we've got few options for where to sit. On my side of the room, there's one desk chair and the bed. I swallow in expectation. The bed. As a distraction, I offer Sanford a pop.

"Pop? You mean a coke?"

"Well, we have Coke, but we have Sprite too."

Sanford laughs. "Here we call it all coke, no matter what flavor it is."

I laugh too, realizing I still have a lot to learn about living in the south. I reach into our dorm fridge and pull out two cans, passing one to him. The click of the pull tab opening fills the silence in the room. Sanford must notice the quiet too, as he suggests turning on some music. I walk over to MC's desk and switch on her stereo system, dialing in the R&B FM station. Since it's late evening, the playlist consists of slow songs.

When I turn around, Sanford is sitting on the edge of my bed. He pats the space beside him and motions me over. I set my can on my desk, noticing that Sanford has already placed his there, and approach the bed. Before I can sit down, he extends his arms out toward my waist and pulls me close between his knees. As I stand over him, he gazes up at me. "I had a great time with you tonight."

"I did too. Thank you."

"You're welcome."

He pulls me further toward him, then places his hand on either side of my face, guiding it down toward his own. Our lips meet in a kiss. For a guy, his lips are remarkably soft. He nibbles on my bottom lip, causing me to part my lips slightly, enough that his tongue can slip in. My knees grow weak and my legs start to feel like jelly as I drift further down toward him. His arms come around me again as he simultaneously scoots himself up higher on the bed and guides me down on top of him, bending backward to recline us both on the bed.

We continue to kiss and I relish the contact of our bodies. I can't resist threading my fingers through his soft, silky hair. I'm lost, drowning in the scent and feel of him. Donna Summer's "Love to Love You Baby" comes on the radio. The moans and rhythms from the song echo in my head until I can't tell if they are coming from the radio or from me.

I'm not sure when or how it happened, but we're now lying on our sides, face-to-face. His arms are still wrapped around me, putting subtle pressure on my butt, so that my crotch is rubbing against him. The rough fabrics of his jeans and my corduroys cause a pleasurable friction, sending tingles of pleasure down low. I break our kiss in an attempt to catch my breath and slow the rapid beating of my heart. It doesn't work.

MAJORING IN LOVE

As I tuck my head under his chin, I can feel the race of his heartbeat as well.

"Sanford." I say his name on a sigh.

"Linda," he breathes back. "You feel so good. Taste so good. Beyond my dreams."

"Your dreams?"

"Yes. I've been dreaming of you since the first moment I saw you."

My heart swells. I want more. What and how much more, I don't yet know, but I want to get closer, feel him closer. "Sanford. Take off your shirt. Please."

I feel a momentary loss as he unwraps his arms from me and pulls the hem of his shirt out from his jeans and begins unbuttoning it. I do the same with my plaid shirt with the goal of feeling his skin next to mine. I lift up from the bed just enough to shrug out of my shirt completely, leaving my top half covered only by my black lacy bra. I hear Sanford's breath catch when he sees me minus my shirt. He sheds his own shirt as our eyes meet. I tug his white undershirt up, signaling that I want him to remove it as well. He whips it over his head in one smooth movement, revealing a chest with a smattering of sandy-colored hair and a thin trail that begins at his navel and disappears below the waist of his jeans. Sanford takes his index finger and drags it below my chin, down my neck, and lower still between my breasts, stopping at the edge of my bra between the cups. My breath catches in my throat as he utters four words.

"You are so beautiful."

I shiver in anticipation as he resumes the connection between our bodies, joining our lips once again and aligning our torsos in skin-to-skin contact. I can't help myself as I wrap one leg around his hip in order to press my female parts to him as close as possible. Our tongues begin a dance and I can't seem to get enough. My hands make their way once again to Sanford's hair. I love the feeling of it through my fingers. His hands wander all over my body, massaging, gliding, kneading. Sensations abound everywhere, bombarding my brain. The sounds of our breathing commingle and overshadow the music on the stereo. My body is humming like a hundred bees, and down low my body is throbbing and pounding, my blood rushing in my ears. I am desperate for a release. I want—need—something. "Sanford, please."

His mouth leaves mine as he kisses his way toward my breasts. Between kisses he responds. "Linda, hun, tell me what you want."

My mind is mush. I try to make a coherent statement, but can't seem to get the words out. I want to fly. I want to soar. I turn on my back and grab Sanford's hands, guiding them toward the
waistband of my cords. "Off."

He appears to comprehend my plea as he releases the button fastener and pulls the zipper down. I help him by wriggling out of my pants and kicking them down my legs, only to realize my shoes are still on. Sanford quickly removes them for me and pulls off his own as I kick the Levi's away. He turns his attention back to me and we resume the exploration of each other's bodies. Our eyes meet and I can't look away as I focus on his touch while getting caught up in the depths of his sea blue eyes. His fingers trail along my breasts, before pinching each nipple in turn. I moan in pleasure as he replaces his fingers with his tongue. As he continues licking and sucking there, his hands continue their exploration and they slowly make their way downward, across my stomach, toward my core.

MAJORING IN LOVE

I arch upward, my body's way of begging for release. Sanford answers the plea, as his fingers find my heat, gently stroking, then going faster and harder as I urge him on. *Finally!* I ascend and burst apart, gasping for air, then gradually float back down. I cling to him, whimpering, not from fear or pain, but from something I've never felt before. A mixture of joy, ecstasy, and rapture. Sanford holds me, whispering words I can't make out, but are comforting just the same. His soft but firm hands rub my skin, enveloping me in a cocoon of comfort. My eyes grow heavy and I'm mesmerized by the steady *thump, thump, thump* of Sanford's heart. Sleep claims me.

***

I've settled into the routine of college life. Classes, meetings, volunteer work, and whenever possible, spending time with Sanford. I'm the only Black girl on my hall, and one of the things my dorm mates like to do between classes is watch their favorite soap operas. I don't have a one o'clock class, so I usually grab my lunch and gather with some of the girls in front of the TV in the rec room to watch. At one, the channel is always set to *Days of Our Lives*. I never watched it at home, so the characters are new to me. On this particular day, we're all gathered ready to tune in. I've already noticed there's only one Black family on the show. A new storyline has David Banning, a white character, interested in the daughter from the Black family, Valerie Grant. As we view the unfolding relationship on the screen, I feel like all eyes are on me. The actor portraying David resembles Sanford in hair color and features. Do they know about me and him? Would they be cool with it or not?

Later, I read in a magazine in the library that this storyline is the first interracial relationship in the history of daytime television, and has been fraught with controversy. People have been writing to the network expressing their agreement or disagreement with showing an interracial couple. There's been so much backlash that the writers canned their plan to have the couple marry. It saddens me to think that even though the U.S. Supreme Court unanimously ruled in 1967 that laws banning interracial marriage violate the Equal Protection and Due Process Clauses of the Fourteenth Amendment, now eight years later, very little has changed. Is this why I'm hesitant to go public with my relationship? Am I worried about what other people think? How they'll treat us? I keep telling myself we're just friends. It's just hanging out. But deep down, I know there's more to it than that.

Chapter Twelve - Sandy

Sandy began volunteering with several organizations as a way to spend more time with Linda. It also helped his standing with the service fraternity and his business school portfolio, but it was mostly about being with Linda. He knew she was hesitant about taking their relationship public, and he wanted to respect her wishes, but damn, it hurt. He also knew she cared for him, and an interracial relationship would not be easy, especially in the south. But he felt like together they could conquer anything. He was in awe of her beauty, her spirit, her drive. She had opened his eyes to so many things over the past few months. He was starting to see the world differently, and it felt good.

Winter break was coming up soon and they'd both be going home for the holidays. It would be their first time apart since they met. He intended to tell his family he'd met someone special when he got home. He wanted everyone to know that for the first time in his life, he was in love. He planned to give her something special for Christmas before they left school to show her how he felt, and to remind her of him.

Chapter Thirteen - Linda

The first few months of college have been the best days of my life. I enjoy living in Atlanta, and don't really see myself returning to Chicago once I graduate. I'm committed to my classes and volunteer work, and I hold my relationship with Sanford close to my heart.

I finally confessed my feelings about him to MC, because it was getting too stressful trying to figure out how to spend time with Sanford when my roommate is within eight feet of me most of the time. I was shocked when she essentially shrugged her shoulders and said she knew about it all along. Would it be this easy with everyone else? Is it time to publicly step out as a couple?

The fall semester ends today and the dorms close down this weekend for the holidays. MC is leaving tonight since she doesn't have far to go. We've said our goodbyes already so I can spend the last night at school with Sanford. I'm already starting to feel an ache at the thought of being away from him for six weeks. We've promised to write each other every day, and he said he would call me once or twice a week using his father's long-distance business line. My train to Chicago leaves tomorrow and I'll spend two days on my journey home, travelling via Washington, DC. Normally, I would be excited to see the nation's capital and other cities through the train window, but all I can think about right now is how much I'm going to miss my first love. Yes, I admit it. I am in love with Sanford Patrick.

Our plan for our last night is to eat dinner together in the dining hall, and come back to my dorm room for the evening. We figured out a while back that as long as we keep things discreet and no one complains, the RAs don't really enforce the rule about a member of the opposite sex spending the night, and I'm more comfortable here than in Sanford's frat house full of guys.

Since we're going to be apart for six weeks, there's a sense of urgency in our lovemaking, even though we have all night. As we're wrapped in each other's arms resting after an intense coupling, I tell Sanford I need to get up for a moment. Upon my return from the bathroom, I reach into my desk drawer for his Christmas gift. I clear my throat in an attempt to banish my nervousness as I hand him the carefully wrapped present.

"This is for you. I hope you like it."

Sanford sits up against the headboard and pulls me to his side. Draping one arm around me, he pulls off the ribbon and tears open the wrapping paper, unveiling a small white box. He then lifts off the lid to reveal my gift to him: a stainless-steel chain-link ID bracelet engraved with the name *Sanford* on the name plate.

"Thank you. This is awesome."

"There's something engraved on the back as well."

He turns it over and reads the inscription. "LJ+SP. Does this mean what I think it means?"

"What do you think it means?"

"That we are a couple."

"Yes, Sanford. We are a couple. I'm done hiding. I want the world to know how I feel about you."

He grins at me. "And how do you feel?"

I know he's teasing me, but I don't mind playing along, as my heart is bursting with joy.

"I love you, Sanford Patrick. Do you want me to shout it from the quad?"

He tweaks me on my nose. "That won't be necessary. If I need to hear it, I can just look at my bracelet. Which will be easy to do since once you put it on my wrist, I don't plan to take it off."

Before I can say any more, Sanford gets up and goes over to his jacket draped on my desk chair, pulling something from the pocket. He scoots back onto the bed and hands me a beautifully wrapped small box about the same size as the one I just gave him.

"This wrapping is so pretty. Did you do this yourself?"

"Are you kidding? My talents don't extend to gift wrapping. Go ahead, open it."

Normally I take my time unwrapping presents, but I can't wait to see what's inside. I rip apart the wrapping and open the box, gasping at what I find. I lift out a beautiful emerald pendant on a silver chain. I feel tears coming on as he says, "here, let me put it on you."

He opens the chain and drapes it across my chest as I lift my hair so he can secure the clasp around my neck.

MAJORING IN LOVE

He hooks the chain and turns me around to face him. "Sanford, this is so beautiful. Thank you. I'll never take it off."

He grasps my hands and speaks. "I wanted to get you something special as a symbol of how I feel about you. Did you know the emerald signifies truth, hope, and love?"

I shake my head in the negative and will the tears in my eyes not to fall.

He continues. "The truth is, Linda Jones, you are my love, and you are my hope for the future."

So much for not crying. I can no longer hold back my tears of happiness. "Thank you. I love it. But you've already given me the best gift of all."

"What's that?"

"The gift of love and a realization. The realization that you shouldn't have to hide who you love. And I'm not hiding anymore."

The End

I hope you enjoyed Linda and Sandy's story. If you'd like to read their daughter Salynda's love story, you'll find it in *Be One with Me*, Book 2 in my *Finding Love in Green Springs* series.

CA MICONI

About the Author – CA Miconi

CA Miconi began reading at the age of five and has never stopped. Her childhood was filled with multiple readings of Gone with the Wind, the ultimate tragic romance. CA got her own happily ever after when she married her retired military hero, Gary, in 2010. She began her author services company, Lucky 13, in 2015 as a result of her love of reviewing, sharing, and talking about her favorite books, mostly romantic suspense and stories featuring strong alpha heroes, especially law enforcement and military. CA also hosts and sponsors author and reader events, and never dreamed she'd one day attend as a signing author. When she's not reading, writing, or working with authors, CA enjoys traveling, spending time with her grandchildren, boating, motorcycling, and cheering on her beloved Baltimore Ravens.

Stay Connected with CA
Facebook:
https://www.facebook.com/camiconiauthor/
Twitter:
https://twitter.com/ca_miconi
Instagram:
https://www.instagram.com/camiconiauthor/
Website:
http://www.camiconiwrites.com/
Bookbub:
https://www.bookbub.com/profile/ca-miconi

Books by CA Miconi:
Finding Love in Green Springs Series:
Book 1 – Be Brave with Me
Book 2 – Be One with Me
Suspenseful Seduction World:
Waiting for Him Too

COMING TO SAPPHIRE CREEK

Carmen Cook

CHAPTER ONE

Deanna Perry took a deep breath and tried to relax while she leaned against the bar, waiting for Brandon, the owner of the Bitterroot Tavern, to get her a glass of wine. She didn't typically have the down time to spend at the tavern with friends and wasn't completely comfortable being here without them. She'd tried to back out of coming tonight, but Gwen had insisted.

"No excuses," Gwen had said, pointing her sandwich as they shared a takeout lunch at Deanna's desk at the security firm, which Gwen's brother owned. "We need to get together to plan."

"Plan what?" The only thing Deanna had been planning on was curling up with a good book while her teenage son was out with friends for the night.

Gwen had just smiled a wicked little grin that made Deanna both apprehensive about what the petite brunette was thinking and a little excited to try out whatever it was she had up her sleeve. She needed to get out of her current rut. She knew it, but that didn't mean she was comfortable doing it.

Deanna had been working two or three jobs for more years than she had fingers on both hands to count, and she'd done it willingly. Happily even, in order to keep food on the table and a roof over her and her son's head after her no-good boyfriend had left her alone and pregnant as a teenager and her drunk of a father had kicked her out, claiming she was bringing shame to the family name.

But she'd done it.

She'd always had more pride than was good for her, but in this instance it had served her well. And now that she didn't have to work multiple jobs thanks to being hired on as the office manager for Skyhawk Security's local office, she should be enjoying her nights and weekends off.

Instead she was standing here, feeling incredibly overdressed in her new flutter-sleeve shirtdress that was the exact same shade of red as her favorite lipstick, while the other patrons were all wearing jeans and cowboy boots. She was resisting the urge to tug at her perfectly respectable hemline when Brandon brought her drink. "Here you go," he said, setting the glass of red wine on the cocktail napkin in front of her. "Are you celebrating tonight? You're all dressed up."

Brandon was the former NFL tight end whose family had owned the Bitterroot Tavern since it had opened generations before. When he retired from playing football, he'd come back and seemed to have taken up right where he left off without missing a beat. He had an easy way with people that Deanna envied. She always felt like she was being judged. That people had an opinion about her, even if they didn't know her, so she tended to keep to herself.

That was another thing that was changing with her new job.

"No, not celebrating," she answered Brandon. "Just meeting some friends."

"And changing her life," Gwen announced as she bounded up to the bar with her limitless energy, throwing an arm over Deanna's shoulder. "But she does look amazing, doesn't she?"

"She does," Brandon agreed with a smile. "And you too. Although if you're going to plot world domination or whatever it is you do when you women get together, you should grab a booth. What'll you have? I'll bring it over."

Gwen gave her order and led the way between the

patrons to one of the booths that lined the walls. With the shiplap high backs, each booth offered a little cocoon of privacy in the busy room. Deanna gratefully sank down onto the wooden bench and slid in. "Isn't Cassidy coming?"

"She's waiting for the babysitter."

"Who was late," Cassidy announced as she slid into the booth next to Deanna, offering her a quick hug. "I'm trying not to be too irritated about her being late, but this is the first time since coming to Sapphire Creek I've had a chance to go out. I was ready, like, three hours ago."

Deanna couldn't help but laugh. "I understand that all too well. But you're here now, so we'll get you a drink and you can enjoy your night off. Then we'll listen to whatever plot Gwen is hatching and make sure we won't get arrested for skinny dipping in the lake."

"One time," Gwen objected. "And thanks to my brother being the responding officer and not daring to look when he ordered me to get out, I didn't get arrested."

Cassidy beamed a sunny smile across the table toward Gwen while Deanna just shook her head laughing. "It's been a long time since I was involved in any type of a plot," Cassidy admitted, swiping Deanna's glass of wine and taking a sip.

"This time it's more of a scheme, really," Gwen said with a twinkle in her eye.

Brandon picked that moment to deliver Gwen's gin and tonic, causing them all to fall abruptly silent. He looked around the table, only pulling his eyes away from Cassidy with difficulty, Deanna noticed. "A scheme," he finally said to Gwen. "Do I need to put Connor on alert again?"

She blew a raspberry at him. "Are you the one who called the cops on me? I wouldn't have thought you'd be such a prude. And no, Connor doesn't need to know."

"Know what?" Connor, one of Gwen's older brothers and Sapphire Creek's chief of police, popped up at their table as though summoned.

Deanna tried to contain her laughter at Gwen's exasperated expression. "Where did you come from?"

"Uh, the bar." He pointed his thumb over his shoulder

and shot a look of male—or maybe it was more brotherly—confusion toward Brandon, who shrugged and started to step away.

"Wait. Cassidy needs a drink."

"Oh, I don't…"

"Of course," Brandon leveled his gaze at her one more time. "What'll you have?"

Cassidy turned bright pink and looked away. Deanna was going to have to get to the bottom of this, she thought, as Cassidy stammered out a request for a Diet Coke. She was about to ask what was going on between the two of them when Gwen's question drew her attention. "What are you doing here?"

"I'm meeting Zach, who's bringing our old sergeant. He just moved here."

Gwen threw her hands in the air. "Why are you guys always around?"

"It is a pretty small town, sis," Connor said, tongue in cheek. "But don't worry. We won't break up your girls' night."

"We're crashing girls' night?" Zach appeared next to Connor, his eyes alight with mischief as he tossed his arm casually across his brother-in-law's shoulders.

Gwen gently thunked her head back against the booth. "You guys always show up to ruin my best plans."

"And what plans would those be?"

"We're going to find men." She pointed a finger at her brother and Zach in turn. "And I don't want any interference from either of you."

Deanna's jaw dropped, but she appeared to be the only one who was surprised. Connor barked out a laugh while Zach raised his hands in mock surrender. "God forbid I interfere with a manhunt. I'll grab Bas and we'll stay far, *far* out of your way."

"Stay out of the way of what?" a new voice asked, and Deanna felt the booth shift sideways and her stomach drop all the way to her fancy new shoes.

200

"Sebastian?" she asked, her voice a hoarse croak while she tried to see around the two men blocking her view.

They shifted and there he stood. Taller and broader than Zach's leanly muscled frame, his dark skin glimmering in the soft light and as handsome as ever while he appeared just as shocked as she felt. "Oh my god. Dee."

CHAPTER TWO

Sebastian Dunn couldn't help but stare. Dee, the woman he'd been dreaming about for much longer than was reasonable, considering they'd only been together once before when he'd come to Sapphire Creek on leave, was sitting right here in front of him. She looked amazing with her nearly black hair curled loosely around her face and falling to her shoulders, one side being held back on by a sparkling clip. Her bright red lipstick seemed to be the same shade as her dress and made her porcelain skin glow in the dim light of the bar.

Most important, she wasn't wearing a wedding ring. He was both overjoyed and a little saddened by that. Part of him hoped she'd found love in the ten years since they'd seen each other.

Realizing he was just standing there staring, he cleared his throat. "How've you been?"

"Hang on," Zach said, interrupting before Deanna could answer. "You two know each other? How?"

Since he was still looking at Dee, he couldn't miss the way she blushed at the question and how her tongue darted out to wet her lips. His groin tightened in response. "Yes," he answered. "We met that time you guys dragged me up here to go fishing."

He could tell both Connor and Zach were remembering how he'd disappeared on them for a full day before they'd had to head back to base. He'd been tired of fishing, tired of seeing Connor and his young wife make moon eyes at one another while Zach bounced their toddler, his nephew and the light of his life, on his knee. He knew they'd invited him along because they considered him part of their families, but he'd never felt so alone in those moments.

Needing to get away from it all, he'd escaped—to this very bar, this very same booth, as a matter of fact—and had met Deanna. Standing here now, he couldn't help but wonder if that was a sign that she was sitting in the same place he'd first seen her.

"Oh my gosh," the petite brunette sitting across from Dee said, sounding awed. "He's the one."

Deanna blushed again, but nodded. "Gwen was babysitting for me that night," she explained, gesturing to her friend. She said it mostly to him, but everyone was hanging on every word so both Connor and Zach nodded. He understood what she was telling him. That babysitter had kept Deanna's young son overnight and late into the next morning so they'd been able to get to know one another more intimately. Warmth spread through him at the memory.

"Then I owe you a thank-you, at least," he said, extending his hand to Deanna's friend. "I'm Sebastian Dunn. Bas to most everyone."

She slid her hand into his for a shake and offered him a cheeky smile. "I'm Gwen McCabe, and this is Cassidy…Wylde." The pause was barely noticeable, but he didn't have time to dwell on that. "And you know Deanna," she continued, dropping his hand. "It appears my plan is useless now," she said in mock exasperation. "At least for Deanna. You might as well join us." She leveled a look across the booth to Deanna, who was still staring. "Is that okay with you?"

"Oh my gosh, yes. Sit, yes. Please." Spurred out of her stupor by Gwen's question, Deanna made an ass of herself, tripping over her words and fluttering her hands like she was trying to take flight. "I just—I never expected…" she gave up, dropping her hands back to the table. "I'm making a mess of everything."

"No." Bas slid in next to Gwen and reached across the

table, taking one of Dee's hands in his as the rest of the party shuffled around, pulling chairs up to the table and scooting so everyone had room.

Her skin looked even paler next to the rich, dark brown of his work-calloused hands. She remembered their contrasts vividly and felt herself flush again. When he'd approached her all those years ago all she'd been able to think was that he was, without a doubt, the sexiest man she'd ever seen. Not just because he had muscles on top of muscles, or the dimple in his left cheek that made her insides all fluttery. It hadn't been the deep reddish brown of his skin that reminded her of aged mahogany or the freckles scattered across his broad nose. Not his flashing white smile or a jaw that looked like it had been sculpted from marble.

More than all of that was the way he looked at her. Like he was able to peer deep into her soul and see her deepest dreams and desires all spelled out. And he hadn't judged her for them. Over the years she'd talked herself into believing that part had been her imagination. That her infatuation with the mysterious stranger made her think she'd felt things that hadn't really been there.

But now, as he was sitting across from her holding her hand and the dim lights shining off his shaved head—that was new—she had to admit to herself it hadn't been her imagination at all. It was him. His quiet, solid presence that soothed a part of her she'd long neglected. The way he chose his words carefully, not minding the uncomfortable silence that sometimes fell before he spoke. Something about his very existence touched her in a way that made her feel so much more than she'd felt a few minutes before.

"You're not making a mess of anything," he assured her, giving her hand a little squeeze. "I know it must be a surprise, for me to pop up like this out of nowhere."

She couldn't help it. She laughed outright at that, so much so that tears filled her eyes and a stitch started in her side. "A surprise? You could say that."

He grinned at her laughter. "I've been thinking of you. I'd planned to ask one of the guys if they knew you once I got the garage open."

"You should have asked," Connor said, sitting in a chair at the end of the table and still looking around like he was trying to figure out what had happened. "Deanna works for my brother, Gavin. She's practically family."

Another flush crept up Deanna's cheeks, but this time for a very different reason. For years she'd longed to be part of a larger family, but had to rely solely on herself. To hear Connor refer to her as such soothed an ache she wasn't even aware still existed.

She had so many questions that she was having trouble thinking of what to ask...especially with their current audience hanging on every word.

"Why?"

Tilting his head, he held her gaze, silently asking her to elaborate on her question. To ask what she really wanted to know, regardless of the crowd around them. He had done that the last time they were together, too, she remembered. Seemed to be able to understand when she was struggling to put her thoughts into words and would patiently wait while she figured it out. "You could have anyone," she said, measuring her words. "Be anywhere in the world. Why are you here? And why would you ask about me? We don't even know each other. Not really."

He released her hand and he leaned back against the wooden back of the booth. "I liked it here," he said simply. "And you're right, I could have gone anywhere after I got out of the military. But I was hoping for a fresh start. A place that held a sense of community, where people look out for one another. Maybe I was hoping to start something new in a place that held fond memories for me. Maybe see if my memory of all those years ago was real or if I was just dreaming about what could be."

Deanna picked up her wine to take a sip, her mouth suddenly gone dry as he voiced the very thoughts she'd been having minutes ago. "And?" she asked. Not sure she wanted to know the truth, but refusing to hide from it.

"I think that depends on you," he answered, a small smile playing over his full lips. "You're not wearing a wedding band, but that doesn't mean there isn't someone who has your heart."

He said the words lightly, but she felt the power of them. "No!" she exclaimed. Realizing everyone was staring, she lowered her voice. "No. I'm not married. Or involved. I haven't—" she paused to look around before admitting the truth. "I haven't been in a relationship in a long time."

Shock showed on his face as he leaned forward, bracing his elbows on the table. "You, what? Why?" Sorrow clouded his dark eyes and he shook his head.

Their friends weren't making this reunion easy for either of them, she realized. Shifting slightly in her seat, she searched for something to say, but Gwen chimed in. "Deanna has been focusing on being a mother. She's put everyone's needs above her own for years." There was a slight edge to her voice and Dee had to suppress a grin. She'd never been on the receiving end of Gwen's protective instincts, and despite feeling like they weren't needed at the moment, it felt nice to have someone rush to her aid.

There was so much she wanted to say to him. So many thoughts and emotions running through her mind, but she wasn't willing to say them in front of her friends.

Not yet, anyway.

Bas apparently felt the same way. He offered her a small smile of understanding. "I'd like to take you out, to get to know one another again. Would you have dinner with me? Just the two of us," he said, giving the group a pointed look.

Before Deanna could answer, Cassidy stood, pushing Zach a little so he'd move out of her way. "Let's go to the restroom."

The guys all looked at one another blankly, but both Gwen and Deanna started to move, sliding out of their seats, which also had Sebastian standing.

"Oh," Zach said, sounding bewildered. "This going to the bathroom in groups is a real thing."

"Are you new?" Gwen asked, giving him a little hip-check as she passed him. "Of course it's a thing. I have questions and want details. I can ask my questions here, or..."

"No," Deanna said with a laugh, shoving her friend away from the table. "No asking anything here. We'll be back in a few minutes." Offering a small smile to Sebastian—she was still having trouble wrapping her mind around the fact that he was here—she paused. "When I come back I'll take care of my tab and you can take me home." Heat flooded her face. "To talk," she blurted. Good God, she was so bad at this.

But he didn't seem to mind. "To talk," he agreed, offering her a blinding smile that had her knees quivering as she wove her way through the crowd to the restrooms.

CHAPTER THREE

The bar was a dark walnut wood with a live edge Bas couldn't help but admire as he approached to settle his and Deanna's tab. Within seconds Connor and Zach flanked him, having abandoned the booth to get the scoop. They'd always been nosy as hell. "Well?" Connor asked, ever impatient.

"Well what?" Bas asked, as he handed his credit card to the man behind the bar. "Mine and Deanna's drinks."

"Are you going to tell us what's going on with you and Deanna? How come you never said anything?"

Zach snorted. "You were so caught up with Bethany and Andy, you barely noticed anything that trip home."

"That might be true," Connor agreed. "But there was plenty of time later. The whole flight back. When we were badgering you to move to Sapphire Creek and re-open the garage. Any of the ten years in between."

Connor wasn't really annoyed, Sebastian knew, he just hated not being in the know of all things. It was part of what made him such a good cop. "There was no reason to fill you in, then or now. What Deanna and I shared was only meant to last a night. It was a mirage in the midst of everything we were dealing with in our day-to-day lives. We'd just gotten back from the Sandbox," he said, referring to the Middle East. "She was dealing with being a single mom and whatever else was going on in her life. We met. We clicked. That was it. We deserved a little break from it all to enjoy ourselves." He paused and thought back for a moment.

"I'm realizing now that I had no real idea what all she had going on at the time."

"A lot," a new voice said from the other side of Zach, drawing all of their attention. "That poor girl has always had to deal with a lot."

Sebastian went on high alert, every muscle tensing as he realized their conversation was being overheard. "You know about her troubles?" he inquired, keeping his voice mild.

"Hell, we all knew about her troubles," the old man continued, tossing his hand in the air to emphasize his point. "I know I'm not supposed to speak ill of the dead. But her father was a world-class jackass who kicked her out after that Sanchez boy went running for the hills rather than stepping up and being a daddy to their baby boy."

Sebastian raised a brow at Zach, who nodded. Zach had brought a young man, Julian Sanchez, by the garage earlier in the day, where the boy had applied for the job of being an all-around gofer in order to learn what he could and eventually become a mechanic. He was going to the local vocational-technical school already, so he had a good start, but nothing beat a hands-on education. Bas had no idea he'd been interviewing Dee's son.

Maybe it would have been good to share their connection before now.

"Deanna is made of sterner stuff than that old bastard realized," the old man continued. "She picked herself up by her bootstraps and made a life for herself and her son." The man huffed out a chuckle and took a slug of beer before setting his pint glass down, slopping on the shiny bar, making Sebastian wince at the abuse. "And that boy has given her a run for her money, let me tell you. He's just as stubborn as she ever was. But they seem to be doing all right now."

The man leveled a look at Bas, which had him sitting up just a bit straighter. "What I'm wondering now, though, is about you. Are you good enough for our girl?"

"Sir?" Bas stopped himself from rocking back on his

heels. It had been a long time since he'd been challenged. And this man had to be closer to a hundred pounds rather than Bas's own two hundred. Not to mention he also looked to be older than dirt.

The man waved his hand through the air and continued. "What type of man are you? Are you one of those who likes to drown worms? Or do you know how to fish the way man was meant to?"

Zach covered his mouth to hide his grin and Sebastian was pretty sure he could hear Connor chuckling on his other side, but he didn't mind. It was nice to know Dee had someone looking out for her—even if the guy wasn't much of a deterrent. "It's been a few years, but I can cast," he answered the question about fishing. It didn't seem right to discuss his relationship status with a stranger before he and Dee had a chance to figure out what they were going to do.

"Well then," the man said, taking another drink of his beer, lowering the pint glass to the bar with another thunk, but thankfully not spilling any this time. "I guess you'll do. Be sure to bring some business cards by the hardware store when you're ready to start working on cars. The transmission on my wife's Buick needs some work."

"I'll do that."

Zach slapped him on the back as the older man moved away. "Welcome to Sapphire Creek, man."

CHAPTER FOUR

Deanna followed Gwen into the bathroom, not at all surprised to find Cassidy already waiting, her arms crossed and toe tapping.

The outer door was barely closed before she started in. "Well?" Cassidy demanded. "You've been holding out on us. How could you have a man like that waiting for you and not tell us? I need details! Don't you understand that I'm living vicariously through you guys?"

"Yeah," Gwen echoed. "You failed to mention all those years ago that your mystery man was a sexy Idris Elba lookalike. Why didn't you mention that part at least?"

Deanna couldn't help the grin that spread across her face as memories of her previous encounter with Sebastian played through her mind like a movie. They'd met here, at the Bitterroot Tavern. She'd been feeling restless—and a little bit reckless if she was honest with herself. Being a single mom working two or three jobs at a time had been exhausting. Not just physically, but emotionally as well.

She'd taken a rare night off and hired Gwen to watch Julian so she could go out. She hadn't had any real plans. All she knew was that she wanted to dance. To lose herself in the music, maybe hook up with someone for a few hours and forget all about being a responsible adult. Just one night of not having anyone rely on her.

But by the time she'd arrived at the tavern she'd lost some of her resolve, so she'd sat in a booth sipping some house wine, which had been all she'd been able to afford. Still she'd enjoyed the music, even if she decided she didn't have the gumption to ask someone to dance. And then he'd shown up.

He'd asked her to dance, holding her close while they swayed to the music. But even more, he'd looked at her in a way she never dreamed anyone would look at her.

Like she mattered. He'd listened to her with his full being and she'd basked in being the center of his attention. They'd spent the rest of the evening lost in one another. She'd shared everything with him. Her biggest dreams and her darkest regrets.

She'd told him how devastated she'd been when Julian's father left and how that had been nothing compared to her father kicking her out. How scared she'd been being pregnant and alone. How scared she still was when she paused long enough to allow the emotion in.

She'd shared her dreams of being a dancer and her reality of working a string of minimum wage jobs and living paycheck to paycheck in order to make ends meet.

Through it all, he hadn't judged her. Instead, he'd praised her strength and fortitude. He'd told her she had the heart of a warrior and he was proud of her. And he'd made her feel complete in a way she'd never dreamed.

"I..." Now, standing here with her friends waiting for an answer, what could she say? That she'd wanted to keep those memories to herself? That she was afraid if she'd said it out loud the whole thing would disappear like the morning mist over the river?

Deanna took a deep breath, puffing out her cheeks while she slowly blew it out. "The truth is, I never thought I'd see him again," she admitted, a little saddened at the thought. "So I didn't want to talk about the evening we spent together. It was so special and he made me feel things I'd only read about in novels. I guess I wanted to keep something for myself."

She moved to the sink and put her purse down to

wash her hands. More for something to do while she was lost in her memories than anything else. "My life was completely focused on Julian. Making sure he knew he was loved and supported while he got his school work done so he could make something of himself. Keeping a roof over our heads and food in the fridge meant I didn't have time to pine away for a man I barely knew."

Looking in the mirror she avoided her own reflection. Instead, she focused on her friends flanking her, understanding blazing in their eyes.

"You're an amazing mother," Gwen said seriously, laying a hand on her arm. "And there's nothing at all wrong with taking something for yourself. You know that right?"

"Besides," Cassidy chimed in, "that was then. Julian is nearly grown now. You can't keep living your life for him. That's not healthy."

Deanna grinned. "Says the woman whose world revolves around her little girl."

"That's different. My daughter is only five. And our situation was…difficult."

"I know." Cassidy had inherited her grandmother's floral shop the year before, which brought her to Sapphire Creek and gave her the means to escape an abusive marriage. Deanna didn't know the details—she'd been waiting for when Cassidy was ready to share—but she sensed a kindred spirit in the younger woman and her heart ached at the obvious pain her friend was still going through. "I was teasing.

"It didn't matter anyway," she told her friends, shifting the topic back to her one night in Bas's arms. "He had to go back to his life in the military. And I had to go back to mine. There wasn't room for us to continue anything at the time."

"And now?"

The idea of being able to start a relationship, a real relationship, with Sebastian set off a whole kaleidoscope of butterflies off in her stomach. "I really don't know."

She turned back around and faced her friends while she wiped her hands and wadded up the paper towel. "That night with him was magical. It's like a dream I've held on to for so long. What if the real thing isn't everything I want it to be? That would not only suck in the now, but it would take away the memory I've cherished."

"Listen to me," Gwen ordered, putting her own purse on the counter and placing her hands on Deanna's shoulders. "You deserve the very best. And if this guy isn't the one to give it to you, then that's on him, not you. But right now, the fact that he's here and seems to be interested in starting something up…" she paused with her eyebrow raised and Deanna felt her cheeks heat in response. Yes, he seemed to be very interested. "That's what I thought," her friend continued. "Since he's here, don't you think you owe it to yourself to go for it? To see if it could be everything you'd ever imagined, rather than thinking it might not live up to your memories?"

Deanna heard what her friend was saying, but couldn't help but shake her head. "I'm not like you," she said, sadness creeping in. "I don't date a lot. I don't take risks. Not anymore."

Gwen made an annoyed sound. "If you aren't willing to take a risk, you're giving up on yourself. And you are not someone who gives up. Ever. Just think about it," she urged.

Nodding, Deanna had a feeling she'd be thinking of little else as she exited the bathroom and made her way back toward Sebastian.

Here goes nothing.

CHAPTER FIVE

After Deanna finally emerged from the restroom with the other women, Sebastian led the way to his truck to take her home. He followed her directions through the sleepy mountain town and pulled his restored Ford Bronco into her driveway beside an old Toyota Camry. She'd been quiet since they left the bar and he couldn't help but wonder where her mind was as he navigated the streets into an unassuming, blue-collar area. The houses here were small, but well kept. The lots were large, a few overgrown with cars up on blocks and various appliances littering the surrounding area. But Deanna's house was tidy. Orderly flower beds lined the walk up to her front door, which had been painted a bright blue. It offset the pale gray of her siding and looked cheerful. A little oasis.

He could imagine her out here tending the flowers on a lazy Sunday morning while her son worked on her car or mowed the lawn. It was obvious she cared for her surroundings.

But now that he'd cut the engine, they sat there listening to the night sounds, and he wasn't sure what to say. Which was ridiculous. He always knew the next move. Hell, he'd made a career of being three steps ahead at any given moment. But somehow, this felt more important than anything else.

"I never thought I'd run into you tonight," he started, resisting the urge to reach over and take her hand in his. "I can only imagine how unexpected it was for you, since you didn't even know I'd moved to town."

Deanna laughed and turned to face him, reaching over and taking his hand in hers and loosening the band that had tightened around his chest each mile that had passed in silence. "Unexpected is a bit of an understatement," she admitted. "I never thought I would see you again. And then, right when I'm starting to think about the next phase of my life, you show up out of the blue. It's going to take some getting used to."

"I can understand that," he said, bringing their linked hands to his mouth and gently kissing her fingers. "But I'd be lying if I said I hadn't hoped to see you again. To see about starting something that lasted more than just a night."

She let out a breath and tugged her hand away, tightening that band around his chest without even saying a word. She was silent for a few minutes, obviously weighing her words.

Bas resisted pushing her. It was true she'd been a factor in his decision to move to Sapphire Creek, but that was a decision he'd made without her. He'd made it not even knowing if she was even available to pursue a relationship. He needed to allow her time to get used to the idea that he was back in town.

Or not. Dread filled him at the thought. What would he do if she sent him on his way saying she didn't want to try?

Refusing to even think of it until she said the words, he studied her profile. She was softer than she'd been ten years before. Her cheeks were a little fuller and there were faint lines around her eyes. She was beautiful. It seemed the years had eased the edges of the fierce determination she'd tackled life with.

She'd settled in, he thought suddenly. When he'd met her before, she'd been adrift. But now, sitting in front of her tidy little house and seeing her wrestle with her heart he could tell she'd found a place for herself and her son. And she was scared to risk the peace she'd fought so hard for.

Thinking of her son, he realized he needed to tell her about the job. "Zach brought Julian in to see me today," he said, keeping his voice low in an effort to soothe whatever doubts she was having. Her gaze swung to him and speared him with a laser intensity. When it came to her son, she obviously would take no prisoners. It didn't matter if she held fond memories of him or not, she would eviscerate him if he messed with her boy.

That shouldn't be such an attractive quality, but it was. She was still fierce as ever. A survivor. And the most beautiful woman he'd seen. Pushing his attraction to the back burner he continued, "I didn't know he was your son until a little bit ago."

"When?" she asked, her voice tight.

"When I was paying our bill at the tavern," he admitted. "Zach brought him to the garage to meet me and help him apply for a job. He wants to learn about cars and become a mechanic."

She released a breath he hadn't realized she'd been holding and nodded. "So he didn't know who you were? That we'd—?"

"No. Heck, if I didn't know he was your kid, there was no way he knew about our connection, right? Anyway, I told him to bring me his school schedule and I'd hire him to do odd jobs around the garage and that I'd teach him what I could."

She studied him for another heartbeat before speaking. "Why are you telling me this?"

He rubbed his head before dropping his hand to rest on his thigh. "Because I want to do the right thing here," he admitted. "I know my showing up has thrown you for a loop and I'm doing everything I can to resist the urge to kiss you so hard you forget your own name." She made a little sound that had his gut tightening again, but he ignored it. "I don't want you to be surprised again, so I'm going to lay it all out there.

"I want to start something with you. And I know we have this weird foundation of a memory to build on, so we need to make something completely new. Something solid that's real and not a dream." Her eyes were blazing and her breathing had quickened. He hoped like hell that meant she wanted the same thing he did, but he wasn't going to leave anything unsaid. Not now.

"I'm also building a life here. The next phase of my life. That means I'm creating a home and a business, which your son has applied to be a part of. I don't know him, but I know you. And I can only imagine he's as tenacious and a hard worker. I'm willing to stick by my word and teach him what he wants to know, even if you decide you don't want to pursue this, whatever this is, between us."

"No," she exclaimed, biting her lip like she regretted how the word erupted out of her. "It's fine for Julian to work for you," she said slowly. "But Sebastian, you have to understand why I'm nervous. You have this plan for the next part of your life and you've already thought about how I would fit into it. I barely know what I'm going to have for breakfast in the morning, let alone what my life is going to be like next year or five years from now."

He opened his mouth to explain, but she held up her hand, halting his words. "I've spent so long reacting to my current situation, just trying to stay afloat and do whatever I needed to do to get by. I never had the chance to really think about what I wanted.

"And now you're here. And I want to get to know you again, I do, but I'm finding it all a little overwhelming. I think I just need a little time to sort it all out." Her hands were folded tightly in her lap and her head was hanging so low while she made the admission that her chin was buried in her chest.

His heart gave a slow roll as he looked at her, so dejected and prepared for rejection for simply stating what she needed. Slowly, he reached over and took her clenched hands in his. "I'm not pushing you," he told her softly. "And as much as I'd like to jump right into a relationship with you, I'm willing to go slow so you can make sure it's what you want."

Her head jerked up, her eyes wide with surprise. "You are?"

"I am. So how about this? I'll walk you to your pretty blue door and I'll kiss you good night. And next Friday, I'll pick you up for a date."

"A date?"

Amusement tugged at his lips. "Yes, a date. Dinner. Maybe dancing."

"But…Friday's nearly a full week away."

He had to laugh at her objection. "I know. So we'll have to make our good-night kiss good enough to last."

CHAPTER SIX

The week became a new brand of torture for Deanna, filled with trying to be patient while each minute was edged with anticipation. In her more generous moments, she was thrilled that Sebastian seemed to understand that she needed time to process the idea of him being in her life on a more permanent basis. In her less generous moments she fought off an overwhelming desire to drive straight over to his garage and insist he kiss her again, her own request for time and space be damned.

She tried to keep busy to keep her mind off the upcoming date by picking up some extra shifts at the grocery store, where she still worked as a cashier a couple evenings a week.

But by Thursday, Gwen wasn't going to be put off any longer. "We have to decide what you're going to wear," she announced when Deanna opened the door to her pounding. She hitched the canvas grocery bag, which looked like it carried a bottle of wine along with a liter of soda, higher onto her shoulder and held out the two pizza boxes in her hands. "Cassidy and her mini are on their way. I've taken care of dinner, so we're going to ransack your closet and then we're going to stuff our faces."

Deanna laughed and stepped back, allowing her friend to enter her tiny living room. "How did you know that's exactly what I needed?" Taking the pizzas, she led the way to the kitchen, where Julian was seated at the table studying some type of car manual. She once again resisted the urge to ask him too many specifics about his new job. She was trying hard to respect his space as he navigated balancing his job and schoolwork by not grilling him for information about Sebastian every time he came home.

Gwen followed her in and plopped down in the seat next to Julian. "Whatcha working on?" she asked, helping herself to a couple of chips from the bowl in front of him.

"I'm studying how to replace a muffler and exhaust system. Bas said that's probably what Mom's car needs when I told him the noise it's making. He ordered the parts and said he'd teach me how to do it when they come in, but I want to make sure I know what he's talking about."

Deanna's head had whipped around at the casual mention of Sebastian. They talked about her? She didn't know what to think of that at all, but Gwen was grinning like a loon and waved her quiet. "You know your boss is interested in your mom, right?"

"Yeah. He told me that he's asked her out. But I knew before that too, because I found her all dreamy-eyed staring after his truck the other night after he dropped her off."

"Okay," Deanna interrupted, pulling some paper plates from the stash she kept for when she didn't feel like doing dishes. "That's enough of that." Gwen was laughing at Julian's exaggerated eyelash batting and puckered-up fish lips. "You're just encouraging him." She placed the plates and a pile of napkins on the table.

"Darn straight I'm encouraging him," Gwen said with a wide smile. "It's the first time in…well, ever…you've been interested in a man. And I know you, Dee. I know if Julian here wasn't okay with it, you'd shut Sebastian down so fast he'd have no chance for recovery."

This time Julian's head whipped around while he speared her with an intense look. "You would?" he asked, sounding more like the little boy he used to be than the young man he'd become.

"Well, yeah," Deanna admitted. "It's important to me that you like whoever I wind up with. And this thing with Sebastian is complicated, so I'm nervous. We met before, a long time ago. Plus he's your boss." She waved a hand through the air, indicating there was more but she wasn't going to give it voice. "It's been just you and me for a long time, so I want to make sure you're happy with whatever happens."

"Mom." Julian stood, his lanky frame several inches taller than her own respectable five foot seven, but he still had that rangy leanness of adolescence that indicated he wasn't done growing. His dark hair fell across his forehead and into his all too serious eyes when he took her hands, gripping them lightly in both of his. "You get to be happy." He waited for her nod before he continued. "And if Bas makes you happy, then I'm good with it.

"He's a nice guy. I've been working with him a lot these past few days and he seems like someone who says what he means. Not in a mean way, but he's a straight shooter. Doesn't play games with people. I like him," he said with a shrug, making Deanna's heart swell up even while she tried to suppress a smile. Her son might be rough around the edges, but he had a heart of gold when it came to those he cared about. She couldn't wait to see the type of man he would become.

"Thank you," she said sincerely, wrapping her arms around his waist and giving him a quick squeeze. "When did you get to be so smart?"

He grinned and took his seat again, popping open the lid of the pizza box and taking an appreciative sniff. "I had a good mom," he said over his shoulder. "A few things sunk in."

Deanna's eyes welled with tears, and Gwen pushed to her feet. "Okay, enough of the mushy stuff. You're on babysitting duty when Cassidy gets here, okay?" She pointed at Julian, and when he nodded, she pulled the bottle of wine from her bag. "There are some crayons and coloring pages in here. And save us some pizza." He nodded again, already taking a huge bite from the slice he'd pulled free.

222

"Let's go find something sexy for you to wear," Gwen said, grabbing the wine glasses and corkscrew on her way out of the kitchen and down the hall.

"TMI, Mom," Julian said around the crust and Deanna laughed, feeling lighter than she had in a very long time.

CHAPTER SEVEN

Deanna's closet had erupted all over her bed, with clothes trailing onto the floor by the time the bottle of wine was gone and the women had each managed to snag a couple of pieces of pizza. But they'd finally agreed on the perfect outfit.

Not knowing exactly what Sebastian had in mind for the date, they'd settled on a vintage-style swing dress with three quarter–length sleeves that oozed old Hollywood glamour. Deanna had always loved how the dress made her feel as it emphasized her curves and accentuated her waist. It was a dark, charcoal gray, which sounded like it should be dull, but paired with Cassidy's peacock blue chunky necklace and the stud earrings that matched her blue eyes, it was anything but drab. It was perfect and understated.

Some kitten heels with a T-strap, a clutch borrowed from Gwen, and a turquoise bracelet completed the look.

Now, as she waited for Sebastian to arrive to pick her up, Deanna spun a slow circle in front of the full-length mirror hanging on her closet door and smoothed her hands down the skirt. Nerves raced along her skin as she eyed the clock.

Three minutes to seven and she'd already been ready for half an hour. Flopping back onto the bed, she threw her arms wide and let out a groan. What was she doing? She hadn't been on a date practically since she conceived Julian. Although if she was honest, that was

224

less of a date and more of a hookup in the back of her father's Chevy after the high school football game.

Now she was sitting here, waiting for a man to arrive at her door, as excited as Julian had been his first day of pre-school. The memory of her son sitting at the kitchen table, eating his bowl of generic oat cereal while wearing a backpack that was nearly bigger than he was had her choking back a watery laugh.

They'd made a happy home together. It hadn't always been easy—heck, most of the time it had been downright hard. But she and Julian were a team. They'd faced every curveball that life had thrown their way and come out winners.

And now she was hiding in her bedroom, scared to go on a date? She snorted and pushed herself to her feet. She hadn't backed away from a challenge yet. She wasn't about to start now.

Blowing out a breath, she threw her shoulders back and lifted her chin.

There. Confident. Poised. Dare she hope sexy? She tried to shoot herself a come-hither look in the mirror but winced at the result. "I look like I'm having a seizure," she muttered as she grabbed the clutch and strode from the room.

Julian looked up from his slouched position on the sofa, the car manual once again in his hand, a pen gripped in his mouth, and did a double take. "Wow. Mom. You look great."

There was a knock at the door and Deanna blew out another breath. "I'll get it," Julian said, standing up and walking around the sofa. He opened the door and revealed Sebastian. "Are those for me?" the boy said, indicating the bouquet of wildflowers gripped in Bas's hand.

"Smartaleck. They're for your mom." When Julian didn't step aside, Sebastian raised a brow. "Are you going to let me in. Or call your mom?"

"In a minute," Julian said, standing a bit taller in the doorway and widening his stance. "First, I need to ask about your intentions with my mom."

"Julian!" Deanna was aghast, but Julian waved at her behind his back.

Sebastian's voice rumbled low as he said something to her son she couldn't hear. Something that made Julian take a step back and clear the way for Sebastian to step over the threshold. Her breath caught as she got a good look at him, the apology for her son's behavior dying on her lips. Dove-gray slacks and a black button-down shirt that showed off his broad shoulders and narrow waist. The sleeves of the shirt were rolled up to reveal his muscular forearms, making Deanna's mouth go dry. "Wow," she breathed before she could stop herself.

"I think that's supposed to be my line," Bas said around the pile of sand that filled his mouth at the sight of her. "You look spectacular."

They stood there, staring at each other until Julian cleared his throat. And just like that, the mood lifted to a celebratory feel. "These are for you." Bas held out the bouquet he'd purchased at the small florist in town, not realizing until he'd walked in that her friend Cassidy worked there. But she'd nodded at his request for a wildflower bouquet and set to work, clearly approving of the choice.

Now that he saw the colors of the kittentails, knapweed, and camas sprinkled liberally throughout the mix, all of which matched her accessories, he guessed he'd scored a point there without even realizing it.

"Thank you so much," she murmured, bringing the flowers to her nose for a sniff. "They're beautiful."

"They pale compared to you." The words left his mouth before he remembered they had an audience. Deanna blushed prettily at the compliment while Julian whispered, "Smooth man."

"I'll just put these in water and then we can go." She left the room and Julian once more turned to him.

"Good call on the flowers." The kid shoved his hands deep into the pockets of his worn jeans. "She loves them, but never buys any for herself."

Recognizing Julian was offering him an inside glance into his mother's heart, Bas nodded. "That's good to know."

"You seem like the type of guy who would want to know things like that."

Sebastian studied the young man for a moment. "You are correct. I want to know everything about her. What makes her happy, what makes her sad. If she gets angry when cars drive too slow in front of her, her favorite meal...all of it."

Julian smiled the first real smile Bas had seen on the kid's face since he walked in the door. His protective instincts calmed for the moment, he reached out and shook the kid's hand. "I meant what I told her earlier. I'm all in."

Nodding, Julian shook Bas's hand. "Good."

Deanna strolled back into the room, picking up her jacket that had been draped over the back of a chair. "Ready?" she asked, looking at her son curiously, but not saying anything.

"Ready." Sebastian opened the door for her and gave Julian one last nod before they headed out.

CHAPTER EIGHT

Sebastian pulled into the gravel parking lot at the back of the Bitterroot Tavern and killed the engine. The drive from Deanna's house had been easy. They'd talked about their week. He'd told her about the county inspector coming by and that he'd be ready to open the garage in another week or two.

He needed to come up with a new name, so Deanna spent the majority of the ride suggesting the most ridiculous names she could think of. "I have it," she announced, back lit by the setting sun and looking so much like one of those old-style pin-up girls he'd always loved that his heart did a slow roll in his chest.

Her last suggestion of "Wrench It" had nearly had him driving off the road. Not just because of the name, but because she'd said it with such relish and a lewd eyebrow waggle and hand motions.

"I'm not sure I can take another of your suggestions," he commented, exiting the Bronco and walking around to open her door for her. He offered a hand down and threaded his fingers through hers once her feet were on the ground. "Not that I don't appreciate the memorable suggestions, but I'm trying to run a serious business here."

"I know," she said, falling into step beside him while navigating the gravel path with ease. "That's why this one is perfect."

"Okay, hit me." He'd paused in front of the side

door to the tavern, but she didn't seem to realize they'd reached their destination.

"Dunn's Way Garage."

Sebastian mulled it over. "I like it."

Offering him a cheeky grin, she nodded. "Me too. It's simple. Straightforward. Julian said something about how you are with people. That you're a straight shooter. So, it's 'Dunn's Way.'" She started to walk again, but he stopped her by tightening his fingers around hers.

"We're here," he told her at her questioning look.

She shook her head. "The backroom of the tavern has been closed. Zach has been refinishing it for Brandon so he can rent it out for parties."

He smothered a smile as he nodded. "I know. I didn't think about the fact that living in a small town would have everyone up in my personal business all the time. But by the time the fourth person stopped by the garage to find out where I was taking you on our date, I knew I had to find a place that would offer some privacy so we could get to know one another again without all your friends and neighbors watching."

"Wait." She held up her hand while she processed his words. "People tried to warn you away from me?"

"No. People were more warning me that you deserve to be taken care of and they were already lining up to kick my ass if I dare hurt you."

She was shaking her head before he was done speaking. "That doesn't make any sense."

"People love you here," he told her quietly. "They respect your work ethic and cherish your friendship. They don't want anything bad to happen to you."

Once again she was shaking her head. Bas realized he was going to have to show her rather than just tell her. "Trust me?" he asked, his free hand on the doorknob.

This time she looked at him and nodded, uncertainty still lingering in her eyes.

He opened the door and soft strands of jazz floated out to greet them. Knowing what the room looked like, Bas kept his eyes on hers as she took it all in. The floors and bar were gleaming to a high shine thanks to Zach. There were white linen tablecloths covering the high boys, decorated with small bouquets of the same wild flowers he'd given Deanna when he'd picked her up. Electric votive candles offered sparkling light, highlighting the delicate petals and greenery centered on strips of burlap and lace.

At her small gasp he led her farther into the room and closed the door to the outside world. "I hope you like it," he said sincerely.

"Like it?" She turned in a slow circle, trying to take it all in. "This is amazing. How did you do this? Why did you do this? I mean, don't get me wrong, it's all amazing. But I'm a simple woman, Sebastian. I don't need all this effort."

"Ah." He stepped forward, bringing her into his arms and started swaying to the beat. "That's where you're wrong. By the time the third person showed up at the garage to find out about the date, I realized how invested everyone is in your happiness."

She started to protest, but he kept talking. "They know you deserve to be cherished and loved. They just wanted to make sure I knew it too."

Tears welled in her eyes, but he caught them with his fingertips before they fell. "It's all so overwhelming," she whispered.

"You are overwhelming," he countered. "You captured my heart ten years ago and refused to budge. Your wit and sass make me laugh when I have nothing to laugh about. Dreams of spending more than just one night with you have kept me going for years."

"Sebastian." She breathed his name as she leaned closer. "I had no idea."

He smiled again and tipped her chin up to meet his eyes. "I'm coming alive with you. Becoming the man I've always wanted to be," he admitted. "I know this is our first official date, but if you'll let me, I will spend as much time as it takes to get you to believe exactly how amazing you are."

Lifting herself to her toes, she claimed his mouth in a searing kiss that stole his breath. When she finally pulled back her heart was in her eyes and he felt invincible. "Only if you'll let me do the same for you," she said, biting her lip.

"This calls for a toast." He steered her to the bar tucked into the back corner of the room where two sparkling glasses of champagne had been poured and were standing next to the frosty bucket holding the bottle.

"That wasn't there when we walked in," she said, looking around.

"Brandon brought it in while we were dancing," he said, handing her a flute.

"I didn't even notice." She held her glass aloft. "To amazing memories and new beginnings."

He leaned down to press another kiss to her lips before he added, "To coming back to Sapphire Creek."

SAVING US

Summer Souls Series

Danielle Pearl

Chapter One

I drag my feet from the car and hesitantly enter the recreation building, the heavy door swooshing closed behind me. The smell of chlorine hits hard, but it doesn't have its usual uplifting effect. It still invokes thoughts of summer, but a season that has always meant freedom and fun now only induces anxiety.

An itch nudges at my nose, and my hand lifts half-way to scratch it, before I remember the splint and surgical tape. I make a fist instead, digging my nails into my palm as a distraction.

I make my way into the locker room and change into a swimsuit for absolutely no reason I can fathom, since I can't actually get in the water with this thing on my face. But it's already caused me to miss some of the lifeguarding courses I need to pass in order to accept the last-minute summer job my dad procured me at Aqualina Beach Club, thanks to his longtime friendship with the owner. My broken nose smarts on cue, as if to remind me my previous summer plans are no longer viable, and failing simply isn't an option.

"Welcome back, Miss Goodman," the instructor says lazily as I enter the small room adjacent to the county park's indoor pool. I choose one of the chairs haphazardly situated in a circle, like this is some kind of group therapy meeting or something.

I nod, forcing an unconvincing smile.

"I hope you've studied your CPR Certification Guide. You've missed a lot from the last two sessions, and," she gestures to my nose, "we don't go into the water for the first few classes, but if you miss much more, it will be hard for you to pass the course."

"It comes off next week," I murmur, trying to pretend the other eight or so students aren't staring. It's only my third class, but it's the fifth for the rest of them. I missed a couple thanks to the surgery that repaired the damage to my nose.

It wasn't all that long ago that I ran more or less under the social radar, but that has certainly changed, and their not-so-subtle whispers indicate they've heard the gossip—and the reason for the current state of my face. In the course of my last week of high school, I've managed to go from entirely unknown to infamous. And I hate it.

The instructor sighs. "Well, you may have to watch from the side for a class or two. I hope you don't fall behind." It sounds like a warning.

I don't need one. I will pass this course and my lifeguarding test come hell or high water. I sure as hell can't spend the summer being a day camp counselor at the Gold Coast Beach Club with my former friends as planned. My nose smarts again as if in agreement. Fuck those assholes.

***

I shower quickly and braid my wet hair before making my way out of the women's locker room. Three of the girls from my class—the same ones who were clearly whispering about me last week—are lurking between me and the exit, chatting and giggling. My stomach squirms and my cheeks flush, but when I follow the line of sight of their not-so-surreptitious glances, they don't lead to me, but to the lap pool.

There are only two swimmers, and it's obvious they're not stealing peeks at the elderly woman in the floral swim cap. And I immediately see what has their attention.

Wow.

A long, athletic body clad in only a speedo is barreling the butterfly down the middle lane. Muscles ripple beneath glistening russet limbs as they crash through the water, and

I'm as enthralled as the rest of them, until one of the girls—Melody, or Melanie, or something—calls my name.

"Hey, Remy!"

I grit my teeth. She's never tried to talk to me before. I drag my feet toward where they're standing and offer what I hope passes for a cursory smile. "Hi Mel..." I trail off.

"Melanie," she corrects me, unbothered. "So, what happened, anyway?" she gestures vaguely to my obvious injury. "Graduation gift?"

Her cohorts barely suppress their giggles. I have no doubt she knows very well what happened, and there was no elective surgery involved. I've actually always rather liked my nose.

"Skydiving accident," I quip, deadpan, earning more giggles, but at least they're not at my expense. The lack of follow-up questions affirm my suspicions that they've already heard the gossip, and require no confirmation from me.

I turn to leave, but one of the girls stops me.

"Hey, I know you missed some classes, so if you want to meet up and go over CPR or something, I'd be happy to help. And I could probably use the practice myself." She seems earnest, and it surprises me.

"Thanks...?" I don't know her name, but fortunately she fills it in for me.

"Kira."

"Thanks, Kira. I guess—"

"Here, give me your number." She hands me her phone, and I dutifully add myself to her contacts. I don't miss the vague look of judgment Mel—whatever shoots her friend. She literally *just* told me her name and I've already forgotten it, but I don't particularly care, so there's that.

When I peek back at the pool, the water adonis is gone. I make an excuse to extract myself and beeline for the exit.

Mel-whatever is clearly getting a kick out of my current social status—or lack of status—and I don't even blame her. I let myself get caught up in an illusion of popularity and "best friendship", and it ended up biting me in the ass.

Or, more accurately, punching me in the nose.

I always knew who Shay McHale was. Everyone in Oceanside does. The New York City suburb on Long Island isn't small, per se, but every town has people everyone knows, and the McHales—and Shay in particular—are definitely those people. We didn't even go to the same school. I went to Ocean High North and she went to South, but kids from both schools have always hung out and partied together.

It was hard for anyone to miss the 5'10" princess of popularity, and even harder to avoid rumors of her modeling stint in Milan (which turned out not to be true) and her trips to fashion week (only partially true).

I still don't know what it was exactly that made her and her best friend since middle school, Brooke, take an interest in me barely months before the end of our senior year. I suspect it had something to do with Chase Martin flirting with me at that party at the pier—something that made even less sense than the girls suddenly pursuing my friendship.

I was so damn naïve.

I am so focused on getting to my car that I don't notice the large mass of muscle emerging from between two parking spots, and, like the klutz that I am, I slam right into it.

Well, not *it*…*him*.

"I'm so sorry," I mumble, mortified as I start to gather the contents of my purse, which are now scattered on the concrete. It isn't until he speaks that I even look up.

"No worries," he murmurs as I finally make eye contact, and something about his warm, ochre gaze snatches my stomach and quickens my pulse.

It's the guy from the pool—the adonis—and he is even more attractive up close.

His jawline and cheekbones are all strong, hard edges beneath short-cropped, tightly-curled, dark hair. He's built like the swimmer he obviously is, his skin dark and warm, smooth and taut, over lean, sculpted muscles.

He proceeds to help me, picking up a lip gloss and—of course—a tampon, and awkwardly hands them over. It takes me a second to even accept them.

I clumsily thank him, and I'm surprised by the half-smirk that plays on his lips as we both stand. He's tall—well over six feet.

"So, do you regularly walk into things? Or do you just have bad luck?" he nods toward my injured face. At least he didn't assume I've had a nose job.

"Definitely both," I retort honestly, and it earns me a smile. He has a lovely smile.

I don't hear the girls approaching until they're barely feet away. "Hey, Remy, want to introduce us to your friend?" Mel-whatever looks the gorgeous swimmer up and down like he's her next meal.

"I—uh, don't—" I stammer.

"Jacob," he offers.

They all exchange introductions, but I'm quiet. As pleasant as Jacob is to look at, all I want is to extract myself. My trust in other humans is at an all-time low, as is my desire to be around them.

Kira says something about needing to be home for her little brother, and I take my opportunity to escape as they disperse toward their respective cars.

"Hey!" Jacob jogs up behind me, stopping several feet away, palms presented as if to show he's not a threat. He bites his bottom lip, and I don't know why that is so damn attractive. "I didn't get your name..."

I blink at him a moment. He's right, of course. I was too preoccupied with getting away from Mel-whatever and her gossipy, predatory manner.

"Goodman," I say, giving him my last name first for no reason I can discern. My *God* am I awkward. "Remy Goodman." *And now I sound like I think I'm James fucking Bond.*

"Remy Goodman." He turns my name over on his

tongue like it's something to savor.

I want to say something more. Something witty, and smart, and impressive.

But words don't come, and Jacob's full lips slip into an easy smile. "See you around, Goodman."

Chapter Two

I didn't even want to go to the party that night. The parties at the old marina pier had never been my thing— no offense to those who lived for beer pong and shady hookups under the boardwalk. But it was the last night before my best friend, Laura, was leaving for Italy with the Latin club. She'd be gone not just for graduation, but the entire summer, and she'd romanticized a plan to see Luke, her crush, one last time, in the hopes he would suddenly declare his undying love after four years of not so much as acknowledging her existence. She didn't actually believe this would happen, but just the idea of its possibility was enough to get her high on *what-ifs*, and, as usual, I gave into her overwhelming positivity. That's why we worked so well. We were polar opposites in so many ways.

The party wasn't exactly unbearable. The spring night was mild, and I was perfectly content reading a crime thriller on the Kindle app on my phone, pretending to text at random intervals so my antisocial behavior at least appeared as if I was ignoring people for other actual people, rather than the fictional characters I admittedly preferred.

Laura had strategically positioned herself between Luke and the keg, and I watched her feign interest in her conversation with that girl who used to cheat off of me in pre-calculus, while unsuccessfully trying to catch his eye. I didn't drink, but chatted with a few casual friends and kids I knew from school, including the semi-popular guy from the lacrosse team who would always flirt with me on the rare occasions I showed up to these things.

Shay McHale took ownership of the far rail, talking, and just existing in a way that always seemed like a performance. And it was a brilliant one, with a built-in audience, perpetually led by her loyal bestie, Brooke, and, inevitably, a rapt fan club of guys.

I'd heard she had some mysterious boyfriend who went to one of the local colleges, but it didn't stop her from bogarting any male attention in her vicinity—or from aggressively flirting with Chase Martin.

Chase and I went to the same high school. We'd been in the same grade for years, and while I'd thought I'd caught him checking me out in the senior hallway after gym class one time, I don't think we'd ever had a direct exchange before that night.

Chase was attractive in the usual way. Dark blonde hair that fell into periwinkle eyes, a delicate nose and a wide jaw. Handsome, for sure, but a boring, expected kind of handsome. Although I seemed to be alone in that opinion, because girls and guys alike all but swooned over him. It probably didn't hurt that he was captain of the lacrosse team, and riding an athletic scholarship to Hofstra University in the fall. Or that his family had money. Lots of it.

Oceanside is one of those towns that attracts all kinds of people, from working class and small business owners, to rich people in beachside mansions. My family was somewhere in the middle (the lower middle, but we were always comfortable), but people like Chase, and Shay, and Brooke? They were all expensive cars, designer clothes, and exotic family vacations—all captured and shared all over Snapchat and Instagram, naturally.

I didn't notice him approach me at first. Chase had spent most of the night holding court in a corner by the far rail, opposite Shay, only taking breaks to defend his flip-cup champion title.

"Who you texting with, quiet girl?" His tone was flirty and teasing, which is why I didn't register it was directed at me at first—although *quiet girl* probably should have given it away. "Must be important, huh?" If he thought so, he certainly didn't think it was more important than himself, or he would have left me to it.

"Just a friend," I murmured when I finally looked up to realize I had Chase Martin's full attention.

"A boyfriend?" He dragged out the word like we were still in middle school and every romantic relationship was inherently scandalous. Of course, I've only ever had one boyfriend, and our *relationship* was more of a platonic friendship with some light hooking up. He dumped me after three months when I wasn't ready to have sex with him. I wasn't upset.

"Just a friend," I repeated.

Chase wasn't at all discouraged by my terse response, and I finally slipped my phone in my bag and let him chat me up, still surprised at having his attention in the first place.

He was vaguely amusing, I suppose, and I was flattered to have the temporary distraction of his interest. But Chase attracted people like flies, and his minions joined us one by one, until Shay, and Brooke, and several others had joined the conversation. It wasn't very long before it felt as if I was no longer even a part of it myself. Which was fine with me.

But Chase didn't let me slip away. He kept bringing his attention back to me, asking if I wanted a beer, if I liked to surf, if I wanted to hang out this summer. My vague non-answers did little to deter him.

There was a part of me that almost wanted to return his flirtations—to believe his interest was earnest. But we'd had the same homeroom freshman year, and I'd casually observed from the comfort of the sidelines while he'd burned girl after girl, first convincing them his affections were real, and then moving on to the next when he'd inevitably get bored. Rinse and repeat.

No. Thanks.

So, I chatted, and smiled vaguely, ever careful never to give the impression that I'd be interested in falling for his game.

But the more attention Chase gave me, the more Shay seemed to take her own interest in me. And the more Shay showed me interest, the more Brooke followed. And then we were all talking. And I surprised myself by thinking that Shay wasn't all that awful.

She was smart. Beautiful, obviously, but in a natural, easy way. Her energy was all about fun, and adventure, and enjoying the universe that somehow existed just for her. And now, it seemed, she wanted it to exist for me, too.

That night had more than one surprise in store. Laura had somehow accomplished her mission, and she threw me a wink and mouthed "don't wait up" as she and Luke made their way under the pier.

I would have just gone home—I probably *should* have gone home—but, well, I was having fun. Shay and Brooke were *fun*. We laughed, and danced, and everyone watched. Everyone suddenly liked me. Everyone suddenly knew my name, and cared to remember it. I'm not proud of how caught up I let myself become, but what was the danger in one night of fun?

But then Laura went abroad.

I had other friends, but they were closer with Laura than with me, and with her temporarily gone, even though they did try to include me, it just wasn't the same. I was lonely. It turned out, being alone was less preferable when it didn't feel like my choice.

It was after that first lonely week that Shay first messaged. She'd tagged me in a Snapchat story of a video someone had taken of us dancing the weekend before. I remember being taken aback by how natural it all looked— the three of us dancing and laughing together, like we'd known one another a lifetime and not just a few hours. Like nothing or no one could touch us.

Logically I knew I was the outsider among a pair of "besties", but it didn't *look* like that in the video. And more importantly, they hadn't made me *feel* that way. Not that night, and not in their comments on the Snapchat story, where   they   shared   hashtags   like

"#myfriendsarebetterthanyours" and "#betterwith3".

People noticed, too. Kids I'd never even heard of were commenting on how hot we all looked, and guys with no self awareness (or respect) whatsoever joked about wanting to watch us in some imaginary threesome. Tons of people added me on both SnapChat and Instagram.

And then Shay messaged me, and you would never have known we'd only hung out the one time. She sent me a pic from that night. "Someone was lookin hot last Fri! Wanna come out with us tonight?" Like it was all completely normal.

I'd accepted.

I'd suspected that first night at the pier was likely a fluke, but no. My first impression seemed to prove correct—these girls were fun, and cool, and suddenly seemed all but enamored with me.

These girls didn't just attend high school parties, either. New York City was only a forty-minute train ride away, and Shay and Brooke took full advantage. We didn't even need fake I.D.'s. When you looked like them, you just walked right to the front of the line, and once they got me into some of their clubbing outfits, I had to admit, I looked the part myself. Shay knew just how to play up my small waist with crop tops, and make my modest chest seem curvier. The four-inch heels she lent me also helped mask my more petite frame. When I went out with them, I felt beautiful. Sexy, even.

But it wasn't all partying.

We hung out, and gossiped, and it wasn't long before they were calling me their *bestie*, too.

It was weird, I know. I knew it even then. But my discomfort at what felt like premature intimacy was overpowered by the drug of popularity and companionship. And what was the danger in that?

Unfortunately, I would find out.

Chapter Three

I learn that I've passed my lifeguarding course, written test, and practical right on the spot, and a wave of relief washes over me. The ocean waters off the south shore of Long Island are still ice cold this early in the season, and enduring them turned out to be the hardest part.

Kira shoots me a smile that tells me she's passed as well, and I return it warmly. I was feeling a little lost after our fourth class and ended up texting her, and she helped me prepare for the practical exam. She's nicer than I expected, and I realize I'd probably judged her by her association with Mel—I'm going to just call her Mel. I was pleased to find out she'll be working at Aqualina Beach Club with me this summer.

We make arrangements to ride together to the club, which is two towns over and no more than a ten minute drive, and we walk into our first staff meeting together. The season officially started a couple of weeks ago, but it doesn't get particularly busy until the end of June—now—so the club has been running on a skeleton crew up until this week.

"Hey! Quiet girl!"

I'm not expecting to see Chase at the staff meeting, and I'm taken aback. My hand automatically flies to my face, as if to remind myself the splint is no longer there.

He notices. "Good as new," he remarks. His smile is more of a smirk, and I can't tell if he's making fun of me or being friendly.

Kira pinches my arm and gives me a look that reminds me of my obligation to introduce my new friend to our attractive coworker, so I find my composure.

"Kira, Chase. Chase, Kira." I gesture between them and explain that we went to high school together. Nothing else. There isn't anything more to explain, other than him flirting with me a time or two and commenting heart emojis on a couple of Instagram posts I was tagged in with Shay and Brooke.

Once Chase's attention is elsewhere, Kira gives me a not-so-subtle look, as if playfully censuring me for hiding him from her. It always seemed to me as if Chase was harboring a secret thing for Shay, but, hey, to each her own.

And then *he* walks in.

The hot swimmer from the county pool.

Jacob.

He sets down his gym bag and turns to the group, my jaw still slack at the surprise of seeing him again. "For anyone who doesn't know, I'm Jacob Canon, the head lifeguard, and your boss." He hands a stack of papers to Chase. "Pass these schedules around."

It's then that he finally looks around at the group of us, and part of me isn't even expecting him to recognize me.

But he does. I know he does. His eyes linger on mine for just a second longer than the others, and a small smile plays on his lips before he bites it away. I flush all over until my skin mirrors the red of my official lifeguard one-piece swimsuit.

I try not to stare as Jacob goes through a short orientation and goes over our schedules. He really is almost shockingly good looking. Lean, but built, and athletic in a way that would be obvious even if I hadn't seen him owning the pool like an Olympian a couple of weeks ago—or if his South Shore University Swim Team hoodie wasn't currently draped over his gym bag.

Jacob then leads us on a tour of the pool equipment and goes over opening and closing routines. He quizzes us on safety protocols before returning us to our break room above the café. I find myself fascinated with the way his muscles flex as he moves, almost as if they are dancing beneath his skin, and I vaguely hear him tell us each to grab a locker before he gets up to end the meeting. I try to look unaffected, but it's rare that I'm attracted to someone, and it gives me untold anxiety.

"Goodman?"

I blink a moment before I realize he's been addressing me. A small smile pulls at his lip, but he shows me mercy.

"I was just asking if you preferred to open or close?"

Kira is waiting for me by the door, looking inquisitive and teasing—after all, she met Jacob that day at the pool, too—and a quick glance around shows he's singled me out with this question. I don't know why.

"Whatever works for the schedule, I guess?" I reply, uncertain. I'm certainly not a morning person, and whoever opens for the day has to vacuum and skim the pool, but the two people who close have to stay until the last member has left, which is often unpredictable, and can go well into the evening. Either way, I want to be a team player, especially on day one at a new job.

Jacob's eyes are dark and warm like his smooth, umber skin, and they seem to know something about me I somehow don't know myself.

"I'll stay late and close with her." Chase's flirtatious voice comes from behind me, and I roll my eyes.

Jacob's glare takes me by surprise. Chase heeds it quickly, making a quick exit, and I move to follow him. Our shift starts in ten minutes and I want to get an iced coffee from the café before then. But Jacob stops me with a hand on my shoulder, and his touch sends a wave of goosebumps down my arm—the good kind.

He nods in Chase's direction. "If he says or does anything to make you uncomfortable, report him to me immediately, okay?"

I blink at him before recovering. "Oh, that's just Chase," I explain, blowing off Jacob's concern. "He doesn't mean anything by it." *I don't think*, I add silently.

Jacob is unappeased. "Only *he* knows what he means by

it, but either way, this is a place of work."

I swallow hard. Any hint of a smile is long gone, and I start to wonder if he's talking about Chase, or if he's caught me lusting after him and is issuing me a warning about professionalism.

My blush returns with a vengeance.

"Canon!" Jack, the club's manager, calls Jacob from outside, and he makes a hasty exit.

Right. A place of work. Got it.

Chapter Four

Kira's obsession with each Chase and Jacob is both amusing and annoying. Chase seems to flirt with any woman with a pulse, and Kira is no exception, but Jacob is something different. He's only two years ahead of the rest of us, but something about him makes him seem older. More mature. I've learned that he attends the pre-law program at South Shore U on a swimming scholarship. I bet he'll make a great lawyer. I don't think I know anyone else around our age who actually knows what they want to do with their life.

I only know this because our lunch breaks are scheduled at the same time on alternate days, and we eat together sometimes. I can't say I don't enjoy looking at him, but he's also surprisingly easy to talk to.

I try not to be too obvious as I watch him clean the pool, his sculpted muscles tensing as he reaches the skimmer across the water. We're all here earlier than usual for training—something we have to do every few weeks to satisfy safety protocols. This morning we're supposed to be practicing back-boarding unconscious victims, and it's by far my least favorite training exercise.

Or it was.

Something about the way Jacob moves in the water—how he handles the life-saving equipment like an absolute pro—has me lost in admiration. And when he asks for a volunteer—something I never, ever do—I inexplicably raise my hand.

I'm climbing into the heated pool water before I even process what I'm doing, and Jacob positions me in front of him. He instructs me to float on my back, and I dutifully comply.

"Unconscious victim. Who wants to demonstrate?" Jacob asks the group.

Chase starts to step forward, his cocky gait matching his smirk.

"Kira and Pavel," Jacob calls instead, leaving Chase's expression suspiciously disgruntled as they make their way into the pool.

"Okay, guys. Victim went off the diving board. You didn't see her hit anything, but she emerges face down." Jacob nods to me, and I position myself into a dead man's float.

I only hear muffled voices from under the water, but I can feel clumsy hands struggle to maneuver correctly to turn me, moving me in ways that would be dangerous for a suspected head or spinal injury. When Pavel finally gets me turned over, Jacob is already chiding him.

"And now she's paralyzed. Great job, Pavel."

Pavel grits his teeth, but he knows he messed up. It's only been a couple of weeks since we passed our certification, and he should still have this down. Literal lives are at stake.

"Kira," Jacob says, motioning me to return to my position.

Kira does a much better job stabilizing my neck while I'm still face-down, but she isn't quite fluid enough when she rolls to flip me, and Jacob's frustration is palpable.

"Everyone in the water, side of the pool," he summons. Everyone complies, but Jacob stops me with a hand on my shoulder. His touch makes me suddenly aware of our proximity, of my swimsuit-exposed skin. "Still need you, Goodman," he murmurs, the shyest hint of a smile peeking out from beneath his aggravation. I know he means for the demonstration, of course, but something about the phrase makes me vibrate with something unknown—something entirely unprofessional.

Jacob faces the group. "You are lifeguards, " he reminds us. "Life. Guards. You guard lives. Your job is to save lives. Not just to prevent death." He glares at the group, his sober eyes fixing on one person then the next, making sure his point is hitting each and every one of us with enough punch. "These moments after a potential head, neck, or spine injury are absolutely crucial. Your actions—your training—can be the difference in someone's quality of life, forever. 'Good enough' is unacceptable."

Pavel looks away. Kira hangs her head.

Jacob nods to me, and I return to my dead man's float.

And then strong, smooth arms are securing my neck from my sternum to the base of my skull and chin, and his whole, powerful body cradles mine as we turn together, his capable hands never slipping even a fraction. He never stops moving, swimming me around in that position, in wide circles, the motion keeping my spine a perfectly straight line.

I swallow hard. I don't know if it's him holding me this way, or the perfection with which he demonstrated the move, but Jacob's warning the first day of work rings hollowly in my mind: *this is a place of work.*

I need to get it together.

I excuse myself to use the restroom as Jacob has everyone practice just this move, over and over, ad nauseam.

He's an adept leader, giving positive reinforcement when earned, and passionately correcting when necessary. I think I've practiced near thirty times by the time he calls training over so we can prepare for guests to arrive at the club. We spent so much time perfecting neck stabilization that we never even got to the backboard, and Chase and Pavel groan dramatically when Jacob tells us we'll all be staying late today to make sure we have that down, too.

"Yeah, working late sucks," he says almost dismissively, "but not as much as fucking up at your job when lives depend on you."

***

It isn't until later that day, when I was having lunch with Kira, that I learned exactly why Jacob took our morning training so seriously—besides it being his job, of course. Kira called Chase over to join us before I could think of a valid reason to object.

"Fucking ridiculous," Chase grumbled over his massive cheeseburger. "Early training, *and* we have to stay late? It's bullshit."

"Is it, though?" I ask him as he shoves a handful of fries into his mouth. "What if something happened tomorrow and we weren't prepared?" True, most of us still had our training mostly down, Chase and myself in particular if I'm honest, but Jacob was right—*mostly* isn't good enough.

Chase waves me off dismissively. "The people who don't know their shit should have to stay late then; not all of us. And, anyway, Canon is just bugging because of that kid at his school. I mean, not to be a dick—I get it's fucked up—but I don't know why he has to take it out on us."

"Kid at his school?" I ask, confused.

Chase continues to talk with his mouth full, barely looking up, as if what he's about to say is common knowledge, but a glance at Kira reveals she's equally confused. "Yeah. You didn't hear about that kid at Long Beach High last year? Hit his head on the high dive at the school pool. Canon was there at swim team practice and saved him or something, but the kid ended up paralyzed, I think."

Kira and I exchange glances. I had heard about a kid getting hurt at diving practice at Long Beach High last year, but I had no idea that Jacob had been there when it happened.

That must have been traumatic for him. No wonder he takes these things particularly seriously. My phone is currently in my locker in the break room, but I make a mental note to Google the incident as soon as I have the chance.

Chapter Five

I don't even get near my phone until after we've practiced back-boarding one another for nearly two hours. I spent my last two breaks finishing the latest Kennedy Ryan novel, and then wondering if I should be indulging in swoon-worthy romance lit when I've been inappropriately lusting after my boss for weeks. Maybe I need a good murder mystery to put me off all things love and dating for a while. At least until I can figure out how to control the way I always seem to feel around Jacob.

Kira and I grab our bags from our respective lockers and head to the showers. She already confirmed after lunch that while she had also heard the story of the diving injury at Long Beach last year, she had no idea Jacob had been there at the time. She does, however, remember the name of the kid who got hurt—Spencer Task—which should make my Googling easier once I have a private moment to myself.

I'm brushing my just-washed hair and Kira is scrolling through her phone when her jaw drops.

"Oh. My. God," she says, playing up the melodrama.

"What'd I miss?" I ask, only half interested. I do really like Kira, but she tends to be particularly invested in the social lives of others, including people I'd rather forget existed. This turns out to be no exception.

"So you know how Shay McHale ditched Brooke Lewis in the beginning of the summer?"

254

"Mmm," I respond, noncommittal. Kira had kept me informed of the local drama. Shay and Brooke had gotten jobs as camp counselors at the Gold Coast Beach Club down the road. It had been my plan, too, of course, before. But Shay, in true Shay fashion, decided at the very last minute she had a better offer, and left to spend a few weeks in Paris, supposedly going on model castings, and leaving Brooke without her bestie. I'd suspected Brooke would've been pissed, but that her desperation for Shay's approval would win out in the end.

"So, anyway, you know how Melanie told me they still weren't speaking? Well, they just unfollowed each other. On everything." Kira holds her phone screen out to me, switching from Instagram to Snapchat to Tiktok to show me they had, in fact, fallen out—on social media anyway.

A phantom pain stings my nose, and a belated wave of anger rushes through my chest. But I say nothing. I just shake my head. They deserve whatever they get. People who purport friendship and connection, but whose loyalties only last as long as you serve a purpose—people who suck you in and betray your trust—they get no sympathy from me.

We exit the locker room and run right into Chase. He invites us both to go surfing, but he's looking at me. I politely decline, even when Kira tries to subtly elbow me in the ribs.

I laugh. "Kira, just go if you want to go. Maybe I'll meet you guys later," I tell her. She looks uncertainly at Chase, who shrugs. "Or I'll just take an Uber home. It's really no big deal." Kira drove us in today, but we take ride-shares when our plans change all the time, and she has no reason to feel responsible for me. I'm an adult, after all.

"Yeah, come on. A bunch of us are going down to Gold Coast." Chase nods toward Pavel and a few of the cabana boys.

"You sure you don't want to come?" Kira asks, already starting to follow behind Chase.

"No thanks," I assure her. I didn't want to go surfing with Chase and his friends anyway, but even if I did, there's no way I'm going to Gold Coast. According to Kira, Shay will be abroad for another week or so, but even without her fearless leader, Brooke can be dangerous. Maybe even more so.

***

I'm waiting for my Uber on the bench outside the club's main lobby when I finally have a minute to Google "Spencer Task + Long Beach High School".

The local articles are plentiful, but few give many details. They all credit a "hero", though: *local boy Jacob Canon.*

The most thorough article simply says that Jacob rushed into the water and stabilized the boy while the diving coach got the backboard. They credit him with saving Spencer's life.

Wow.

There's very little on Spencer's recovery, though. The press seems to have lost interest in the story pretty quickly, and the most recent article, still from over a year ago, simply mentions "a long road ahead".

"You know him?" Jacob's warm, smooth voice startles me from behind, and I jump in my seat. "I didn't mean to scare you."

"You didn't," I promise, and he throws me a skeptical half-smile. "I just didn't hear you approach. And I don't know him," I answer his original question, nodding to the article on my phone.

Jacob nods understandingly. "So you get why today's training was so important."

I offer him a shy smile. "So we can be heroes like you?" I tease.

But Jacob looks mildly bewildered. "Don't believe everything you read."

What's that supposed to mean?

My phone rings with an Uber notification, informing me that my ride has been cancelled by the driver.

"Damn," I murmur, hitting the button to order another car.

"Everything okay?" Jacob asks, brown eyes full of sincerity and concern.

"Just my Uber cancelling," I tell him. "I'll order another."

"I could give you a ride," he offers unexpectedly, and I look up at him, tempted. Too tempted. "You're in Oceanside, right? It's not out of the way."

"Are you sure?" I ask. "I don't want to impose."

Jacob hits me with his full smile—wide, bright, and infectious. I find myself smiling in return. "No problem at all. Do you have a few minutes first? I'd like to show you something."

***

Jacob leads me back through the club, and down the stairs into the sand as twilight calms the sky. He offers me his hand as I make my way up the lifeguard tower I climb multiple times daily. His touch has the usual effect.

He follows me and sits beside me, looking out at the ocean just as the sun begins to set.

"What'd you want to show me?" I ask.

He gestures to the horizon. "This."

The sunset?

But he's right, of course. Despite spending almost every day here this summer, not once have I taken the time to sit and watch the explosion of fluorescent oranges and pinks as the day turned to night, and I find myself mesmerized.

"It's beautiful," I whisper.

"Yeah," he breathes, and out of the corner of my eye, I convince myself he's watching me as much as the night sky. Moments pass in a comfortable silence before he speaks again. "He's still in a wheelchair."

I don't know who Jacob means at first, distracted as I am by the view and his company, and I meet his gaze to find it serious and meaningful.

"Spencer," he clarifies

"You saved his life," I remind him.

"Or ruined it," Jacob says under his breath.

I blink at him.

Jacob sighs. "I was the one who got him out of the pool. I was the one who stabilized his neck for the backboard. I thought I did everything right, but…"

"It's not your fault he was injured, Jacob," I remind him.

He looks at me fiercely. "No, but I wasn't experienced. I'll never know if I'd done something different—if someone else had got to him first…"

"You think he'd be walking?" The articles made it sound like there was a serious spinal injury, but Jacob was right earlier—those first moments are crucial. Still, I get the feeling he's putting undue pressure on himself. He was a teenager, still in high school himself.

Jacob shrugs, and the weight on his dark, broad shoulders is obvious.

"Or, he could be dead," I say pointedly.

Jacob bites his lip thoughtfully.

"All I know is, if I ever ended up in trouble in the water, you are the absolute first person I'd want to rescue me."

Oh my God. I just said that. Out loud.

Jacob's gaze swings to mine as my entire body flushes read.

"I—I mean…because…because you're such a good lifeguard," I stammer, mortified. "You know what I mean." I hope.

He blows out a deep, calming breath, that gorgeous smile of his playing on his lips. "I know what you mean," he promises.

And without even understanding why I do it, I reach for his hand, taking it tentatively into mine, my pulse beating a mile a minute as he squeezes, offering me something I don't yet understand.

We don't say much else. But I marvel at the sight of my small, freckled hand against his calloused, ochre skin, like complementary pieces of a puzzle, suddenly clicking into place.

Chapter Six

The past week has been both exhilarating and anxiety inducing, and it has everything to do with Jacob. But Jacob is still my boss, and while it's more than clear I've been developing more than just a crush, his feelings remain vague, and I wonder if it's because of his position of power, or if he's only vaguely into me.

The first day my schedule matched his own seemed like a coincidence. After all, we've shared lunch breaks before, but that day, not only did we close together, but all of our breaks lined up. He asked me at the end of the day if I preferred my old schedule, and promised that it was entirely my choice.

But it shouldn't be my choice. While Jacob takes requests into consideration—he really is a thoughtful boss—I don't think he asks anyone else for their preferred schedule. But then, him switching mine to align with his could be extremely problematic if I wasn't totally on board.

And I *am* totally on board, but how to communicate that without giving away my feelings?

I told him I liked my new schedule just fine, which earned me one of his perfect, broad smiles—the ones that always seems to spur a flutter in my belly.

"You having lunch with Jacob again today?" Kira asks, her tone all friendly teasing. She has already formed an entire romantic relationship between Jacob and me in her own mind, and I suspect her imagined drama is far more thrilling than the reality of the thing.

"She is if she wants to," Jacob says, startling me from behind not for the first time, something that always makes us both laugh. "No pressure, though."

I nudge him playfully with my elbow, before quipping "maybe if you're lucky." I'm not usually much of a flirt. I'm usually all awkwardness and missed social cues, but Jacob has a warmness about him that gives me a confidence I never knew I had.

Jacob's ochre eyes dance with amusement as he tells me he has to grab his phone from his locker, and promises to meet me in the café in five minutes.

Kira heads to the beach to take her shift on ocean watch. I hang back by the pool to wait for Jacob, laughing at Chase as he checks out the hot yoga moms trailing after their preschoolers.

And then my stomach rolls with nausea at the sudden, unmistakable sight of Brooke Lewis.

She stomps up the steps from the beach, her sunglasses-clad face searching purposefully until she obviously spots Chase. For a moment he tries to shrink into his lifeguard chair, before seeming to steel himself with an almost bored resolve.

I flatten myself behind a wide pillar for cover, but I can still see them.

Brooke looks pissed, and I can make out her voice, but not her words. It isn't until Chase waves to shoo her away that Brooke unleashes her wrath. Voices raised, they carry over the breeze.

"Who do you think you are not to text me back, anyway? You're lucky I ever let you touch me!" Brooke seethes.

Wow, I had no idea Brooke and Chase ever hooked up. But then, why would I?

Chase responds with exaggerated rambunctious laughter, only riling Brooke up more. "I. Was. Bored," he all but growls.

Brooke drops her jaw in dramatic fashion before squaring her shoulders again. "Well, we're both done with you anyway." She pretends to turn to walk away, but it's a pitiful attempt. Not that Chase could leave his post to chase after her anyway.

Both?

Does she mean her and Shay? That they've made up and now they're both revoking their friendship because Chase is blowing Brooke off? I guess that wouldn't be out of the ordinary. I've heard that Shay will be back in town this week, if she isn't already, so it would certainly be a convenient time for the besties to rekindle their alliance, I suppose. One thing I learned during our short-lived friendship is that their dynamic is no accident. They both serve a purpose to each other, and whether or not they like it that way, they certainly *need* it that way.

"Hey," Chase calls after Brooke, practically hissing through his teeth.

Brooke doesn't come back, but she turns slowly in place, revealing a knowing sneer.

"What did you tell her?" Chase demands.

Brooke simply shrugs, sneer still in place.

I'm not surprised Chase cares so much about Shay's opinion of him. I've always suspected a crush, but Shay has always been clear that she "doesn't do high school boys". And, of course, she's had that college boyfriend, Marty, since I've known her—or *of* her—the one I've never once met.

The absolute irony in that.

Because despite never meeting him—never even seeing a photo since Shay made such a big deal about keeping him a secret—he is what sent my life up in smoke.

I didn't even need to meet the elusive Marty to have a relatively low opinion of him. The reason Shay kept him secret isn't so much their three year age difference, but because she was only sixteen when they'd started dating. Something about that always creeped me out, but that sure wasn't something I ever felt comfortable enough in our friendship voicing. Shay and Brooke may have called me "bestie" within two weeks of us hanging out, but I was never under the illusion that my place with them wasn't conditional, even if I never actually understood what those conditions were.

It happened out of the blue. One day we were binging Oreos and trying on each other's clothes—or, rather, they were dressing me in *their* clothes—and the next day they were giving me the cold shoulder at a pier party.

It was strange, but subtle. At first, at least. But after an hour or so, it was hard to deny they weren't only blatantly ignoring me, but shooting me eye rolls and dirty looks.

And whispering. There was lots of whispering.

So, I left, only to find vague Snapchat stories about some unnamed "slut"—a word I hate and never use—and "traitorous bitches".

I had no real reason to think it was about me. But then, why were they ignoring me out of nowhere? It wasn't until the next morning, when I'd found myself blocked by both of them on both Snapchat and Instagram, that I knew.

I didn't *understand*, but I knew.

And then the whole school knew. They knew something I didn't, and all I could think was there must have been some gross misunderstanding. Because even if the word *slut* wasn't just some misogynistic bullshit invented by the patriarchy to shame girls for doing the exact same things as guys, *I* hadn't been doing any of those things. In fact, the most action I'd gotten in months was vaguely and awkwardly returning Chase's flirtations at a party or two.

It just didn't make any sense, and because it didn't make any sense, I naïvely assumed it was fixable.

I'd begged Shay and Brooke to talk in person. I'd ignored the harassing posts and snide comments they were obviously behind, some directly, some less so. I'd managed to gather that I'd been accused of "fucking around with Shay's man", which made even less sense. Because, again, I'd never even *met* Marty. So, I begged.

And I cried. As ashamed as I was that I even cared about what these two girls I'd barely known a couple of months thought of me, I'd started to believe in their friendship, and it hurt. And the worst part was that I was absolutely certain that given the opportunity to tell my side of the story—that there *was* no story—I could make everything right.

That was my downfall.

A week after our inexplicable falling out, they were ready to talk. Or, rather, Brooke was. Shay, deeply hurt by my supposed betrayal as she was, couldn't bear to so much as look at me. So Brooke would be our mediator.

Or so I'd thought.

Brooke drove to my house and I got in her car willingly. She was on the phone with Shay when I did. I should have known something was up when I heard Shay say "She deserves it," and Brooke replied, "I got this."

So fucking naïve.

The moment she'd hung up, I launched into my rehearsed speech. "I don't know why you think I hooked up—"

I didn't make it through a full sentence before she sucker-punched me.

I sat there for a moment in absolute shock as blood sprayed from my nose, gushing all over the brand new NYU sweatshirt I'd excitedly purchased at my pre-freshman tour.

No one had ever hit me before, and it took me a beat to even register what had happened. And then all hell broke loose.

Brooke went for my hair next as I got my bearings and realized I'd been set up—lured and attacked. *Was this even real life?*

Utter rage filled my veins as I grabbed for Brooke's hair and screamed for her to *let me go.*

"You let me go first!" she'd squealed, but I wasn't falling for her tricks again.

My fingers dug in further, gripping viciously, and, all on instinct, I slammed her forehead into her own dashboard. It stunned her long enough for me to jump from the car and flee back into the relative safety of my house, Brooke's tires screeching as she fled the scene.

SAVING US

It had all gone down in a matter of mere minutes.

My mother was horrified, and, after getting me cleaned up, took me directly to the police station to file a report. But because Brooke had gone to the hospital for her dashboard—concussion, and because it was my word against hers as far as who had first attacked whom, there were no real consequences. Not for Brooke, anyway. Even the warning to stay away from each other seemed cursory at best.

According to the police, it was a draw. But according to the rumor mill at school—no doubt carefully curated by Brooke and Shay themselves—I had gotten my ass kicked, and deservedly, too. I didn't even have Laura here for comfort, although she'd stay up late most nights to let me vent on the phone.

I was a social pariah, and I had no one to blame but myself. It didn't even matter that I'd never met Marty, or that the entire fiasco had been fabricated, for reasons that—to this day—I don't understand.

But it *was* my fault, and once I took ownership of that, I was able to start to heal.

I had known all along something wasn't right. Their sudden, unexplained interest in me, the expedited, forced intimacy...the red flags were there; I just chose not to see them.

I will never know what their motives were—I accept that now. Whether they had simply gotten bored with me and this was their creative, attention-seeking way of getting rid of me, or they had been setting me up from the outset for their own sick entertainment—it changes nothing.

I should have trusted my gut, and I shouldn't have been taken in by flattery and faux acceptance. A part of me had always known it was temporary—that it wasn't real—and I'd let myself get so caught up in the attention and popularity that I lost sight of reality.

I didn't see it coming.

That won't happen again.

I don't know if Brooke knows I work here or not, but the last thing I want is some kind of confrontation at my workplace.

I see Jacob skipping down the stairs from our break room, and I'm about to slink around the back of the café so I can meet him for our lunch while still avoiding Brooke, when I hear a scream.

I find its source immediately when I spot a familiar preschooler vaguely struggling to make it to the side of the pool after jumping from the diving board. It's a pretty common occurrence. I've even seen this particular kid in this same position many times, and he always makes it.

But Chase is still distracted by Brooke, and, seeing this, the child's mother acts, her screech echoing around the entire deck as she jumps in after him, fully clothed.

Chase follows, leaping from his guard chair after them both, just as the child makes it to the ladder, all on his own. It is ultimately the mother—a loud gossip of a woman named Carol—who ends up needing saving, and Chase expertly slings his rescue buoy beneath her arms and swims her to safety.

A crowd has gathered, and Jacob has emerged to comfort the child with a towel and help Carol from the water. Chase follows behind, red-faced, likely more from embarrassment than exertion.

I rush to help with the boy, James, who is more confused than anything else. I wrap him in the towel and tell him everything is okay, on repeat.

Carol catches her breath with dramatic heaves that seem exaggerated, but I chalk it up to the fear of a mother who believed her child in danger—whether or not he ever actually was.

I feel for Chase. It's always a judgment call to jump in the water to help a struggling kid, especially one we know can make it if given the chance. Of course, the diving board rules explicitly state that only competent swimmers are allowed, and that parents are required to make sure it's followed. But Aqualina is a private club, one people pay thousands every summer for the privilege of membership, and rules are usually only enforced when absolutely necessary—if even then.

Still, a parent jumping in to rescue their child is bad. At the very least, Chase should have registered Carol's distress, even if James's was debatable. He should have acted. He should have at least made it into the pool before the child's mother did, and, I suspect, if he hadn't been so distracted by Brooke and her curious threat, he would have. And that is entirely unacceptable.

"I'm sorry," Chase says shamefully to no one in particular. "He's okay."

"He. Almost. Drowned!" Carol points to her son, whom I've still got bundled in a towel on my lap. But she's not addressing Chase at all; she's staring pointedly at Jacob.

Carol, her wild, aggrieved expression almost comical amid her sopping wet hair, streaking makeup, and disheveled clothing, jumps quickly to her feet. She still makes no move to comfort her son, who seems to be just fine. In fact, he looks almost bored, as if his mother's fury is nothing out of the ordinary. To be fair, she *has* been known to make a scene or two over minor complaints in the café, or over cabana boys not quite positioning her beach chairs in direct enough sunlight. But in this situation, I can't exactly blame her. Right or wrong, she at least believed her child to be in danger.

I am surprised, however, that she isn't directing her anger at Chase.

"I want to speak to your fucking supervisor!" she demands, her voice reaching new pitches.

Jacob nods, patiently validating her distress, while signaling for her to calm down. "I know you're upset, but there are kids around here. Please don't use that language."

He's right, of course. A large group has circled, and parents are suddenly covering their children's ears.

Carol doesn't care.

"How fucking *dare* you?" she shoots back to Jacob before turning suddenly to me. "Who is the head lifeguard?" she demands.

Jacob grits his teeth as if he knows something the rest of us don't.

I offer her the most sympathetic smile I can muster before directing her right back to Jacob. "Jacob *is* our head lifeguard," I tell her.

Carol's eyes glare wide, her mouth gaping in obvious outrage, but she continues to address me as if Jacob isn't even here. "How can he be the head lifeguard?" she seethes. "They can't even swim!"

I blink at her. It takes me a second to even understand her meaning. But Jacob understands immediately, and his discomfort of a moment ago makes instant sense.

He was expecting this.

But he doesn't back away.

"Who is *they*, ma'am?" he asks, deadpan. "Do you mean lifeguards? Is it lifeguards who can't swim, ma'am?"

Carol seems taken aback for only a split second before she regains what, I suppose, she thinks passes for composure. She waves her hand flippantly, "you know what I mean."

And then *everyone* knows what she means.

The crowd changes shape, some dispersing, others hanging around in some kind of collective shock. Carol appeals to friends nearby, vaguely addressing a couple of women I've seen her hanging around with. "You *know* what I mean! Most of them can't even swim, so even if he *can* swim, he shouldn't be *in charge*! My son almost drowned! *I* almost drowned!"

One of the women puts a comforting hand on Carol's back, whether to calm her down or to express likemindedness, I don't know. Others take barely perceptible steps back as if to distance themselves from her disgusting words.

I want to stand up for Jacob. I want to tell Carol she's a terrible, ignorant racist, but shock holds me hostage, and all I can do is watch the scene unfold.

Jacob maintains a level of decorum I wouldn't even expect from a member of the Queen's Guard outside

Buckingham Palace. "Well, ma'am, if that's how you feel, you're welcome to voice it to the club's management. Be sure to tell them you're questioning my qualifications solely based on the color of my skin. I'm sure they will give your concerns the consideration they deserve." His words are clear, his tone pointed, but his mask of professionalism never wavers.

Carol is obviously angered by this response, but she can't seem to find the right words to express it in a way that won't make her look even worse, and, thankfully, they die in her throat. Instead, she just kind of huffs out sounds of indignation before not-so-gently grabbing James from my lap, and turning on her heels. She stomps away from the pool, muttering to the same woman who had offered her comfort about "disrespect" and "political correctness".

I am still in shock.

But most shocking is Jacob's lack thereof.

He's not surprised. He saw this coming. And I know without having to ask that this has happened before. If not exactly this, similar incidents—enough that, if I hadn't gotten to know Jacob personally over these past weeks, I wouldn't even know he was affected at all.

Most of the crowd dissipates, and a few members do step up to apologize on Carol's behalf—to tell Jacob how uncalled for her outburst was. As if Jacob doesn't already know that. One member promises to talk to the club owner, his "close, personal friend", and have Carol "dealt with". He swears "this isn't who we are," speaking of the club's patronage.

But if he's the only one to say so, if the vast majority of them simply stopped to watch the show before walking away, aren't they condoning Carol's behavior? And doesn't that mean, in fact, that *this* is exactly *who they are*?

Jacob asks me to take the rest of Chase's shift, presumably so he can give him a well-earned lecture on distractions and doing his job, promising to find me another lunch break within the hour. I assure him I'm fine, and will do whatever he needs.

It's a long half hour. From the solace of my perch, I

watch the water with due attention, but my mind races.
I still can't believe that just happened.

Chapter Seven

The last several hours have lasted a lifetime. All I want to do is talk to Jacob, and I'm even more grateful we'll be closing together today.

But when the time comes, Jacob is all business. We do our respective jobs, making casual conversation, and I wait for him to bring up what happened earlier…but he doesn't.

I don't want to be the one to do so in case he doesn't want to talk about it. That's certainly his prerogative.

Even though a big part of me is desperate to make sure he knows how horrified I am—how much I don't condone Carol's actions today—the other part wonders if that's even about offering comfort to Jacob, or if I'm just trying to make myself feel better. If Jacob is trying not to dwell on it, who am I to make him relive it? It isn't about me. So I follow his lead.

It's when we're walking to our cars that Jacob stops me.

"Hey, Goodman," he says softly, and I think he finally wants to talk about what happened. "What are you doing later?"

"I…what?" I stammer like a fool, and it earns me my favorite Jacob smile.

"Later. Like, do you have plans, or…?" He worries his lip between his teeth, and, for a second, I wonder if, somehow, I might make him as nervous as he does me.

I shake my head, a blush rising to my cheeks as I keep eye contact.

"Want to come to a party with me?"

***

Jacob picks me up from my house at nine.

I tried on four outfits before deciding on a simple black sundress, leaving my auburn hair long and loose.

As excited as I am for our…evening, I guess—since I'm not sure this is technically even a date—I can't shake the feeling of indignation on Jacob's behalf that's been plaguing me ever since this afternoon.

I try to ignore it—to tamper it down and just enjoy his easy company—but my poker face has always been lacking.

"You good, Goodman?" Jacob gives me a smirk, and it earns him a smile.

"Yeah. I am. I just…"

"This about earlier?" He knows. Of course he knows.

"I'm sorry," I blurt, and I'm not even sure what I'm apologizing for.

"You don't have anything to be sorry for," he counters, offering me side-glances as he drives toward the Atlantic Beach Bridge. "But it seems like you want to ask me something…"

I guess I do. "I just can't believe she said that. I can't believe she even *thinks* that," I admit.

Jacob throws me another glance, as if to gauge how much he wants to say, and I cringe inwardly at the thought, again, that I might be pressuring him to discuss something he'd rather not. But then his lips pull into an empathetic smile, and he blows out a long breath.

"Well, you wouldn't, would you?" he says, not unkindly.

And I get it. I do.

I find I'm mortified at my own shock. I'm mortified that I have lived my life believing that those kinds of thoughts, those kind of people—people not just like Carol, but those who comfort and enable her—were a thing of another time or place. But they're not. They're merely hiding in plain sight. Some not even hiding at all.

Somewhere deep, it hits me hard how precarious it is. Today it was a *Karen* at the pool, but tomorrow it could be a police officer judging Jacob a danger merely because he happens to be a Black man. My stomach rolls with nausea. What a privilege it is to grow up in such ignorance.

Jacob doesn't have that privilege. He never has.

"Can I ask you something?" I say tentatively.

Jacob smiles, as if amused by my naïvety, and I don't blame him.

"You're not just the head lifeguard; you're, like, the best swimmer around. You made All-City. You're nationally ranked, for God's sake." I gratuitously remind him of things he very much already knows.

"You been reading up on me, huh?" Jacob's smirk is the widest I've ever seen, and my skin flushes scarlet as I realize my mistake.

Well, I guess now he knows. I sure have been reading up on him, and it gives me untold satisfaction that he seems pleased by this news.

I swallow down my anxiety and nod.

"And you want to know why I didn't throw my swimming achievements in her face." It isn't a question. Jacob shrugs. "Simple. I didn't owe her any more than she demanded of the white kid—who was actually on duty at the time—which, of course—"

"Was nothing." I finish for him.

He offers me another smile as if to say *now you're getting it.*

"You knew what she was going to say," I recall. "Before she said it."

Jacob huffs out a short, ironic chuckle. "I had an inkling."

I blink at him, and he smirks that playful smirk that makes my heart rate skip. "It's not my first day being Black, Goodman." He winks, and whatever tension might have been—whatever resentment at the unfairness of it all—takes a backseat to his perfect Jacobness, and I can do nothing but return his smile.

He takes my hand as he continues driving. I don't have words to fix anything—they don't exist, of course. All I have in this moment is my hand in his, and I squeeze his back, trying desperately to communicate with that one touch what I don't know how to say—that I am here, that I hear him, and that I want to know more. I want to know everything. I want to know *Jacob*.

***

I don't even know where this party is. I assumed it would be in Long Beach at one of Jacob's friends' houses, and it isn't until we're pulling into the pier parking lot that I realize our destination.

My pulse races, anxiety rolling my stomach. I haven't been to a pier party since that last night with Brooke and Shay—when they'd ignored me and launched their cruel rumor campaign.

Jacob must register my nerves, because he asks if everything's okay, and I simply nod mutely, still not getting out of the car.

"Look, if you changed your mind. It's cool. I can take you home, or we can just hang out as friends. I know I'm your boss. I know it's—"

I cut him off. "No, it's not that," I assure him. "I just…" I trail off. I just *what*? I'm just a loser who's spent the past month hiding from mean girls? I'm about to start college at NYU next month, in one of the world's biggest, most exciting cities, and I'm still scared of a few high school bullies?

A wave of confidence straightens my spine, and I plaster on a steeling smile. "You know what?" I tell him, "let's go."

We walk down the pier and I'm relieved when I spot Kira. She stopped inviting me to these things a while ago when I kept declining, and I'm warmed by her open excitement at seeing me.

"Yes! Finally!" she squeals, giving me an

exaggerated hug, as if we hadn't just spent a good portion of the day together. She turns to Jacob. "I should've known all it would take to get this one to come out is you asking her," she smirks.

I elbow her less than subtly, and we all laugh. She's not wrong.

The night is mild, the breeze warm and light. I do a thorough scan for Brooke or any of her close lackeys, and am relieved she's nowhere in sight.

There are kids from a few of the different local high schools, and Jacob introduces me to a few of his friends. They seem pretty nice, and a part of me wonders why I ever let myself believe the world so small that two mean girls—popular as they were—had the power to end my entire social life.

I don't think Jacob ever heard the rumors about me. If he did, he certainly never acted like he believed them—or cared if he did.

He offers to get me a drink from the keg, and even though I'm not much of a drinker, there's something unburdening about tonight, and I accept.

My comfort comes too soon.

My heart leaps into my throat as I spot Shay McHale standing by the keg, approaching Jacob. She meets my stunned gaze, smiles mischievously, and licks her lips.

She's back.

I knew she'd be back, but I didn't realize she'd be *here*. After seeing Brooke at the club earlier, she was the one on my radar—not Shay.

Shay flips her long, highlighted hair over her shoulder and touches Jacob's arm, saying something to him with her most flirtatious smile. She obviously saw us walk in together, hand in hand, and she wants me to know it.

Jacob's back is to me, so I can't see his face, but his body language is friendly as he says something in reply. Shay throws me a look that tells me everything I need to know.

She's still out for vengeance.

It doesn't matter that I haven't done anything to warrant

it. It never did. I watch as she leans into Jacob, whispering something lengthy into his ear, and they both turn to glance back at me before continuing their conversation.

My stomach rolls, fear and disappointment freezing my veins and wetting my eyes. And it's fucking humiliating.

I don't have to hear their words to know Shay is repeating the same catastrophic rumors, and I know Jacob doesn't know me well enough to know they're false.

Suddenly the breeze is too humid—suffocating—and I can't catch my breath.

"You okay, Remy?" Kira asks, but one good look tells her I'm very much not okay.

"I don't feel well," I manage to get out. "Drive me home? Please"

"But what about Jacob—"

"Please," I beg.

And, once again, I flee.

Chapter Eight

My mood is low as ever as I suffer through my last shift of the day. This has been the slowest passing day of the summer, and the one thing I looked forward to every day—Jacob—seems to be quite done with me.

I texted him after leaving the party to tell him it was because I wasn't feeling well, but promised I'd be at work today. And he was perfectly nice about it. But I arrived this morning to find my schedule altered just enough that we no longer share any breaks.

I don't blame Jacob. It hurts, but I've lived this before. I know how persuasive Shay can be, and Jacob barely knows me, really.

But the lack of shared breaks and my anxiety have made it impossible to even try to talk to him—to explain. Not that I'd even know where to begin.

Still, I've had the day to think, and I've decided I will no longer be a bystander in my own life. If Jacob is no longer interested in me, that's his prerogative, but one way or another, I'm going to tell him my side of things. Maybe I can't blame him for not knowing who to believe in a she-said/she-said situation like this, but it can't be she said/she said until I actually *say* something.

After my shift, I shower and change, pulling my damp hair into a long braid. I grab my bag from my locker and check my phone, and am about to head down to find Jacob when Chase nearly barrels right into me.

"You being chased, *Chase*?" I tease, but then I register his expression, and I start to think he is, in fact, being

277

pursued.

"Remy, you gotta hide me from her," he says, half desperate, half amused.

Of course, everything is a joke to him. But then his words hit me.

"Hide me *from her*."

Shay.

And then I hear shouting from outside. "Excuse me, Miss, you can't go up there. It's for employees only," Jacob calls just as not Shay, but Brooke struts into the room, with Jacob, Kira, and Pavel all racing in behind her. "Do I seriously need to call security on you?" Jacob asks Brooke, who ignores him.

Instead, Brooke sets her focus on me. "You! Of course *you're* here!" she screeches.

The memory of her attack in the car comes rushing back, fast and without mercy, but instead of fear, I find myself overcome with overwhelming anger. Strangely, it manifests in an unexpected, confident calm.

"Well, I do *work* here," I deadpan.

Brooke is obviously taken aback by my response, no doubt expecting me to cower.

I'm done cowering.

She turns her wrath on Chase. "You never told me *she* works here! Shay had to tell me, and she fucking loved doing it, let me tell you!"

"You never asked." Chase, for all his amused fear of moments ago, seems almost bored, as if Brooke is more of an inconvenience than anything.

I peek over at Jacob, who looks like he's trying to work out what's going on. He's not alone.

"So you hook up with me all summer, make me lie to my best friend about it, and all the time you're fucking around with this…this…fucking *whore*!"

"Hey, now!" Jacob steps forward, but I don't need my boss to speak for me.

I open my mouth to defend myself, but instead, out comes a laugh. And then another. I laugh outwardly and openly, letting myself feel every ounce of the sheer comedy of the idea that I would even want to hook up with Chase Martin.

Chase, to his mild credit, looks vaguely offended. He shouldn't. I've always made it abundantly clear that, despite flirting with him a time or two, I had no intention of ever, ever doing anything with him.

"What's so fucking funny," Brooke demands.

I point at Chase, barely managing to get my words out through my laughter. "You—you thinking I would fuck around with Chase." I laugh so hard I snort, and out of the corner of my eye, I catch Jacob's reluctant smile.

"Why not?" Brooke isn't deterred. "You fucked him when he was still with Shay." Her eyes subtly drop to my nose, and my humor evaporates in one fell swoop.

I fucked Chase?

Chase was with Shay?

What?

I'm about to tell her how ridiculous her words are, but then I catch Chase's face.

He looks guilty. Really guilty.

And then something clicks, and I understand.

You fucked him when he was still with Shay.

Marty. Chase *Martin.*

There never was a college boyfriend.

Does Shay really think herself so far above high school boys that she made Marty up? That she made Chase lie about their relationship? For *years?*

It doesn't explain why Brooke thinks Chase and I hooked up, though, but Chase's expression tells me the answer lies with him.

"The fuck, Chase?" I mean to sound commanding, but my voice cracks.

For a moment, everyone stares at Chase, waiting for him to give us the missing piece of the puzzle he's obviously holding.

And then he sighs. "Okay, I lied. I'm sorry," he mumbles.

He *what?*

Brooke's jaw drops, but she's the last thing I care about right now.

He. What?

Chase suddenly changes tact, shifting from sheepish to defensive in an instant. "I said I lied! Okay? I fucking lied, but it had nothing to do with *you*, Brooke. I was trying to make *Shay* jealous." He seems pleased with his confession, and it only enrages me more.

I take a step toward him.

Chase meets my gaze, and offers me some kind of conciliatory smile. "I *am* sorry, though, Remy. I really never meant for you to get—"

I don't hear the rest—I swing.

My fist makes direct contact with Chase's nose, and the déjà vu isn't lost on me as blood sprays, blending right into his red lifeguard hoodie. Chase brings his hands up to block himself from further blows, but the one is all I was interested in, and I glare at him, dumbfounded.

I bite back my whimper as pain radiates through my knuckles, and I shake out my fist, cursing and gritting my teeth.

A strong hand lands hesitantly on my back, and immediately I know it's Jacob's. I lean into his comfort, and his warmth spreads through me, calming my breaths.

But fuck does my hand hurt.

I glare at Chase. He did this to me. He was willing to sacrifice my entire reputation, my friendships— shallow as they were—to make Shay jealous?

Jacob takes a step between Chase and me, and I'm not sure which of us he's trying to protect from the other. He sucks in a long breath, rolling his shoulders like he's trying to release his own anger.

"Real quick," he says, his eyes never leaving Chase, "you made up and spread lies about a coworker, of a sexual nature?" His words are all professional, but his tone is entirely personal. And threatening.

Chase holds his busted nose with both hands. "She fucking hit me!"

For a moment I wonder if I might have just jeopardized my job.

If I did, it was worth it.

I'm about to defend myself when Jacob speaks again, his voice nearly shaking with rage. "I asked you a question."

Chase, wisely, proceeds with trepidation. "I, uh... It was before we even started work here, and it was really just a joke that—" Chase starts to explain.

Jacob isn't having it. "You're fired. You get that, right?"

Chase's eyes go wide. "Seriously, bro?"

Jacob lets out a sardonic laugh. "I am not your *bro*. And now, I'm no longer your boss. Take your nasty little friend," he points to Brooke, "get your shit, and get the fuck off club property. We'll mail you your last paycheck."

Chase looks like he wants to argue. But blood is still running from his nose, painting his hands red, and with one final glance in my direction that looks equal parts resentment and remorse, he leaves.

Brooke doesn't follow at first; she just stands there looking affronted.

"Again, do I need to get security? I already plan to submit a warning notice to the members who allowed you in on their guest pass, and you won't be allowed back, but we could make this scene way more embarrassing for you, if you prefer?"

Brooke huffs indignantly, and she offers me no apologies—not even acknowledgement that she assaulted me because of a stupid lie—before stomping her way out.

Jacob signals for Pavel to follow them and make sure they leave, and despite implying otherwise, Jacob takes out his walkie-talkie and calls security to escort Brooke Lewis from the property, giving them a full physical description I know she'd find less than flattering.

Kira, who's been looking on in some semblance of shock, finally comes forward. "Holy fucking shit," she whispers.

Holy fucking shit, indeed.

She wraps her arm around my shoulder and starts to ask if I'm okay, but all I want is to take the chance I've been waiting for all day to talk to Jacob.

"Can you give us a minute?" I ask her, and with an understanding nod, she leaves, promising to wait for me in the lobby.

"Are you okay, Goodman?" Jacob asks, his gorgeous ochre eyes swimming with genuine concern.

But I'm better than okay. I'm better than I've been in a long time. Because things are finally starting to make sense. Still, that's not what I want to talk to Jacob about.

"Look, about last night—"

Jacob stops me. "It's cool. I shouldn't have pressured you to go out with me in the first place. It was totally inappropriate."

"Pressure me?" What is he talking about?

Jacob looks surprised at my confusion. "Well, when you left last night, I figured…"

"Oh, wow. No. Not even a little bit," I assure him. "Is that why you changed my schedule today?"

He shakes his head, but his words tell me I'm right. "I never should have lined up our breaks in the first place. I know better than to pursue someone who works under me. I really do, Goodman. This was on me, not you, okay?"

"I'm pretty sure I told you I wanted that schedule," I remind him.

He chews his bottom lip pensively. "You didn't feel pressured to say that?"

"Pressured!" I laugh, and it earns me a hesitant smile. "You're probably the most thoughtful guy I've ever met."

Jacob sighs. "But last night—"

"Last night I saw you at the keg talking to Shay— the girl they just mentioned," I gesture vaguely to where that mortifying scene just played out. "And I just figured she told you the rumors."

Jacob looks like he's waiting for the rest of the explanation, but there is no rest. "Wait…you saw me talking to some girl who talked shit about you, and thought I would…what? Listen to her talk shit about you *to me*? And *judge* you over it?" He looks offended.

And he's not wrong. What about Jacob ever made me think he would just believe Shay? Like I just said, he's one of the most thoughtful people I know.

He shakes his head. "She asked me if I was there with anyone, and I pointed you out. Other than that, she was rambling about seeing me swim at a meet once."

Shame colors my cheeks and I swallow hard. "Can we sit?" I ask him, and he leads me to the bench.

I tell Jacob everything.

I tell him about Chase flirting with me, about Brooke and Shay's sudden friendship, and how I fell for all of it. I tell him how Brooke lured me into her car with promises of reconciliation, only to attack me, both physically in the car, and my reputation all over social media. I tell him all of it.

Jacob listens not only with rapt attention, but with deep compassion. He looks hurt for me, angry on my behalf. And when I fill in the final piece—the revelation we all just witnessed just minutes earlier, he smiles.

"Crazy, huh?" I ask.

"More like badass," he counters, and I blink at him, until he gestures to the small trail of blood on the floor. "I should've made him clean that shit up before firing him, huh?" He posits, and we both burst into laughter.

Fuck Chase Martin.

I don't know when Jacob's arm came around my shoulders, or when I melted into his comfort, but here we are. I can't remember ever feeling so safe.

"Can we try last night again?" I ask softly.

"Depends which part," he says. "The date part, or the part where you run away because you think I care what other people might say about you." He raises an eyebrow, and I dig my shoulder into his chest playfully.

"The first part," I promise.

***

Jacob picks me up for our first official date at eight thirty that evening. He rings the doorbell, and introduces himself to my parents and everything. He hands me a single daisy.

He looks breathtaking. His hair has grown longer these past weeks, and his tight curls stand at attention, his fresh shave offering smooth, umber skin I want nothing more than to feel against my cheek. I have wanted to kiss him for too long.

It's still hard to believe he thought he'd been pressuring me to accept our date. He won't make that mistake again. I won't let him.

He opens the passenger door for me, but I don't get in at first. Instead, I take his hand.

Jacob accepts and laces his fingers through mine, his lips pulling into a contented smile that gives me the confidence I need.

"I'm going to kiss you," I announce, my voice soft, but, somehow, not nervous.

His smile grows tenfold and he doesn't let me lean in far before he meets my lips, tentative at first.

They are so very soft as they dance against mine, gentle but hungry, and my hands come around his neck as his fingers find their way to my hair.

We kiss and kiss, in no rush, and all I can think is that I can't believe I waited this long to do this.

The salty breeze feels lighter tonight. With just a few weeks left of summer before I start college at NYU, new beginnings are on the horizon. And with Jacob just a short train ride away at South Shore U, the possibilities seem endless, and tonight feels like a dream.

And I know, without question, that it is very much only the beginning.

About the Author

Danielle Pearl

Danielle Pearl is the Amazon and iBooks best selling author of the Something More series. She lives in New Jersey with her three delicious children and ever-supportive husband, who--luckily--doesn't mind sharing her with an array of fictional men. She did a brief stint at Boston University and worked in marketing before publishing her debut novel, Normal. She writes mature Young Adult and New Adult Contemporary Romance. Danielle enjoys coffee, wine, and cupcakes, and not in moderation.

Learn more at Daniellepearl.com

Like her Facebook page for updates -- Facebook.com/daniellepearlauthor

Follow her on:

twitter.com/danipearlauthor

Instagram.com/daniellepearlauthor

LOVE JONES

By
Eden Butler

©2020

LOVE JONES

Want to be the first to get a look at covers, sneak peeks and excerpts?
Join my newsletter.

Want to hear all about my pre-orders?
Follow me on BookBub.

Interested in meeting my fellow Saints & Sinners?
Come hang out with me and my exclusive reader group.

If you're looking for me elsewhere, I'm always hanging out on social
media at the following.
I'd love to hear from you!

Facebook   Twitter   Instagram   Pinterest

www.edenbutler.com

LOVE JONES

The first time.
The last time.
It all aches the same.
—Kiera Riley-Hale, Songwriter

DANIELLE PEARL

DEDICATION

For TB and those dances on dusty streets.

ONE

Mia

New Orleans
2013

D'Angelo shredded my soul with the low growl of his voice.

The song was an anthem, the seductive plea to a faceless woman begging her to let him love her down. It was over a decade old when I heard it pumping from Aly King's busted stereo in the tiny Tremé cottage she shared with her drunk father. I was seventeen and clueless. Ignorant. Naive. But that song and the velvet smooth voice woke something inside me I hadn't known lay sleeping.

"The video is *way* better," Aly promised, laughing when I stared at the man on the screen standing on a turntable in a low-lit room, the focus on his naked body. The camera angled dangerously close, panning over curves and tendons, sinewy muscles, lithe ridges over bone and glorious brown skin, the deep contours that suggested he held more power, more promise below the lens. "Tifi," she said, using the Creole endearment for me with a smirk pulling her mouth to the right, "wipe your mouth. You're slobbering."

I'd never seen anyone so beautiful.

Aly's laughter was soft, but got louder when I swiped at my bottom lip, reaching for the laptop to replay the video. Six times and a final seventh and I knew his body, the flex of his stomach muscles as he exhaled, the press of his fingers denting his chest, and how often he passed his thick tongue over his bottom lip.

That man worked a flame inside me with his voice, his body. Stirred an inferno and nothing else had matched it.

I was sure nothing ever would.

Until the next night.

Until Aly brought me to Armstrong Park to hear a jazz band play, something my father would have never allowed. It changed everything. Even my thinking about D'Angelo and his place as the most beautiful man in my heart.

"Come on, we need to get to the park. My Papa wants me to meet some old man he thinks I should marry, and I don't wanna risk running into him."

Old was only about thirty-five, but to us, still teenagers, that was ancient.

Her grip was tight, leading me through a dancing, thick crowd as she passed a bottle of Mad Dog 20/20 to me, the only bottle she figured her father wouldn't miss from the back of the cabinet filled with bourbon and tequila above the fridge.

"Why is it purple?" There was disappointment in the roll of her eyes, but we were close enough, knew each other enough that I'd gotten used to the expression. "Oh, so this is another of my stupid questions, right?"

"It's a 'I'm a rich judge's kid' question." Aly took a swig, not blinking at the too sweet taste as it moved down her throat. "Purple is better than orange. That shit is nasty."

The next drink I took got hidden behind a grin I didn't mean and the glance I shot toward the crowd three blocks down from Aly's neighborhood. "We aren't rich," I promised, hating how defensive I sounded.

"Tifi, your daddy will win his election and you and your people will be Uptown and away from the Quarter before you know it." She looped her arm in mine and took back the bottle. "You don't live *here*."

She wasn't wrong. Tremé was a special place, filled

with Creole cottages and families who'd spent decades passing down their homes from one generation to the next. It was the oldest African American neighborhood in the city, founded for free people of color back when most black folks weren't allowed to own property at all. Now there was music and culture, musicians and artists of every race, from every country, a welcoming neighborhood that celebrated its past by honoring its roots. But as friendly as her neighbors were, as comfortable as I was in Tremé, it still wasn't like the life my father forced me into, in his bid to move out of the middle class. Here I wasn't expected to kiss anyone's ass or pretend to be someone I wasn't, wearing designer clothes he'd charged on his maxed-out credit cards because it made him look good. Here, with my best friend, I could be myself.

A loud cat call sounded behind us and Aly shot a glare over my head, but kept walking, finishing her small speech. "And soon you'll forget all about us at St. Margaret's and go off to your fancy college because you're the smartest person on the planet and then one day when you're singing on Broadway *and* sitting on the Supreme Court, because you gotta do what you love and keep your papa happy too, I'll be all 'Mia Love? Wi? I knew her. We went to hear Rebirth play at Armstrong Park the summer before senior year and drank purple Mad Dog together.'"

"Shut up," I said, laughing, swiping at her side so quickly that the bottle slipped from my fingers. I caught it, holding it in both hands, feet apart. "Shit!"

"That would have been a disaster." Aly grabbed the bottle from me, twisting the cap back on.

"Nah. That would have been a blessing." The voice was deep, slipping into my ears, just as we stood outside a tiny house that edged the corner of St. Phillip Street and the park. "Aly King, why the hell are you making this white girl drink that shit?"

"She can handle it." A smile froze on Aly's face, then lowered as the guy behind me moved and I caught a whiff of something sweet like sandalwood and the expensive scent of rich cologne that filtered into my sinuses.

"That true?" he asked me, the smell sweeter, richer the

closer he came. "You can handle this mess?"

"I can hold my…" Thick gulps of air choked me as he moved, shifting from the darkness behind me into the glow of the streetlight overhead. "Own."

I'd heard of lightning bolt moments—thunderous clarity where a look, the smallest notice does something to you. It changes you with little effort, like a dandelion fracturing in the slightest breeze. One small whisper of movement, and everything falls apart.

That's what happened to me then. With the smell of his cologne and the smooth stretch of his full mouth as he smiled at me, I was transfixed. I was changed. D'Angelo had woken me. This guy shot fire and energy into my soul.

His was a smile that would shame a daydream—imperfect, but mostly straight teeth, white and well-kept peeking out behind two wide, thick lips, the bottom dented in the middle where he nibbled on it.

When the guy tilted his head, and Aly elbowed me in the side, I stopped gawking at him, did my best to ignore the flame I was sure brightened my face.

"You good?" There was a smugness to my best friend's expression, something that was mostly amusement with a hint of worry.

"Fine," I tried, looking away from them both, fussing with my hair and the curl hitting my bare arm as I stepped off the sidewalk. "Should…we…go?"

"Shit!" Aly ignored my likely bright pink cheeks and how I couldn't quite look at her or the guy standing to her left. She jogged off the sidewalk to duck between two thick crepe myrtles.

Ignoring my still thundering heartbeat, I watched my friend, giving her a head shake for the weird way she skulked behind those thick-limbed trees. "What's the problem?" She waved me over, grabbing at my wrist before she pulled me to her side.

"Zay! Come here," she told the sweet-smelling guy and he followed.

"Here we go. Aly King and her drama…" he said.

"Non, not drama." When Aly glanced around the tree, Zay followed, looking over her head, his eyes squinted before she pushed him back against my side. "Don't let him see you."

"Who?" I leaned forward, curious, but Aly shook her head. "You think your dad found out we took the Mad Dog?"

"Ain't nobody gonna get mad at their kids for ganking Mad Dog, boo." Zay's voice vibrated against my back and I looked up, something tight in my chest making me breathless. If I was still blushing, still looked like an idiot for staring at him, he didn't seem to mind. "That's why her pops bought that shit. It's cheap, and he doesn't care if she takes it."

"How do you…know?" His skin was darker than Aly's light brown Creole complexion, reminding me of Alfie, my father's clerk from Sierra Leone, though Zay's skin was younger, his bearing smoother. He also didn't have the same West African lilt as Alfie, and his eyes were brown, not black and there was a small scar just along the curve of his right cheek. His cedar and sandalwood scent was thicker now, standing so close to him and the heat from his wide body made the scorching July temperatures around us thick and the air heavy.

"There's a lot of shit I know." Eyes tilted, Zay moved his gaze down, over my face, keeping it on my mouth before that slow, sweet smile advertised a lot my imagination could fill in for what he was thinking.

"It's not my papa," Aly said, shooing us away from whoever had her spooked. "It's that old man he wants me to meet." We came to the other side of the sidewalk, the music fading, the crowd thinning before Zay stopped us. "What?" Aly rubbed her neck, keeping her attention toward the park.

"You wanna stay out of sight, I can hook you up." When Aly cocked an eyebrow at him, Zay laughed, his head shaking. "So suspicious. Some shit hasn't changed since we were in primary. Hell, woman."

"Where we going?" she asked, walking backward, her attention still on the street behind us.

"You know Rebirth is headlining in the park. My cousin works sound for them." Zay stretched, his tall, wide body like a boxer relaxing as he dropped his hands to his side when Aly folded her arms, still looking skeptical. "Would I lie?"

My friend was fearless, but she wasn't stupid. She'd stopped Alicia Maddox and Portia Reynolds from beating the hell out of us when we were freshmen just by screaming at them like a crazy woman. I'd done the only thing I could do: followed her lead. Aly taught me to be fearless too, but we were both still cautious.

When Zay nodded toward the park, taking a few steps, and Aly didn't follow, he turned, head shaking like he couldn't believe how stubborn she was being. "What now?"

"What do you want in return?" He frowned, moving back to stand in front of her, his hands on his hips when Aly offered him the bottle in her hands.

"Oh, hell no. Keep that shit." Zay pulled out a small flask from his back pocket, drumming his fingers against the ornate filigree covering it. "My daddy keeps the good shit in his cabinet." Aly waved away his offered flask, relaxing her shoulders when he shrugged. Then Zay glanced at me, holding his drink between his long fingers, his pink tongue sliding along that thick bottom lip as he watched me. "You gotta a name white girl…"

"It's not white girl," I said, moving my chin toward his flask. Hell, I was thirsty, and if he kept looking at me the way he was, I was going to need whatever he was drinking to calm my nerves.

"Fair enough, boo."

His fingers were soft, warm when I took the flask he offered, the whiskey inside biting all the way down. It burned so much that the noise of Aly's obvious throat clearing didn't register until I pulled the flask away from my lips.

"It's Mia," I finally said, feeling a little calmer.

"Mia Love."

"The judge's daughter?" Zay laughed, a short, sharp humorless sound before he took a step away from me.

I waved off the question, returning his flask. "I take it your folks didn't name you Zay?"

"Isiah Jones," he said, shooting a glare at Aly when she clicked her tongue to the roof of her mouth. "But nobody but my Granny T calls me that."

"Y'all done?" she asked, walking between us to grab my arm. "I want to get off the street."

"Come on, dramas." Zay nodded toward the park, tucking his flask into his back pocket as he moved off the sidewalk. "I'll hook you up."

The flask was empty three hours later just as Aly discovered a bouncer with big enough arms and a small enough brain to hide her from anyone she didn't want finding her. Rebirth's horns and the buzzing vibration of their music shouted across the black sky, penetrating the hot summer night like a whip. I was drunk on the city, on that place and the people there, laughing and dancing, filling me up in a way my father's friends and social circle never could. Those people were Krewe balls and cotillions. They were country clubs and status.

Tremé was sound and sweetness. It was life and laughter. With Aly and this crowd around us, I was never freer.

"You dance, Lil Love?"

Zay Jones had swagger. He could call me by my last name, not bother with the first, and have me forgetting to be offended. Hopping off the speakers at the back of the stage, he held out his hand, long fingers stretching, nails flat and trimmed. "Can't be scared of a dance."

"I'm not scared of anything." I'd never told a bigger lie, but I still took his hand, let him curl his free one around my waist and followed the two-step he made when the music went slow.

His body was warm, solid and the whiskey buzz in my blood loosened my inhibitions. Without realizing it, I started to hum, letting the sound vibrate, rattle up my throat, until I sang along with the chords and melody, until Zay went still, leaned back to look down at me.

"Well, shit. Who knew?"

"What?"

"Lil Love can sing."

Eyes rounding, my face heated and I dipped my head, realizing that I'd given myself an audience.

"Oh, what, now you're embarrassed?" I shook my head, looking away from him, my arms stiffening when Zay pushed my chin up with his knuckle. "You got no reason to be. That's a sweet voice you got there, boo." He shook his head, that beautiful smile so wide, dimples dented in his cheeks. "See? I knew you were a little scared," Zay said, that voice a rumble into my chest, fracturing any hesitation I had about instant attraction. Until this night, I'd never believed it existed. Not in the real world. Not when it didn't involve a nearly naked D'Angelo singing on a screen.

"Is that what you think?" He didn't back away when I looked up at him. Zay held onto me like there wasn't a challenge in my eyes, like we weren't grabbing the attention of anyone who happened to spot Judge Love's daughter and some kid nobody knew dancing on the backstage as Rebirth played for the crowd.

"What I think," he said, working his thumb over my forehead, his gaze following the movement until it stopped, catching my eyes and staying there. "What I think is maybe you're looking to be rebellious and you figure you'll start right here. With me."

"On a stage in Armstrong Park where my dad will never visit?"

He wasn't wrong. Nothing would be more rebellious than for me to date Zay. It wouldn't fit the plan my father had for me. An interracial couple at his precious country club would raise eyebrows and kick in the little boxes the social climbers liked to live in.

"So you're saying you're not looking to rebel?"

I had never cared about being a rebel. Until I met

Aly, I'd never cared much about anything but breaking free from the expectations my father had for me. She dragged me onto a stage and made me sing. Now Zay dragged me on a stage and let me dance. This wasn't a rebellion. It was something belly deep I'd never felt before. I didn't know much, but understood I liked the way he smelled and the feel of Zay's hand pressed against my back.

I knew I wanted to keep feeling everything inside of that moment.

"I'm eighteen. I live to rebel but no, not with you and not right now."

"That's good." He pulled me close and that belly-deep feeling went lower, turned into a twinge that had me stretching against him, had Zay biting his bottom lip harder than he had all night.

"Why's that... good?" The question came out sounding like a whisper, feeling like an ache.

"Because I got no use for rebels."

On that stage, dancing close with a guy who smelled like cedar and sandalwood and felt like freedom, I forgot myself and enjoyed the dance, hoping the sensation would last. Praying it wouldn't wreck me completely. It was the initiation of my undoing. It was the start of everything that changed who I'd always be, and it began with that one sweet, slow dance.

TWO

Mia

New Orleans
Fifteen Years Later

Kelsey Densely wanted attention, craved it like a junky waiting a fix, and the notice of the crowd-- older, bellies rounder, hair grayer, faces fixed with fillers and Botox, her classmate's attention-- seemed enough for Kelsey. But attention on the microphone and the grip she kept tight to the envelope in her hand wasn't what held my interest.

"He see you yet?" I heard, closing my eyes when my cousin Matt stood next to me.

"How should I know?"

Actually, I did know, but I wouldn't give my annoying cousin the satisfaction of knowing that Zay Jones hadn't bothered to glance around the club even once. My old high school boyfriend seemed too caught up in the attention our classmates gave him and, I noticed, pouring back another glass of champagne, and hearing whatever it was the beautiful woman hanging on his arm whispered into his ear.

"Looks like he's forgotten all about your little crush."

"You are a smug asshole, Matthew."

I didn't bother acknowledging my cousin's laugh or how he called after me as I moved through the crowd and away from the stage.

Away from Zay Jones and his inattention.

300

Fifteen years was a long time to put New Orleans and the promises we made to each other out of his head.

"Mia!"

Shit.

"Amanda, hi." I let the woman kiss my cheeks, both of them, because my cousin watched me. He always did when my father was in D.C. Thirty-three years old and I still had a sitter. "How are you?" I forced the pleasantries because Amanda's husband, the third one she's had before the age of thirty-five, was a client my father wanted our firm to land. "I hear Rick is opening a new hotel on Canal?"

"Oh, he is. It's all he talks about. Bores me silly with all that talk of permits and the city getting in his way…"

"That's a pain." The waitress paused when I stopped her, offering Amanda a glass of champagne. "You know my cousin Matt has lunch every month with the Mayor." It wasn't a lie, and, even if he was an insufferable asshole, he had his uses. A glance over to him and he was at my side. "Didn't you say the Mayor was looking to invest in some new projects?"

"He might be…"

"Amanda's husband—"

It was business. It was New Orleans business, and, in this city, politics and business went hand in hand. Matt spent a good half hour talking, likely flirting with Amanda, and I slipped away from them, hoping to keep him busy and the woman interested enough that she'd mention our firm to her number three.

Did Zay have to do that? Work the room? Move people around like pieces on a chess board?

A nod to two CPAs I knew from the Club, one of which tried to feel me up in tenth grade before I socked him in the nose, and I moved away from the crowd, glancing at the stage, eyeing Kelsey before my attention shot back to Zay.

No fillers, that much I could tell. The beginning of gray at his temples, but nothing else that gave away his age. That melanin was a gift, he'd always teased.

"Black don't crack, Lil Love," he'd joked one afternoon when his Granny T had stopped by school to drop off his

house key. He'd confessed she was pushing sixty. The woman's smooth skin and thick black hair gave nothing away. I'd have guessed her to be inching closer to forty.

"There's no way. Sixty?"

He'd shrugged, looking cool and bored, his go-to response when he tried to impress me. And he was always trying to impress me. "We got that good, good *stuff. Island genes, Granny T says."*

"She's beautiful." The woman herself stopped at the door, staring between us before she left, waving and then paused. Two football players pushed on each other fighting over who got to hold open the door for her and the older woman's smile stretched as she strutted out of the room.

"Hell, don't let her hear you say that." Zay pinched the bridge of his nose, but still smiled, like he was proud but didn't want me to know he was.

"Why?"

"She's too big headed already. She catches you talking about how good she looks, and she'll be on me all the time talking about 'when you gonna bring that sweet white girl over to see me?' I'll never get rid of you."

"Oh," I teased, folding my arms. "So, you want to get rid of me?"

"Nah, not you." Zay grabbed my hand under the table, holding it between his fingers. "Not just yet."

He hadn't gotten rid of me. Someone else did that dirty work for us.

My family had no loyalty except when it suited them. And for Matt, that loyalty only extended as far as it would earn my father's favor.

He laughed at Amanda, brushing something from her shoulder, giving her all the attention he had and the familiar brimming anger that always bubbled in my chest when I thought of the past, of Matt and my past, began to surface.

"What's this Matthew says about you and this

boy?" my father said one afternoon not long after we'd been discovered in the library. *"This...this Jones boy? That...that* activist's *son?* Anytime my dad mentioned Zay's father, it came with a tone of criticism. Speak out against unfair wages and sub-par housing and you got labeled. At least, Mr. Jones had. It was enough for my father's disapproval to be weighty and final.

It was enough for his disapproval of me to last years.

"I won't have it, Mia. Not my daughter. Not in this lifetime."

Then, everything changed.

They made sure of it. My father's reach. My cousin's scheming. How much I loved Zay. What I'd do to keep that reach from touching him.

They knew it all.

"Promise me, one day, Love." He'd held me so tight. It would be the last time and his grip came with a kiss that told me what he felt. The press of his mouth. His breath panting. Fingers digging into my arms. Voice breaking, desperate. "Please. Tell me one day we'll find a way."

"One day, Zay." I believed that promise when I spoke it. I believed it every night after that. "I promise we will. When they aren't controlling us. When we're our own people. I promise." Then, I stopped believing.

"That's my girl."

And I was.

His girl.

Only his.

But Zay Jones didn't belong to me anymore.

And I wasn't my own person.

"Amanda's husband is going to call me in the morning." Matt held out another glass to me and, automatically, I took it. It was habit how we worked together, a puppet show, though I didn't know who was pulling the strings most days. "That was a good catch."

"Dad wants to land his account." Demanded. He demanded I land Rick Reynolds's business and two more high profile companies before the end of the year. Fund raising for his campaign would begin in the spring, and no one was backing the party anymore. "I was just following through."

"Aren't you the good little soldier?"

Replacing the glass on the bar behind me, I faced my cousin, not caring that my face was tight, that it was likely obvious what I thought of him just from the expression on my face. "Have I ever told you how much I hate you?"

"Often and repeatedly." He laughed behind the drink he took. "It fills me with a warm sort of glee."

"You're disgusting." I expected him to follow me when I left the bar. He usually did. Matt wasn't one to walk away when provoked, and he'd never let me have the last word.

"If I was your brother and not your cousin, you could run off and do whatever the hell you want to do." Blocking my way into the hallway that led to the bathrooms he nodded toward the crowd waving with his glass. "Including finding your old love and begging him to take you back. But, *big* cousin, I'm not your brother, and your father hated my parents, even if my mother was his sister. I have not spent the past twenty years of my life kissing the Senator's ass for shits and giggles."

I grabbed his glass, taking a large sip for myself. "You're more calculating than he is."

"I'm not stupid." The crowd parted, and I caught sight of Zay laughing. Matt stood in front of me. "I for one listen when he wants something done and what he wants tonight, is for you to keep clear of Isiah Jones. You, on the other hand, are crazy if you think for one second your father will ever allow you to rekindle something that should stay buried." He turned, shaking his head when Zay stood to greet Father Michaels. The older man had coached his football team to a district win the year we graduated. Matt scratched his chin, his attention moving from the two men, then back to me. "You should have never come here tonight."

"How would that have looked? I'm on the

committee. So are you."

Grabbing a passing waitress, Matt stole a fresh glass and stood at my side. "Then *he* shouldn't have gotten an invitation."

A small crowd emerged from the hallway and I moved closer to the bar, ignoring Matt as he watched me, as his focus seemed devoted to where my attention landed. When I rested against the bar, glass in hand, my cousin stood in front of me, standing so I couldn't see who Zay spoke to or if he remained at the same table near the stage.

It was ridiculous. Frustrating, but Matt was adamant. He'd never be a derelict in whatever task my father gave him. "Zay's the fourth richest man in the country and the most famous graduate St. Margaret's has ever produced. He's contributed thousands to the school, and you think we shouldn't have invited him?"

"Just stay clear," he said, rubbing his eyes. "Please. To save me the headache."

"Guard duty must suck, little cousin."

Mouth dropping open and, no doubt, a catty, cruel insult at the ready, Matt rolled his eyes, patting his jacket pocket when his cell vibrated. "Don't move," he told me after glancing at the screen and taking the call. "Uncle Bobby…"

I managed the only relaxing breath that came from me that night when Matt was at the back of the club and most of the champagne in my glass was gone. Around me the crowd was growing and Kelsey had been joined by two other committee members, both of whom were bickering with the woman over the envelopes in her hand.

Zay courted the attention he got from women and men, older, richer versions of the assholes they'd been as kids, the same assholes who were only friendly to him when he was scoring touchdowns or letting them cheat off his Bio tests. Now they wanted pictures and his ear to bend for one thing or another.

Now they wanted everything he had.

From the back of the room, I spotted Matt waving his hands as he continued to talk to my father, gesturing like an idiot, ignoring the looks he made as he paced. God knew what they discussed. Likely me. They were exhausting.

I could say goodbye. One phone call to my banker, and it would be over. I would be poor by my father's standards. But I could learn to live modestly. I could be free. Away from my family's expectations. Away from everything I hated and still did anyway.

But where would I be?

On my own?

Spending the occasional weekend with Aly and her new husband when they had the free time? I'd isolated myself so much, away from anyone who wasn't connected to my father or his business that there was no one left for me alone.

The only one who would be—Zay—probably wouldn't want to be with me once he learned the truth. Once he discovered that I'd done everything I promised him I wouldn't do.

Across the club, Richard Melancon patted Zay on the shoulder, laughing louder at something the man said and my ex only stared at him. Melancon had been Matt's friend our senior year. He'd discovered us in the library. Now he was looking for an investor for his tech start up and seemed to forget all the damage he'd done.

But the glare on Zay's face told me he hadn't forgotten a thing.

The memory came back like a windstorm. Ripping apart the small calm I had. Watching Zay and Richard brought me back to that day. To that darkened corner and I closed my eyes, dipping my head, letting that lost moment consume me.

His lips on my skin, wide and warm. My fingernails against his scalp, loving how fast he breathed against me, how the hot, moist pants of his breath against my skin shot chills over my body.

"I could do this here. Right here. I don't care who sees." The library was low-lit. The corners nearly black, but it was risky being there with him. We were tempting fate.

"We'll get caught," I told him. *"You can't get detention again."*

"Neither can you, Lil Love."

We did anyway.

That day in the library. The night at Aly's when she left her father's home and moved into the tiny apartment above the dance studio where she worked.

She hid me and Zay from the world. She covered for us when my father came looking.

But the world found us.

It always would.

"Reynolds is interested in two more hotels over the next ten years. Your dad got a call from Mac Eldridge at Chase…" I didn't care what Matt found out and ignored my cousin as he went on about how he planned to score the man's account.

Zay's security ushered Richard from his table and that beautiful brunette whispered in his ear. He didn't smile. Didn't do much more than disturb the ice in his glass, staring at it like he was disappointed all the whiskey had disappeared.

"Are you listening to me?"

"No."

"You should be." Matt glanced over his shoulder before he stared back at me, his mouth tight as he scrubbed a hand through his hair. "Forget about this shit, Mia, for your own sake. Your father will never let you walk away. Besides, Isiah Jones can have any woman he wants in the world. What the hell makes you think he'd still want you?"

He wasn't wrong. Models and actresses. Women of means. Women with advanced degrees from the finest universities in the world. They all wanted him, and he could get them with very little effort.

I was smart. I was educated, but I'd given up every dream I'd dreamed for myself to come back to New Orleans and run my father's firm after his first run for the Senate. Zay had left, chased from the city by dirty cops and dirtier politicians who wanted favors from my father.

"You have to get out," he'd told me. *"Don't let them*

control you."

But I hadn't. I'd done exactly what I promised Zay I wouldn't.

Matt was right.

He wouldn't want me now. I wasn't the same girl.

I was the disappointment he'd left behind.

A glance up and my chest felt tight, a sensation I hadn't experienced in fifteen years. Not since that first time at Armstrong Park. The first time I danced with Zay. When he looked at me and stole my breath.

Like he was doing right now.

THREE

Zay

She had me sprung.

Got drunk on her. Full body whipped. One dance, the thick hum of Kermit's horn vibrating against my feet and that fine, sweet girl wrapped up in my arms.

Eighteen years old and I was sprung.

Heart. Head. Body and soul. Gave all that shit to her and let her do what she would.

Lost it all.

Time looked good on her. Those hips, that ass still lush. Still wide. Legs that were tight and curved, small waist. Face like a fucking angel. Eyes green like a magnolia leaf, all wide and anxious as she watched me.

Mia Love. *My* love. First I'd ever had.

"Mr. Jones, your drink."

My assistant stood too close, her hair brushed against my neck as she set another gin and tonic in front of me, and the heady mix of her perfume overwhelmed me. It was too much, just like the woman. We'd have to have a conversation.

"This Kelsey Densely woman asked if you could say something to the crowd." She brushed her hand over my arm, resting her hand on my shoulder like we weren't employee and employer and didn't move it away when I shifted my glance up. The woman had been doing this shit for a week straight, despite my warnings to watch how she touched me. It felt a little like she was staking a claim. Nobody had rights to that shit.

"Miss Nelson, you can go."

"Sir…" Whatever the hell she thought she didn't tell me. She should have known better, seemed to when I cut that question with a silent glance back at her. I did warn her, more than once. She was being unprofessional. I needed an assistant, not a date.

Benny, my security, was behind me, not there to do anything but keep drunk assholes from working my nerves, but he still stepped up. Kept the woman in check. One look at the man and she nodded, kept even a quiet good night to herself.

It happened sometimes. Some of the assistants were young. Eager.

They could get a little reckless stupid.

Or, in Mia's case. They forgot they had a backbone. "Zay!"

Kelsey. This chick. She spent four years in high school pretending not to know my name. Now I'm 'Zay' and not 'Elijah' like she called me the half dozen times she asked to copy my homework in Sister Frances' fourth period Geometry class.

"What can I do for you?"

"Would you mind saying a little something to everyone?" The smile was veneered. Tits were fake. Whole lot of that shit going on in this place. None of our classmates wanted to get old, and it showed.

"Hmm, I'd love to," I told her, not meaning it, "but I'm afraid I just don't have the time." I glanced at my cell, then back at her, making sure to look her in the eye. "I'm headed out in about an hour and will be leaving soon." She opened her mouth, ready to say something and I stopped her, patting her hand and shooting her a wink. "But I'd love to set up the foundation with another donation. Father Michael said there was a deficit in this year's donations. Maybe our classmates would appreciate that more than hearing my boring ass talk about shit that doesn't matter, right?" I threw a wink at her, counting on the charms I'd worked to perfect to win her over.

"Oh, that would be great," Kelsey said, her cheeks going pink. "I'll be sure to announce your donation when I do the awards." She squeezed my hand, her smile widening before she walked off.

Deflection. I'd learned that was key to getting out of situations you didn't want to be in. Sometimes, it was necessary. When you have money, especially when you've made that money on your own, people tended to believe you were a pushover. Maybe they thought you had rich asshole guilt.

I don't. Every cent I made came to me hard.

I gave up a lot to earn it.

Me and Mia both did.

She looked away from me, ignoring whatever it was that asshole cousin of hers whispered into her ear. Some things never changed. Like how that prick followed after her. I'm guessing it was because the Senator told him to.

"Hi everyone!" Kelsey was back on stage, bringing the attention of the crowd to her. "Welcome St. Margaret's alumni!" The woman was nervous, glanced at me, but didn't linger. "We've got a few small awards to give away, voted on by y'all in the past few weeks leading up to tonight so thanks to everyone who participated…"

I tuned out the bullshit she said, my attention on the stage, those thick, red curtains and the small wooden flooring. Fifteen years ago, we'd been here, all alone, just me and Mia fighting over whether she had the nerve to get up there and sing.

"Bet you won't do it. I mean, I'm sayin', you should. But I'm guessing you won't." It was my dumbass try at challenging her. She wasn't stupid. My Lil Love was fierce, except when it came to singing in public.

"Are you calling me a coward, Isiah Jones?"

What kind of man would I be if I didn't challenge the woman I loved?

"You, boo? Never." I'd leaned across that table, pulling her onto my lap. *"But I'm betting you're gonna lose your nerve before you manage a single note."*

"To hell with that."

And she was off, up there, mic in hand, belting out Bonnie Raitt's old "Angel from Montgomery" like the song was hers and no one knew it like she did. That voice, that girl smiling and singing right on that stage broke something loose inside me.

Did she still sing?

It'd be a damn shame if she locked that part of herself away too.

Her damn daddy had expected so much.

He took even more and from the looks of her cousin fussing at her in her ear, I suspected shit hadn't changed. That tore at my insides. Damn shame.

"You're good, Love. Don't let anyone tell you you're not."

"You're biased."

I was, but I also had ears. I knew what I'd heard was something special. She came to me easily, resting against my chest in the middle of the empty street outside the club. It felt good to have her there. Just us. No worries about who would see us. Not sweating if somebody would run off and tell her damn daddy she was stepping out with me.

Just me and my girl on that empty street.

"Dance with me, Songbird," I told her, already pulling out my phone, my thumb scrolling to the app, hitting the song I knew would do something to her.

"Here? There's no mus—" She pushed back, the glare she forced on her face faker than the tits those rich bitches from the club she was always sneaking away from every chance she got. "You're playing dirty now." "That's the plan." D'Angelo started in on his promises and my girl came back to me, arms around my neck, lips against my throat. All the females went stupid over this dude, but I wasn't mad at him. Hell, I benefited.

"You really think I was good?" she asked, her voice quiet.

"Baby, ain't nobody better." She came easy to me. Soft like a whisper and we got a little lost right there on

312

that empty street. She'd tasted like amaretto. Sweet and silky and I got drunk off her. I'd have killed to stay in that moment forever. Given every cent I had to be back there now.

The memory slipped through the noise of the crowd, through whatever bullshit Kelsey said and I looked past the faces, wondering about the girl I loved. Hoping there was something left of her in the woman across the room.

But Matt leaned down to Mia's ear, and the expression on her face told me he said something that had her itching to slap him. I wished like hell she would. I'd been wanting to do that shit for fifteen years. Since he'd called the cops and lied, saying I'd taken Mia against her will.

They were the ones who interrupted our dance.

And threatened my future.

Mia watched me, and for a second the frown faded. Something flashed in her eyes. It came and went, disappeared before I knew what to call it. Then she turned away, let her cousin go back to whatever bullshit he said that made her flag down the bartender and ignored the look I gave her.

Fucking pity.

From the looks of her, there was nothing left of the songbird I loved.

FOUR

Mia

Aly wasn't a King anymore. She'd left her father's Tremé cottage and the prison of that life right after we graduated. Seeing her coming for me, seeing Ransom Riley-Hale, her husband and former NFL darling on her arm, I got why she fought like hell to keep free from the past. The man was beautiful, a wide, confident presence that kept the attention of everyone in the room, but who only had eyes for his wife.

She wouldn't have that if she hadn't fought to free herself from her father's tight reins. Something I hadn't even attempted.

It had been five years since I'd seen her, but when she spotted me hunched on the bar, looking scared and small, my friend Aly came to the rescue. She seemed to make several observations at once: a glance at me, then to my bourbon, meant I was drinking to dull the pain. One look at Matt and me ignoring him, said I was still being watched. A sweep of her gaze across the club, toward where Zay held the notice of our classmates, not paying me a lick of attention, advertised I hadn't bothered with speaking to him.

Aly whispered in Ransom's ear, nodded to Matt, then they both approached.

"Shoushou," she said, greeting Matt with an endearment she didn't mean before he could respond. "You look good!" He didn't. He looked pale and tired, but she didn't give him time to explain that. "This is my husband, Ransom." She nodded, stretching her smile.

"This is Matt Williams, Mia's cousin. Remember I told you about them?"

"I do." Ransom held out a hand, and my cousin's demeanor changed. Blessedly, he seemed to forget about me. "You seriously left the Dolphins? And your dad is coaching at CPU?"

"Let me tell you about their chances at the SEC championships this year. You need a drink?"

Aly was smart, and by the way her man took control, I figured her husband was too. There wasn't a red-blooded southern man, lawyer or otherwise, who could resist a football conversation with a bonafide NFL player, retired or not.

I started to say as much, nodding toward Ransom's back, as Aly sat on the stool next to me, but my friend cut me off, snapping her fingers like there was serious business that needed to be handled and no time for dawdling.

"What?" I asked when the frown on her face tightened as I reached for my glass.

"You have got to be shitting me."

"I never thought you'd show," I said, hiding my embarrassment behind my glass, then groaning when Aly took it from me.

"Wi. I showed." She looked over her shoulder, leaning toward the corner of the club, where Ransom stood talking to Matt and the two other men, I couldn't make out, who joined their conversation. Then Aly faced me and the hard edges of her expression had not softened. "The question is, why the hell are you over here with that asshole and not at that table with Zay?"

"You know why."

"Tifi, please." Shoulders lowering, Aly pushed the frown from her features and grabbed my hand. "Modi, I don't know why you think they can control you. That shit was a lifetime ago."

"And Zay's family…"

"His family's protected by his gobs of money." She shook her head, brushing the hair from her shoulder. "You haven't figured that out by now? He can't be hurt by your father and his threats." Everything my dad forced me into—all the warnings, I'd confided to Aly about. I had to. Our friendship was another casualty of my father's demands. "Shoushou, you know that Zay's reach is pretty damn far. My father and mother-in-law, they run in those same rich celebrity circles. It happens when you're in the NFL and win Grammys for famous country singers. I told you this before, but Kona and Kiera, they say it all the time. Rich folk like to stay rich and connected. No one is richer than Zay." She looked back to his table, to the attention he still held. There were so many women converged around him. So many men in fine suits trying to pass over their business cards. But everyone was held back by the beefy security guard at his side and maybe the steely expression on Zay's face.

"You agreed to stay here to keep him out of jail and to keep his Granny T off of Immigration Services' radar. But your father is lying to you if he still says he can do damage to them."

But it wasn't just doing his bidding that kept me from walking across the room and telling Zay I wanted to keep my promise to him now.

"It's not just that," I told Aly, fiddling with clasp on my bracelet. For some reason I couldn't find the strength to look at her. "I'm...a coward. He'll... think I'm a coward." Aly grabbed my hand, and I glanced at her, eyebrows lifting when she stared at me like that. There was nothing I couldn't say to her, even now. Even after all this time. "I...never told him about any of this. I don't want him or anyone else thinking I'm playing the martyr here. I did nothing. I took the coward's way out. I stayed in my father's good graces and still got to go to a good college and live a life of privilege. That isn't what I promised him I'd do. He won't want me anymore. Not after all of that."

"How the hell will you know if you don't even speak to him?"

LOVE JONES

Jerking a look toward my cousin, I shook my head. "Matt will have my father on the phone in under five minutes."

"Who the hell cares?" Aly was fierce. Still. She was a soldier, always had been. I'd always craved the same strength she had. I'd always dreamed of being that brave.

"It's not that simple…"

"Wi," the Creole word accentuated with a definite nod, "it is, tifi." She stood, downing what remained of my drink. "It's real damn simple. You either live what's left of your life for yourself, or grow old regretting not even trying. We don't get much time, Mia. It goes by damn fast. You better hurry up before everything you want for yourself passes you right by."

Overhead the music lowered and the band on stage began to play. They were a decent five-piece bar band that kicked off their set with a Van Morrison classic, and within seconds, the crowd was on their feet dancing. Zay took them all in, not smiling, just observing, looking for all the world like he was waiting.

"If he tells me it's too late…"

"Then it's too late." She took my elbow, and I stood, ignoring how she pushed me toward the dancing mass of people. "But at least you won't spend the rest of your life wondering."

The crowd was thick, bustling, arms flaying, hips and legs moving as they danced. I couldn't move through them without getting lost. I couldn't move around them without Matt spotting me, and if I was going to make a stand, it would have to be a big one. The band was good and three songs in, they might be due for a slower tempo number. Taking a gamble that they'd humor me, I took a breath and moved backstage, catching the eye of the guitarist. A quick smile and brief explanation landed me a spot at the mic, and in a dizzying ten minutes, I stood there in front of men I didn't know, hearing the same sweet melody of "Angel of Montgomery" playing me in.

The stage lights were blinding, and I couldn't make out more than shapes and sounds five feet in front of me, but I hoped Zay could see me, hear every word. I prayed he remembered us at this place, just kids being rebellious, dreaming the biggest dreams we were bold enough to believe were sure to come true.

There were low whistles from the crowd when I started, a few laughs doubting I could carry a tune very far and then one loud, loving, "You got this, tifi!" from Aly that stretched my mouth into a proud smile.

The first verse went by like a secret, memory and hope flooding out of me into the chorus, seeing us together in all those lost moments. But the past was dimmed by sweet memory, the scars and sorrow not visible. Just then, I didn't want them to be. At that moment, singing everything I was and wanted, I only brought the sweetness into my mind.

Zay and me and a feeling that I hadn't buried.

He'd remember. Only he could.

The last note vibrated. The last breath drifted into silence, and the applause sounded before I opened my eyes, blinking as the lights lowered, and I smiled, my attention shooting right to his table, hoping, praying...

But Zay wasn't there.

"Mia..."

"I have to go." Aly followed me through the club, not letting anyone get more than a passing glance at me, as I made angry, irritated swipes at my wet face. "I'll call you tomorrow." It was a promise I'd keep, but, for now, I couldn't breathe. Couldn't fight the embarrassment that grew the louder Matt's laughter got when I left the stage.

"Please wait. Let us..."

"No, really," I told her reaching for the door. Head lifted, I turned, kissing her cheek. "It's fine. I'll be fine."

The street wasn't empty. No New Orleans street was ever empty this early in the night, but I didn't notice anything other than the small line waiting to get in the door and the free space on the sidewalk. That was my focus—to put as much distance between me and this place as I could.

He wasn't there. Of course he wasn't. Why would he be?

Zay wouldn't wait for me. What was there to wait for?

The tires crunched against the street and I only half recognized the low thump of music behind me, nearly a block from the club before I stopped, realizing for the first time I'd passed the lot where I'd parked and had ended up in a dark section of the street on my own.

"Shit…"

Then the music got louder with the opening of a door and I stopped walking, adjusting my keys so that the teeth peeked out between my fingers. But the footsteps behind me weren't running, and the music I heard was slow, seductive and so damn familiar.

D'Angelo was still my favorite.

"Songbird." Zay's voice was still smooth, still deep and vibrating.

"You heard that?" I said, turning to find him standing in front of me. He looked even better up close. "I didn't see you. I thought you left."

"The crowd was thick. They have a balcony. You took off."

"I…" Shaking my head, I held up a hand, hating how my eyes burned, but I had to tell him. He had to know what I'd done. "When they arrested you—"

"It doesn't matter." Zay's mouth was lifted on one side, and those deep, brown eyes moved like it took effort to take in my features. Like he was trying to see what had changed in me and what was the same.

"It does to me. It's why I stayed."

"I know why you stayed." I opened my mouth, but he covered it with his thumb moving over my bottom lip. "I know about your father's ultimatum and what he thought he had on my Granny T."

"You knew?"

"Money buys information, boo."

"You never said anything…"

"You wanted me to come back?" His eyes were

squinted, hard. "After you made me promise not to look back?" He took a step, clenching his jaw. "I don't break my promises. You made me swear, remember? You said you'd find me first."

Head down, I inhaled, letting that sweet smell become solid, something that would remain if I never got to see him again. "I'm a coward. I haven't done much to…" I exhaled wanting to explain. Wishing all the words would come, knowing they'd never be enough. I had to try anyway. "I let you go because I believed he could get in your way." Zay nodded, but didn't speak, let me take his hand, move my fingers between his. "I've seen my father destroy so many people just because he wanted to. You have no idea…" When he lifted his eyebrows, his expression, amused, I understood, remembering what Aly told me. The well connected and wealthy understood how the game is played and Zay had been playing it a long time.

"Well…I didn't want to be the one putting you in the middle of that. You already had a target on your back because of me." He looked away, head shaking but moved his attention back to me when I tugged on his hand. "But I stayed because I figured you…would have forgotten…" There was no excuse for my staying. No excuse for staying stagnant for so long. No excuse for never keeping my promise. "Shit, Zay, I was scared of breaking out the stupid little box I lived in. I've been scared a long time. I told you. I'm a coward."

The music filtered into the air, coiling around me like a spell and I closed my eyes, letting it calm me, waiting for Zay to step away, expecting his disappointment. But the seconds passed and his scent came closer right along with warm, soft press of his lips on my forehead.

"You planning to stay a coward?" he said, pulling my chin up.

"I…"

"It's a simple question, Lil Love."

The burn in my eyes got sharper, and I grabbed his hand when he pressed his fingers against my face, like he was a lifeline, the only lifeline that would save me. "I can't breathe here. Not for a long time."

Zay nodded, moving his hand to my back, holding my fingers against his chest to dance with me. There was no one here to threaten us. There was nothing to fracture this moment or interrupt this dance.

"This better?"

"Almost."

Then Zay bent his knuckle under my chin, pulling me closer, pressing his body against me, slipping his lips on mine and righted my world with one sweet kiss.

EPILOGUE

Zay

There was nothing like freedom.

That soul-sweet moment a body relaxes. When it lets loose from the stresses weighing it down, when the heaviness of the world gives way and every damn restriction fractures into nothing but weightlessness.

Mia's body was light, naked, her full, heavy breasts moving against my fingers as she rode me. "Zay…*ah*…"

"You and me, Lil Love…this is how it was always meant to be."

She clenched around me, those tight, wet walls holding my dick like she owned it, and she did, harder, sweeter than any woman ever had.

"Come here. Baby…kiss me."

I was sprung…again. Had I ever stopped? She asked, I gave and inhaled her—nipples hard, rubbing against my bare chest as she rode me, her round, soft ass in my hands as she moved.

"I…could die here…right here with you, Songbird…fuck, you feel good. Did you always feel this good?"

"Nothing has…ever been like this…not ever."

She squeezed me, that heat warming, the wetness slick and I was drunk, knocked out by this woman, this body. Mia gasped when I turned, pushing her to her back, hovering over her, my fingers digging between her hair and the pillow she laid on.

"Go deep," she said, pushing me closer with her

leg, arching up when I moved my hips. "I want you deep, Zay."

"Anything, boo…anything you want."

It took ten minutes for us to fall apart. Ten minutes of working inside her, my body sweaty, my head full of Mia Love, *my* Lil Love and the memory of the sweet girl I left behind in New Orleans was nothing compared to the woman wrapped around me. A flick of my tongue on her nipple and me pistoning harder, wilder and we both shot over the edge, holding onto each other like we were the only ones who would keep us tethered to the earth.

"Zay…" She said my name in a sated moan, and it told me enough what was in her head.

"I feel you." Mia curled against me, kissing my chest, relaxing her weight on top of me, and I got the feeling that it was the first time she'd let go in years. "What do you want to—" My question died on my tongue when Mia lifted, reaching onto the bedside table for her cell and the tightness that had bunched up her shoulders all night returned. A glance at the screen, and I spotted her daddy's face, telling me all I needed to know about where my sated happy Songbird went.

"Duty calling?" I asked, resting back against the pillow, wondering how long it would take for her to make an excuse and leave.

But Mia didn't move. Her gaze locked on that screen, her body sinking into me as her eyes went wide and my mouth stayed closed.

"You remember what you said to me?"

It had been forever ago, the night before I left New Orleans. We'd hoped for a day when no one controlled us. I wanted that day to be now.

Mia dropped the phone and moved her gaze to me, smoothing her fingers over my mouth as she watched me. "I made you a promise?"

"You did." I held my breath, sure whatever she said next would change my world one way or another.

There was a glint of moisture on her bottom lip when she pressed them together, then Mia smiled, a soft, sugary sweet look that left me a little punch drunk. "It took me a long time, but now I plan to keep it."

Shit. This woman would wreck me without even trying.

That smile got wider when I exhaled and pulled her on top of me, close enough to take her mouth and own it. "That's my girl."

"I am…and I always will be.

THE END

Find out more about Aly and Ransom in Eden Butler's THIN LOVE series
available exclusively in KINDLE UNLIMITED.

THIN LOVE (Thin Love #1)

Love isn't supposed to be an addiction. It isn't supposed to leave you bleeding.

Kona pushed, Keira pulled, and in their wake, they left behind destruction.

She sacrificed everything for him.

It wasn't enough.

But the wounds of the past can never be completely forgotten and still the flame remains, slumbers between the pleasure of yesterday and the thought of what might have been.

Now, sixteen years later, Keira returns home to bury the mother who betrayed her, just as Kona tries to hold onto what remains of his NFL career with the New Orleans Steamers. Across the crowded bustle of a busy French Market, their paths collide, conjuring forgotten memories of a consuming touch, skin on skin, and the still smoldering fire that begs to be rekindled.

When Kona realizes the trifecta of betrayal—his, Keira's and those lies told to keep them apart—his life is irrevocably changed and he once again takes Keira down with him into the fire that threatens to ignite them both.

ALSO BY EDEN BUTLER

FROM CITY OWL PRESS / PARANORMAL & FANTASY ROMANCE
Infinite Us
CRIMSON COVE SERIES
Forgotten Magic
Love and Magic
Haunted Magic

INDEPENDENT TITLES / CONTEMPORARY ROMANCE
THE SERENITY SERIES
Chasing Serenity
Behind the Pitch
Finding Serenity
Claiming Serenity
Catching Serenity

THE THIN LOVE SERIES
Thin Love
My Beloved
Thick Love
Thick & Thin
My Always

SAINTS & SINNERS SERIES
The Last Love of Luka Hale
Roughing the Kicker
Offsides

GOD OF ROCK SERIES
Kneel
Beg

STANDALONES
I've Seen You Naked and Didn't Laugh
Platform Four

Fall

COLLABORATIONS
Nailed Down, Nailed Down Book One, with Chelle Bliss
Tied Down, Nailed Down Book Two, with Chelle Bliss
Kneel Down, Nailed Down Book Three, with Chelle Bliss
Stripped, Nailed Down Book Four, with Chelle Bliss
Santa, Baby, A Carelli Family Christmas Novella with
Chelle Bliss

ABOUT THE AUTHOR

Eden Butler is a writer of contemporary, fantasy and romantic suspense novels and the nine-times great-granddaughter of an honest-to-God English pirate. This could explain her affinity for rule breaking and rum.

When she's not writing or wondering about her possibly Jack Sparrowesque ancestor, Eden patiently waits for her Hogwarts letter, reads, and spends too much time in her garden perfecting her green thumb while waiting for the next New Orleans Saints Super Bowl win.

She is currently living under teenage rule alongside her husband in southeast Louisiana.

Please send help.

Social Media Links:
Newsletter: http://eepurl.com/VXQXD
Twitter: https://twitter.com/edenbutler_
Facebook: www.facebook.com/eden.butler.184
Instagram: https://www.instagram.com/edenbutlerwrites/
GoodReads:
www.goodreads.com/author/show/7275168.Eden_Butler
Saints & Sinners Reader Group:
https://www.facebook.com/groups/345844502509364/

Find out more about Eden's books on her site www.edenbutler.com

YOU'VE GOT THE LOVE

LOVE

CHICAGO SPORTS ROMANCE BOOK 4

ELIZABETH MARX

YOU'VE GOT THE LOVE

ELIZABETH MARX BOOKS

Editor: Melissa Ringsted, There For You Book Editing
http://thereforyoumelissa.blogspot.com

For Jasmine & Jade who know that love is color blind.

1

A BRIEF REPRIEVE FROM MISERY

Flannery Flame
Chicago, Hotel Rouge

Grief steals more than your joy for living, it robs you of all your deepest desires too.

Requiring a drink, a diversion, and a bit of relief from the war waging within myself I reclined on the red velvet booth in the dimly lit hotel bar and sipped my Old-Fashioned. My best friend, Isla, had signed an author whose new book was my entertainment. The book had produced a few outbursts of laugh-out-loud hilarity in the last hour. I'd finally arrived at the good part—the hot, heavy, sigh worthy sentences where the hero satisfies the heroine in some incredibly mouth watering way. My foot jiggled in anticipation as it rested on the corner of the table. This was as close as I'd been to a climax in a long time.

"Ma'am, if you'd like to take your sexy shoes off my table," a baritone voice said, as the feel of an assertive presence swirled around me.

Reading words like breathlessness, bliss, and burning desire made adjusting the height of my book impossible even if it blocked my view of the seductive speaker. "Are you a bar Nazi?" I asked as I continued speed-reading, my toes curling inside of my stacked suede heels.

"This isn't your room, you can't sprawl around unnoticed."

I held up a finger. The wait a second finger, not the fuck

off finger, because I was in the middle of the juicy part where fingers and other appendages were working diligently toward completion. In spite of his his deep baritone voice distracting me, I worked my way through all the good stuff quickly before I snapped the pages of the book together and met his expression.

Okay, wow, wasn't expecting that! A striking Black man towered over me. His hair was braided away from his face in perfectly aligned rows, and he had a sharply trimmed beard that hid his white teeth until he gave me a coy smile that hinted that his mouth might cause spontaneous combustion. *Temptation.* I bit into my bottom lip because the last thing I'd ever been was impulsive when enticement presented itself.

I crossed one ankle over the other ankle, which was still resting on the corner of the table, while he watched the sheer fabric of my dress slide down my legs to the middle of my thighs. Then his vibrant eyes took a leisurely stroll up my torso before he gave me a hard stare. "This isn't a library …" His eyes betrayed him as they wandered to the necklaces hanging in the deep V between my breasts. "I have one in the penthouse I'd be happy to show you though."

That come on made me exclaim, "Wowza!" and several heads at the bar turned in my direction. "That's almost funnier than my book."

He slipped into the booth alongside me—not on the side where there was more room but in the small area between the edge of the seat and myself. His rock-hard body rubbed against mine, and I could smell his expensive sandalwood aftershave and a hint of minty mouthwash. "What's so funny in the book?"

"The heroine verbally slayed the hero."

"Is she cutting her teeth on those washboard abs or the chiseled jaw?" His hazel-colored eyes studied the cover of the book for a moment longer, and then my face at this closer position. "Sometimes men are willing to take a few hits to accomplish their goal."

"No fang sharpening, this is more of a linguistic fight-club beat down."

"Are you here for the book signing?"

"I'm one of the romance authors, but I also wrote a memoir."

"Romance." He groaned, as if romance was a dirty word; not the fun, filthy words one might whisper to turn on your partner, but a mythical word that existed outside of his frame of masculine reference. Examining his self-assured demeanor cozying up alongside me, I decided love was probably not part of his emotional quotient, unless it was self-love. "You can't loiter in the lobby bar."

"I bought a drink." I picked up my whiskey glass, and the giant ice cube clattered in the glass as I saluted him.

"Buy more," he suggested. "We like to see at least two per patron per hour."

"Did you learn that in bar management one-oh-one?" The cocktail waitress happened to be passing, and I caught her attention. She glanced at the man and cringed for an infinitesimal second—I guess he spread his prickiness around beyond the parameters of the patrons. "What can I get you?" she asked gripping her tray in front of herself as if it was a shield warding off frisky businessmen who thought ordering complicated cocktails might be considered foreplay.

Removing my shoes from the corner of the table, they had to skim his lap in order for me to get them under the table. I might have been a little more aggressive than necessary, making sure the thick heels found flesh at a couple of points. He grunted once but then chuckled deep in his throat. Once I planted my feet on the floor, I pulled away from the back of the booth as I assessed the confines of the dark bar. I pointed to a group of three young women in another booth. "Send them another round and give them these." I pulled three romance titles from my oversized tote, quickly autographed them, and handed them to the waitress. "You can bring me another Old-Fashioned, too, so I'll be over your boss's minimum." Turning toward him, I gave him my best fake smile, the one I reserved for intrusive assholes of the highest magnitude.

He settled against the plush velvet and raised his arm over the edge of the back of the booth right over my shoulders, as if settling in to wrap me up like a nightcap. "Bring me my regular, and put it on Miss …"

"Flame," I said to the waitress.

"Flame's room." He reached out with his other hand as if to brush his fingertips over the ends of my long, red hair right above my breast, but his hand stalled, dropped to the tabletop and he gripped the edge of the table instead. I felt my traitorous nipples go hard. "Is that where the flame comes from?" he asked, eyeing my hair.

"Flame is a nom de plume." The allure of his voice had me leaning toward the intimate caress, but something about the way he freely touched me made my hackles rise, so I drew away and hissed, "Meaning you're going down in flames."

His face transformed into something formidable when he cocked an eyebrow and angled his head. The curled edges of his lips indicated my challenge might have activated his hunter DNA. "Ms. Flame and I are only in the first quarter of what I expect to be a game for the record books," he scolded as the waitress scuttled away.

"Do you usually harass the clientele?" I asked, holding his direct gaze, which wasn't easy because of the predatory way he watched me as if I was a foregone conclusion to a string of nightly walks of shame from his penthouse to the lobby.

"Just the gorgeous ones who put themselves on full display."

Shuffling the pages of the book, I said, "I'm sure they're usually an easy score."

"I have been known to run with the ball, but I haven't even thrown my first pass yet."

"So the penthouse library wasn't an itty bitty pass?"

"There's nothing itty bitty about me." He laughed,

and my traitorous eyes went to his hands. My mind wandered to what those masculine but elegant hands would feel like exploring my body free-range style. "I like calling my own plays."

"Ex military?" I asked.

He laughed and adjusted the lapel on his blazer.

I tried again. "Ex cop?"

"Why would you think that?" he asked, picking at his shirt collar.

"You like rules and you need a uniform, the one you're wearing isn't comfortable." He chortled, but it had an edge to it, making me certain I was onto something. "Are you going to tell me who you are or do you like the man of mystery fantasy?"

"Hotel owner."

The wide shoulders, trimmed to perfection core, and cocky assuredness read more like state-of-the-art soldier of war or professional athlete, but I gave up checking out other men years ago because I had the man of my dreams. A sharp ache registered under my rib cage. These days I didn't check out men because it felt as if it was a betrayal to a beautiful memory that died way before its time.

The three young women in the booth across the way received their books and drinks, and they bounced in their seats before they searched the bar for me. They noticed him, the good-looking Black man practically overpowering me mentally and physically, and they tittered behind their hands.

"Adoring fans?" he asked me as the waitress sat our drinks down.

"Everyone can use a bit of hero worship." I picked up the stirrer from my drink and stuck the cocktail cherry in my mouth, pulling it off slowly. "In a world where there's very little real romance anymore we writers do what we can."

He took a sip of his coffee as the robust scent swirled around us. "Set up ridiculous expectations men have no desire to live up to?"

"Haven't been able to satisfy your woman?" I slid a copy of one of my romances in his direction. I wouldn't dream of sharing my memoir with him, he would pick it apart and have way too much advantage over me. "Read a romance and you'll leave all the ladies gratified."

"I don't need an instruction manual to satisfy a woman, I was built to do it." His phone buzzed, he pulled it out and examined the screen. "I have to take this."

When he connected the call was on speaker but he didn't move away for privacy. I raised an eyebrow and waited.

"Sweetheart," a woman's voice said, "wanted to check on your speech and make sure that you used the firehouse story?"

"I've got it all worked out, Mom. Thanks for the feedback."

"Everyone at CASA is excited to have you as keynote speaker."

"Looking forward to it." He glanced at me sideways. "Although, can I add a plus one?"

"Of course. Is it someone special?"

He chuckled, and it was a cross between mirth and malevolence. "Only time will tell. Got to go, Mom. Love you."

"Your mother is a court appointed special advocate for kids in the system?"

He ran his fingers up and down the handle of his coffee cup. "You know about CASA?"

"They have a big gala here in Chicago every year, I've attended." The keynote speaker was usually big time businessmen, but sometimes they had kids who grew up in the system speak and they were the ones who had people emptying their wallets.

He nodded his head but then his eyes went to my lips and he gave me a coy pout of his own. "Why don't you come up to my penthouse and point out the romances?" He took a sip of his coffee, which was about as stout as his posture but something about the abrupt change of subject rattled me … or maybe that was the strength of the whiskey. "You could curate a to-be-read pile for me."

"You don't strike me as the type of guy who has a library card, much less a library."

He fished around inside of his breast pocket, pulling out his wallet and laying it on the table between our drinks. "Want to wager on it?"

"What's the bet?" I asked, cautiously trying to calculate if he was a gambler doubling down or just cocky enough to try to con me.

"If I have a library card you come to my penthouse tonight and go with me to CASA next Saturday night."

I'd avoided recklessness my whole life, and long-term commitments for the past year and a half, but the liquor was relaxing my judgment because something deep inside of me screamed at me to take him up on both. *Do it.*

He thrummed the leather of his wallet with his fingertips, not in agitation, but perhaps anticipation. "If I don't, I'll comp your room and your bar tab."

"Seems like I don't have a lot to lose either way."

He shrugged, but his eyes strayed to the necklaces hanging between my breasts again and his gaze lingered there. "Maybe just your panties."

2

SEX WITH A STRANGER

RAND COLLINS

Of course the exquisite Flame took the wager and then proceeded to lose the bet. I didn't make wagers unless I knew they were a sure thing. It's one of the things my time in the American Football League taught me: don't gamble with your future. The league paid me out after a massive lawsuit, and now I had more money than Midas. My head was concussion free, unlike so many of the guys who gave all to the game, but the AFL had sleazed up my sterling reputation. At one point, I was the most hated Black man in football. I knelt for what was a righteous cause but that didn't always sit well with affluent owners. I didn't go out as an esteemed football legend in spite of it being my goal, the one I hoped would bring me the love and utter devotion I craved. However, I did exit the field as a proud Black man willing to play football as long as I could serve it with a side of social justice. My terms were non negotiable.

Flame trailed me off the elevator and over the zebra patterned carpet toward my door. She paused for a moment and glanced down at her shoes; one of the leather ties around her ankle had come undone.

Before she could fasten it, I dropped to my knees in front of her, fishing around her ankle for the leather cords.

338

"This flooring makes me dizzy," she said.

Laughing deep and throaty, I caressed her smooth skin and wrapped my hand around her ankle and squeezed. "That's not what's making you dizzy."

Flame reached out with one of her hands and measured the texture of the wallpaper in a sensual movement that reminded me of a dancer but seemed natural for her. "Well, it's not too much whiskey," she insisted. "Although all these patterns are supposed to rev you up." She quickly pulled her hand away from the wallpaper and pranced down the hall. "I especially like the retro vending machine mini bar in my room."

Ambling to my feet, I caught her in a few strides and directed her to my door by the small of her back. I swiped my key card over the lock and asked, "Have you tried the chilled condoms yet?"

She froze at the threshold and tossed a section of her pomegranate-colored hair over her shoulder, narrowed her green eyes, and pouted. "I was more interested in the wax lips."

Extending my hand, I asked for her permission to pull her into the suite. Then I closed the door behind her. Finally, alone in a private moment, I was eager to explore her body the way I had imagined from the first moment I saw her on a security camera. She'd waltzed through the lobby with that fiery hair that begged to be fisted in my hands as I rocked inside of the deepest recesses of her body. "Your lips are perfect, they don't need plumping."

"I'm here to examine your leather-bound romance section."

The thrill running through me made it impossible to drop her hand, so I twirled her so her body collided against mine. Anticipation flowed through my limbs and settled deep in my groin. "That red hair will be a perfect complement to the animal print robes."

She drew in a startled breath at the contact, the way her long dancer's frame met with my muscled, sturdy one, but she said half-heartedly, "I am not taking off my clothes."

"I can work within those confines," I whispered as I

brought her fingertips to my mouth. When my tongue grazed her fingers, her body jolted against mine.

She licked her bottom lip for an infinitesimal second before she glanced around at the lavish neutral interior. My private apartment was aesthetically different from the rest of the hotel, which was mostly black and white with splashes of red leather; there were belts, buckles, and the threat of bondage on every surface. "Show me your books," she whispered.

After removing my blazer, I took her tote off her shoulder and dropped them on the sofa on the way to the library. The bookcase lighting merged with the light radiating off the lakefront skyline, bathing the room in a soft blue haze. Flame went to the collection of first editions and examined them. She clenched and unclenched her fists at her side. "These are incredible."

Moving across the room, I went to my own mini bar. "Touch them," I whispered as I slipped the chilled packets into my pant's pocket.

Her hands rose in a tentative gesture, similar to how she touched the wallpaper, and I knew at some point in her life she'd been a dancer. Her lithe movements were that mesmerizing. "You've read all of these?"

"Every romance you've ever loved and a ton of classics."

She selected a book, opened it, and leaned her face into the pages. Her eyes fluttered closed for a moment before she glanced at me leaning on the glossy surface of the desk. "Why are you watching me like that?"

"I'm trying to decide whether to take you with the dress on or off the first time."

Her fingers traced the pages but she laughed nervously. "The first time?"

Standing to my full height, I tossed the chilled, metallic condom packets on the bare desktop in challenge. "We both know we didn't come here for the books."

She snapped the book shut and drew the bound

leather toward her breasts. "I don't like being a foregone conclusion."

I took a leisurely visual stroll up her body. "You need something I can give you."

"What's that?" she asked, taking a step closer to me.

"Release," I said seductively, my voice drawing her closer still.

"What do you get out of it?" she asked, standing on the other side of the desk so close but still too far to capture her lush mouth.

Reaching out, I wrapped my arm around the back of her neck, while my thumb caressed the fine skin under her ear. "I get to discover if you're as fiery as I've imagined since I saw your red hair streaming through my lobby like liquid fire."

"You're a voyeur."

"Not for just anybody." I pulled her torso over the desk, our mouths so close, but not quite touching. She inhaled a startled breath and then exhaled a seductive sigh right before we collided. Her lips were warm, soft, and tentative. I moved slowly, rhythmically, wanting to savor her. Feast on her outer beauty and the pain I sensed under the hard exterior. She was an ache forged in fire and this overwhelming desire pulled at me from the moment I first saw her.

While our tongues danced with each other, she climbed onto the desk to get closer, making it easy to tug her to my side and one step closer to the finish line. Our bodies rubbed against each other from thighs to mouths. My hands explored the length of her frame while she held onto me for dear life by my shirt collar. My fingertips skimmed up inside of the hem of her dress and over her taut thighs to the edge of her panties that I tugged on tentatively. "Let me undress you?" I panted against her ear.

"No," she hissed. "Hurry or I'll come to my senses."

Too far gone with lust to allow her escape, I maneuvered her down on her ass with a thump. She was insistent as she unbelted my pants, but before going for the zipper she ran her hand over the length of me through my slacks. She mewled a soft, urgent, "Please," as she reclined against the hard surface of the desk on her shoulders. I stripped her panties off and dropped them in my desk drawer. Rolling on the condom, the cool sensation tempered me and I resolved to make this good for her. I slowly stroked the length of her entrance with the tip of my cock a few times before slipping inside of her just a bit.

"Now." She arched her back.

She was so fucking hot and tight I'd need a Polar Vortex to cool the fever burning at the base of my spine. I moved to pull away a bit so she could adjust, but she wrapped her legs around my hips and drew me deeper. I grunted as the pleasure built.

"Sweet baby Jesus that's cold," she hissed.

Her words drew my attention to her wanton display, her wavy hair fanned around her head like a flaming halo. My hands moved from her hips to her torso where I peeled the sides of her dress apart farther so I could see the black, lacey bra that had teased me over coffee. Pushing her necklaces away, I peeled both cups down, revealing her perfectly pert nipples, the color a shade or so shy of her hair. I wanted those nipples in my mouth.

She put her hands over mine, guiding them to mold her breasts, as her whole body seemed to tremble in anticipation of my next caress. "But so hot at the same time."

Not moving deeper into her quite yet, giving her time to accommodate me, was torturous. I distracted myself from going all primitive caveman by scoring her nipples, they pebbled, and her response made me go harder.

She arched her back, offering me her supple body and flexing her hips so I slipped deeper, and then deeper still, until I was so deep I wasn't sure where she began and I ended. If she didn't stop clutching me like that I'd blow this play a yard shy of her end zone. Slipping my arms under her ass, I picked her up and sat down in my desk chair.

"Oh God, that's a lot," she strangled out as her

weight came down on me hard.

"You call the plays now, Flame." I took her nipple in my mouth and let my fingertips roam her thighs, making the tiny hairs stand on end. Then I examined the spot where we were joined.

Something about her seemed to break open with my words, and she thrust and panted like a wild women, coming down one final time on a scream that reverberated through me and made me come at the same time.

After several long moments she was able to catch her breath. "Sex with a stranger isn't all that bad," she whispered as she wiped at her eyes.

"You've never had a one-night stand?" I exhaled heavily.

"I've only slept with one man until now."

"Are you crying?" I asked, unable to conceal the real concern in my voice. "Did I hurt you?"

"No, I've been unfaithful to my husband."

Those words felt like a cold dagger in my back. The shock spilled out of me in a harsh question. "You're married?"

"Not any more." She swiped away the tears streaming down both her cheeks as I sat her back on the desk. "But I betrayed his memory."

Adjusting my pants and my he-man attitude, I said, "Let me get you some tissues." Slipping into the bathroom, I heard a soft keen of pain erupt in the other room. I dropped the clump of tissues in my hand and picked up the entire box, but when I stepped back into to the library she was gone. "Totally ran with the ball when I should have passed," I shouted to myself, followed by, "For fuck's sake," which echoed through the empty room.

3

SIGN ON THE DOTTED LINE

FLANNERY

Escaping to my room where I could empty my profound sorrow into my pillowcase was the only thing I could think to do after our encounter. I didn't want to pour my heart out to a stranger, especially to a casual-sex connoisseur. Everything about the way he moved, from unzipping his pants in a single, slow, confident stroke to the way his abs contracted with purpose when he thrust indicated that he had plenty of experience seducing women in the sack, or in this case on his desk and office chair. I'd never done immediate gratification before, and as reckless experiences went it was pretty fabulous. My room phone rang several times during the evening but I didn't answer it. I wasn't up for an awkward phone conversation about panty-melting sex with a complete stranger. *Where are my panties?*

The following morning I was eager to set up my table display at the book signing, glad that my reckless Lothario was only a classic romance fan so he'd stay far away. Once the event started, I lost myself in excited fans, autographs, and various male cover models who stopped by. One of which spent a considerable amount of time loitering at my table with some of his adoring fans. His handsome face and chiseled torso on the cover of one of my titles continued to pay dividends.

The book universe knew my tragic backstory, they

knew a man swept me off my feet because my memoir laid it all bare. Readers also knew the heartbreak that followed because the object of my bestselling memoir died while his inspiration still lingered on the bestseller's list. Many times I supposed the extra kindness I was shown was due to my personal tragedy.

The model, Dicky Schlongstocking, had changed his legal last name to Schlongstocking and his sexual appeal certainly helped make that particular romance title a bestseller. In between booklovers he flirted with me, and I'd felt myself go into a partial blush a couple of times but I wasn't falling into bed with a guy who'd capitalize on it the moment it was over with an Instagram post. I'd taken my risky shot with the beautiful Black man, and the guilt I felt gnawing in my gut told me the experience was a one and done.

Hearing a groan from the crowd lined up in front of my table, I searched in between the bodies of the two young women flirting with Dicky. There was a tall, wide-shouldered man setting up two brass stanchions with velvet ropes in front of the booklovers in my line.

"Um, excuse me," I called, getting to my feet and wondering why he was cordoning off my fans from me. "Who told you to do that?"

He turned on me. My Lothario with a library. One of his eyes twitched. I instinctively sat back down, pretty sure it was an angry eye twitch. I couldn't imagine what I'd done. Didn't Lotharios like it when their conquests got lost on their own? He turned back toward the women behind the rope, instructed them to stay put, and took up the distance between the velvet ropes and my table in three long strides. He bore down on Dicky, took the measure of the model, and very simply asked, "Who are you?"

"I'm Dicky, Dicky Schlongstocking."

I had to hand it to my hit-it-and-quit-it, he didn't burst out laughing the way I did the first time Isla told me the name, but he was quick witted. "You must work for Pornrub."

Dicky didn't comprehend the insult because he sat up a

little straighter. "You think I'm porn material?"

My Lothario angled his head in a clear warning gesture. "Hit the locker room."

Dicky, obviously not the brightest book on the romance shelf said, "Huh? Wait, aren't you—"

"Yes, I am," he said, pulling Schlongstocking to his feet by one of his beefy arms. "Pound the porn circuit, she's way above your pay grade."

Dicky leaned around him, cracked his thick neck, and searched my face as if deciding on how much of a fuss to put up so he could keep his macho-man card. I had no idea what this was all about, so I shrugged my shoulders. Lothario patted Dicky's back roughly, encouraging him to move faster, and as soon as Dicky was out from behind the table, he leaned his ass on the spot where Schlongstocking's forearms had been moments ago. "He's a meat head and too young for you," he growled.

"Since I'm only interested in his meat, then I'd like it young and tender." I cocked my head in challenge even as I watched the women behind the ropes titter in some sort of recognition that eluded me. "Isn't that what men are after?"

Then in the bright lights of the ballroom it dawned on me who *he* was. I was used to seeing him with a throwback fro that paid homage to the seventies Black Power Movement. "Oh my God, you're Rand Collins."

"The one and only." He tugged on the cuffs of his dress shirt so I could see the expensive cufflinks.

"You, you—" Realizing he was a professional football player, didn't make it any less preposterous to accuse him of performing a sexual act on me that I clearly enjoyed, so I snapped my mouth shut.

"Yes, I did, and I plan on doing it again," he replied matter-of-factly.

"You're in the AFL. Why are you running a hotel?"

"Did you miss the ruckus I caused when cops disrespected my brothers on the streets Monday through

Saturday after worshiping us in our uniforms on Sundays?" Rand crossed one ankle over his other in a relaxed stance.

"I tend to stay away from the news."

Rand tilted his head in my direction. "Either way, Pornrub's not rebound material."

"And you are?" I asked in equal parts exasperation and distraction as I observed the women standing along the red rope line; they were studying me as I nervously organized the piles of books. Rand had positioned himself with his back to our audience who wouldn't be able to see a single expression that flashed over his expressive face.

"At least satisfaction is guaranteed with an athlete."

"That's not what my sorority sisters said. Some of them tried multiple sports for a frame of reference."

He chuckled low and deep in his chest. "How'd the ballers stack up?"

"Notoriously at the bottom of the pack." I organized the markers into neat rows. "The table tennis team had incredibly high productivity ratios though."

He tugged on his earlobe. "Productivity ratios?"

"The female climax ratio was two to one." I laughed nervously when he thrust out his chest and clarified, "Must be the magical fingers."

"Finger placement is fundamental in football, too." He leaned in close so his minty breath washed my neckline. "And *my* fingers got you off."

The flush on my face went to DEFCON 2.

"You're not the kind of woman that has sex with a strange guy who's just in it to score." He cracked his neck, and I wasn't sure if that was a statement or a question he wanted me to answer.

"Um …" I said, buying time as I read the signs the women at the rope line were now holding up. The first sign read 'Rand Collin's smoking HOT!' and I had to drag my gaze away to survey the man who made me suddenly feel flustered, vulnerable, and exposed. "Why have you separated me from my fans?"

He glanced over his shoulder for a second and beamed at them with a megawatt smile, completely ignoring the *Love*

Actually signage before laser focusing on my boobs in my low cut sweater. "I'm *your* number one fan after last night."

I laughed nervously, unsure if he was making fun of me or flirting.

Rand's large hand covered mine as they nervously fidgeted with the markers. He strummed his fingertips over the back of my hand before he picked up my hand and brought it to his mouth, swiping my knuckle with a gentle kiss right below the thick, gold band that replaced my wedding ring. "Come back tonight. Stay longer."

One of the ladies at the ropes sighed dramatically. I read another sign: 'You've Got the Love Again'. I drew my eyes away from the unsteadying idea of anyone ever replacing the love and devotion I felt for Andy. Or for my unborn child. A stranger could never fill that gaping wound. "I have a book event tonight."

"The lingerie party in the lobby bar?"

"It's a pajama party," I insisted.

"My bad. I mean my bad imagination." He chuckled as if he knew more about this than I did, and he leaned in close to my ear. "Wear something sexy under your pajamas, I'll meet you in your room afterwards."

Turning to answer him, my jaw rubbed against his and all I could think about were our mouths touching. "Aren't you a hit-it-and-quit-it kind of Lothario?"

"I wasn't finished with you when you rushed off," he said, his lips hovering over mine.

Glancing up at him through my lashes, I bit into my bottom lip so I wouldn't lick them in anticipation. "The tears weren't enough to make you rethink an encore?"

He swiped his lips over mine, but when I instinctively responded his mouth delved deeper. Our audience twittered but he pulled away and said, "I plan on giving you a standing ovation every night."

The elevator opened at the lobby level, and I had to

waft my arms through the air to get the cigar smoke to clear. Rand tried to warn me that the party would be a lingerie party, but here I stood in the regretful floofy, pink-and-white footie bunny pajamas while many of the other partygoers were decked out in costumes ranging from Victoria Secret's Pink to the very scandalous Savage X Fenty. I considered reversing back into the elevator and ditching the party, but before I could kick myself into gear my best friend, and book publicist extraordinaire, slipped alongside of me.

"You clearly didn't read between the lines." Isla laughed and put a rock glass into my hand.

"Why didn't you tell me this was an actual lingerie party?" I slurped at the drink, which made me cough because it was ridiculously strong.

"You would be recoiling in your room if you'd gotten wind of how racy this regatta is." Isla cocked her fishnet stocking clad hip and drew me through the throng to the bar. "Even on the other side of the book signing I heard that the shockingly handsome Rand Collins was at your table and he kissed you in front of everyone. I'm miffed that you didn't text me."

Discarding the straw, I downed the rest of the whiskey, clinking my empty glass against hers before I said, "I screwed him on a desk chair last night so the kiss was hardly earth shattering."

"Crikey, my whorish ways are rubbing off on you," Isla said as her eyes wandered over the hot guy across the way in black satin boxers and a garish T-shirt with a cartoon version of a tuxedo printed on the front.

"You aren't whorish, you're just not afraid of doing whatever the hell you want."

"I found Mr. Saturday Night." Isla tossed her blonde curls over her shoulder and licked her strawberry lips for him before she turned and gave me her motherly scowl. "But since you've spent your adult life dedicated to a single man it might be revelatory."

"All that's left of that are shattered memories. I'm still a living, breathing woman."

Isla gave me a sad frown and she touched the fabric of

my costume. "This isn't worthy of your beauty." Her hand went for the zipper at my neck. "What in flamin' Hell do you have on under this?"

She probably expected the plain black cotton of mourning but it was hot pink ribbons, lace, and screamed bunny-humping bondage. She quickly zipped it back up, patted the zipper, and gave me a lurid once over. "Clearly the man fitter than a Mallee Bull has inspired you."

"I've got the flesh burns to prove it."

"The other authors I represent said he wouldn't even give them an exploratory once over." Isla sipped her drink, and then gave the tuxedo T-shirt guy a provocative pout. "I knew you'd bounce back at a book signing, but I'm impressed that you landed him. He's fucking Grade A stud material."

"I haven't landed him, it was an economy seat on a one-way flight."

"Did you crash land or fly to the heights of ecstasy?"

"He handles women like a football." I glanced around, feeling as if someone monitored me as I signaled the bartender for another whiskey. "Hard, fast, and in complete control. Leading to end zone elation."

Isla threw her arm around my shoulder and squeezed. "Andy wouldn't begrudge you a companion, even if it was just for sexual release."

"I feel like I betrayed his memory." I sipped my drink. "Andy wouldn't have liked Rand."

"Andy would have grounded anyone else you might have been attracted to." Isla adjusted her corset so that her boobs were on point. "You can't feel guilty for being alive."

"But—"

"You weren't meant to die. You paid a heavy enough price for an accident."

"Everything I used to do I did for Andy. Now I cheated on him and it's all because I got all hot and bothered over Rachel's book."

"Rachel's book made you do it?" Isla laughed out loud. Mr. Tuxedo Shirt noticed and started our way. "You've been avoiding this subject but it's time you wrote the follow-up to *You've Got the Love*."

"Nope, no more memoirs for me."

"You need to write it while it's still brutal for you."

"You're totally heartless." I tossed back some of the amber liquid.

"You've got to be strong enough to write this chapter of your life before you can put it away."

"I feel like I'm a ghost dancing over his grave."

"But you're not a ghost—you're a living, breathing woman and you have a right to your own Mr. Saturday Night."

"I don't have to start with someone who makes me scream out in ecstasy."

"*You've Got the Love* is at the very heart of who you are … your religion, deep down and forever. You can't turn your back on the kind of devotion you're capable of." Isla cocked her hip provocatively; however, it wasn't for me but the guy approaching us. "That memoir made your career, this one will make your life."

"Make my life miserable," I mumbled under my breath and turned away toward the bar so the guy would have a chance to deliver his come-on to an audience of one. While I was unable to hear his exact words, he had a deep, trancelike voice. Isla exclaimed something sultry after him as he stalked away.

"What'd you tell him?" I asked Isla when he was gone.

"Room number and expectations."

Expectations? Maybe I should have considered expectations. "So subtle."

"I don't want subtle, I want a no-strings-attached, mind-blowing sexcapade."

"It's hard to believe you sign sweet romance authors."

"Some writers are plain Jane's and they write erotic bondage bullshit, so I guess I'm leveling out the playing field because I like to play hard and fast but I sign the soft and sweet ones like you."

4

QUARTERBACK SNEAK

RAND

After checking on the book signing I returned to my office where I could keep one eye on the ballroom, from several different vantage points without breathing down Flame's throat. Stepping into the outer security office, I found Cyrus Fletch relaxed into one of the ergonomic chairs, his feet up on the counter, observing the cameras. "What a fucking player move," Fletch practically cackled, which could only mean he saw me in the ballroom.

Fletch was my sports agent; he'd signed me right out of college. Most agents would have dropped my ass cold when the AFL black balled me, but not Fletch. The cocky, redheaded bull was as angry as I was and he fought one brilliant legal battle against the AFL, which set me up for life. We're good friends and stuck with each other until one of us retires into obscurity.

"I do not require twenty-four seven monitoring." I folded the sports page in half and slipped it under my arm as I walked into my lavish inner office.

"When you asked me to run a background check I thought it was business related." Fletch stood on the other side of my desk with his hands on his hips, taking in the view and probably trying to take the temperature down. I thought for a second that his red paisley suspenders might actually ricochet off his chest since it was puffed out with condemnation. "Rule number one: never mix business and

353

pleasure."

"This is all about gratification, I assure you." I slipped into my leather office chair, an exact copy of the one Flame had rocked my world in a few floors up. I really wished it was her on the other side of the desk right now. Yeah, she'd give me a verbal throw down, but the pay out afterwards was spectacular. I was actually dizzy after our encounter and I might have drooled down the front of her dress.

Fletch balanced his six foot frame on his fists over my desk. "You don't have time for distractions, especially one as fucked up as she is."

"You saw her ... fistfuls of that fiery hair in my hands." I laughed at his scowl. "You never told me how sexy redheads are."

"I'm certainly not going to share shit about my wife, asshole." Fletch stood to his full height and he adjusted his bow tie. "Of course she's hot, I married her."

"Try not to sound so pleased about it." I picked up my remote and turned on a couple of the security screens and the two screens dedicated to my stock portfolio.

"I'm totally pleased with my wife but what I'm not pleased with is you getting sidetracked while we're trying to negotiate a deal to buy an AFL franchise."

"Do you ride Palowski's ass the way you ride mine?"

"Yes, Aidan's part of this deal, too." Fletch adjusted his pocket square before he went to his briefcase. "And the race car driver is also. Just so we're clear, I wouldn't have to babysit you or Luke if you didn't get speeding tickets for drag racing down Lake Shore Drive."

"Do you consider a Jaguar F Type and a BMW i8 Roadster drag racing?" I accepted the file Fletch handed me across the desk and took in the view of runners near Buckingham Fountain. "I can't believe the Jaguar beat me."

"It's all about the driver. Luke Marshall is a fucking Indy 500 Champion."

I cracked my neck because I still wasn't used to the idea that I'd never be the best of the best in my sport. I would never wear a Super Bowl ring ... of course there was always a chance that the AFL team we're bringing to Chicago could net us all a ring. Even Fletch who only played rugby for fun or Luke who drove cars fast in circles could benefit from a hunk of gold and diamond jewelry signifying our success. "What's fucked up about Flame?"

"She ended up in a roll over crash."

"Okay." I thought cautiously. *This might account for the dead husband.* "Was the accident her fault?"

"No, a semi jackknifed in front of her SUV, and then the car behind them sideswiped them and sent her SUV into a roll over." Fletch dropped his head and danced from foot to foot.

"Just tell me," I snapped.

"She was seven months pregnant." Fletch pulled his head up and rubbed his clean-shaven jawline. "Trapped in the vehicle."

"That's disturbing. Here in Chicago?" I questioned, afraid to even ask about the baby.

"Yes, on Lake Shore Drive within a couple of yards of where you got the ticket." Fletch fished around inside his briefcase again. "She doesn't write about what happened, even on her blog." He handed me a book. "They had to use the Jaws of Life to extract her, but she'd gone into labor by then. She lost her husband and the baby, so if that doesn't fuck with your head I don't know what would."

"She seems normal to me." I examined the cover of the book titled *You've Got the Love ~ A Memoir.* "When did the accident happen?"

"About nineteen months ago," Fletch grumbled. "Leave it alone, Rand. She's not the girl for anyone right now, maybe never."

"There's something about her that's going to make that impossible."

"What's so special about her?"

"She let me have my way with her and she didn't even know I have a Heisman."

"Immediately putting out makes her special?" Fletch played with the spikes of hair over his forehead. "I know you've got mommy issues but leave her alone."

"I don't have mommy issues, my adopted mom is great." Now the piece of white trash that gave birth to me at fifteen and dumped me at a fire station when I was five, she's a real piece of work. However, my Black adoptive mother is a saint.

"You have terrible taste in women. Remember your last girlfriend and the stories she sold to the tabloids when you lost your AFL contract?"

"Flame isn't a fortune hunter, and she has zero interest in being my sugar baby."

"Rand, I'm telling you, she's bad luck."

"That's stupid, you said the accident wasn't her fault."

"Did you know that the Ancient Egyptians considered redheads so unlucky that they sacrificed them?"

"The Romans thought red hair was lucky and they were sought after as slaves." I'd done a quick Internet search on all things with red hair. "It's probably why your line has survived this long. Unless it's because you're a vampire."

"Are you making fun of me?" Fletch grumbled. "I've been a redhead all my life."

"Are we talking discrimination here? 'Cause I was born black, dude," I grumbled back at him with the same tone. "Being black cost me a football career."

"No, your big mouth cost you the career." Fletch slipped his hands into his pant's pockets and rocked in his stance. "Remember when I advised you to leave that alone, too?"

"What else came up in the background check?"

"Everything looks good on paper. Financially

secure, well educated, she only carries a little debt—she's a bit of a shopaholic—but the only other weird thing is that she flies back and forth to Australia a lot."

"Any idea why?"

"Her husband was Australian, he was some golf savant but he came to the U.S. for college, met her, and it seems like she was the love of his life."

"What was the husband like?"

"Stud with a capital S."

"What does that mean?"

"It means he won almost every single golf tournament he ever played in. He was blond, buff, and quite frankly beautiful." Fletch buckled his briefcase and picked it up. "You can't hold a candle, player."

"Fuck you, Fletch. I'm beautiful, too."

"She's used to a guy worshiping her. You're many steps removed from the kind of dedication a woman like her needs, especially with what she's been through."

"Are you saying I'm not sensitive enough?"

"I've known you since you were in college, and if you have an understanding side I've sure as fuck never seen it."

"Rock hard jock on the outside." I pounded on the center of my chest for emphasis. "Soft, gooey center that cries at rom coms and weddings."

"Don't even think about the word marriage without a prenuptial agreement."

"I'm never marrying a woman I'd need a prenup with." I laughed at the dirty look he shot at me but I don't think he believed me, even though I was being one hundred percent honest with him.

"What is it with you jocks? The instant you fall in love your brains seep out of your dicks."

"Once we're in the red zone, we can't stop ourselves from running up the score."

5

YOU GIVE THE LOVE YOU HAVE

FLAME

Isla, Rachel, myself, and another friend left the party shortly after the entertainment ended. Dicky Schlongstocking lived up to his name, performing a raunchy dance that left little to the imagination but gave me zero inspiration. I stumbled into my room because we were all still drunk laughing at the model's *Magic Mike* moment while imagining Mr.-Don't-Have-Your-Feet-On-The-Table's reaction to their dicks flapping on his bar. Flicking on the light switch I froze. Isla and the other girls bum rushed into me from behind, so I landed on my knees at the foot of the bed.

There was a gorgeous, naked man standing in front of the window with his hands on his hips and his back to me. It took my mind several seconds to catch up to *who* stood in my room sculpted with the masculine authority of *The David*. The entirety of his back was covered in a tattoo of angels and demons in a classic good versus evil smackdown.

Isla said, "This is one hell of an encore."

Rand cracked his neck and must have wondered if I told Isla about our previous conversation. Scrambling to my feet, I moved toward the closet. I had no idea Rand would be waiting for me in my room. Sure he said it, but I figured he'd show up later for a booty call not a buck-naked free for all.

Rand flexed his buttock muscles before he slowly turned on us with both his hands over his equipment. If my tender insides were any judge of proportions then he'd need both hands to keep himself covered. "Ladies," he said in a low, seductive voice before he took me in from head to toe. "That's one flaming hot bunny suit."

"You might have tried a little harder to convince me that it wasn't a pajama party." I crossed my arms over my middle.

"Why would I want to share your lingerie with a crowd?" He beamed at my friends with a cocky grin. "Did you ladies enjoy the show?"

"Clearly Schlongstocking is not as impressive as this one," Isla said, "but we had to come back early 'cause Flannery is on the piss."

Rand's eyebrows drew together, and I explained Isla's Australian slang. "She's trying to say I'm drunk, but I'm not."

"What are you doing in Flannery's room?" Isla asked, taking another leisurely stroll up his body from his toes— she loitered in the thigh area for quite a while.

Her exploration gave me time to make out the scrolled letters of the tattoo on his pecks. *My blessing, my curse.*

"Planning a romantic rendezvous." He chuckled malevolently and pointed toward me with his elbow. "I just need to peel her out of that bunny suit."

"Step one of your romance plan is get naked?" I snapped as I reached in the closet for the hotel's leopard print robe. I threw it at him.

He watched the exotic fabric slide down his body as if he was totally okay with being cock-in-hands naked for an audience, and when he pulled his head up his eyes searched my face. "You want to give me a hand?" he asked of me.

"Yeah, 'cause her Mr. Saturday Night's other ones are fully occupied." Isla laughed. When I glared at her, she yawned dramatically and shoved our other friends toward the door. "We're all knackered." Our friends weren't down with exiting the show because they fought her all the way to the door. Isla practically shoved them into the hallway.

"What were you thinking?" I asked Rand as the door

lock clicked.

He let his equipment go, and my traitorous eyes watched him pick up the robe before he slipped it over his shoulders; it was too tight and too short for his frame. "I thought I'd cut to the chase."

In a huff, I crossed my arms over my middle. "I've never been a foregone conclusion before I met you."

"You want to talk first, I'm open to that." He sat down on my bed, leaned against the headboard, and made absolutely no move to cover his pert appendages as he patted the spot alongside him. "I have lots of questions."

I slouched on the end of the bed facing him. "About what?"

He adjusted one of the pillows behind his back. "About the scar you have right over your pelvic bone."

My eyes flew to his. I could tell by his grim expression he already knew most of my sad story. I couldn't understand what he thought he'd get out of knowing the gory details. "You don't need that information for a weekend fling."

"Who said it's a fling?"

"It's certainly not how a forever starts."

Rand examined my face. "Maybe you did something reckless to prove you're still alive."

"Maybe I did it to prove I'm not worth living," I snapped back.

"Why?" he asked in a sharp tone. "Because we were hot and bothered for one another and we rocked each other's world?"

"All within an hour of meeting each other … it's got to be forty yards in four point three seconds."

"I saw you the day before so you were on a twenty-four hour clock."

"And what exactly did you want?"

"I wanted to know if that lithe body could light up my world." He gave me a tentative smile. "And now I want you to tell me what you've lost, so we can move past the imaginary wall you've put up between us and pick up where we left off last night."

"You want my deepest darkest?"

"You'd prefer I go first? Fine." He indicated the spot on the bed next to him. "At least sit alongside me while I confess."

He sat perfectly still waiting for me to move, to accept what he offered or deny him. Of course when he spilled his guts he'd expect me to spill mine, too. Rand played by the rules; he'd blown up his life for what he thought was a righteous cause and he'd demand honesty. I couldn't fault him on that. I crawled up the bed and mirrored his position.

"Any desire to take off the footy pajamas before I tell you?" he asked. "Strictly for motivation's sake."

"Trust me," I gave him a little pout, "if I take off these pajamas you will be completely distracted."

"Sexy?" He laughed out loud when I batted my lashes. "Did you wear it for me?"

I shrugged noncommittally. "I certainly wasn't putting out for Schlongstocking."

Rand scratched the hair on his chin. "You've probably figured out what happened in the AFL already, so we don't need to go into that, but what happened before that is relevant. So is what happened afterwards."

"Which is?" I asked.

"I'm not all black. My birth mom was white, or part white, I'm not really sure. I don't remember her that well. She had me when she was fifteen and she tried to keep me, but by the time I was five she abandoned me at a firehouse."

"I'm sorry."

"That's not the horrible part. The shitty part is she tried to sell me for money for drugs before she dropped me off at the firehouse."

"No mother could be capable of that."

"You mean *you* would have never been that kind of mother."

"I won't be any kind of mother." I frowned. "I can't have children."

"Because of the accident and the jagged scar?"

361

"They tried to perform a C-section while I was still trapped."

Rand's head pivoted toward me in a flash and his eye twitched. I thought it was an angry eye twitch, but now I realized it signaled concern. "Without anesthesia?"

"I was trapped. I begged them to do it to save the baby. I knew Andy was already dead." I fiddled with the zipper on my pajamas. "I wanted to be with him."

Rand let slow seconds tick off. I wondered if my truth about wanting to die in an incredible moment of pain would send him packing, but instead he said, "I read your book, the memoir."

"And you still decided to stand in my room au natural?"

"I'm here, I can remind you that you're still alive." He exhaled a heavy breath. "If you let me I can give you the love you need right now."

"Maybe I don't want what I can have right now, maybe I still want what I had."

"If I'm lucky I can make you rejoice at still being alive. What you make out of what's left has always been up to you."

"This isn't changing careers after a set back." I felt the tears rising behind my eyes. "All I ever wanted was to be a wife and mother."

"All I ever wanted was to be a Super Bowl champion." Rand sighed. "I know those aren't equal. That people are more important than rings and awards."

"It's highly unlikely that I'll ever be a mother, so that's a forever loss."

"Somewhere there's a scared five-year-old kid at a firehouse who probably needs you."

I frowned, maybe I'd become so absorbed with my losses that I stopped seeing life's possibilities.

"The way your book reads it seems like you think Andy's love made you."

"Don't great loves transform people?"

"I'm unsure. I haven't had a great love yet." Rand hesitated, and then he expelled a heavy sigh. "Perhaps he did transform you with his love, but maybe now you're supposed to transform me with it."

"I only learned your name this morning," I grumbled out loud in spite of the pain and the tears streaming down my face. "Why would you need my love anyway?"

Rand moved to touch my hand, but I pulled away. He folded his arms behind his head, leaned against them in the pillows, and examined the ceiling. "You're the first woman in my life who ever shared herself with me without knowing a single one of my accolades. The first, the only."

"You have other accolades?"

"Flame, I won the Heisman in college."

"I'm assuming your last girlfriend, the one who spilled her guts in *US Weekly*, was a gold digger."

"She played for the gold posts."

"My blessing, my curse," I mumbled the words tattooed across his chest out loud. "I guess that means that your gift of jock extraordinaire has also jinxed you."

"Same for you right?" he asked, unthreading his arms and leaning in alongside me. "You wrote that memoir about a once in a lifetime love and then it vanished. Makes you almost believe there's a price to be paid, but I don't believe in a vengeful universe."

"The fact that you've thought about how you fit into the universe means you're more enlightened than I ever imagined."

"You thought I was eager to score." He took a deep breath and almost whispered the rest of his thought. "But maybe I'm in the final play of the most important game of my life."

I was done fighting him so I leaned my head on his shoulder and took the comfort I knew he could give me. "Maybe you do need the love I have to give," I whispered reverently as I picked up his hand and threaded our fingers together.

YOU'VE GOT THE LOVE

THE END

ABOUT THE AUTHOR

Windy city writer, Elizabeth Marx, brings cosmopolitan life alive in her fiction — a blend of romance, fast-paced Chicago living, and a sprinkle of magical realism. Elizabeth resides with her husband and a crazy Aussie named Indiana Jones. She grew up in the city, has traveled extensively, and still says there's no town like Chi town.

You can visit her website www.elizabethmarxbooks.com or http://www.facebook.com/AuthorElizabethMarx

Contact the author at elizabethmarxbooks@gmail.com

Other books in the Chicago Sports Series

CUTTERS VS. JOCKS, BOOK 1

Cutters versus jocks. Small town girl versus big man on campus. Love at first sight versus lust you can't fight.Can anyone win when you don't play your heart out?

https://books2read.com/u/mdnRlR

BINDING ARBITRATION, BOOK 2

Through the corridors of the Windy City's criminal courts, single mother Libby Tucker knows exactly how far she'll go to save her cancer-stricken son's life. The undefeated defense attorney is prepared to fight, but the cost of this victory requires revisiting old heartaches. Can Libby win the battle to save her son without sacrificing her own heart?

https://books2read.com/u/3n8AWx

SIGNING BONUS, BOOK 3

She's the Master of Many Trades. He's thinking she has the skill set he needs just by being female. She'll land him and the signing bonus.
Sometimes what happens in Vegas doesn't end in Vegas.

https://books2read.com/u/47l0XA

MY LOVE, MY LIFE, YOU

By: Janet A. Mota

Chapter 1

Nicki

My phone dings from my night table as I open my eyes to start a new day. It has been a week, and I smile when I realize it is Friday. I know it's my daily morning text from Marcus. Marcus is my best friend. We met in college and hit it off from the moment we met. We both were studying Business Management and shared many classes. We have guided each other through some tough times in our lives. I can't imagine my life without him. A couple of years ago, Marcus was in a bad motorcycle accident. He was injured badly and thankfully he mended quickly and without any lasting effects. It scared me. I never thought I would have to face losing him. It made me realize that my feelings for him go beyond friendship. I love him. I'm in love with him. Unfortunately, my fear of losing him paralyzes me from telling him how I feel. I try not to think about it and check my phone.

Marcus: Good morning. Wishing you a great day.

Me: Good morning. I hope you have a great day too.

Thirty minutes later I am showered, dressed, and pouring coffee into my mug while my bread finishes in the toaster. I pull the bowl of fruit and butter from the refrigerator and prepare my breakfast while watching the news. What a depressing state of events our world is in right now. I turn off the TV, finish my breakfast, and head to work. I work for a Fortune 500 company in downtown Orlando. I have been working for this company since I graduated and have worked my way up to being head of Business Relations. I love my job and the company I work for.

****

Marcus

I need a break. I have been putting out fires all day and need to step away from it all for a moment. Business is booming and I'm happy about that. Some days I wish I wasn't the boss and didn't have ten million questions thrown at me a day. Some days I don't want to be responsible for major decisions in the corporation. But I love my job, and I'm very proud of the work that I do. I'm the vice president of a corporation that builds and distributes medical equipment to hospitals and doctor's offices all over the country and around the world. I started working for them a year after college and have worked my way up to VP.

I step away and head downstairs to the small café. I place an order for a dozen muffins and a power smoothie. Coffee isn't cutting it today. While I wait for my order, I pull out my phone and text Nicki.

Me: Hey. How's your day going?

Nicki: Crazy today. You?

Me: Same. How about dinner tonight?

Nicki: Sounds good. Where?

Me: My place. 7 good?

Nicki: See you then.

I smile and put my phone back into my pocket. Nicki always makes me smile. She's the one person I can always count on. She recently broke up with a guy she was dating. That guy hated me. I have no idea why, and Nicki refused to stop hanging with me. That caused a rift in the relationship. Nicki made it clear that she would always choose me. As much as I hate that her relationship failed because of me, it made me feel good to know that she would never let anything, or anyone, ruin our friendship.

The problem is I feel more than friendship toward her.

I've felt more for her for years. I finally opened up to my family about it, and they agree that I should tell her. They all love her. She's been around my family for years and they consider her a part of the family already. When I told them how I feel, my mother started crying and said she couldn't have picked anyone better. My dad smiled and said, "Tell her, son." My grandmother just nodded at me, but she didn't say anything. So I decided that I'm going to tell her tonight. I need to tell her everything and can't keep this from her. The what-ifs keep eating at me. What if she feels the same? What if she finds out later and gets mad that I never said anything? What if she falls in love with someone else and I lose my chance? I just hope that she takes the news well.

You see, a few years ago, I was in a motorcycle accident. It left me in bad shape. I had a major injury to my spine, and I couldn't walk. The doctors said that I could walk again with a lot of hard work. I was terrified of that never happening. A few times I lost confidence in myself and wanted to give up. Nicki was there every step of the way. She even took leave from work to help me. She helped me with my therapy and was my support system when the therapist was working with me. I fell in love with her then. I want her next to me for the rest of my life.

Chapter 2

Nicki

I don't bother going home since Marcus' apartment is two blocks from my office. I live twenty minutes away. It's not worth it. So I decide to work a little late. On the way, I stop at the bakery and pick up some chocolate-covered strawberries for dessert. They are his favorite. Within minutes, I'm ringing the doorbell. Marcus answers the door wearing an apron. I can't help but think how hot he looks wearing it. Marcus is gorgeous in whatever he wears but that apron gets me every time. He's a six-foot-two black man with green eyes and a muscular build. Women flock to him. Beyond that, he has the biggest heart. He's compassionate, loyal, loving, and selfless. He's the perfect package. Any woman would be lucky to have him by her side. I hope he'll be by my side. I do.

"Hey, come on in." He kisses my cheek. "You look great, as usual." I smile.

"It smells amazing in here," I tell him and hand him the box with the strawberries.

"I made your favorite." He winks and I follow him into the kitchen. "Is this what I think it is?"

"It is. You made spaghetti?"

"I did. I know it's basic and nothing impressive," he responds.

"Stop it. You made my favorite and I can't wait to eat it." He smiles wide and opens the oven. He pulls out a tray of garlic bread and my mouth waters. "Oh, wow."

"Ready to eat?" he asks.

"So ready." He laughs and follows me to the table with the bowl of spaghetti. A minute later he comes back with the breadbasket. He takes the seat across from me and tells me to dig in. We make our plates and talk about our day. Dinner is delicious.

***

An hour later, I'm loading the dishwasher. Marcus insists that I go relax, but he cooked so I clean. He's picking out something to watch on television.

"Do you want to watch a movie or start a series?" he asks as he walks into the kitchen. He grabs popcorn and puts it in the microwave.

"Either. Doesn't matter to me." I put the last of the dishes into the dishwasher.

"I wanted to talk to you about something before we get started with the television. Do you mind if we talk for a few minutes?"

"Of course." I look up at him. "Are you okay?"

"Oh, yes, I'm fine."

"I'm going to wipe everything down and will be there in a few minutes." Marcus nods, grabs the popcorn out of the microwave, and pours it into a bowl. I finish up quickly and head into the living room. Marcus is sitting on one end of the couch, a bowl of popcorn on the middle cushion. He smiles at me as I walk into the living room. I sit, slip off my shoes, and tuck my feet under me as I face him.

"What's up?"

"I have a confession. I've been wanting to confess for some time, but I don't know the best way to tell you this so I'm just going to say it." He takes a deep breath and I'm holding mine. "I have feelings for you."

I stare at him for a minute. *Did he just say that? No, my mind is playing tricks on me.* My heart is racing and feels like it's going to break right out of my chest.

"Say something," he urges. His eyes are pleading

with mine.

"Did you just say you have feelings for me?" I ask, still in shock.

"Yes." I start laughing because I don't know what else to do. I start to laugh so hard tears fall from my eyes. "I don't think it's very funny."

"Yes, it is."

"Why is it so funny?"

I compose myself and look at him. I can't wipe the smile from my face. Marcus doesn't think any of this is funny, and I can't blame him. He must be mortified with my reaction. Well, he's about to find out how funny it is.

"It's funny for two reasons. One, I was going to tell you that I had feelings for you very soon too. Second, I'm so excited and happy that you feel the same way. I've been harboring these feelings for so long. It's a relief that you finally know." I sober and look at him. "I was so scared to tell you. I thought our friendship would be over. My heart couldn't bear it, so I kept my feelings bottled up. I recently decided I couldn't keep it locked up anymore."

Marcus stands and reaches for my hands. I put my hands in his and he helps me up. He looks me in the eyes and asks, "Can we do this?"

"I think so. I want to try," I whisper.

"Me, too." He lets go of my hands and gathers me to him. He envelops me and a calm comes over me. Marcus feels for me the way I feel for him. No more wondering what could be. We are going to try this out. I close my eyes and inhale his scent. His scent has always brought me to a calm place. Knowing he will be by my side as a partner makes my heart soar. I pull away and look up at him.

"I'm scared," I confess.

"Me, too, but we need to do this. I don't want to have regrets." I reach for his hand and bring it to my lips. I kiss his palm.

"I'm ready."

Chapter 3

Marcus

After we calm down, we sit to watch a movie. I can't tell you what movie is on. My mind is reeling from what we both just shared and decided. Telling Nicki about my feelings has weighed on my mind for a long time and finding out she feels the same is mind-blowing. I prayed I would get that reaction, but I admit I was shocked to hear it. I thought she was going to get angry or tell me it couldn't happen. When she started laughing, I didn't know what to think. It felt like getting sucker-punched in the stomach. I was certain she was going to reject me and tell me to stop being crazy. I expected her to tell me to never utter those words again. When she stopped laughing and said she felt the same, I thought my heart would burst.

"I can't concentrate on the movie. I don't know what we're watching," she says as she stares at the television.

"Me neither." She picks up the remote and turns off the TV. She turns on the couch to face me and places the bowl of popcorn in her lap.

"Tell me when you first realized you wanted more with me. I want all of this out in the open. I want to know if you've told your family how you feel. I want to know it all and I'll reciprocate."

For the next couple of hours, we share our stories. We put everything out in the open but one thing.

"Are you sure you want to deal with the

controversy of dating a black man?" I ask. I hope she's thought this through.

"I know there will be people that don't agree with our choices, but I don't give a damn what they think. I want to be with you. I will always stand by you and I think we'll make a great team. Are you having issues with dating a white woman?" The look in her eyes nearly breaks me. I can see she's worried.

"I think we're going to have our challenges, but I think we can get through them as a united front. There will always be racism, but I'm hoping we can set an example. The color of our skin doesn't mean anything. I would be proud to have you by my side. There is no one else in the world I would rather battle with." She smiles wide and leans into me.

"Kiss me." I place my hands on her face and lean into her. My lips brush hers very lightly. Her breath is shallow, and her eyes are closed. I don't hold back. My mouth comes down on hers. I run my tongue along the seam of her lips, and she opens for me. My tongue meets hers. I feast, devour and taste her. She's sweet, and her sweetness is something I'll always want. It's a slow and sensual meeting. I'm completely addicted. As long as I live, I'll never forget this kiss.

I pull away slowly and watch as she opens her eyes. "Wow," she says as she places a hand to her lips. "That was the most amazing kiss I've ever had." I smile and place light, tender kisses all over her face. "I need to go."

"Why?" I ask as I continue kissing her face.

"Because if I don't, we will end up in your bed," she whispers.

"What's wrong with that?" I stop kissing her and look into her eyes.

"Let's not rush this. I don't want to ruin it before it starts. I want it to be the right time." Her eyes search mine and I smile.

"You're right."

She stands abruptly and heads toward the door. She picks up her bag from the foyer table and opens the front door. "Thank you so much for dinner and tonight."

"The pleasure was all mine." I wink at her and she stares.

"You don't play fair." She opens the door, rushes out, and slams the door behind her. I can't help but laugh.

Chapter 4

Nicki

Marcus will be here to pick me up any minute. We do Sunday brunch once a month, but this time feels different. This is our first official outing as a couple. I haven't been able to get this goofy smile off my face. I haven't seen him since Friday night, and I'm dying to see his gorgeous face. I need to be sure nothing has changed. He already had some appointments yesterday, so we decided to get together this morning. I've missed him. I always miss him when we're not together.

I stop pacing when the knock on the door startles me. I check my reflection in the mirror as I walk to the door. I take a deep breath and open the door. Marcus is standing there in jeans and a black polo shirt. This man is all kinds of sexy. My eyes take him in, and he licks his lips. Before I have a chance to say hello, he takes my mouth. His kisses make my knees buckle. His arm circles my waist and brings me close to his body. I melt into him. His taste is intoxicating. He breaks the kiss and I slowly open my eyes.

"Good morning," he breathes.

"Hi," I croak out.

"I've been dying to do that again. I hope it was okay." Marcus' shy side appears and it's adorable.

"You can do that any time you want."

"Good. Kissing you has become something I can't go without," he says as I close the door behind me. I quickly lock the door and we head toward his car.

"Me, too."

***

Sunday dinner is a tradition for the Thomas family. I have joined them numerous times but tonight I'm extremely nervous. Being Marcus' friend is completely different than being his girlfriend. Marcus told me his family is happy about us, but I still wonder. He has plenty of black women to choose from, but he picked a white one. I wonder if it makes his family unhappy. I would never want to make them uncomfortable or put them in a position where they need to defend me all the time. I don't want that.

"Are you sure your family is okay with this?" I ask, gesturing between us.

"Yes. Why wouldn't they be?"

"I need to be sure. I love your family as if they're my own. I couldn't bear it if something caused them to hate me," I confess. Marcus glances my way and pulls the car over to the side of the road. I'm staring straight ahead, and my mind keeps picturing all the worst-case scenarios.

"Look at me," Marcus instructs, and I do. "My family has known for some time how I feel about you. They were the ones who pushed me to tell you. They're thrilled. They love you and already see you as a part of our family."

"Okay," I say and take a hold of his hand. He kisses my hand and pulls back on the road. Five minutes later, we turn into his parents' driveway. We climb out of the car and head toward the front door. As we approach, the door opens and Mrs. Thomas appears. Her arms are extended.

"My sweet girl." Her arms wrap around me in the warmest hug. "I'm so happy you're here."

"I appreciate the invitation, as always," I tell her as we break apart.

"Sweetheart, you never need an invitation." Marcus

kisses her cheek and we follow her into the house.

.

Chapter 5

Marcus

Dinner was delicious, as usual. Momma brings out her famous chocolate cake and we all dig in. Nobody makes a chocolate cake like her. She has a secret ingredient she doesn't share with anyone. I wonder who she will pass the famous recipe to since I'm the worst baker on the planet. Maybe she'll give it to Nicki. I hope she does. I don't have any siblings, so she'll have to give it to her future daughter-in-law. I plan on marrying Nicki.

"Nicki, you've been very quiet this evening. Are you doin' okay?" my dad asks her. Nicki slowly puts her fork down and wipes her mouth.

"I have something weighing on my mind," she responds.

"Let's hear it," Dad coaxes.

"Marcus told me he spoke to all of you regarding his feelings for me." She looks around the table as she says this.

"He did," Momma states.

"He also told me you were okay with us being in a relationship. I just need to be sure. I need to hear how you feel about it." She looks around, reading everyone's expressions.

"You, my dear, are an extraordinary human being. You love with every part of you. You have an enormous heart and you allow everyone in. You are also one of the most intelligent people I've enjoyed conversing with.

MY LOVE, MY LIFE, YOU

My grandson is a smart man. He couldn't have made a better choice by picking you to be by his side," Grandma said. When she speaks, everyone stops talking and listens. "I'm not saying it'll be easy. I'm saying that if anyone can handle it, it's the two of you. You're going to come across a lot of ugly and it won't be an easy pill to swallow. Some people will embrace you as a couple and some people will try to break you. That's just how it is. You have made it this far with a strong and solid friendship. I've seen you stand up for us and never let anyone break the bond. I believe you are a perfect fit for Marcus. We love you and are so happy Marcus finally told you how he feels. We are even more thrilled you feel the same."

Nicki has tears falling down her face as she stands. She goes to my grandma and hugs her. "I love you."

Grandma rubs Nicki's back as she hugs her tightly. Momma is crying and Dad is taking the whole scene in. Nicki pulls away and kneels in front of Grandma. "I promise I will always honor and defend Marcus. He's my everything. He always has been." Grandma pat's Nicki's cheek and smiles. Nicki stands and comes back to her chair.

"When Marcus was in the accident, you were by his side day and night. No one could get you to leave his side. You have been at every important incident in Marcus' life. I have no doubt you'll stand by my son," Momma chimed in.

"When you first started coming around, I was afraid we had to be sensitive to you. I was afraid to introduce you to our customs and traditions because I thought you wouldn't be receptive to them. You never did. You love hearing the stories, sharing our traditions, and taking part in them. I don't know where this relationship will lead, but I'm confident that if you marry my son you will carry on our traditions for my grandchildren," Dad said.

Tears pour down Nicki's face now. She stands quickly and embraces Momma and Dad. She needed this from them and I'm so glad they understood that she needed it.

Chapter 6

Marcus

An hour later, I'm walking Nicki to her apartment door. She hasn't said much on the ride. I let her have her time. I know she needs to ponder what was discussed at dinner. It's part of why I love her so much. She never does things or acts on a whim. She makes sure to think everything through. When she decides, she sticks to it. She's amazing like that.

We reach her door and she unlocks it. She doesn't say a word, just grabs my hand and tugs me inside. She closes the door behind us, pushes me up against the adjacent wall, and slams her lips to mine. Her kiss is hungry and possessive. I get lost in the kiss quickly. The feelings she elicits with just a kiss has me burning for her. One of my hands finds its way into her long, lush hair. My other hand wraps around her waist and brings her closer. I know she can feel how much I want her. The moan she releases makes me crazy and I kiss her deeper. Her hands find their way under my shirt and to the flesh of my stomach. The feel of her hands on my skin is incredible. I'm about to pick her up and head to the bedroom when I realize she may not be ready for that. It's like a bucket of cold water was poured over my head. I pull away suddenly and she looks stunned.

"What's wrong? Why did you stop?" She's trying to catch her breath.

"I was about to lose all control," I say.

"I wasn't objecting," she mutters, and I pull her into

me.

"I want you more than anything. I just want to be sure you're ready. We just now decided to start dating, and I don't want to rush anything." I run my hand along her cheek, and she turns her face into it.

"I've wanted to be with you for years. I think we've waited long enough." The want and need in her eyes have me rethinking the decision to stop.

"You're right, but what if we jump in too fast?"

"I don't think there is such a thing as too fast for us." She smiles and I lead her to the couch. We sit and I turn on the television. The movie "*The Hitman's Bodyguard*" is on, and we start watching it. It's our favorite movie.

Nicki scoots over on the couch. She lays her head on my shoulder as we watch the movie. I look over at her and she's watching me. She smiles and I lean in and peck her lips. I do it again and she grabs my face to keep me in place. The kiss grows deeper and hotter. Before I know it, she's straddling my lap and we are deep into a make-out session. Kissing this woman has become my favorite thing to do. I can't get enough of her. The heat coming from her body is making me crazy, and I want all of her.

"Baby, we're getting carried away again," I say.

"You're right." She climbs off my lap and I immediately miss her heat.

"I promise we'll be together soon. Let's just give our relationship a little more time," I say, and she nods.

"Okay," she says, and walks into the kitchen. I watch her retreating and immediately regret stopping. I've been dying to get my hands on that delectable ass. I finally have her and put the brakes on it. I must be losing my mind.

Chapter 7

Nicki

It's been two weeks since we've started dating. It's been an amazing two weeks. My love for Marcus grows every day. He's a wonderful man and I'm lucky he picked me. I never wonder what he's thinking or how he's feeling. He's the perfect boyfriend, and many of my friends have shared how rare it is. He shares himself with me in every way but the one way I've been wanting for years. I know why he's putting the brakes on sex and I understand, but I don't want to wait anymore. He doesn't want sex to be all our relationship is built on. It certainly won't be because we have spent the last ten years by each other's side. He knows everything about me, and I know him. We have been there for each other in both the good times and bad.

Right now, I'm at my dad's house, doing my weekly cleaning. My mom passed away when I was seven and Dad raised me all alone. He was such a great dad. He worked hard and provided everything I needed. He couldn't afford much but there was never a lack of food or love. He hasn't been doing very well lately. He was recently diagnosed with a mild heart condition that makes him very tired. I've been coming over twice a week to do his laundry and to clean the house. Dad hates it but I come over anyway. He needs help, and I'm happy I can do it for him. He's done so much for me over the years and it's the least I can do.

I'm finishing up in the kitchen when Dad walks in.

"Are you almost done?" he asks.

"Yes. Why are you in such a hurry to get rid of me?"

"I'm not. You have your own life to deal with and you don't need to fuss over me." He huffs as he makes his way to the refrigerator. He pulls out a beer and I place my hands on my hips.

"Dad, don't you think you should stop with the beer?"

"No, I don't, and the doctor didn't say anything about it. One or two beers every once in a while, never killed anyone." He pulls out a chair at the table and sits. I join him.

"Okay fine, I won't bother you about it again." I smile and he pats my hand.

"How are things between you and Marcus?" he asks, a huge smile on his face.

"They're great. I'm so happy we decided to tell each other how we felt. It was weighing on me."

"As soon as I met Marcus, I knew he was the one for you. The way he looked at you made me so happy. I knew he would be there for you through it all. He looks at you like you hung the moon, sweetheart. He's a good man." I smile. My dad has always loved Marcus. Marcus feels the same way about him. The two of them completely upgraded this house a few years ago. Dad wanted to do it and Marcus refused to let him do it alone. When Marcus had the accident, my dad felt it like it was his own son. "You know, when he was in the hospital, I was so afraid for you. I was so afraid you were going to lose him without the love I know the two of you could have together. Your mom and I were so happy. I wouldn't trade those years for anything in the world even if I knew I was going to lose her. I want you to have that kind of love. Marcus is your forever love. Enjoy every moment you're blessed to have together."

"I will, Dad. I'm so happy you approve of our relationship."

"Why wouldn't I?"

"No reason."

"Listen to me. You and Marcus will have your challenges with ridiculous people. Unfortunately, that's how the world goes round. You and Marcus are making a powerful statement. I'm so proud of both of you. You have the power to change how people view the world. Love each other through all the difficult times. In the end, that's all that matters." He stands and kisses my forehead. "I love you. Now go home." I start laughing.

"Love you, too."

Chapter 8

Nicki

Later that evening, I'm pulling brownies out of the oven. I smile because I know Marcus is going to be very excited to see them. He had a busy day today. Every year, his company has a retreat and spends a Saturday doing team-building things. I don't remember all the details but it's something to that nature. He says it's fun but exhausting. Anyway, he's heading over. He's already had dinner and wanted to stop by to see me before heading home. I've missed him so much today. We've spent so much time together in the last two weeks. Being without him all day today has me missing him like crazy.

The knock on the door startles me and I almost drop the pan. I place it on the stovetop, take off the oven mitts, and head toward the door. I check the peephole and see him. I swing the door open and jump into his arms.

"Whoa!" he exclaims as he catches me. My lips find his and I kiss him hard. He responds immediately and our kiss quickly gets hot. Somehow, he gets us back into my apartment and manages to get the door closed. He pulls away abruptly and smiles. "Hi, baby. I've missed you, too."

His mouth comes down over mine again. He carries me to the couch and lays me down and comes down on top of me. His weight over me feels wonderful. My hands move to the hem of his shirt and I push it up. He breaks away from me long enough to pull it over his head. His mouth goes to my neck and he kisses a spot that makes my eyes roll back in my head. My heart is pounding, and I'm hoping we are finally going to take our relationship to the next level. I don't want to wake up without him anymore.

I feel him moving down to my chest and suddenly he stops. "Are you sure this is okay?"

"I want you." The look in his eyes is smoldering. The want in them makes my heart skip a beat and my breathing increases.

He pulls at the hem of my shirt and I sit up. The t-shirt comes over my head. Marcus throws the shirt behind him and stares at me. "You're beautiful."

I can feel the blush as my eyes roam over his chest. I've seen him without a shirt many times, but I could never openly look at him. The rippling muscles. The tight abs. He's perfection, and I can't wait to lick every groove. The thought of that makes my body hot all over. I run my hands along his chest and Marcus watches every move I make. I lean over and kiss his chest and his breath quickens. His hands run along my back as I kiss his chest. His hands make their way to my face and pull me away from his chest. He kisses me softly.

"I want you so much, but I want to go slow," he whispers.

"Don't hold back. We've waited so long for this."

He stands abruptly and helps me up. Once I'm on my feet, he bends and picks me up. He kisses me as he walks us to my bedroom. He sets me on my feet next to the bed. I take a step back from him and take off my bra. His breath catches as he takes me in. His hand comes up to cup my right breast. His thumb flicks my nipple and a moan escapes me.

"Shit, baby. That sound drives me insane." His hand trails down my stomach to the button on my jeans. His eyes lock with mine as he unbuttons it. "Sit on the bed." I do as he asks and he makes quick work of the zipper, pulling the jeans down my legs. He stands and takes off his jeans as he stares at me in nothing but panties. His boxer briefs are sexy and the bulge makes my mouth go dry. My hands go to the waistband of my panties and I push them down my legs and off.

"Lean back," he commands. I do as he says, and my arousal kicks up a notch. That was hot. "Spread your legs." I do so, and he licks his lips. I know he can see the wetness and I need to feel him. I don't feel embarrassed. He makes me feel sexy and wanted. Within seconds, he's on his knees in front of me. My breath hitches as his mouth descends onto my most intimate place. I gasp at the sensation and fall back on the bed.

Chapter 9

Marcus

I knew when Nicki and I finally made love it would be incredible, but this is beyond anything I could've dreamed up. Her taste is mesmerizing. I'm so hard. I need her wrapped around me. I need to be inside her right now. I flick my tongue on her little bundle of nerves and she goes off like a rocket. I watch her and I'm hooked. I want to see her like this all the time. She's magnificent.

I stand and pull off my briefs. She licks her lips as she takes me in and I lose all control. She crawls back on the bed to make room for me and I slide over her. Her legs come up and wrap around my waist. Her heat against mine makes me even harder. I'm at her entrance but don't push in.

"Do you have condoms?" I ask and she shakes her head.

"I don't. I'm on the pill and don't want any barriers with you." She watches my face and I see the blush on her cheeks. "I'm clean and have only had one other partner. We always used a condom," she adds quickly.

"I've never had sex without a condom and I'm clean, too. Are you sure?" I need to ask.

"Very sure." I kiss her like my life depends on this kiss. I push in a little and she gasps. I can already feel how tight she is.

"I need you to know I'm in love with you," I tell

her, and I see a tear escape her eye.

"I'm very much in love with you, too," she says, and I lose it. I push all the way in and we both let out a moan. She's so tight and feels amazing.

"You feel so good." I start to move, and I know I'm not going to last long. No woman has ever made me come this fast. My thrusting becomes frantic. The moans coming from her are driving me crazy. "Baby, I need you to come."

As soon as the words are out of my mouth, her inner walls squeeze around me.

"Marcus!"

I shatter. My orgasm hits me and I feel it everywhere. A loud groan escapes my mouth and I pump all of myself into her. I collapse on top of her, breathing hard. Her legs tighten around me and I kiss her shoulder. I lift my head and place my hands on both sides of her head.

"Nothing has ever felt like that."

"For me, too." I kiss her slowly and thoroughly. "I love you."

"I love you too," I tell her as I run my nose along hers.

***

I'm addicted. I was addicted to her before sleeping with her. Now, I cannot be without her and her body. People always said sex was different when you found the right person and it's true. I never believed it, but it's true.

"We need to get some sleep." She snuggles deeper into me and I smile.

"I know." She looks up at me and smiles. "I'm looking forward to waking up with you."

"Me too. I don't think I can live with not waking up next to you again," I admit. Maybe it's too fast, but she needs to know where my head is. I'm not letting her go.

"I feel the same." I kiss her and reach up to turn off the light. "Are you sure you don't want to go for round four?" I laugh and wrap her up tightly in my arms.

Chapter 10

Nicki

The next morning, we're headed to my dad's house for brunch. Marcus hasn't seen my dad in a while. He's excited and nervous. It's different now because he's dating me. I told him my dad is happy with it but, like me, he has to see it for himself. I turn into my dad's driveway and we make our way out of the car. Marcus takes my hand and we head toward the house.

"It's about damn time, son." We both turn to see my dad coming from the back of the house. Marcus starts laughing and embraces my old man.

"You're right. I should've done it a long time ago," Marcus says.

"Hi, beautiful." My dad leans towards me and kisses my cheek.

"Hi, Dad." He leads us into the house, and I get started with brunch. My dad can't cook, and I make brunch here for us at least once a month. He and Marcus sit at the kitchen table while I pour us all some much-needed coffee.

"Talk to me," Dad says as he looks at Marcus.

The two of them catch up on life's happenings since the last time they saw each other. They've always gotten along great and I smile to myself. I'm so happy with the turn my life has taken. I'm lucky to have a man like Marcus by my side, and an amazing support system in our families. It certainly could've gone another way. They could've supported a friendship but not a romantic relationship. It's not right but the possibility was there. I was so deep in thought I didn't hear the guys talking to me.

"I'm sorry, what?"

"Whatever you're making over there smells wonderful," Dad states.

"It'll be done in a few more minutes."

"Do you need any help? I can set the table." Marcus starts to stand, and I stop him.

"You and Dad talk and catch up. I've got this." Marcus winks at me and I keep working.

***

An hour later, we are coming out of dad's house to continue with our day. As we're approaching the car, my father's neighbor appears. She's walking her dog and stops when she sees us.

"Hello, Nicki!" she hollers.

"Hi, Mrs. Wilks," I say. "How are you doing?"

"I'm well," she replies, but her eyes are on Marcus. "Who's this?"

"This is my boyfriend, Marcus. Marcus, this is Mrs. Wilks. She lives just down the street," I say, and Marcus nods toward her.

"It's nice to meet you, ma'am."

The look on Mrs. Wilks' face is pure hatred. Her whole demeanor changes, and she looks at me with disdain. "How dare you disgrace your race!"

What the hell? Is she serious? The rage starts at my toes and goes up my legs. I feel my face get hot as I spew, "How dare I what? You are a disgusting human being. He is no different than you or me. I don't give a damn about my race. If my race has that big of an issue with me being with a black man, then it can kiss my ass. Neither you nor anyone else has a reason to look at him any differently than anyone else. The only thing that makes him different from us is the color of his skin. I love the color of his skin. He's beautiful, inside and out. If you don't like it, too bad. People like you disgust me, and you should be ashamed of yourself."

I don't give her the chance to respond. We climb into the car and I start the engine. I see my dad heading her way and can see the anger on his face. Marcus rolls down the window.

"Get off my property. You are no longer welcome here. If you ever speak to my daughter and her man in that way again, I promise you will not like what comes out of my mouth. Leave now."

Chapter 11

Marcus

"I love you," I say as Nicki speeds out of her father's neighborhood. I've never seen her this angry. She looks over at me and her features soften a little.

"I love you, too. Very much. I'm sorry about that."

"Why are you apologizing? None of that was your fault."

"I want to know what my race has against black people. Why do they see you as a threat? I don't understand." I see the tears fall from her eyes.

"Baby, pull over." She does as I ask, and I pull her into my arms. "Thank you for being in my corner and defending me. Thank you for loving all of me, including the color of my skin. Most of all, thank you for getting so angry at racism. We need more people like us fighting for what's right. But you need to understand that we are going to encounter many more like that." She pulls away and looks at me.

"I know, and I will do what I just did all over again. I'm not afraid to fight for what's right. I'm not afraid to speak up against racism. I'll always fight. I promise you."

I take her mouth in a searing kiss. I need to feel her. Within seconds, we are pulling at each other's clothes. She stops abruptly and looks around.

"We're on the side of the road. We can't do this here."

"Get to your apartment fast." I need her now. The fierceness she has to protect me and the promise she just made me awoke a need inside me. No one has ever jumped to my defense like that or promised to always have my back. I need to make this woman my wife sooner rather than later.

She smiles at me and the tires squeal as she pulls back onto the road. That's my girl!

Epilogue

Five Years Later

Nicki

"Marcus!" I cry out. I'm holding onto the kitchen counter for dear life. My contractions are getting stronger and they are now five minutes apart. He is in the back room with his parents getting our son, Leon, set up. I called them earlier and told them I was having contractions. From the time I called them until now, the contractions have increased tremendously. Marcus comes running into the kitchen.

"You okay?" he asks as he grabs my hand.

"They're five minutes apart now." His expression goes from calm to nervous in the blink of an eye.

"An hour ago, they were twenty minutes apart."

"This little one is in a hurry to get here." He quickly leads me to the front door. Momma comes rushing from the back. When she reaches me, she places her hands on my face and I bring my eyes to hers.

"May God bless you and watch over you. I pray He helps you have an easy delivery and my beautiful grandchild is born healthy."

"Amen," I say, and she kisses my cheek. "I love you."

"I love you, too, honey."

***

The screaming of a healthy baby girl fills the hospital

room. I'm sweating, crying, and breathing hard as my daughter is placed on my chest. I look up at Marcus. He smiles down at me as a tear falls down his cheek. He leans down and kisses me. We each take in our baby girl. She's perfect and already snuggling up to me. The nurse takes her from me, and she starts screaming again. We start laughing. Marcus follows the nurse while the doctor cleans me up. We waited to find out the sex of the baby. We didn't know with Leon either and it was such a special moment. The surprise of finding out when they are born is indescribable.

I lean my head back and thank God the delivery went well and for blessing us with another healthy baby. Leon is an incredible little boy. He's the light of my world and now I have a little girl to light it up even more. Marcus and I have created a beautiful life and I wouldn't trade it for anything in the world.

"Hey, baby," Marcus says. I open my eyes and find him standing there with a little bundle in his arms. "Someone wants her momma." He places the little beauty in my arms and tears well in my eyes.

"Hi, beautiful. Welcome to the world." I kiss her forehead. Marcus leans in and kisses my forehead. "Do you think the name we picked out suits her?"

"No, it doesn't seem to fit her."

"Do you have a name?" I ask.

"Grace."

I look down at her and smile. "Welcome to the world, Grace." She opens her eyes and looks around. We start to laugh.

"Thank you," Marcus whispers in my ear. When I look at him, he smiles and kisses me. It's a passionate kiss, and certainly not appropriate in a hospital room, but I don't give a damn. "Thank you for leaping with me. It was the best decision I ever made."

"If you hadn't done it, I would have." I wink at him and we start to laugh.

"I love you."

"I love you more."

Thirty minutes later, the whole family is in the room with us. Leon is sitting on the bed with me while Grace is being passed around between her three grandparents. It's the second time I've been able to witness such a special moment. There is nothing better than this.

The End

About the Author

Janet A. Mota lives in Jacksonville, Florida with her husband and two children. She works in the legal field during the day and only writes when all duties are completed for the day. She has a passion for writing and reading. She picked up her first romance novel when she was eighteen years old and never parted from the genre. She published her first book five years ago and has written eight more since. Below is a list of her published works.

Unexpected Surprises
Shattered
Undeniable
Attraction
Chances
Sweet Destiny
Believe In Love
Through It All
Santiago: Book 1 in The Almeida Brothers Trilogy – Social Rejects Syndicate

QUEEN OF THE DARK

DARK

Kenna Rey

For permission requests, submit via email at KennaReyWrites@gmail.com
A sincere thank you to my diversity/inclusion editor, Renita McKinney, at A Book A Day, and Michele Ficht for the proofread.

Chapter 1

Night's Calling

"Hurry, Nadia. I'm about to bust," Claud ground out, his English accent thicker than normal as I rode his cock. He thrust up into me as I watched his face, anticipating the power I'd feel with him coming apart beneath me. Using the black leather headboard as leverage, I shoved deeper onto his length and watched as his face went from ecstasy to concentration, doing his best to hold out for me.

"Almost there. Don't you dare come." I moaned, throwing my head back. I was rising towards the climax, and I needed just another second before … "Fuck, Claud, I fucking love your cock!"

And as I came, I thought I may love him too. Dark brown sex ruffled hair framed his pale face, a startling contrast to my own onyx complexion. If my job didn't put a damper on our time together, I might even tell him.

"Fuck, baby," he groaned as he let go himself, and I reveled in the power he yielded to me. His muscular frame shifted upon the silky sheets, and he rolled atop me, lips pressing gently to mine as he leaned in. "Move in, Nadia. We've been seeing each other for over a year. I need you to be here when I get home."

"I don't know, Claud," I whispered, grabbing for his cock again to distract him. "I have enough time for another round before I head back to meetings. You're leaving in a few hours for a long work-trip, my big bad security guard. Let's talk about this later."

His disarming smile as he grabbed at my thighs and

thrust them above my head made me seriously consider his words.

If sex was a language, Claud spoke it fluently.

***

Last night was one for the record books. The dark encompassed me like a blanket, comforting me with sweet nothings. Wedged in the shadows between a building and some shrubbery, I allowed my senses to take over. Soaking up the sounds of the waves crashing to shore in the heat of a June Miami night, I released the tension in my face and listened. Relaxed. That is, until the sounds of my assignment had me grinding my teeth, fighting my instincts to bring about justice on my own. My comfort-zone was stealth, and my resume spoke for itself. But the replay of the evening weighed heavily on my conscience as I began my post-shift workout. I often found myself in that very spot when I needed to reset the balance in my brain. Working off the aggression I couldn't dole out during my shift was the only way I'd catch a few hours of sleep. Today, I found myself daydreaming about moving forward to light up the night with firefights. But my job was stealth – the quiet strike of knowledge seeking until we had enough information to attack. On a female-led team, my girls and I were dangerous at night and boss ass chicks in the daylight. We served our country in the Special Forces. But on paper, we were retired. With our top-secret clearances, we wouldn't receive public accolades for our hard work.

The government liked it that way.

During the daylight, my vampire tendencies caught up with me. Most days, the sunlight burned my eyes as I made my way to my daytime business, Queen of the Dark. We were a fashion house built for the active lady boss. Obviously running your own business with some of the most affluential women is a massive accomplishment on its own. I love my team, and I've learned that women are some of the biggest assets the world has to offer. We run a tight ship, and I couldn't do it without them.

My night team is built from your nightmares, and we don't apologize for doing whatever it takes to keep our country safe. My day team is built from your wet dreams, but my girls will tear you apart for undermining them.

I like it that way.

"Asia, wait. Let me spot you," Norway, my partner and best friend, said as she stepped up behind me. Probably a good thing, since I was testing my own limits on the squat rack. "Rough night? This must be a personal record."

"Yeah, I got caught up near the docks," I grunted out as I got the bar on my shoulders and stepped away from the rack.

"Figured. You always go too heavy after a rough night. How'd your newest stealth machine work?" Norway asked as I pushed through one last rep and re-racked the bar. As a designer, I had been experimenting with fabrics that would keep me and my team hidden.

Raising my water to my lips, I paused as memories flooded my head. The newest design, made from a mix of Kevlar and polyester, was designed for both protection and stealth. It was a good defense, one of the best I've designed, and I was damn proud of the prototype. Mixed with years of training, I felt good about moving forward with the design for the rest of my team.

The trafficking ring we were following preyed on women and children, and the urge to barge onto their boats and save them was stronger now than ever.

Soon.

They weren't just trafficking women and children, though. They were weaponizing at alarming rates, and we didn't know why. We did know they were so big even the scum in Hollywood and some government officials were vying for a spot with these bastards.

As whimpers echoed across the bay, a white-hot rage rolled through me. The urge to barge in solo warred with years of conditioning and training, and I almost lost touch with the mission. As I moved, quieter than normal thanks to my new design, I was ready to abort the protocol. But movement to my right distracted my thoughts. A crate was moved onto the large yacht, handled by a man I hadn't seen entering or leaving the vessel within the last few days. His broad shoulders and untrimmed beard under the streetlight caught my attention, but any other distinguishing features were muted in the cloak of night.

"Great. Quieter and cooler than I expected, but still hot." I didn't elaborate further. I wanted to protect the integrity of our mission, and quietly handling our business would help. Especially if we were comfortable. Norway knew that. When I finally looked up at her, I studied her beautiful deep blue eyes and warm sepia complexion. She did the same, scanning me to determine if she should push, but she let it go.

"Now that I have your attention, Bazzle wants us to meet up with the men's team for lunch." Norway dropped the news like the bomb it was. Our boss had a stronghold on this organization, and he knew we'd do whatever it took to take them down. The look in her eyes matched the disgust I felt as she said, "They're catering at headquarters, and it sounds like they have an in with the ring we've been working to dismantle."

"Is that a good idea?" Grabbing a towel from the bench, I wiped the sweat from my face and headed to the treadmill for a cooldown. "I want to catch these guys just as badly, but blowing our covers isn't good for anyone."

The treadmill beeped as I clicked through the settings, and Norway joined on the elliptical next to me, warming up for her own post-shift workout. We couldn't very well carry the burden of our evenings home to the people who didn't even know our organization existed. I tended to push myself hard after a shift, hoping to wear myself out for a couple hours of rest before heading into my own office.

"With one of them on the inside, Asia, we could use the extra intel. You know we work independently because we bring different... assets ... to the table. But Bazzle hasn't led us astray yet and he believes it's time to bring our teams together." Norway said clearly, her exertion on the elliptical not straining her words. "Anyway, we'll talk about that at lunch. Clear your schedule."

"I have a lunch date already. I needed that dick appointment." I pouted, but resolved to miss out on a romp with Claud.

"Are you still seeing that white boy?" Norway gave me a look that begged for details, but I wasn't giving in. "Maybe you can move that dick appointment up a few hours."

"Yes I am, and I won't say another word," I said through a smirk, knowing it would wind her up. "Well, except that he wants me to move in with him and I keep stalling. He doesn't know why I haven't spent the night."

"Asia, plenty of us have relationships. My lady knows I have a security clearance and that's all she needs to know. She doesn't ask any more questions, which is good because I won't give her answers."

"I know." Reaching for the red stop button, I pressed it and leaned onto the rail closest to her. Glaring, I continued, "I'm going to hit the showers. I have a billion meetings I have to reschedule now, dick appointment included. See you in a few hours."

"Get some sleep, Asia."

"I'll sleep when I'm dead."

Chapter 2

Just Lunch

- Hey gorgeous. Something came up. Can we reschedule our lunch date?

Relief flooded me as I read Claud's text. My assistant was taking over the other meetings, but I didn't want to disappoint Claud. I missed him.

- Yes. Something came up on my end too. Dinner?
- Sounds good. 8?

But the relief was short-lived as my own disappointment flowed through me. One whole week. I was so wrapped up in fantasizing about Claud's dark tousled hair and green eyes – and what did that say about me? I wasn't the fantasy type, right? Images of his cock and how he worked me over last week flooded my mind as I stared at his name for a few more seconds. He was the most laid-back guy I had ever dated, and yet, the most sexually dominant. I never saw myself with someone like him, but how could I resist? Job complications be damned.

Grabbing my purse, I checked my makeup one last time before heading to the last-minute lunch. Presentation was important, and as a fashion director, I loved flaunting my body in beautiful clothing. I typed out a quick response as I exited the elevator in my building into the private garage underneath. My baby was parked just steps from the open doors, a royal purple Bugatti. It was an extension of the aesthetic, but of course, my speed demon tendencies were well documented by the paparazzi who normally followed the up-and-coming fashion designer. My very own alter-ego.

Thank God for fast cars.

I was running a few minutes behind as I entered the nondescript federal building off a backroad just outside of Miami, the longer route a necessity to prevent being followed. I smoothed down the fitted black dress while my heels tapped the concrete, but stopped as a second set of heels mimicked my own. I smiled, waiting for Norway in the underground garage.

"Lookin' sharp, Asia," Norway said as she headed over to me. Her red pencil skirt and black top came from my fashion line, and I returned the smile. That outfit was made for her. Quite literally, I even made space for the knife sheath to be hidden underneath that form fitting skirt. "I can tell you've been hitting the gym harder. Your quads look great."

"Flattery gets you everywhere," I sing-songed, mocking the flip of my braids over my shoulder. "I see you chose well for the occasion too. I hope they underestimate us."

"Girl, I can't wait. That would make my whole day." Norway joked, eyes glittering.

Our laughter continued as we strode into the featureless hallway with the lithe grace of the well-trained. The badge scanner beeped, letting me know the fingerprint scanner was now ready for secondary security. I entered quickly and tilted my body to watch both the room and for Norway's entry. The expanse of hardwood tables and leather-padded chairs of the dining hall greeted us, and I stopped in my tracks as a familiar pair of green eyes raked over my body. The lust painted stare caught us both off guard.

Claud.

My eyes zeroed in on his green tie – matching his gorgeous gaze – and his lust spurred my own. Had it always been like this between us? The week since I felt his hardness or heard his voice was only over-shadowed by my desire to break up this ring. But why the fuck was he in my domain? I looked around the hall, hoping for a dark corner to escape towards to catch my breath. Norway pulled at my arm, a what-the-fuck look crossing her blue eyes as I tried quickly to pull myself together.

Shit was about to get extra messy.

"Asia! Norway! I'm glad you're both here. This is Brazil, and he's part of the three agent-team who has infiltrated the dock ring. He's been working his way up their hierarchy for the last several months, and he is finally in a position that we need your help for. Grab some food and let's get started."

"Several *months*, Bazzle?" Norway interjected, but I nudged her with my elbow before she overstepped her bounds.

Norway reached out a hand to shake with Claud, I mean Brazil, and I stood still. His eyes left mine briefly to scan over Norway before he smiled, his English manners always the first to show their stripes, and offered his hand as well. Those dark tousled locks still caused my heart to contract, but I didn't have time to catalogue his looks. The rough beard *did* look great on him, though. Holding my head high, I offered him my hand.

As we shook, I leaned in and whispered, "Hey *Brazil*. Nice to make your acquaintance." I watched as my favorite smile graced his face – the one that softened those green eyes – before he leaned back into me. The confusion radiating through my pores eased a bit at that smile, but hadn't I been hiding this from him, too? "I guess we aren't missing our lunch date after all."

"I am going to rip that fucking dress off of you, Nadia. Or should I say, 'The Infamous Asia'? Does your team know how you like to submit to me? I wonder if I could make that happen during this very meeting." He growled back into my ear, took his hand from mine, and brushed off his suit jacket. An audible breathing infiltrated the room before I realized it was me, and I was pissed all over again. Who was he to come in here and undermine me at my own game? Motioning towards the buffet, I headed towards the food and tried to pretend my fucking boyfriend wasn't part of this organization.

Or that he just made me wetter than the Niagara Falls.

This changed everything.

***

That Tie Though

Security firm, my ass.

Naturally, I had looked into Claud's security business. Sal Palo Security managed large private security geared towards senators and other high-end clientele. If I was watching, Brazil would have been obvious to me. Envy washed through me with the realization that Claud had used his front to glean information from clients for our employer, but I wasn't normally a jealous person. I had to check that attitude, turning it into begrudged respect.

Genius.

I was the best in the business for a reason, but maybe Claud was more cunning than I gave him credit for.

But the way he adjusted the damn tie I gave him as Bazzle spoke distracted me, which meant I needed more than a post-shift workout to clear my mind. Brazil's baritone response rumbled through me like a remembered vibrato between my legs. He exuded calm, relaxing into his description of the inner workings within the organization. Meanwhile, I wanted to rip off his clothes. The myriad of desires played havoc on my mind, and I wondered if I seemed as outwardly collected. But as I chewed on my lip to remind myself to stay present, his eyes caught my lips as he stuttered through an explanation of how he broke through the barrier of the crime ring and made his way through the ranks.

I sat up straighter, leaning forward to focus on his words. His usually collected demeanor was dented with stuttered words as he pretended not to watch me, and I took the inward joy as a victory. But enough was enough. It was time to put on my professional pants. His gaze hardened on me momentarily, but I didn't back down. Naturally submissive to him in bed, I wasn't giving him that benefit here in my domain.

We had been photographed together at dining establishments or entering my condo. It was good because people didn't tend to fuck with me – they assumed the big, bad Claud was my bodyguard. But it was too public, which meant we were both discreet, if you didn't count the subtle conversation we were making. An image of the Golden Crow flashed through my mind, with its white linens and black-tie servers, Claud's eyes were locked on me across the table. My favorite red dress was accompanied by black pumps with red bottoms – you know the ones – and I held a glass of red wine to my lips to cover a smirk. In the same breath, it was risky. People like Bazzle probably already knew about our relationship. That he hadn't brought it up before today was puzzling.

"Asia, you've been sneaking around the docks and collecting evidence. I'd like for you and Brazil to meet up and compare notes," Bazzle said as his gaze bounced between us, bringing me back to the present. "And Brazil, I need you to figure out a way for Asia to infiltrate as well. Norway, I need you on the docks in case shit burns down."

"Not happening, Bazzle. The only women in the organization come in as sex slaves. They're not respected within the organization and Asia's reputation precedes her. She is too good for that role." Brazil watched me as he spoke the words, but I wasn't willing to give him the benefit of the doubt.

"I will do what it takes, Brazil." I sat up straighter and looked towards Bazzle. "I didn't sign up for this without knowing the risks. If you believe that I'm needed inside, I'll do it."

"I respectfully disagree, sir." Claud's stare could catch me on fire. "Asia, this isn't about pride. If something goes wrong, we may not be able to get you out."

"You know my reputation, Brazil. It was hard-won. We have a common goal and I want us to succeed. I trust

Bazzle, and to work with our team, you need to trust us to do our jobs."

I could almost taste the flames of his displeasure. Good. Let him stew. I needed a way in, and I wasn't too proud to help someone else. My reputation was built through grit and determination. I stopped, listened, and asked questions. I'd never been quiet enough to be forgotten. Brazil's reputation was as ruthless as mine, but he had a bad habit of relying on only himself. I was never going to be the girlfriend sitting on the sidelines.

Adjusting my necklace, I looked away towards Bazzle. His jaw was clinched, eyes hardening as I put a blank look on my face.

"I know the two of you have been seen together," Bazzle gritted out, "but maybe that's your in. It's between the two of you to figure it out."

"Wait, what? *Brazil* is the dick you've been fucking?" Norway looked between us, and I smirked as I took Claud in. Hell, I was right in assuming Bazzle knew, there was no room for shame now. Norway laughed as she continued, looking towards Bazzle and then me, "Sorry, Bazzle. But *girl*."

"*Asia* didn't know I had this position, just as I didn't know she was in the organization," Claud gritted out. "Our relationship is none of your business."

"Don't forget, Brazil.

Business isn't personal," I said, collecting my things.

But I was about to make it *very* personal.

Chapter 3

You Got Me Fucked Up

"What game are you playing, *Asia*?" Claud ground out as he pulled into his subdivision and smoothly into his garage. As he put the car in park, he glanced at me with *that* twinkle in his eye.

"I don't know, *Brazil*," I mimicked. "Why is my *boyfriend* undermining me in a meeting with *our* boss? Afraid your girl will break up the ring you've been working with before you?" I taunted him. I knew it, he knew it, and my wet panties knew it.

I was playing with fire. But I needed to be burned. I needed him inside me immediately, and as he moved the car into park, his eyes hooded, I knew he was thinking the same thing.

"Get naked. Now, Nadia," he rasped out. "I was hard as soon as I saw you in that dress. Take. It. Off."

I never felt like less than a Goddess in his presence. He may have taken the control, but I held the power with him and we both knew it. He respected it, and I needed his commands to get out of my own head. I reveled in it.

Moving slowly, I pulled the dress up inch by inch, exposing the tops of my lacy stockings to his hungry eyes. He didn't flinch, but the flame in his green eyes spoke of his affection. I took in a deep breath just as slowly, accepting the role I played between us. Two could play it cool, even if I was going to make him cum so hard he saw stars.

"Beautiful," he complimented, and I preened. I didn't recognize this girl, the one who desired his compliments. But I learned a long time ago not to question what I enjoyed. "Hand me your dress, Nadia."

I did as he asked, eyes downcast. My core clenched at the gravel in his voice, the second tell that he wanted me as much as I needed him. My eyes followed his hands as he pulled the dress up to his face and inhaled. I wanted nothing more than to give him everything that he needed. The realization that he and I knew the same things, that I could move in with him here and make a life together, made me hotter for our connection.

"Good girl. Wait here," he said as he opened his door and came around to my side. He opened my door, reached in, and picked me up.

As his mouth collided with mine, I delighted in the feel of his arms. The strength, the certainty that I could let go with him and that he would have my back. I kissed him back with fervor, barely restraining myself from climbing him like a tree. My fingers ran across the green tie before I grabbed it and pulled his lips tighter to mine. He groaned as he opened the door to his house, and it almost undid me.

"Beauty, I missed you," he said as his lips moved down my neck, ratcheting up my desire. He put my legs down and pushed me against the door before saying, "Tell me you missed me, baby."

"Don't you dare leave me for that long again," I moaned as his palm found my breast, fingers tightening as his lust colored his face. "I need you, Claud."

"Patience," he groaned as his lips surrounded a nipple and his hand covered my mouth, silencing me. The warmth of his mouth didn't compare to the heat in my core. I was about to take things into my own hands, and I knew he would punish me for it.

My hands skimmed the belt on his Armani suit. I released the buckle, and he groaned as he nipped my nipple. I yelped into his hand, and could feel his smile against my skin. My own lips tilted up, and I gave in to his demands as his hands moved down my body, grabbing my ass hard and lifting me against his erection. He was harder than steel, and my hips bucked of their own accord as another groan escaped him.

"This is going to be fast, Nadia. I need you too." He pulled out his cock, not giving me a chance to respond. His hands pulled my hips forward and he thrust in deep. The coolness of the wall contrasted with the heat of my core and his mouth, and I tightened against him before he could pull back to thrust again. I screamed, and his moan followed as he hammered into me. My head fell against the wall as his mouth found my throat, nipping, sucking and licking. I couldn't do anything more than breathe through the pleasure.

"Let go," he groaned. "Now, Nadia."

Giving in, I allowed myself the release that had been building since I realized he'd be home today. His husky moan followed after a few more rough thrusts, and his lips found mine gently as we caught our breath.

My fingers untied the beautiful green silk, an idea percolating to get his attention. His eyes glittered as he recognized the look, and I pulled the tie away to push him into a nearby chair in his home. Our home soon. Excitement had me moving quickly. I wanted to tell him while he was still inside me.

"Nadia," he groaned my name like a warning. I smirked.

"Hands behind your back, handsome." He complied, challenge written in his playful greens. I reached behind him with my breasts in his face, and worked the tie around his hands. His training would make this child's play, so I tied them a bit tighter than normal.

Claud quirked a dark eyebrow as I grabbed his already hardened cock and sat, rolling my hips.

"I couldn't stop picturing you bending me over the table and spanking me in front of Bazzle," I said as I pushed back against him. His dark hair called to me, and I grabbed a handful, pulling his head back as my lips met his chest and moved up over his jaw.

"Dirty," he growled as he raised his hips to meet mine. "I bet you'd like it if I let another man get you ready for me too, huh?"

"Judging by how hard you just got saying that, I'm thinking I wouldn't be the only one who enjoyed that," I countered before he elicited another scream from me.

I counted the minutes that he submitted to me, feeling powerful as I continued to grind my pussy against his hard cock. I was loud, praising him, waiting until he did what he did best. Take over. Loosen that tie and make me completely his.

I already was.

Six minutes. I didn't even feel his hands moving as I continued to ride him. The song changed, but Claud had untied himself, grabbed me and lifted me higher to slam my hips against him, burying his cock deeper than I could get it on my own.

We were going to set the world on fire.

***

Queen of the Dark

"I'm coming, Claud," I shouted. I'd rather it was in ecstasy. "I may allow you to see my vulnerabilities while you fuck me, but don't forget who I am."

"I can't let you put yourself at risk, *Asia,*" Brazil said with exasperation. Make no mistake, at this point, we were no longer Nadia and Claud. A muscle twitched in his forehead, and I zeroed in. "The initiation is brutal for the sex slaves."

"Brutal how? You are in Brazil mode – I see that now. But Brazil is still Claud, and if you can't see that Claud is still running the show, maybe I'll go to Bazzle." I picked at my nail, and glanced at him through my lashes. I forced calm into my voice for my next words, "This is my specialty, Claud. You have to let go of your protective instincts. I won't bow for this."

417

He ran his large hands through his thick hair, and I bit the inside of my cheek with my head cocked. I knew he was fighting his own demons, but I could also see I was getting through to him. Business wasn't personal. I wasn't going to allow any relationship to get between me and my job. Those women and children needed us to work together.

"The first day, you'll be inspected by several men on the first boat. I'll be there, but I'll have to watch them strip you naked, search you for devices, and prep your body for … abuse." His eyes hardened as he turned away from me again.

"God. Why are they such pigs?" I ran a hand down my face. But I said I'd do it, and I needed the intel. "What's my role here, Claud? Who do I need to pretend to be?"

"Move in with me, Nadia," he demanded. It wasn't a question, it was Claud's version of control. "I won't say more until you agree."

"That's some bullshit, Claud. You can't control my work life. I will walk away right now." I told him, allowing the authority I fought hard for to shine through. I could see him fighting himself, and I wasn't trying to push him. But I wasn't going to let him push me either. "If you'd asked, you'd already know I was planning to move in the second I saw you at the office. Instead, you've decided that you're going to manipulate me, and that ain't happening. What is my role? I won't ask again."

I never saw this side of him, but he was allowing his love for me to shine through. I could be gentle – needed to be. It was clear this was hard for him to let go. He grabbed me by the hips, pulling me into an embrace, and I reveled in my rightness. I squeezed him back, but we weren't finished with business and I wasn't going to give in until we had a plan in place. I pushed back against his chest to move away from him, and a look of disappointment marred his features. He respected the space, though, and it made me want to jump him all over again.

Fuck, this man was my weakness.

"You'll be coming in as *my* woman. No one will touch you without my permission, but we can't get past the inspection. You will need to remain quiet, docile. Use the stealth that you're known for. Act like a ... pet." He cringed and ducked as I gasped.

"I am no one's pet, Claud, and I can't pretend to be. But I will be quiet, docile. This will be a one and done, though." I fumed, angry for the women and children who were forced into this abuse. "I saw a man with your shoulders at the dock last night. He was carrying a box full of what I can only assume was more ammunition. That boat is being filled quickly. What's going on in there, Brazil? What role are you playing?"

"That *was* me. I don't touch the women or children," he confirmed. "I have been letting them know we are there to protect them, though. They don't trust me, but one woman in particular has been listening. I will make sure she knows to gather the others once help arrives."

"You better," I said reverently. "I'd trade my life for theirs, you know?"

His shoulders fell, and as he took a deep breath, I knew I had said what he'd been worrying about. He nodded towards the fridge and walked over for a bottle of water, tossing one to me before shutting the door. The crack of his bottle opening before he threw his head back and emptied the contents made me sad. This was always his tell. He was about to give in to my demands, and I slowly opened my bottle to watch his reactions. He crumpled his own bottle, throwing it into the recycling bin before looking back at me.

"Is this consensual, Nadia? I won't have my girl upset with me for putting her in a situation I don't want her in. It's a boys' club, beautiful. They don't believe in consent – taking what they want is obvious. But if we enter this with you as *my* woman, one I want to share with the guys, it's the closest to consent you're going to get."

"How can you bring in a woman who wasn't sold,

though? Is this a common occurrence?" I asked.

"Common? No. It's the dumbest idea I've ever heard," Claud's distress was still showing on his face, but as the reality of what we were doing trickled, I could see his normal cool exterior start to harden his features. "It's the safest way we could have a group of men, uh… play while I watch."

I wasn't pleased with this situation either. I didn't want these sexual abusers to put their hands on me. But Claud wouldn't let them touch after the initial inspection, and I knew his instincts to protect would kick in. I knew I'd be a distraction for Claud if we didn't iron out the details, and I didn't want him to get hurt either. Being distracted had almost cost me once already, and this was a battle I refused to lose.

"Let's do it. I need more information though. Who are the key players, what do they enjoy, what's our escape plan? If we do this, it'll be within the week we tear this whole charade to pieces."

"I am so in love with you," Claud said as he pulled me into him for a sweet kiss. "This may be the craziest thing I've ever agreed to, but I love you. Let's get down to business."

Chapter 4

Fix Your Crown, Sis

"Bitch, you're crazy," Norway flipped me off as she walked away. She turned around long enough to say, "Our jobs are dangerous enough. This is a death sentence, Asia, and I won't take part in it."

"It's crazy, but we need some crazy shit to exorcise these assholes," I shouted after her. I almost whispered the next part, but I knew she could still hear me, "I know this is coming from a place of love, but I will do *anything* to get those women and children out of that situation, Norway. Anything."

Claud and I had spent the last fifteen hours concocting a plan. It would be incredibly risky, but I knew I had to do it. We had exit strategies in place, I was educated on everyone involved, and I was given blueprints of the yacht -- giving us the opportunity to get all the kids to safety. I would not actually come into any danger with these dickbags, fantasy or no. We would go in, they would strip me down and check for recording devices, but they wouldn't be allowed to get any farther. Of course, they could turn on Brazil, but he and I were both top performers in hand-to-hand combat. I was only second to Norway, but we trained together.

Confidence could get us far, but I wasn't getting cocky.

Norway's steps halted a few feet farther, and I watched as she dropped her shoulders, her head falling into her hands. As her back rose from a deep breath, my heart stuttered. I didn't want this to come between us. She was the best person to help, and her agreement would increase the odds of success. She knew I wouldn't do anything to risk her life, and even though it was crazy, it was our best shot at taking these bastards down safely.

"I know you would," Norway began, her back still to me. "And that's what scares me the most, Asia. I know you'd put them ahead of you. You've always been soft-hearted when kids are involved."

"And that soft-heart has saved so many children just like these. This situation is different from those. There are too many powerful people at play, and that includes judges and military. It may even go higher into the government, but Brazil hasn't seen any of them – even though he has heard their names dropped a couple times. If we don't get to the heart of this, it'll be swept under the rug and they will get slapped on the wrist. You know the drill."

Her onyx hair shook on her back again as she kept her face in her hands. I heard an audible intake of breath as she spun back towards me on the heels of her feet. When she pulled her face out of her hands, she hardened her stare on me.

"I'm not saying yes, Asia. But I'll hear you out. You deserve at least that." She couldn't exactly say no, but she could ask Bazzle to take her off the assignment.

After a few hours of debating, I called Brazil and asked him to come in and discuss the inner workings of the sex ring. We would be including top officials of other alphabet government organizations to get the kids to safety, divest the boat of the criminals, and clean up the scene by collecting evidence and guns. This was going to take more than just the few of us. And since Norway agreed to help, I needed to ensure that she was going to understand the whole plan that would be taking place in two days, on the Fourth of July. At least any gunfire would be brushed off as fireworks.

Our timeline was quick, but we would be ready. Brazil entered the room in a cloud of palpable confidence, leaving a click of the door hatch to echo through the room. I didn't take my eyes off Norway. His steps echoed in the nearly empty room, and she looked away first. Right towards my man. I bit back a laugh as she gauged him before I felt his arms wrap around me from behind and his lips press on the top of my head.

Finally, I looked over my shoulder and allowed myself to take him in. His black pants hugged his hips, and butterflies fluttered wildly in my stomach as he smiled down at me wickedly. I had to force myself back into work mode. It was clear that he was putting on a show for my best friend, and I laughed as Norway cleared her throat across from us. Claud winked, pulling the chair out next to me.

"Norway." Brazil nodded to her as he took his place at the table. "Asia tells me that you two have been discussing our ... infiltration technique."

"Well, she certainly wasn't discussing your penetration technique," Norway deadpanned. I smirked, sitting back to watch the show-off.

"She hasn't complained," he retorted.

"Before we get started," Norway interjected, "I need to know you will keep my girl safe. She is my sister without the blood relation, and I am still not convinced this is a good idea."

"I love her, Norway. I don't want her involved either, but you're her best friend. She told me all about the two of you yesterday, which means you know I don't get to say shit when it comes to work."

Norway continued to face Brazil as her eyes swung to me. She silently asked if we could trust him. I nodded. After over a year of dating on our crazy schedules, he had never let me down. Not in the bedroom, not through disrespect, never. I squeezed his hand under the table, and his gaze shifted towards mine, softening as he took me in.

"You still look insanely beautiful, baby," he whispered in my ear. Goosebumps rose on my skin and I smiled back at him.

"I will personally dispose of you, Brazil," Norway interrupted. "If she dies in this stupid venture, I'll come for you."

"I would question your friendship if you didn't."

***

Hunger for the Night

I strapped on my last heel, the only protection I would have tonight. Brazil would be here any minute to pick me up, and staying busy kept my mind from making up scenarios that would distract me from the mission. These victims needed me to be the Asia I cultivated in my career, not the girl so deep inside her head that she got sloppy.

We needed Claud engaged, too. Not that he would go off or act a fool. I knew he wouldn't, but he had a claim on me that no one else would ever have. I swung the door open after the bell chimed and pulled Claud into my arms without thinking. I kissed him deeply. His arms swooped around my waist, pulling me deeper into the kiss.

"Are you ready for this?" His gruff voice rumbled through my body, and I took a deep breath, giving him nothing else.

"Of course. Let's take down these assholes."

He led me towards the vehicle he had hired for the night, as we would be leaving the docks with the organization and not in our own vehicles. He waved off the chauffeur and opened the door for me, grabbing my ass, almost slipping it out of the short blue dress I wore. Ignoring him, I stepped into the luxurious vehicle and sat on the far side, Claud entering behind me. He gave instructions to our driver and slid the screen up between us.

His hands immediately found my bare clit, stroking gently as he leaned into me. His lips found my neck, and I spread my legs wider for him. I needed this from him, the opportunity to come from his hands, away from prying eyes. I needed his hands, his dominance, and I refused to feel ashamed as we made our way to the docks.

His fingers deftly worked my clit, forefinger slipping into my wetness as he let out a groan and moved to the floor. His perfect suit, perfect hair, and perfect eyes looked up to me. He scooted me further towards the edge of the seat as I ached for his mouth. He gave me what I wanted, licking up my cleft like his life depended on it. I guess it did. If things didn't go as we expected tonight, we could both lose our lives.

His tongue moved with an expertise, working me up to a climax immediately. Maybe it was the nerves for the evening, but nothing was going to stop me. He nipped at my lips before sucking my clit into his mouth, and I gasped as he buried his face in my core. His tongue entered me, and I gasped, moaning aloud before he thrust his fingers in my mouth. I sucked, using my feet to stroke his cock in the prison of his pants.

"I love you, Claud," I screamed as I came, oblivious to the world around us. He kept at it until the last of my orgasm passed. The pleasure in his green eyes as I finally admitted my feelings for him spurred me on, and I clinched harder for him.

"On your knees, Nadia," Claud rasped out as he unbuckled his pants and pulled his cock out. He stroked it a few times as I complied. "Get it out of your system, baby. I need you to take the edge off. We can't show them weakness."

I crawled forward, prepared to ruin my lipstick as I grabbed his length and stroked a few times before wrapping my lips around him. I reveled in the sound of his groan, living for the moment. We only had a few more minutes before we arrived to the docks, and I needed to give him the best of me before we entered the dragon's lair.

Dropping down hard, I sucked him to the back of my throat and moaned, hoping he could feel the vibrations. He grabbed the back of my head and pushed me a little deeper, and I drew my tongue out and dragged it the rest of the way down his length. His groan had me wetter than a rainy day, and I bobbed my head quickly.

"Nadiaaaa," he groaned, pushing me a little deeper. "I'm going to cum. Swallow all of it, baby."

I did exactly what he said, reveling in his lust. I swallowed hard, making a scene of licking the rest off my lips before he pulled me off the floor and into his lap, kissing me deeply.

***

Classy bitch

A large white yacht sat at the end of the dock, dark tints lining the windows. Claud led me down the thin dock and held my hand as I stepped onto the boat. I knew what was coming, and I wasn't exactly ready, but would anyone ever be ready for something like this?

An older man greeted us, saying, "Gio, who is this?"

"This is my fiancé, Dessa. Dessa, this is George," Claud said with an Italian accent, shocking me. He had explained that he went by Gio here, but not the accent.

"No women are allowed to board with clothing, Gio. Make her strip," George demanded. I expected this, but not at the edge of the boat.

"Strip, Des. Now." Claud's tone gave no room to argue, and I had to trust what we had built. I knew that Norway was waiting for us outside, and if I couldn't trust my boyfriend, I could definitely trust her and the rest of my team to come for me.

I grabbed the hem of my dress and pulled it over my head. Claud didn't make a sound behind me as I bared myself to him and the man in front of me. My breasts hung heavily in front of them, and the man grabbed them tightly as I whined and Claud growled behind me.

"She is mine, George. You will ask for permission or I will go to Savion. He'll cut your hands off before I finish speaking." Claud's tone again left no room for fucking around, and George immediately dropped his hands and pointed towards a door that led towards the inside of the boat. I breathed a short sigh of relief as Claud stepped in front of me and opened the door.

Once inside, I took a quick look around. We weren't in the bowels of the ship quite yet, but aside from the décor inside, I was confident in the layout. Another few guards approached us, and I moved a little closer to Claud. He pulled me to his side, hand sliding up my ribcage as he led me towards the larger living space. The tinted windows I recognized from outside lined the room, but I knew my team couldn't see me.

Three men stepped up to me, and Claud stepped back. They nodded to him before one checked my hair for wires, one ran his hands along my upper body, and the last started to paw at my pussy and my ass. He wasn't gentle as he shoved his fingers into me, and I let out a sharp squeal of pain. He laughed and dug in further, until *Gio* put a stop to it.

"Not this one, Senator. This one is mine. You can watch, but you're not allowed to play tonight."

"One of these days, Gio, you'll learn how much fun it is to *share*," the senator replied, following it up with a hard smack to my ass. I wanted to throttle him, but I had to remind myself of the mission. I looked over towards Claud, noted his clenched fist, and breathed in a sigh of relief.

"That day isn't today, *Senator*," he sneered back. The goal was to keep the conversation going as Norway and the rest of the team snuck onto the boat. They were tasked with getting to the kids before we would get off the boat. They would give us a signal through the window – a laser that would penetrate the tint – and then we'd be safe to take these fuckers out. "It's initiation night, fellas. Go gather the other men. Savion should know we're here now."

I couldn't turn off my training, though, and saw movement out of the corner of my eye. I coughed to clear my stiffening muscles, not turning towards the movement as I followed it in my periphery. Claud came to my side, pulling me in and squeezed my ass – his acknowledgement in this hell-hole that he saw what I did. It was one of our team members ducking under the surveillance system to get towards the back of the boat.

Claud pulled me with him into a chair and shoved me roughly to the floor to sit at his feet. I let my rage continue to boil quietly under the surface, only getting a slim taste of what an *initiation night* looked like, and ground my teeth. I let my displeasure show on my face, giving another distraction as one of the men laughed, looking directly at me.

"You've got a wild one, Gio," he mocked. "I can't wait to watch you break her. What's taking Savion so long?"

"He's probably balls deep in a bitch," another man with a teal button-down shirt laughed. "You know he likes to test out the new crop before they move on."

Disgusted, I continued to glare as Claud ran a finger down my neck before grabbing the back of it in a protective manner. Before he could speak, four more men entered the room, dressed in flashy gear meant to subdue their prey. It's likely how they got these women and children to trust them in the first place before ruining their lives.

"She is feisty. I like a good challenge," *Gio* replied, standing to greet the new men. "Savion, Ciao. Anyone else aboard today?"

In his green tie, Claud had a hidden chip that transmitted the conversation to our team outside and onboard. I was grateful for thinking of it. His subtlety in conversation would hopefully go unnoticed by those in the room, but spoke volumes to our team. Since he had been working his way up the ranks, no one here thought anything of checking him when he came onboard.

"No, brother. Just us tonight. Michaels and Davidson are celebrating Independence Day with their wives. Why they'd want to miss out on this evening's … festivities …" Savion said as he looked directly at me, "is beyond me."

My skin crawled with unease as tension ratcheted up in the room. The men here were openly ogling me, and I had to fight the urge to cover myself. Fireworks exploded nearby, and I jumped, creating a trickle of chuckles in the small space. Claud and Savion made their way back towards me, Claud sauntering in the way that always made me anticipate a heavy hand. Normally, I'd be soaking for him, but here, not so much. What was taking our team so long? Ten more minutes, tops. I repeated it like a mantra.

"The party is just starting, my friend," Claud said jovially, the next notification for our team that they would only have ten minutes remaining to get to the women and children. "Let's pour a round and light some cigars. I'm in the mood for a great Cuban tonight."

I sent up a prayer of thanks as they walked past me and towards a liquor cabinet, and settled in to watch their interactions. I'd take out the old guy first, George, for being the first to paw at me. He'd be easy. Next would be ol' teal shirt, who stood near him laughing as he clipped the end of his cigar.

"The girl is a bit exotic for your usual tastes, eh? I didn't think the girl you were bringing would be so … dark." Savion said, dripping disdain without a hint of remorse. Fuck these racist bastards. Savion just made it to the top of my list.

"I hope they underestimate us. Bazzle knows what we can do."

"Girl, I can't wait. That would make my whole day."

The conversation just a few days ago between Norway and me played through my mind, and I held onto that reminder. Claud warned me that this could happen, and he wasn't far off. These criminals were acting civilized while they harbored human beings like cattle, and I would take them down.

As promised, Claud kept the group distracted as I did my best to remain unappealing. I spotted a metal pipe tamper on a nearby table, a tool with a scoop on one side and a pointy edge on the other used to assist in smoking pipe tobacco, and decided it would do well enough. I grabbed it discreetly, and looked towards Claud who gave a subtle nod in approval as he continued to speak with the other men in the room.

"What do you say, gentlemen? A shot for courage?" Claud projected for the men in the room. It was the sixty-second warning for our team. I held my breath as he grabbed a bottle of tequila from the rack and started pouring shots for each of them. Before he could finish pouring, four quick dots of red touched the wall, and Claud smashed the bottle over George's head, knocking him clean out as I jumped from my perch and grabbed for Savion.

The cowards in the room grabbed for guns, but they were no match for us. Our unit broke down the door and barged in, Norway throwing another dress to me as they entered. I backed into a wall and she blocked me as I slid the dress over my head quickly. She passed me my gun as our team read Miranda Rights aloud.

"We got them, Asia. The kids are safe."

"Where are they?"

"Already on the bus. Which one said the shit about you being *exotic?"* Norway said with a look of malice. "I'm going to hurt him first."

Chapter 5

Only by the Night

"The last box is unpacked," I yelled downstairs to Claud as I took in our mixed things. "My girly shit looks weird next to your bachelor décor."

I laughed as I heard him pop the cork on a bottle of champagne and stood to head downstairs. After two months of rounding up more evidence and surveillance footage, we had taken down what we were estimating to be at least 85 percent of the organization within the United States. The US alphabet organizations, like the FBI, handled the remaining cases and Norway and I worked with organizations to get the women and children back on their feet.

It was going to be a long road to recovery for them, but I had all the confidence that they'd succeed. I'd made as much room for them as I could within my company, trying to help the women with stable positions to start their new journeys.

I made my way down the wooden stairs, white handrail gripped in my right hand, and smiled as Claud offered a flute of champagne as I hit the bottom step. His eyes were glittering with mischief, and my heart stuttered as he pulled me into a simmering kiss.

"So, what's next, gorgeous? Netflix and chill? You, cooking dinner naked?" Claud nuzzled into my neck, dragging a laugh out of me.

"What are you in the mood for?" I flirted back, ready for anything this man wanted to give. We both had the night off after several months without much of a break. "I have some ideas, but they don't involve TV or food."

"Ah, but we have guests coming in a few hours."

I stared back at him for a minute, confused. We hadn't discussed guests or, well, anything really. I had been so focused on moving my belongings into his home that I hadn't really planned anything that would lead to spending time with anyone besides Claud.

"Oh? Who's coming over?"

"Just some friends, babe," he smirked. "I think you'll be excited to see them. Finish your champagne, go upstairs and run a bath, relax for a bit. You have a couple hours. I'm just finishing up a few contracts. I'll come up and get you before they get here."

"O....kaaay," I said slowly, confused but willing to go along with the surprise. I needed a break, and he was giving me the opportunity to take one. I shouldn't complain – even if he was working on his day off.

Upstairs, I found a note on the bathroom counter that he must have put in there before he came downstairs for the champagne.

Nadia,

Take a bath. Shave everything. Use the soap I left on the side. There are shower caps in the cabinet should you need one. I love you. When you're done, I'll have an outfit ready. Wear only that.

Claud

I smiled at his thoughtfulness and filled the tub. I walked to our room to grab some essentials, and came back to a full tub. Stopping the water, I stepped in and sighed at the feeling. I grabbed the book I brought in and leaned back against the tub.

As the water cooled, I drained it and walked into our room. Getting used to sharing a space was going to be weird, but I was grateful that Claud was becoming more accustomed to my crazy schedule, especially since his was pretty erratic as well.

On the bed was another note next to a white box wrapped with a bow. I didn't know what to think of it, still curious to what his plans were for the night.

This box is for you. I hid it so you wouldn't unpack it too early. Put this on and come downstairs. I ordered dinner, and I'm starving. I miss you.

"Claud, what do you have planned?" I said aloud as I opened the box, careful not to break the edges. The bottom slid out slowly, and the contents were wrapped in tissue paper. I broke the sticker seal and peeled it apart to find a royal purple negligee, matching my beautiful car parked beside his in the garage. I laughed as I placed the towel on the bed and slid into the tiny fabric.

If we had company coming over, and this is all I was wearing, I had no idea what kind of company we were keeping. He didn't leave any shoes, so I touched up my appearance a bit and walked downstairs, eager to find out what he had planned.

"Claud," I called as I walked down the stairs. The table was set for four, a solitary candle lit atop it. "Baby, where are you?"

"In the living room," he called to me, and I wandered towards his voice.

As I walked into the room, I stopped in my tracks as two other men sat in the chairs opposite the couch. I started to walk back out of the room, but Claud used *that* voice on me – the one that told me this was a game, and that I could trust him.

"I remember this beautiful woman standing in my kitchen a few months back, taunting me with images of other men touching her. Getting her ready for me," he said as he stood and walked towards me. He leaned in and whispered, "Surprise. Welcome home, Nadia. Let's make it memorable."

About the Author

Kenna Rey is a compassionate romantic. She is always dreaming up stories about love and fulfilling relationships. She writes a multitude of romantic genres and loves to write about powerful female friendships. In her obsession over the human dynamic, she leaves nothing to chance.

Kenna resides in the suburbs of St. Louis, Missouri with her high school sweetheart, a kiddo and three snuggly doggos. She loves to host get-togethers with family and friends, hiking, camping or riding roller coasters. She is also a big fan of anything chocolate.

Keep up with Kenna at her website:
www.kennarey.com

For more information about human trafficking in the United States and to seek assistance, please visit: www.humantraffickinghotline.org or call 1-888-373-7888

SIENNA'S SENTINEL

By Lori Ryan

Chapter One

"Sure took your sweet time," Sienna Evans crooned in a singsong voice, surprised the refrain from their youth came out as easily as it had when she was ten and he was eleven.

"He" being Boon Montgomery, who most definitely was not eleven anymore. Nor was he the scrawny long-limbed boy back in Tennessee who'd once upon a time been her best friend. The boy over the fence.

Boon's head shot up and she looked into blue eyes she hadn't seen in more than a decade, eyes that now held an unreadable gaze.

Sienna let out a slow breath. She wasn't sure what she expected. That he might open those big warm arms and draw her in for a hug? That he might scowl and ask her what she was doing at HALO Security? That he wouldn't even remember who she was?

Her one-time friend's face was closed off to her and she thought she'd made a mistake in coming to him. She should have hired a different company, never mind that HALO was the best.

Then his face cleared and he gave her a crooked smile as he took two long strides to stand in front of her.

Still, she could see the hesitation in him. He wasn't happy to see her. Not the way she'd thought he might be.

She felt her own smile go brittle but she kept it in place and tilted her head to look him in the eyes.

She'd thought about finding him over the years.

Her cousin Booker heard through a friend of a friend he relocated to Austin when his tour in the Army was over, but she hadn't looked him up.

Seeing him now, it was hard not to wonder if all soldiers came out of the Army looking like him. Surely not?

He looked like he could easily lift a truck with one hand and something about the way he moved, how he took up the space in the room, seemed to say he could. There was a confident ease to his movements that told anyone looking at him that he wasn't to be messed with or taken lightly.

It was the kind of surety that said he didn't have to prove himself.

"I got here as fast as I could," he said in a low voice that gave her shivers. It was the same line they'd given each other as kids over the fence, but it sounded distinctly different now.

"Sienna Evans," he said, crossing his arms and shaking his head at her. "Can't believe Sienna Evans is standing in front of me after all these years."

She punched him in the bicep and then had to resist the urge to blow on her knuckles to soothe the hurt. The man was hard as a rock. "You're bigger."

"You're not," he said, putting a hand out toward her head and bringing it back to mark the spot below his chin where she might reach if they stood chest to chest.

Lord, if that didn't make her body get all happy warm in just the right places. She took a step back just as the door to the room opened and a woman entered.

"Ms. Evans, sorry to keep you waiting," the woman said as she breezed into the room on heels that had Sienna drooling.

She and this woman could be friends.

The woman offered her hand. "I'm Gin Gentry. My brother, Loid, would have been here but he was called away for an emergency." She smiled in Boon's direction. "But since you requested Boon, I'm guessing you're fine with skipping the intro from Loid."

Sienna shook the woman's hand, carefully avoiding looking at Boon in that moment. She didn't want to know what he thought of her seeking him out.

Gin gestured to a table and chairs, and Sienna realized she'd barely taken in her surroundings. Probably not all that smart given what she'd been through recently.

The room was a pretty basic conference room with a round table and four black chairs. There was a large ficus in the corner similar to the kind her service maintained in her condo. A side table offered single serve coffee pods and maker, a pitcher of water and glasses, and a box of tissues.

From what Sienna had read, the company did the typical private security work, but they were hired more and more to do overseas kidnap rescue missions including one well-publicized case recently, when they were sent to bring home a child whose non-custodial parent had fled the country with him.

She would guess the tissues were for those cases.

"Why don't we sit," Gin said, drawing Sienna's focus back. Sienna could feel Boon's eyes on her as she pulled out a chair and sat, nervous now at having to explain why she'd come to him for help after all these years.

***

Boon took in the woman before him, still trying to handle the fact Sienna Evans was in his office. Apparently, he should have put more than the 900 miles between himself and his childhood.

Hair that had once always been pulled into braids of one pattern or another was now cut close-cropped to her head. It might not look sexy on another woman, but with her it drew all the focus to her large eyes and full lips.

Legs that once boasted a collection of scrapes and bruises that bore witness to her ability to climb the highest trees in the neighborhood, were now long and shapely leading up to curved hips that drew his eyes more than they should.

He pulled his eyes away from her body before he studied other changes too hard. He was ogling her like a drunk frat boy and he didn't want to be that man.

She was gorgeous. And she was here.

She and her family moved to Austin when they were still kids, but when Loid offered him the job here, he hadn't ever imagined she was still in the area.

Then it hit him. Gin said Sienna asked for him. So she'd known he was here?

He waited until she and Gin sat before taking a seat to the right of Sienna with Gin on the other side of the table. He shouldn't care that she was in trouble, but hell if he didn't.

"What's going on, Sienna? You're in some kind of trouble?" He thought back to the notation in his calendar. This was a private protection case.

Her dark eyes went stormy for a minute, but she met his gaze and nodded. "The police are looking into it, but I feel like I need some kind of protection until they catch the guy."

Boon stiffened. "What guy?"

Okay, so that came out a lot more growl than inquiry, but so be it.

As much as he wanted nothing to do with his past, he couldn't help but feel protective of the woman before him. This was Sienna. If she was in trouble, he had to help her.

Sienna sighed and pulled her phone from her shoulder bag. "I was at a protest two weeks ago," she glanced Gin's way, then looked back to him. "A Black Lives Matter protest."

Boon nodded. He and some of the guys had gone down to one of the protests in Austin before he'd been sent on an assignment in another city last week. They had wanted to support the movement but also knew they could put themselves between protesters and any counter-protesters who came to cause trouble. Their presence could usually shut down any threatening or antagonistic behavior pretty quickly.

She held her phone out to Gin and Boon fought the urge

to swipe it away so he could see for himself what was on the screen.

"There was a man there who was really worked up. He got in our faces."

Fuck this. Boon grabbed the phone. On the screen was a shot of Sienna holding a protest sign. Towering over her was a big ass white man and she wasn't kidding when she said he got in their faces. The man's face was red with rage, mouth open as he screamed at her.

But, God, there was Sienna, standing tall and staring him dead in the eye. Her face was still. She was in control, even though he could see the edge of fear in her eyes. She faced that man down.

The picture gave him chills for so many reasons. For the danger she might have been in if this asshole lost control. For the sorrow of knowing she had to look at this man who hated her so much simply because of the color of her skin. For the way he wanted to step between her and this motherfucker to keep her safe.

Not that she would have wanted him to step between her and the man. She would have been furious with Boon if he did something like that, but at least he could have stood at her back and glared the asshole away.

"He's not letting this go?" He asked. Had the guy somehow tracked her down and was harassing her?

She shook her head, taking back the phone. "My friend posted this picture and it went viral. Most of the comments and things have been positive and really supportive. But some..." she shook her head. "My name is out there as the woman in the image. At first, it was fine, but in the last week, I started getting some really threatening messages."

"Through Facepage?" Gin asked.

Sienna nodded. "And now email. Some of them are just angry rants, but there's one guy that just keeps messaging and he's pretty specific about the way he wants to put me in my place."

Boon growled again. He would kill this asshole.

"And you can tell this is the same person?" Gin asked.

"Yes. The threats always include some of the same details." Sienna pulled up her emails and moved to hand the phone to Gin.

Boon thrust out his hand and she turned the phone over to him instead. God damn if he didn't sound like a caveman as he read the emails and boiled at the words he saw on the screen. The person sending them was describing in gruesome detail the way he hoped to torture and maim her before ending her existence in a country that "never wanted her scrub-ass here in the first place."

Holy hell, had the lunatic skipped the slave trade lesson in school all together? Did he think her ancestors had come over on a pleasure cruise and loved the place so much they decided to stay?

He scrolled through the emails. They were rife with the N-word and some other terms for Black people Boon had only heard used by the absolute lowest of people. Disgust crept up, trying to block out his anger.

Gin interrupted his reading.

"What brought you here to us today?"

Sienna shifted in her seat. "He started calling."

"He has your phone number?" Boon bit out.

Sienna nodded. "The police think it's the man in the picture. He was arrested for disorderly conduct but released on bail shortly after."

"They haven't been able to trace the phone calls or emails?" Gin asked.

"Pre-paid cell phone," Sienna said. "The emails are coming from a generic account with what seems to be a fake name associated with it. I wanted to hire you for security until they find him or he loses interest. Surely that will happen eventually."

Boon met her gaze. "We need to pull our tech guy in and let him look at all those emails. And Gin can look at them, too. She's got a degree in forensic psychology. She might be able to tell us something about what he might do next."

"The police are looking into it," Sienna offered.

He nodded. "And they can keep looking into it. But it won't hurt to let our people chase down any leads, too. We can share anything we find with the police."

Boon looked at the woman who'd once been his best friend. She was a reminder of a time in his life he'd long ago left behind and had zero interest in revisiting.

Even so, he couldn't help but want to be sure she was safe. Reminder or not, he would do what it took to protect her, then walk away and hope to never see her again.

Chapter Two

He looked around her apartment. "What do you do, exactly?"

If his mother was there, she'd smack him upside the head and tell him to mind his manners.

But really, the woman lived in a penthouse apartment with a garden rooftop overlooking downtown Austin. He turned in a circle taking in the gleaming granite of the kitchen and the soft cushy couches that filled the open living space.

She laughed, shaking her head. "Marketing."

"You must be good at it."

That smile widened. "I am, thank you very much."

He barked a laugh. "And not afraid to say so."

She lifted a shoulder. "In the right company, no I'm not. And I don't mind telling an old friend I've made it to a VP position in Austin's biggest marketing firm."

He whistled and shook his head. "I'm not surprised in the least, Sennie," he said, falling into using an old childhood nickname. "You always knew what you wanted and went after it. You got what you set your heart on."

She smiled his way. "Can I get you anything? Water? Coffee?"

"Coffee would be great." He put out a hand to stop her. "But let me check the place first."

She looked over her shoulder, then gave him a raised brow. That one she'd perfected that said she thought he was crazy.

"You think someone got past the doorman and the alarm and got in here?"

He gave her his own look. He'd perfected this one on the battlefield so he'd toss it up against hers any day of the week.

She relented and stepped aside, sweeping an arm out.

He started with the two doors off the front entry: a bathroom and closet that showed him she was either a neat freak or she paid a cleaning service to keep the place in shape. Probably both.

He'd already visually scanned the open living room and kitchen, but he moved into the kitchen since the island between the living room and cooking area blocked his view of the whole room.

Dark woods and granite were set off by stainless steel appliances including a range any professional chef would drool over. He stepped into a large pantry that boasted a restaurant style refrigerator with three glass doors. If he had that thing in his house, people would discover what a mess his fridge was.

Hers was organized within an inch of its life, matching the shelves in the pantry.

He went back to the living room where he easily scanned the rooftop garden through the floor to ceiling windows that took up the whole back side of the space.

The bedrooms were all that was left. He hit the one at the back of the space first, betting it would be hers since it would share the back wall that opened out onto the garden.

Bingo. King sized bed piled high with pillows and flowery comforter and a too-damned-large walk-in closet and master bathroom with a tub that could have doubled as a pool.

He went to the next bedroom. This room had a large window that overlooked the city and was almost as impressive a view as the one outside her window. He checked the closet, finding only empty hangers and a few boxes neatly stacked in one corner of it.

He went back to the living room and found she'd

moved into the kitchen, starting coffee. She looked his way and smiled.

"Everything all clear?"

He rolled his eyes. "You hired me and now you're giving me shit about doing my job?"

Her smile fell. "Yeah, sorry. I guess I've just felt like I'm pretty safe here with the security we have in the building."

"Your neighbors don't ever prop open a side door for a friend or anything?"

She shook her head. "No, there are alarms on the doors and video cameras. If a door is open for an extended period, the doorman hears an alarm and checks it. Besides, it's not a building filled with college kids who do that kind of thing. The people who move here value their privacy and want the security the building offers."

He took a seat at the island and pulled the mug she'd poured toward him, waving off the milk and sugar she offered.

She went to the refrigerator and began taking out vegetables, lining them up on the counter before grabbing a cutting board and knife.

"How does stir-fry sound for lunch?"

"You don't have to feed me, Sienna. I'm here to do a job."

He saw the stiffening of her shoulders but she forced a smile anyway.

"It's no big deal. If I'm cooking for myself, I might as well cook for you."

He nodded. "Appreciate it. And yes, stir fry is fine."

He only had his go-bag with him for now. One of the other guys would be relieving him for a few hours so he could go home and pack what he needed. He planned to grab a few cold sandwiches to stick in the fridge when he came back.

"Tell me what you've been doing all this time," she said. "You went into the Army?"

He gave her the quick and dirty version, skipping over his time as a Delta operative. "Yup. Army for three tours. Buddy of mine from basic knew my boss at HALO and got me the job when I left the military. Been with them for the last two years."

Questioning eyes met his. "And you like it?"

The question didn't take any thought to answer. "Love it." He shrugged. "Most of the time."

"When you don't?"

She'd always been one to press for more.

"Some of the work we do can be boring. Protecting spoiled heiresses, that kind of thing."

"Like right now?" There was no judgment in her tone. She was simply asking the question.

He grinned. "You're not an heiress."

She plated their food. "You were supposed to say I'm not spoiled."

He laughed at that, but when he spoke, he was dead serious. "You're not spoiled. And you sure as hell aren't boring, Sienna Evans."

She lifted the plates and led the way to the dining table at the other end of the kitchen.

The table was too big for one person, but anything smaller in this apartment would have looked out of place.

Boon went to sit but froze when he saw the photos on the wall. They were black and white images in glossy white frames and even he could tell they were taken by someone who knew what they were doing. But that wasn't what stopped him.

He looked to her and back to the image. "That's our fence."

He'd know that fence anywhere with the way the rails on half of it had fallen to the ground and someone had replaced one or two of the upright posts with metal ones instead of wood.

He could still hear her voice calling out to him. "Sure took your sweet time, Boon Montgomery. Been here near on twenty minutes waiting for you!"

"I got here as fast as I could," he'd say, not telling her he'd had to stay with his little sister until his mom got home because his dad was drunk again and Boon hadn't ever wanted to leave Julia in his dad's care when he was like that. Too easy for him to pass out and leave the two-year-old unsupervised.

She grinned. "It is."

His eyes scanned the rest of the pictures as he sat, hating the way his skin started to crawl at the nudge toward a past he didn't like to revisit. There was the fence they'd met over, another of a nearby field with the big tree and the rope swing they'd played on, but the rest he didn't recognize.

He took a bite of the food, not noticing the flavors as he gestured at the wall. "What are the other ones?"

She pointed to a picture of a swing set with an old car in the background up on blocks. "That's the playground me and my sisters played on when we moved to Austin."

Her aim went next to the back door of what looked to be a diner or restaurant. "The place my mama got work at when I was in middle school. My sister and I would go there after school and she'd bring a snack out to the back. We'd sit on that wall there and eat it before walking ourselves home and mama would ask us about our days."

The last picture showed the outside of a shoe store Boon recognized as being in downtown Austin.

"I got my first job in that shoe store stocking the shelves." She sighed in an overly dramatic way. "It's where I developed my love of Jimmy Choos."

Boon grinned and shook his head, knowing it was the response she would be expecting. "Who took the pictures?"

"My cousin Booker gave them to me for Christmas one year. You remember Booker? He stayed in Tennessee after we moved here. I'd go visit him but you weren't there anymore."

"We moved," Boon said, pushing back his plate. "Another trailer park."

There'd been an endless string of trailer parks.

He looked at the pictures again. Why would she want to remember any of that, especially now that she lived like this? The one with their fence in it showed other things, too. A rusted-out car and the trailer park where he lived.

If it had been taken from another angle, it would have showed the apartment building she lived in and the playground with the broken swings and merry-go-round that didn't go round anymore because one side of it tilted all the way to the ground.

He tried to nudge the conversation another way. "Booker's got talent."

She beamed at that. "He does. He's a photographer in New York City now. He's freelance but he sells his pictures to a lot of big name newspapers and magazines. He's won the World Journal Digital Award and the Umlaut Award."

Boon nodded, remembering the quiet boy who'd sometimes trailed them when they were ten and he was only five or six.

Maybe that was why she kept the pictures. If her cousin gave them to her, she could hardly throw them away. Of course, she could take them down and only put them up when Booker came for a visit.

"How was the stir fry?" she asked when the silence stretched.

Boon grabbed onto the question like a lifeline that could pull him from the sea of memories swamping his boat. "It was great, thank you."

It was a lie, but it was a harmless one and it was better than telling her it had turned to sawdust in his mouth, each bite seeming to clog his throat as he tried to shove it and the memories down.

With any luck, the police would catch the guy stalking her and Boon could walk away from this forced trip down memory lane.

Chapter Three

Sienna knew she would get questions when she walked into her office with Boon at her back. But bad luck had Jung walking through the lobby as she and Boon got off the elevator.

Jung's face was straight when he said he needed her help in his office for a moment, but she knew damned well what this was. This was her best friend being a nosy ass and not being shy about it.

She glanced apologetically at Boon. "Do you want to wait in my office?"

He gave a single shake, no, of his head and followed her as she and Jung went to the right side of the receptionist's desk rather than the left toward her office.

Boon took up a post outside the office door as Jung shut it and turned to her with a shit-eating grin.

"This is the guy from your childhood?" he asked in a whisper.

At least he had the sense to whisper. She waved him away from the door and over to the small table in the corner of his office where his sketches and mockups of ads lay haphazardly on the table. Her best friend was a slob.

"Shush," she said, sending him a glare meant to cow him. "He'll hear you."

Jung raised a brow. "You mean he has supersonic super hearing on top of all those muscles and perfect teeth?"

Sienna couldn't help the laugh that burst out. "He'll hear us whispering and know we're talking about him."

Jung grinned at that. He liked nothing more than causing trouble. "Probably."

Sienna rolled her eyes. "How did I end up with you as my best friend?"

"I know," Jung said, not bothering to whisper now. "I'm not even gay and I'm useless in the fashion advice department. There's really no explaining it."

"None," Sienna said, gathering her purse and briefcase with a smile of her own. She shook her head at him but she was laughing. "You're an idiot."

He shrugged. "That I am."

"I'll see you at our two o'clock," she said. "I have to finish the pitch for Gingham Paper Products."

He waved off her comments. "Bah, you know you had that pitch ready three days ago. You'll nail it."

She didn't bother to answer as she opened the door and felt heat hit her cheeks as she saw Boon. She hoped he hadn't heard any of that.

***

Boon watched as a flustered Sienna left the office of the man she'd called Jung. The stab of jealousy that hit him was ridiculous. He didn't know if she had anything going on with the man with the dimpled smile and just right hair and it shouldn't matter to him.

Just because he'd had more than one thought about how it would feel to have her curves pressed against him or what her mouth would taste like, didn't mean he should go anywhere near there with this woman. She was a job. And an old friend.

Not to mention a constant reminder of where he'd come from. That was a reminder he didn't need.

The attraction was laughable, anyway. He was anything but the type of man she'd go for. He was paid muscle. Her type would be more like this Jung guy. Someone as successful as she was who would know how to travel in the kinds of circles she did.

He shook off the thoughts and focused on his job. Sienna might feel like she was safe in her home and at work, but he knew the reality. If the guy threatening her wanted to get to her, he could and would.

Sienna walked down the hall, passing back by the receptionist's desk and going around to the other side of the floor. He scanned the area as they walked. While she nodded greetings to people, he watched the faces of the people around her, looking into every office they passed. The offices on the interior of the space were smaller with no windows. He would guess they belonged to assistants and newer associates in the firm.

She went to an office at the back of the space on the window side. They were on the top floor of a ten story building, but he would treat it as though they were on the first floor and anyone could enter at any time.

The space was bigger than Jung's office had been and its style matched the style she'd had in her home. Clean, gleaming surfaces with modern lines. Everything was simple and elegant, matching the woman before him.

As expected, the office was neat with none of the paperwork on the surfaces that might typically be on a desk. There was a slim letter-sized envelope in the middle that couldn't hold more than a few pages, a pen holder with three pens and a tablet on a stand displaying a calendar.

Sienna went to a coat rack in one corner and took off her coat, hanging it before turning to him.

"Uh, so if you want, you can probably take off. I won't need to leave the building until two for a meeting with a client."

"You won't go out for coffee or lunch?"

She glanced toward the door. "My assistant can bring me anything I need."

He looked at his watch. "I'm going to go down and talk to the guys at the security desk and then maybe take a walk around the block, but I'll be back well before two."

She was giving him a strange look but then she laughed. "Same old Boon. You were always trying to protect me when we were little, too."

He knew what she was talking about. He'd jump between her and a bully and she'd turn around and shove

Boon to the ground, talking about not needing anyone to do her fighting for her.

He crossed his arms. "You're paying me to be here."

She gave him a small smile and waved him off. "You don't have to be by my side every second of every minute. You got me here safe and sound. Take a break. Shoo. I need to get some work done and I can't do that with you standing over my shoulder."

He grinned at her then turned to go, but his movement was stopped when he heard Sienna suck in a too-fast breath behind him.

Boon spun to find her standing at her desk with the envelope he'd seen there in hand. And she looked good and shook.

He crossed to her in two long strides and took the paper from her shaking hands.

"He got in here. He got into my office." Now she sounded pissed and he was glad. Having her pissed off was a lot better than the panic and terror he'd seen in her eyes a moment ago. If she was ticked off and fighting back, she was beating this guy as far as Boon was concerned.

The page showed the same image of her facing down the man at the rally only this time it had the markings from the sight of a gun drawn over her face.

Boon growled, seeing red. He looked down at Sienna. "This guy's not going to get anywhere near you, you hear me? Not with a gun and not with anything else. I'm not going to let that happen."

She nodded at him, crossing her arms over her chest as if holding herself together.

"You sit tight here. I'm going to talk to your assistant and the head of security and find out how this got in here. Can you lock this door?"

She gave another nod, but the motion was stiff.

He moved her over to her chair and gently pushed her down into it before kneeling in front of it. "Are you okay to stay in here and lock the door while I look into this or do you want to come with me, Sennie?"

She took a long breath and blew it out. "I'll come with you. I want to know how this guy got past the security desk or if he just dropped this off or what."

Boon gave a nod and held out a hand to her.

Ten minutes later, they had their answer.

"At least he didn't make it up to my office." Sienna was still wrapping her arms around her middle and Boon hated that. He knew she was feeling vulnerable.

The man at the front security desk shook his head. "There wasn't anything unusual about the delivery. Guy delivered it this morning. Asked for a signature and everything."

"Do you record the delivery company on a log or anything?" Boon asked.

"There's no real reason to, until now, I guess." He rubbed the back of his neck. "There are usually only a handful of companies that drop things."

Sienna looked at Boon. "We have a few print shops that send things to us and sometimes there's a document that's delivered by hand."

"Did you recognize a uniform or anything?" Boon asked.

"No. He was wearing street clothes, but that's not out of the ordinary. He was a bike messenger. They don't usually wear a uniform."

"Can you get me video of the lobby for that time?"

Another shake of the man's head. "He didn't come in the lobby. He stopped me on my way in this morning and I brought it in."

"Is that out of the ordinary?" Boon asked, mostly just irritated that this man couldn't tell them a damned thing.

He only got a shrug this time.

He took Sienna's elbow, the contact seeming to settle the agitation in his gut just a little.

"Come on, let's get you back upstairs. We need to report this to the police so they can try and track the guy, and I want to call Reaper and get him on this. Hell," he said, looking over his shoulder at the guard as they moved into the elevator, "I'll bet he can and see if it was a legit messenger or not."

Sienna looked at him as he stabbed the elevator buttons.

"This Reaper guy sounds a little scary, and it's not just the name."

Boon grinned. "That's because he is."

Chapter Four

Reaper didn't find anything useful. No messenger company in the area had a record of a delivery to Sienna's building that day. Boon was starting to think whoever sent the envelope had just grabbed some teenager off the streets and paid them to walk the envelope into the building.

On top of that, the guy in the photo from the protest wasn't likely their guy. For one thing, Reaper had looked through all the threats Sienna received. The guy from the photo had still been in police custody when the first of the threats from her stalker were sent. For another, he had only been visiting the area and had since returned home to Atlanta. From the way her stalker talked, it seemed like he was still in the area.

"I need wine," Sienna said as she slipped her sneakers off at the front door.

They had been at her office late that evening and then she'd changed into more comfortable clothes and they'd met a group of her friends to march with for a few hours downtown at the protests. He was on edge the entire time they were there, knowing the chance of her running into counter protests or getting caught up in any violent flare ups if people who were more interested in causing trouble than in genuine peaceful protest, were high.

"Not before I check the apartment," Boon said, stepping around her, though he didn't blame her for wanting that glass of wine.

"Yes, sir," she said, slumping back against the door to wait in the entryway while he did his thing, but he could hear the sass in her voice.

He cleared the apartment quickly and went back to find her with her eyes closed even though she was standing up.

He found his fingers itching to reach out and brush down her face, wanting to wipe away the exhaustion. He flexed them at his sides instead.

"Hey, Sen. All clear."

She opened her eyes and gave him that warm rich smile he was growing used to seeing each day. "I'm having a glass of red and curling up on the couch. Now that we're locked away in the tower, will you join me?"

He snorted. She was no princess in a tower. She worked too hard for that. He respected the hell out of her for that, but he also worried for her, and that was unexpected as hell.

"Sure. But I'll have water instead."

She made a face, crinkling her nose at him, but when she came out of the kitchen a minute later, she was carrying a bottle of water for him and a glass of wine for herself.

They settled on the couch and he watched as she tucked her feet up under her. He wanted to pull her feet into his lap so she could lay her head back on the armrest and relax. Wasn't going to happen, but it was what his heart and body wanted to do. Thank fucking hell his head was in charge.

"Do you ever take a break?"

She opened her eyes and grinned at him. "You worried about me Boon Montgomery?"

Yeah, he was, but she didn't need to know that.

"You go back to Tennessee a lot?" she asked.

He scowled. "Not if I can help it."

He'd finally gotten his mom to let him buy her a little condo in Austin so there was no real reason for him to go back there. His dad was still in Tennessee but he and Boon hadn't talked in a long time.

"Don't you have friends there?" she asked, brows raised and he could see she truly didn't understand why he wouldn't want to visit.

He lifted a shoulder. "Not so much. Most of the people I was friends with went their separate ways when I joined up and I have enough friends here that I don't miss them."

"Hmmm." She twirled her wine glass but he could see she wanted to say more.

"What does *hmmm* mean?" The Sienna he knew had never been one to keep her opinions to herself.

When they were young, she'd be all up in anyone's business, even if that meant going toe to toe with the older kids on the block. That had been bad news for Boon, who usually had to end up fighting off anyone who tried to come at her when they didn't like what she had to say.

Of course, she'd been right there with him, little fists balled up doing her best to land a punch.

"*Hmmm* means it sounds like you're afraid to go home. I didn't think you were afraid of anything."

Boon laughed at that and his hand that had somehow moved to her leg, stopped the slow circles it had been making there and stilled. "There's a difference between being afraid and just not wanting to visit."

Her brows rose in challenge. "You sure about that Boon?"

He didn't answer.

"Where a person comes from is important."

"Really?" he challenged. "I wouldn't think you'd judge someone for where they come from."

She shook her head, sipping the red liquid in her glass. "I don't mean it that way. I mean it's important for you to remember where you've come from. Who your people are and what made you the person you are today. You wouldn't be the man you are today if it weren't for what you went through as a kid."

He shot her a look. They'd never talked about his family or what his family life was like when they were kids. It was one of the things he liked about her. At school, people made fun of him for living in a trailer and having a dad who couldn't hold a job. A dad who more than once lumbered through town stupid drunk on cheap alcohol, picking fights with anyone he could work into a lather.

But with Sienna, she'd just accepted him. Never cared that he didn't have nice clothes or fancy shoes and shit.

He looked around at her place. "You like to remember where you came from now that you're making so much money, that's fine for you. But I don't need that."

She made a dismissive sound and her eyes narrowed. "That's not at all what I mean. I wouldn't have made it to where I am if it weren't for my mama teaching me that I can take pride in a job and do it well. That I can see something I want and go after it. I wouldn't be the person I am if I didn't have my family surrounding me and cheering me on. If I didn't have good friends to call when I thought I was too tired or things were too hard to keep pushing for what I wanted. My past lifts me up and keeps me moving to my dreams."

He tipped back the water bottle and drained it to avoid answering her. She didn't get it. They'd both grown up poor, but she was different.

She had a family who'd always been there for her. Her mom and dad had worked several jobs but Boon remembered the way they'd smile and pull Sienna into hugs when they came home. He remembered the way Booker and her other cousins had her back no matter what.

His mom had done the best she could, but it had been hard to keep the tension out of their house whenever his dad was around. Boon protected his little sister from it as much as possible when they were kids, but by the time he was eighteen, his mom had kicked his dad out and Boon joined the Army looking for some kind of way to get out of their go-nowhere existence.

There was no way he wanted to revisit that.

"Where is Carrie nowadays?" Sienna asked, leaning forward to put down her glass before settling back on the couch again.

She looked sleepy, but content to snuggle into the couch instead of going into her bed and he moved closer, letting her lean into him instead of the arm of the couch. He wondered if he was going to have to carry her there later.

His body tightened at the thought of it and annoyance flared. He didn't need to be thinking of Sienna that way, but somehow, his body wasn't getting the fucking message. The more time he spent with her, the worse it got.

She was smart and funny and so damned gorgeous. He couldn't stop thinking about the way she'd stood up to that man at the rally. Yeah, it had gotten her into the position she was in now, but that was on that asshole. It wasn't her fault. She'd stood her ground, proud and fierce.

"Boon? You still with me?" she teased.

He shook off his thoughts. "Carrie's in the military, too." He furrowed his brow. "She went Navy. I'll never understand why she didn't choose the Army," he said with a grin, "but she loves it. She's stationed in New Orleans."

"Easy flight for you to visit."

He nodded. That was one visit he didn't mind making. He and his mom flew down a couple of times a year and Carrie came up to Austin when she could get away.

"Is she married? Kids?"

Boon smiled wide at that. "She and I take turns trying to turn mom's push for kids away from us to the other one. Carrie says I'm older so it should be me first."

Boon had no interest in kids, or at least he thought he didn't. Why then was he picturing little girls with Sienna's big brown eyes and her guts and grit?

He stood, probably a lot more abruptly than he should have if the look on her face was any clue.

"I need to make a few calls before bed." He went to the door and double checked the deadbolt and alarm. "You need anything, give a holler."

He didn't need to look to know she had a stunned expression on her face, but he kept moving to the guest room he was using. He needed to put distance between them, pronto.

Chapter Five

A week next to Sienna—opening the door for her, breathing in her scent when they stood close, going home with her at night—was starting to wear him down. More than once, he'd seen a look in her eyes that said she was struggling with the same attraction he was.

He might have to take up Gin on her offer to send one of the other guys over so he could take a break, if for no other reason than to save his sanity.

Problem was, when he thought about anyone else being the one here with Sienna, he went bat-shit crazy. Which just showed how insane he was, since he trusted the people he worked alongside with his life.

There hadn't been any other contact after the picture that was dropped at the office, but Boon was on edge, something in his gut telling him this guy hadn't just given up and walked away.

He scanned the area again as he opened Sienna's car door and put a hand to her lower back to lead her into her office building. He wanted them to be walking into a restaurant like this. Wanted this to be a date, not a job.

He was so damned pitiful.

She'd stopped being a reminder of a painful past he wanted to erase and was now the woman he couldn't get off his mind, and didn't want to.

She smiled at him as they walked, making that dimple in her left cheek show up. He smiled back, winking at her as they moved.

And then shit went to hell. There was a man coming at them, something in his hands.

It didn't take any conscious thought for Boon to process that it was a gun. As the man raised his weapon, Boon moved, pushing Sienna to the ground to cover her with his body.

The sound of the weapon firing reverberated in the air, competing with Sienna's scream as they went down.

Three shots. Within seconds, there was more screaming from those around them.

Boon watched as the man ran around the side of Sienna's office building.

"Are you all right?" He scanned her body, checking for injuries, from either the bullets or the fall. "Sienna, talk to me."

Fuck, if he lost her… He should have been focusing on their surroundings more, not fucking staring at her mouth wondering what it would taste like. He should never have been on this job. Or at least, not alone. He should have taken help when it was offered.

She pushed against him. "I'm okay. I'm good."

Thank fuck. Boon scanned the area again. "Get inside the building." He stood and helped her to her feet, gently pushing her toward the security guards who were coming out before taking off after the asshole who'd dared to fire at Sienna Evans.

He had to assume the guards had called the police, but that guy would be long gone by the time the police arrived.

He circled the building, drawing his weapon from his shoulder holster to carry it low by his side as he moved. The man was halfway across the back parking lot when Boon caught sight of him. He checked the area, saw it was empty, and picked up his pace.

"Hey!" Boon called out.

The man turned, raising his gun toward Boon.

Boon didn't hesitate. He fired, two shots.

Boon kept his eyes on the man as he fell. Sienna's stalker lay crumpled on the ground as Boon moved toward him and kicked the fallen gun away. He holstered his gun before leaning down to check for a pulse. It wasn't the man from the picture at the rally, but Boon would bet it was the man who sent all the messages to Sienna.

The guy had a pulse.

A security guard came around the building holding a Taser on Boon.

Boon raised his hands up, waiting for the guy to recognize him. He did, and lowered the weapon, but when his eyes went to the man on the ground, he went white as a sheet.

"We're gonna need an ambulance. You got cameras back here?" Boon asked. When the police arrived, he'd most likely be taken into custody while they sorted the situation out. If he had video showing the man pointing his weapon at him, things would go a lot more smoothly.

He turned to see the guard wide eyed and shaking his head.

Fuck, this man was useless in an emergency.

"He wasn't supposed to... this wasn't..."

"We need an ambulance," Boon barked, then the man's words registered and he stood.

"No," said the security guard as he backed away, and then he bolted.

Boon moved fast, tackling the heavy-set guard to the ground. This was the man who'd taken the threatening photo from the supposed messenger and Boon started to put things together. Had there even been a messenger or had the guard brought the photo to the office himself.

Boon held the man on the ground as sirens began sounding in the distance as more voices filled the parking lot.

He wanted to get to Sienna. He needed eyes on her to see she was okay. But he couldn't let this scumbag get away.

"Boon!" Sienna's panic was unmistakable as she ran to him, her sharp eyes taking in the scene and realization dawning in her eyes.

When the police arrived there was chaos for a short time until Boon was able to explain what had happened. An ambulance took the shooter away but he had a police escort and Boon knew he would be cuffed to the bed in the hospital.

After seemingly endless questions, he was finally able to wrap his arms around Sienna.

Fuck, he hadn't realized how much he needed that. Needed to feel for himself that she was okay.

He ran his hands over her back, her arms, up to her head as she held tight with her arms around his waist.

He could feel his heart slamming against the bars of its cage and he knew how it felt. He wanted to scream and rail at the danger she'd been in and he knew then that what he was feeling for this woman from his past was no casual attraction.

Chapter Six

Sienna let out a sound that was something of a cross between a sob and a gulp as she melted into Boon's arms.

She lost her battle with tears as he pulled her tight to him. This wasn't like her at all, but she might need to give herself a break after what she'd just been through.

He shushed her, squeezing her before leaning back to look her in the eyes. "I'm okay, Sienna. I'm fine."

"They're not charging you?"

"No. The DA will need to sign off on that for sure, but the security guard is spilling his guts. Turns out, he's friends with a group of guys who call themselves the Equality for Whites Brigade, if that name doesn't just say it all. He was the one who brought that picture to your office and they convinced him to turn off the security cameras in the front and back of the building today. He thought they were just going to try to scare you. Throw paint on you or something."

Boon's chest grumbled with what could only be described as a growl as he spoke and Sienna put a hand to his chest. Anger simmered in her gut at his words. Rage that she would have to go through something like this because of her skin color. But at the same time, this was what she dealt with every day of her life. It was nothing new and it was exhausting.

She almost laughed. Exhausting was too soft a word for it, but she didn't have any others.

Boon lifted her chin and met her gaze. "Let's get you out of here."

She nodded. She should be glad this was over. The man would be going to prison when he got out of the hospital.

Hopefully, the security guard would as well, though she would guess since he was cooperating, maybe he wouldn't. Still, the immediate threat was gone. She should feel relieved.

Instead, she could only think about the fact that this meant it was over. She didn't need a bodyguard anymore. And that probably meant Boon Montgomery was about to be out of her life again.

Chapter Seven

If this were a normal job, Boon might have said goodbye to the client at the station. Or maybe escorted them home one last time, only to say goodbye at the car.

This wasn't normal and this wasn't just any client.

He didn't want to say goodbye to Sienna.

They drove in silence and when he parked her car in the lot and came up with her, she didn't comment on it.

He held her hand in the elevator, liking the way it felt to be with her like this.

And that's when he knew, he wasn't going to be able to walk away. He'd never so much as let himself kiss Sienna, but God he wanted to make love to her tonight. It was so damned many ways of fucked up and wrong.

He wasn't good enough for her, but maybe she'd have him anyway.

"Sienna," he said when she'd opened the door. He tugged her inside and pulled her so she faced him. He wasn't imagining the heat there, was he? He searched her gaze.

She reached up, putting her hand to the back of his head and pulling him down. Her mouth met his.

Fuck. All thought fled as he drew her closer, taking over that kiss and making it his. Theirs.

She was soft against him as her lips parted for him and his tongue swept against hers. He wanted to taste every bit of her. Wanted to know if every inch of her tasted as sweet as her kiss.

He should move them to the bedroom. Should slow them down.

Hell if he could do a damned thing but let his hands

467

explore her curves as she lifted one leg and his cock went harder as she cradled herself against him.

He backed her to the wall and cupped her breast, his thumb grazing and teasing the nipple.

Too fast. It was all too damned fast.

She raked her nails over his shoulder and he groaned. Then he was reaching for his shirt and then hers. She was pulling her skirt up and reaching for the fly of his pants.

His fingers traced the lace of her panties and he slid his fingers over the fabric to feel the wet between her legs. He could smell her and he wanted her with an intensity so damned deep he couldn't have put it into words with a gun to his head.

She freed him from his pants as he stroked her and then he had her panties off and he was sliding inside her.

A week ago, he wanted nothing to do with the woman who'd walked right out of his past, forcing him to revisit a time in his life he wanted no part of. Now, he prayed she would want more than just this one night. That she'd want what he wanted. To see where this could go between them. To see if they had a future together instead of only the painful echoes of the past.

***

Sienna woke, eyes opening as she took in the heat surrounding her and realized the strong arms holding her belonged to Boon.

She smiled as she remembered their night together. It had been a long one, with them waking more than once to make love.

The fact that this was the boy she'd bonded with so many years earlier made her grin. This was her Boon. And he sure as hell was no boy anymore.

She worried her bottom lip, the fact he wanted no reminders of his past making her question whether they could have any kind of future together. Was this only a one-night-stand to him?

Not if she had anything to say about it. She didn't want temporary with Boon. She wanted this man, heart, body, and soul.

Trailing her hands down his back sent shivers through her. Yes, she wanted all of him. She pulled back to look at his face.

Warm eyes met hers and she knew when she saw them that Boon wouldn't be walking away.

She grinned and pulled him closer, wrapping her legs around his and tangling them together in the bed.

They needed coffee and breakfast, but it could wait. She wanted this man even more and she wasn't one to put off what she wanted once she set her sights on something.

And right now, her sights were on a future with the man who'd grabbed her heart.

.

The end.

LORI RYAN

Lori Ryan is a NY Times and USA Today bestselling author of romantic suspense. Sienna's Sentinel is a taste of a new series she'll be writing in as part of Susan Stoker's Special Forces World in February 2022.

In the meantime, if you want to read more of her work, check out the Hereoes of Evers, TX series here: https://bit.ly/EversTX It's one of her favorite series with heroes to die for and heroines strong enough to take them on.

To find Lori on Facebook or Twitter, go to her website at www.loriryanromance.com. Thank you so much for reading!

PACING

by M. JANE COLETTE

Akin felt as if he was in an episode of *The Twilight Zone*—not the new series, which he had never seen, but the old 1959-1964 one, which he had sometimes watched in re-runs with his mom as a kid. Item: he was in a bar with his stepfather. Item: everything around them looked as if it was perfectly normal. As if they were totally existing in a normal universe. But they weren't. They had been transported to the Twilight Zone. Definitely. Proof: his stepfather was asking Akin for dating advice.

This was, Akin thought, proof of how good his relationship with his stepfather was. Frederick had, really, done everything right when he had entered Akin's mother's life when the boy was twelve. He treated him like a man. He made a big deal out of asking Akin's permission to court his mother, which his mother—"Nobody owns me, Freddie, his daddy didn't own me, and this boy sure doesn't!"—had thought was ridiculous... but also charming. He asked Akin's opinion about any contemplated change to the house in which his mother had brought him up ever since he could remember, from painting the outside trim to replacing the aged carpets with laminate. And while he didn't exactly take Akin's side when his mother rode his ass—which was pretty much all the time—Akin knew he was in his corner.

Plus, he was fucking cool. A dreadlocked Rastafarian straight from Jamaica—although, on the balance, he probably smoked less weed than Akin did. A drummer and a guitarist, with a killer voice, who quickly started getting regular gigs in the neighborhood. An incredible cook. A damn good soccer player too, he had spent hours kicking the ball around with Akin, trying to convert his stepson to the game.

Akin, like most of his friends in Calgary, preferred basketball and hockey. Still. Frederick's footwork was impressive.

He had been a good stepfather, and, Akin had

472

thought, a good husband and partner to his demanding, amazing—but so damn demanding—mama. For more than fifteen years.

But now, here they were, Akin twenty-eight, and Frederick and his mama both over fifty.

And, courtesy of Akin's mother's forceful request for a divorce, Frederick was newly single. And asking his stepson for dating advice.

"Boy, I've been off the market for a decade and a half," he was saying now, staring into his beer. "I don't know how anything is done. Dudes at work, they're talking about all these dating sites. I don't want to use a computer or robot to meet a woman."

Akin had no idea what to say.

"How do you meet girls, son? Fine specimen like you. Beating them off with a stick, always." Frederick looked at him with so much affection that Akin blushed.

"Well, I don't, not really, Freds." Frederick had never asked Akin to call him Dad or Papa or anything, but over time, Frederick seemed too formal, so Akin came up with his own nickname and Frederick loved it, signing all of Akin's birthday cards, Love, Your Papa Freds. "Not as much as you always think. But mostly… work, you know. And places like this aren't bad. There are some hot women at the bar."

"Sure." Frederick sighed. Then looked at him, eyes wild. "You talk to your mama lately? You think she changed her mind?"

Akin looked away. He had talked to his mama lately— just that morning, in fact. And he knew she was not going to change her mind. Thrilled that he was going out with his stepfather, her last words to Akin, in fact, were, "Can you get him to move on, Akinlolu, I'm just done telling him that I really am done." And, Sweet Jesus, how was he supposed to get his stepfather to move on?

"You've just got to get back on the horse, man," Akin finally said. "Just you know—find a woman. And do her. God. What did I just say? Excuse me." And, gulping down the rest of his pint, he escaped to the washroom.

Raquelle had lifted her eyes from her proofs just in time to see the tall man run to the washroom as if his bladder was going to explode. This was what she liked about bringing her work to bars like Bijou, despite the noise and intermittent interruptions: the people watching. She imagined how many beers he had drunk and how scintillating his companion had to have been for him to hold it for so long. Had he just started chatting up a gorgeous thing and was afraid to leave lest he get displaced? But, nature always triumphed. The mischievous part of her wondered what he'd do if all the stalls, all the urinals were taken. Was he bold enough to nudge someone over? Say, "Brother, fuck it, sorry, I really, really have to piss?"

The thought made her laugh, and she was still laughing when he came up to her at the bar.

"Before you say anything, yes, I was laughing at you, but I totally didn't expect you to come up to me and call me on it," she said, still laughing, and quickly sliding her papers into her lap.

"Not the reaction I expected, but okay, it works," he said. "Do you feel at all guilty about laughing at me?"

"Not really," Raquelle said. "Did you make it to the urinal on time?"

"You just have absolutely no time for social graces, do you?" he said. "Lovely. I love that in a woman. Akin." He extended a hand.

"Raquelle." She accepted the handshake. "And you are adorable, Akin, but I'm old enough to be your teenage mother, so go scoot."

"In most other situations, I'd say, don't talk smack about my mother, bitch, or I'm gonna sic her on you, but, in this case, I want you to be my teenage mother. Er. Step-stepmother."

"I have no idea what you just said, but I feel like I'm on some kind of Candid Camera or reality TV show here. Porn reality TV show. Which, you know, you'd think there'd be some more of."

PACING

"You're utterly insane," he said. But seemed delighted.

Raquelle smiled. "It's been said," she said. "Although I've never been tested. So tell me, my out-of-wedlock gorgeous baby. What can I do for you? And kudos to me on choice of baby daddy, cause you're so pretty!"

"Funny you should say that," the tall young man said, moving closer to her. "What I was hoping you'd do is…"

She agreed. Akin couldn't believe that she'd agreed. Well, first, he hadn't believed that he had asked. He had seen her sitting at the bar, poking at an olive in her martini glass and frowning at some papers when he and Frederick had entered Bijou. Briefly, he had wished he wasn't babysitting his stepfather so that he could chat her up. Then noticed that she was probably closer to Freds' age than to his. Still. Devilishly attractive, red hair and freckles. Then he noticed her again as he made his escape to the washroom, and then he saw her see him, and start to laugh. And when she was still laughing when he came out, he saw the crinkles around her green eyes and the brown freckles that covered almost all of her nose and her cheeks, and hair the red of which might still have been natural, but probably received some assistance from a bottle—that's when he decided… well, actually, he had no idea what he had decided. He had decided to go over to her. To, what? He wasn't sure. *Not* to pick her up for Frederick.

But. Then it happened.

Well, it was pretty good the way things worked out. She was hilarious and light-hearted, and when she understood what he wanted—he didn't even really understand himself what it was that he wanted as he explained it, really—she laughed more and said, "I'm in, kitten. What a story. But only if your daddy is as hot as you. Is he as tall as you?"

"No," Akin had to confess. "Stepfather, remember? I'm made and born in Canada, but both my parents are Nigerian. Result—this hot, black six-foot-three boy. He's Jamaican and, I don't know, maybe five-eight. Not that there aren't tall Jamaicans. He's just not one of them."

"Well." Raquelle sighed. "I'm not as tall as you either,

but I expect few women are, so I'll try to swallow my disappointment. You have a plan beyond recruiting me?"

"I didn't really plan to recruit you."

She laughed. Then, just as suddenly, frowned.

"You don't by any chance think I'm an escort, do you? And this isn't some kind of sting-operation? You have a bit of a cop look about you."

He looked at her, offended.

"You think I look like a cop?"

"Cop. Lawyer. Definitely an authoritarian vibe," she said. "No?"

"Lawyer," he said. Half-reluctantly.

"Truth?" she said. "Lawyer is better than cop, because then you definitely can't arrest me. Although, kitten, there are definitely scenarios in which you snapping a pair of handcuffs on me would not be appalling."

He had a rather terrifying thought.

"*Are* you an escort?"

"Do you think I'm an escort? I asked before?" She batted her mascara-less eyelashes at him. "I've never been taken for a sex worker or an escort before. It'd be a first."

"Er." He had no idea what to say. "You're very attractive, of course," he said. "But. Um."

"So I just look crazy enough to ask if I'd go and pick up your daddy on a lark? I can work with that." And she laughed again and was up and off. "Don't hurry back to the table," she threw over her shoulder. "I'm magic, but I'll need at least five minutes alone with the man."

By the time Akin made it back to the table, the woman—Raquelle—was sitting in Frederick's lap. Well, not exactly in his lap, but her chair—which used to be Akin's chair—was pulled so close to Frederick's chair that she might as well have been sitting in his lap.

PACING

And she had one hand on his knee. The other moved in a sensual dance between her cheek and Frederick's shoulder.

His stepfather looked entranced.

Akin approached the table and cleared his throat.

"Oh." Frederick looked at him as though he had forgotten his existence. "This is—ah—Raquelle. Raquelle, this is my son. Akin."

"Stepson," Akin was quick to correct. Then hated himself for it—he never did that to Frederick. But Frederick didn't even notice.

"I took your chair. I'm so sorry," Raquelle said. Not taking her eyes—or hands—off Frederick.

"I'll get another one," he said.

"I hope there'll be no need of that," she said, getting up in one fluid, leonine motion. "I've been trying to convince your"—she paused, looked at Akin, and threw him a vamp-like smile—"stepfather to go for a ride with me. On my motorcycle. The weather is perfect for a ride. Don't you think, Frederick?"

Of course she'd have a motorcycle, Akin thought. Oh. And fuck. A pierced tongue. He loved pierced tongues. And vampy, older women. He felt a little… regretful.

"Well, as I was saying," Frederick said, throwing Akin a look the younger man was not sure how to interpret, "it's sort of a father-son date…"

"I'm afraid I don't have a sidecar for your baby," Raquelle purred. Her eyes were laughing, but Akin felt mildly insulted anyway. "But I think… perhaps your son will excuse you? Just this once?" She smiled again, with her entire mouth and body. The piercing in her tongue flashed.

Akin heard his stepfather groan.

"Of course I will excuse you," he said graciously. And then, in a flash, they were gone—and Akin found himself thinking about a pink pierced tongue. Red hair. So many freckles. And, as he noticed when she had led Frederick out of the bar, a rather nice, full ass for a white girl.

He sighed. It all went down just as he had sorta-kinda planned.

He should have no regrets.

477

But. He had to admit that he did.

He avoided texting Frederick the next day. Or the next. He didn't want to know—well, anything, really. And that, he told himself, was as it should be. There are things that were best left unsaid between sons and mothers, sons and fathers. Sons and stepfathers. He did not want to be his step-daddy's wingman. Ever again.

But of course, when Frederick called him the following week, Akin picked up. And of course, he asked—"So. Freds. The last time I saw you, a hot redhead was taking you for a motorcycle ride. How was it?"

"Fine. Just fine. Good." His stepfather sounded tongue-tied, which totally was not like him. Akin tried to decide whether he should prod—or wait. "Thing is," Frederick finally said. "She wants to see me again."

Fuck.

Akin heard himself have the thought. Pushed it away.

"That's great," he said, in a hearty way that he hoped didn't sound fake.

"She said—she said she's got a friend she thinks I should meet."

"That's great," Akin said again. This time more sincerely. The woman was definitely a little—well, whack, really. But good-hearted. He could totally see her setting Frederick up with a...

"Thing is, I'm a bit worried," Frederick said. "You—well, you didn't get a chance to really talk to her that night. She's really something. Very"—a pregnant pause—"different. Free thinker. So I'm not sure... if it's a set-up. Or. You know."

"Sweet Jesus, Freds, you're not sure if it's like a blind date set up or a threesome? You are the lamest Jamaican I know. I take it back. You are the lamest Black man I know. The *squarest man* I know. Do you know how many..." Akin stopped himself. Here he was, again heading into territory he did not want to explore with his stepfather. Ever.

"Yes. I know. I don't do enough drugs, I don't drink enough, I don't fuck enough. Do you know that your mother actually accused me of *not* cheating on her? *Not* cheating on her. As if that was a character flaw. I am who I am, Akin." A long pause followed. "So. Would you come with me, son? In case…"

"No!" Akin screamed. "Absolutely not! You did not actually—wait until I tell Mom, she's gonna tear you a new one and you're really going to wish…"

"God! No! Son! No!" Frederick was as appalled as Akin. "I just meant—she's a little scary. Raquelle. Just—if you could be there to, you know. Help me make sure I don't get in over my head."

It was pathetic. It was adorable. It was so Freds.

"Lamest Jamaican I know," Akin said. But he agreed.

Raquelle didn't exactly have to drag Diane to the date, but she had to use her best powers of persuasion.

"He's cute, he's sweet, he's recently separated, just like you, and already looking for true love, just like you," she said. "You will adore every last inch of him."

"If he's so perfect, why are you setting me up with him instead of going after him yourself?" Diane demanded.

Raquelle flicked her tongue back and forth and fiddled with its piercing. She didn't want to lie.

"He's just not my type," she said. She very carefully did not think about his son. Who also was, really, not her type. Too young. Too tall—okay, she was totally lying, he was perfectly tall. And he looked—well. Delicious. The stepfather was fitter, sweeter… the stepson smarter. More fun. And her brief contact with him rather tainted her planned seduction of the stepfather.

Still. She had given him a fun tour of the city's night spots, listened to his divorce woes, assessed his taste in women—and selected Diane as the woman in her contacts list to best suit Frederick at this stage of his post-divorce dating career.

And now she was dragging Diane—who, really, was going to die alone and get eaten by her cats, because the bitch refused to go anywhere—into the same bar in which she had met Frederick and Akin last week. To the same table.

And there they were, Frederick sitting at the table, Akin leaning against the bar.

She hadn't expected to see the son again. Not at all.

A big grin split her face, and she flicked her tongue piercing twice.

"Well, hello," Raquelle said, joining him at the bar after depositing her friend opposite Frederick. "And how are you going to add to my life's many experiences today? Last week, my first stint as an escort. This week, my first foursome?"

He flinched. She laughed.

"Don't worry, kitten," she said. "My friend is as… unadventurous, shall we say, as your daddy. And you."

"Stepfather, not daddy," Akin corrected her. "And why do you say I'm unadventurous? I'm the one who…" He trailed off. He didn't really want to remind her, or himself, of what he had asked her to do.

"Right," Raquelle nodded. "You. Adventurous. Gonna prove it to me?"

He leaned closer to her.

"Are you hitting on me?" he asked her in a stage-whisper.

"I don't know," she whispered back. "You are my teen-pregnancy son and I did just give your daddy a ride last week—I understand that this is a very popular subgenre in both porn and romance, but it's not really my thing, you know? Still, what I want is to change this foursome into a twosome for Diane and Frederick, because—let's face it, I scared the shit out of your sweet step-daddy and she won't."

They both glanced at the pale, middle-aged blonde, who seemed very happily engaged in conversation with

PACING

Frederick.

"You know her long? Good friend?"

"I met her in the grocery store on Wednesday. Thought she'd be perfect for your dad."

"You're shitting me."

"I'm kidding. Maybe. Does it matter?"

She was very close to him and she smelled like coconut and cocoa butter and...

"Engine oil," she identified the third smell for him. "Bit of bike trouble on the way. So. Kitten. We gonna ditch these two lovebirds?"

"How?" Akin asked.

"Hmm. You're right. We'd better not leave together, because if Frederick feels as icky about the whole father-son thing as I do, he'll freak. Okay, what we do is—you notice any cute girls?"

"You want to add another girl to the mix? I'm barely keeping up as is."

"No—you tell Frederick you hooked a cutie, and she slipped you her number and you've texted her and she's already texted back, and would he mind terribly... He ditched you last time. He owes you. Then you leave, and go find my motorcycle. Pink Harley. It's just down the street."

Pink. And a Harley. Of course.

"What?" she said. "If I'm gonna ride a hog, I'm gonna ride a custom-colored, girl-colored hog."

"And how are you going to make your getaway?"

"First I'm going to moon over Frederick a bit so that Diane gets motivated and competitive. Trust me. I know women. Then I'll fake a child care emergency. Good old stand-by. Diane will buy it, 'cause she's got kids too."

"You've got kids?" Akin asked. But Raquelle was already traipsing back to the table.

The pretty boy was waiting beside the motorcycle when Raquelle made her exit fifteen minutes later. She was excited—too excited. *Down, girl.* This was—just the two of them playing Cupid for his poppa. And Diane, who also deserved some happiness—or at least the company of a

481

sweet, gorgeous man for one Saturday night.

"Tell me the helmets aren't pink," Akin said. She laughed.

"Pink, with pig tails," she teased, reaching for the top box.

"Sweet Jesus, thank God I'm so full of toxic masculinity not even a pink helmet will do me damage," he said. "So. Where are we going to go?"

"I was thinking," she said, tossing him the helmet— black—"that as I am providing the wheels for our adventure, you should provide the destination."

He caught the helmet. Put it on. Looked at her.

"Is this the part where I say, my place?" he asked.

Raquelle shook her head. "Am I going to have to teach you about foreplay and pacing, kitten?" she said. "I'm starting to think I should have stuck with the daddy, not the son. Hop on, little one, and hold on tight."

"You're kind of obnoxious," he said, straddling the bike behind her. He put his arms around her waist. Loosely. Comfortably. They felt good and she was glad he couldn't see her smile or her flush.

"I try," she said. "So? Where am I going?"

"Head east," he said. "We're gonna outrun the city lights."

Thirty minutes later, the bike was parked on a range road, and they were lying next to each other at the edge of a canola field, staring at the sky.

"You're redeeming yourself," Raquelle said. "I hadn't pegged you for an outdoor boy."

"Hey, brothers can like the outdoors too," Akin said. "Especially after we come back from a family trip to Lagos. Somewhere between seventeen and twenty million souls in that city, depending on who is counting. And who is counted." He felt himself becoming broody and he tried to shake it off. He was laying in a Western Canadian prairie field on a blanket of clover under a blanket of stars, next to a beautiful—if weird as all hell—woman. He should—focus. Except, on what?

Was he trying to seduce her? She him? Or were they just… hanging out?

He regretted pulling her into his scheme to launch Frederick back into the dating world. He should have just gotten him drunk and left things at that. Instead…

He sighed.

"Kitten is sad," Raquelle said, rolling onto her side. "Come, tell mama all."

He looked at her. "Why do you keep on doing that?"

"What? If I had played my cards just a little differently, I could be your step-stepmama now. And…"

"Why do you keep on bringing up…" He stopped. There was no point. He shifted a little farther away and looked at the starry sky.

She closed the distance between them.

"Imagine there's a shooting star," she said. "Now make a wish."

He closed his eyes. Made a wish.

Her lips brushed his cheek and she settled, comfortably, naturally, into the crook of his arm. Awkwardly, cautiously, he reached over to stroke her hair.

"What are you thinking?" he whispered. Regretted his words as soon as he spoke them: the moment was fresh and fragile. And she was going to turn it into a joke.

"I'm trying to decide if fucking in a canola field is on your bucket list. Or mine. And whether one or both of us is the kind of pervert who gets turned on by public sex. And how often, or if at all, anyone drives down this road. And also…"

He kissed her. It wasn't a sweet or romantic kiss, but a desperate, anxious one—he just wanted her to stop talking. She responded, parting her lips and letting him find her tongue piercing. He shifted his body to slip his hands under her hips and pulled her onto his torso. Her hair flowed down and covered her face, his. She raised herself and sat up, straddling his hips. He felt, rather than saw, her attempting to tie her mane of hair up.

"Leave it," he said. "I love it."

She leaned back down, her hair covering them both. But now, he did have to push it out of the way to find her lips. Her neck. A round breast. As he started to fumble with her blouse buttons, she put a hand on his. Pushed it off her. And then moved away herself.

"Pacing," she murmured. "Pacing."

His cock was hard and twitched. She sat up. And reached for his hands.

"Make-out session under the stars, check," she said. "But I am a city girl. The mosquitoes are eating me alive, I'm terrified we're going to roll into a cow patty, and I'm pretty sure I heard a coyote howling. Next stop?"

"I'm in actual physical pain," Akin protested. "Like… actual pain."

"It will pass," Raquelle said. "All things do." She leapt up onto her feet and extended her hands towards him again. "Come on, kitten. Up and away."

Akin stood up slowly, unwillingly. Raquelle pulled him towards her. Kissed his chin, then pulled his head down towards her lips. He groaned.

"Pacing," she murmured. "And, kitten? I need you to remember this. Because I'm old enough to be your teenage mama, and you're clearly a romantic. I'm the woman you picked up in a bar to flirt with your step-daddy—cause you kinda sorta thought I was an escort. Or at least a morally flexible cougar."

"You can't really talk while you're kissing me," he murmured back, into her hair, her ears. "Can you please stop talking? And I am not romantic."

"Starlit sky on a summer night? No. Not at all." She kissed him again. Pulled away. "Pacing. Fun. Play." Stepped away. "Don't fall in love, you idiot."

"You're a little full of yourself, aren't you," Akin called after her as she walked towards the Harley. She turned around and shrugged.

His hands around her waist felt good, so good, as

good as the kisses on the clover-covered bank beside the canola field. His body pressed against her back—she shouldn't think about it, any of it. She should ride and feel the wind and speed and night, and just enjoy the moment.

As they entered the city again, and the first red light stopped them, she felt a pang of sadness. The night, the adventure was almost over. She would say now, "Next stop?" And he would say, again, "My place?" And she'd make a joke about pacing again—and either go with him or not go with him. Sleep with him or not sleep with him—well. What Raquelle would usually do is sleep with him—because he was delicious—and happily dance out of his life. She really should have slept with his stepfather, she thought, suddenly angry at herself. Who was sweet and lovely—and totally not right for her, but they would have had a fun night, and now, she would most definitely not be thinking about fucking this boy.

Who was too young. And too cute. And too—she sniffed. He smelled really, really good. Like sandalwood and amber? And lust. She wanted that scent all over her, over and over and over again.

And that way lay pain and grief and loss.

She would definitely *not* sleep with him. That would be better.

The red light seemed to last an eternity.

"Next stop?" she yelled.

"Are you afraid of heights?" he yelled back.

"Terrified," she told him the truth. "Absolutely terrified. But I climb every hill, every ladder. Are we going to scale the Calgary Tower from the outside?"

"Something even better," he yelled. Then yelled a downtown address into her face.

The light turned green.

They left the motorcycle in a well-lit spot in front of a downtown hotel and then, hand-in-hand—Raquelle had tried to evade his hand, but Akin insisted, reaching for it again, and again, until she finally let her still-gloved hand rest in his naked one—walked towards his office tower, which

485

happened to be the tallest building in the city's skyline.

They said nothing as he swiped them into the building.

Into the elevator.

Pushed the button of the top floor.

"You work for Jones Brown?" she asked. "When you said lawyer—I had no idea I was hanging out with royalty! Did I make you pay for my drink? I don't think I made you…"

"Hush," he said. And wrapped his arms around her. Kissed her. "I am a third-year associate. Utterly insignificant."

"Kitten, I know the royalty of this town inside and out, and there are no insignificant lawyers at Jones Brown. They own the whole entire town. Well, their clients. Holy fuck. The holy of holies."

"Trust me," Akin said. "I'm utterly insignificant. One of two Black lawyers in the firm, by the way, which means my face gets slapped on all of the promotional materials to demonstrate that we're not racist assholes even though all our department heads and highest earners are. And—I told you there are two of us? Both of us, we've been here for three years. Chima's mother is white and his father is from Cameroon. He's like half a foot shorter than me, and fifty shades lighter. The managing partner still can't tell us apart."

"I'm sorry." She rested her face against his chest. "I've met your managing partner, you know. At our last meeting, he told one of his lackeys to 'Get that cunt out of my boardroom.' He's a charmer. Must be hell to work for."

"Yeah, well." Akin looked at Raquelle's somber face. "You've been kicked out of a boardroom by the managing partner of Jones Brown? What the hell do you? Are you a lawyer too?"

"I could be a lawyer. Or, a forensic accountant?" she said hopefully. "Or, like, an undercover federal financial crimes kinda guy?"

"You're not a guy." He nuzzled her cheeks. Ears.

"Is sex in your building elevator on your bucket list?" she said. Before he could think about it, the elevator door opened. And she stepped through it, pulling him behind her.

Despite being once booted out of a Jones Brown boardroom, Raquelle was not really familiar with the layout of the firm's offices. Even if she had been, the midnight tour made everything seem eerie and otherworldly. With light-saving measures in place, the hallways and boardrooms were illuminated by the city lights outside coming in through the floor-to-ceiling windows and the occasional humming monitor.

"Is there roof access?" Raquelle asked as Akin maneuvered her towards the lobby's immense window.

"There might be," he whispered into her hair from behind her, then wrapped his arms around her. "Would that be more terrifying than looking out of this window?" He pressed her against the glass. She made herself look down.

"This is pretty damn terrifying," she said. She felt her heart rate elevate and panic start to rise. She was going to fall. She was going to die. She should close her fucking eyes—but she couldn't...

And suddenly, she felt herself being pulled away from the window, and she was in the middle of the lobby, her face pressed against Akin's chest. Moaning.

"Sweet Jesus, I'm so sorry," he was saying. "Christ, Raquelle, I—I didn't realize you were really that afraid. Why would you—you should have told me."

"Would you believe me if I told you I like it?" she said, still breathing hard.

"No," he said. "You were absolutely terrified. There was no joy in what I saw."

"The joy comes now," she said, very simply. She didn't expect him to understand, nobody ever did. She just needed him to keep his arms around her—just like this—tightly—creating a safe place while her heart rate came down and the spinning in her head stopped.

"You are a very odd woman," he said. Kissed her hair.

Forehead. Eyebrows. The tip of her nose and then the tip of her chin. Her neck. She moaned and arched her back, giving him better access to her cleavage. Breasts.

He nuzzled them with his face through the fabric of her blouse before starting to fiddle with the buttons. Raquelle let him, losing herself in the sensation, heart rate still elevated from the terror of the heights, vertigo giving way to a different kind of dizziness.

"I don't get this kink," he mumbled through a mouth full of breast, "but would it be served in a safer way by being fucked with your back against the glass? You wouldn't see... but you'd know it was there?"

He was sweet. He was so fucking sweet, and she was soaked with desire and she wanted to rip his clothes off and take him on the floor of the lobby of this fucking law firm right now.

But then she remembered his story in the elevator—and her own experience with the Jones Brown managing partner.

"It might," she said. "But I have a better idea."

"Why are we going to my managing partner's office?" Akin asked again.

"One, because it's as high as the lobby—I told you, before I was booted out of the boardroom, I got yelled at in his office," Raquelle said. "Two—you'll see when we get there."

"This isn't the kind of sick plot twist where I find out that I thought I was picking you up but actually, you set up the whole thing to pick me up to get into Jones Brown and steal files or sabotage computers or something, is it? Because, like I said, I'm a lowly third-year associate and one, I don't have access to anything and two, I really don't want to get fired."

"It's not. But love the plot twist and the way your mind works. Also, you weren't picking me up. You were propositioning me to proposition your father, which, you know, is the most..."

PACING

He turned around and pulled her towards him. Kissed her.

"Stepfather. And you really need to stop bringing that up."

"Stepfather. So tell me, does the 'step' part really make a difference? I mean, does it…"

"Raquelle!" He pushed her against a filing cabinet now, and covered her mouth with his hand. "Can you please. For the love of god. And my penis. Stop talking."

"Buzz kill?"

"Total buzz kill. Is that what you intend?"

She looked at him. Bit her lips. Shook her head.

"Call it," she murmured, "a defensive mechanism. Now. Let go of me. And let's go to the holy of holiest."

"It's going to be locked," he called after her as she slipped out of his arms and walked ahead.

"Not going to be a problem," she called back.

It was locked, but as Raquelle had anticipated, it was not a problem. Sensitive documents in law firms were, for the most part, digitized and protected that way. Actual secret papers—of which there were not nearly as many as thrillers would make one think—were kept in vaults and bank safety deposit boxes. Locks on individual office doors were mostly for privacy.

She had this one opened in two minutes.

"How the fuck did you know how to do that? Are you a burglar? Lock picker?"

"I researched locksmithing for a project once." Raquelle decided that admission was not damning. "I got really into it. Bought some of the tools."

"And you carry them around with you in your purse?" Akin was staring at her with disbelief.

"Backpack, nor purse. And, you would not believe the number of times I lock myself out of my house," Raquelle told him as she stood up. Pushed the unlocked door open. "Coming?" She stepped over the threshold.

He did not follow.

"Raquelle?" he said. She turned around in the doorway.

"You're gorgeous. And fun. And I'm really into you. Clearly. And I am again thinking that this is the part with the plot twist in which you've engineered this whole…"

She slipped her blouse, still unbuttoned, off. Unclasped her bra, and dropped it behind her. Undid the top button of her jeans.

"This is the part of the night," she said, "where you and I fuck on your racist managing partner's desk. There was no plan. Just serendipity. I too think he's an asshole—and this, let's say, is another one of my kinks. You in?"

She unzipped her jeans, and wished they were loose enough that she could just drop them—but struggling was involved.

He was still standing on the other side of the door. She stood inside the office, wearing only her panties.

She turned around.

Thongs, Akin had often thought, must have been invented by a Black man. Maybe a queer Black woman—he didn't really know what it was that women found attractive about each other. But that little bit of pink lace around that round, freckled ass—he was lost to reason as soon he saw it. She didn't have to say, do, anything else. He was in the office, his jacket, T-shirt, jeans on the floor.

And then they were on that asshole's mahogany desk, and Akin didn't care if this was all a set-up. He didn't care if Raquelle was actually a private eye or a spy in the employ of a competing law firm or client. He didn't care if she was a terrorist wanted by Interpol or just a local blackmailer.

He didn't even care if she had slept with Frederick—no, he kind of cared, please, God, that would be icky and he was pretty sure he couldn't get over it—why the fuck did he ever come up with that stupid, stupid idea?

"What's wrong?" she asked. Her ass, now stripped

even of the thong, was naked against the desk, and he was going to flip her around and take her from behind so that he could look at its lusciousness while he fucked her. "Condoms? No condoms? Cause I have some in my backpack…"

He kissed her.

"I need to ask," he said.

"Tested last time about three months ago. Four partners since then. Always with condoms," she said promptly. "You?"

"Um. Same. Well. Six months. Two partners. Four for you in three months? Really?"

"Don't judge, lawyer boy—your sexual peak is waning and mine is kind of out of control. Come back here."

"No—I—Frederick. What I need to know. I just need to know—you took him for a ride."

"I took him for a ride. We went all around the city. I dropped him off at his rather unattractive apartment building. Chaste kiss on the cheek goodbye. He did not even try to grope my ass, and I…"

Akin flipped her over in one quick motion. Groped her ass.

"Now," he breathed on her neck, "I'm not letting go of you. And you're crawling off the table—yes, like that—to your backpack for the condoms."

They heard the vacuum cleaner in the hallway at the precise moment that Raquelle was crawling around the floor looking for the discarded condom wrapper pieces and Akin, watching her ass rise up and down, was wondering if she had a third, maybe fourth condom in the backpack.

"Shit," he hissed. He was fairly sure the cleaners did not enter locked offices. But then, this office was no longer locked…

"Sshhh." Raquelle pulled him down, and then around to behind the giant mahogany desk they had just thoroughly defiled. "Get dressed. Quick."

They dressed themselves but also each other, Raquelle finding his socks, Akin hooking her bra off the ficus plant where it had fallen. He straightened the handful of knickknacks they had disturbed on top of the desk while she put the two used condoms and wrappers in a Ziploc bag and tossed it into her backpack.

"It's like you've done this before," he said. Then immediately wished he hadn't.

She looked like she wished he hadn't, too, but recovered quickly.

"Former Girl Scout," she quipped. "Always prepared. Now—I have ears like a bat. The vacuum cleaner is still far away. Make a run for it? Or wait them out and hope they don't come in?"

"Make a run for it," he said without thinking.

"When I say run—I mean—go outside very quickly, and you watch for the cleaners while I re-lock the door," Raquelle said apologetically. "Let's not get you fired today, yeah?"

He nodded. Took a deep breath.

In the end, their escape from Jones Brown was anti-climactic. The hum of the vacuum cleaner never came closer, and they saw no one during their furtive walk to the elevators. Out the building. To the pink Harley.

But Akin was clearly shaken, and Raquelle, as she handed him a helmet, decided that the time for teasing was over.

"Your place?" she asked. He nodded, and gave her the address.

They rode in silence, Raquelle very carefully not thinking anything... except wondering what *he* was thinking.

Despite not thinking, by the time she brought the Harley to a stop in front of Akin's apartment building, Raquelle had made a decision. She was not going to go in. There was no point in prolonging the night, or attempting to top the adrenaline or the excitement of the earlier, forbidden encounter.

But when Akin, after dismounting and taking off

his helmet, pulled her off the bike, she didn't resist.

She was, she realized, lost.

They had gentle, languorous sex in the shower—love-making not fucking—scrubbing, soaping, rinsing and licking each other until the water ran cold. Then more vigorous, almost violent sex on the bed. Floor. Briefly, to cool off, on his fifteenth-floor balcony—her fear and arousal both palpable to Akin, and more understandable this time.

When they finally crawled back into bed, Akin couldn't feel his penis.

And he still wanted more of her pussy. Ass.

He decided to content himself with disappearing into her breasts. Which were freckled, like her nose and ass.

"I have never said this before in my life, but I'm pretty sure I won't survive another orgasm," Raquelle said. Nonetheless not pushing him away. He wrapped his arms around her.

"We can just cuddle," he said. "Shut up. You're going to say you don't cuddle. I don't break into my managing partner's office and fuck on his desk. It's a night of firsts for both of us."

"All right," she said. He felt her relax in his arms. "But you're still not supposed to fall in love. You fucking hopeless romantic."

"You talking to me? Or yourself?" His eyelids felt heavy—he was going to disappear into sleep. He fought it: he knew, he knew that if he fell asleep, when he woke up, she'd be gone. And he didn't want her to be gone. Not yet. Not yet...

One last, he thought, one last kiss. He reached for her—or she for him—he wasn't sure. But his last waking memory was of his lips on hers.

When he woke up, the sheets were a tangle and, as he expected, she was gone.

Raquelle sat in her usual spot at Bijou's bar, nursing a martini and staring at the proofs in front of her. "Write drunk, edit sober," Hemingway was supposed to have said. In her

493

experience, it worked better the other way. Writing was exciting. Editing was hard work. And proofing—which was what she was supposed to be doing right now—was boring as all hell, and the only thing that made it endurable was this martini… and the memory of what happened the last time she had a martini here on a Saturday night…

"Before you ask, I made it to the urinal on time."

She looked up, startled. There he was. Standing beside her. Sitting beside her. A hand on the small of her back. Another on her knee. A kiss on the cheek. Lips.

She closed her eyes. It wasn't real. She conjured him up and she imagined him.

"Raquelle? Hello?"

Opening her eyes slowly, she stared into his gorgeous eyes, so brown they almost looked black. The flaring nostrils. The delicious mouth that a week ago had explored every last inch of her body.

"Hi," she croaked out. She was coming apart. Fuck. And she realized—she realized the game she had played with herself. Leaving before he woke up. And then, a week later, coming here, to the place where they had met. To "work."

To pine, and to hope that he'd come, too.

"I've brought you a gift," he said. And then, kissing her again, placed a sheet of paper on top of her proofs.

"What's this?" she asked.

"It's a contract," he said.

"What?"

"I'm a lawyer. It's a contract. It sets out all the rules for all our future encounters and the kind of relationship we're going to have."

She stared at him. Then at the paper.

"It's blank," she said.

"I thought we could write it together. Or, you know. Figure it out together," he said. "As we go. No rules or expectations in the meantime."

PACING

"Akin," she said. And realized that it was the first time she had said his name.

"Raquelle," he said. "I know all the things you might say. Or think. I've thought them too. I'm too young, and you're too fucking crazy, and my mother is definitely going to think you're too old for me, and Frederick…"

"Let's not bring him into this." Raquelle laughed awkwardly.

"Let's not, but we must, because if we're going to," he paused, "hang out," he finished lamely, "you'll see him again, and we'll need to explain that I'm the world's worst wingman, and I ended up getting the girl." He paused. "Did I get the girl?"

She swallowed. Hard.

"I don't really do—relationships. And," she looked at the blank paper in front of her, "contracts."

"It's a contract for a non-relationship then. For… you know. Hanging out together again. Motorcycle riding." He leaned closer to her. "Breaking into law firm offices. There are few other places that I'd like to… defile with you." He kissed her ear.

"You know nothing about me. Nothing," she said. "And I know… like three things about you. There are so many reasons this won't work."

"I know," he said. "But see? There's no pressure this way. We know it won't work. So—we can just. You know. Enjoy it while it does." He kissed her other ear.

"I've always wanted to have sex in the women's washroom here," she murmured. "There are mirrors everywhere."

"I like mirrors," he said. "Okay. Sign."

"What?"

"Sign the contract." He scribbled his name, in large letters, on the blank sheet of paper.

Raquelle laughed.

"You're as crazy as I am," she said. Took the pen from his hands. "You gonna take me as your date to Diane and Frederick's wedding if I sign this?"

"I'm morally obligated to do that even without the

495

contract," he said. Nudged her.

She signed. Smiled.

"Washroom?" she asked.

"Pacing," he said. Kissed the tip of her nose. Looked at the marked-up papers under their "contract." "Um. Raquelle? Now that we're legally bound to *not*-a-relationship—tell me. What the fuck is it that you do for a living?"

"You need to know?"

"I need to know."

Raquelle laughed.

"I write romance novels," she said. "And, Akin? I have this really hot washroom sex scene here that's just not working. I need help fixing it."

She smiled as he pulled her onto his lap. "Pacing," he said. "I think before they go to the washroom, he fondles—then finger-fucks her—at the bar."

"I might want to come back to this bar one day," she purred into his ear.

"Too bad. My plan for the night is to get us banned from every place we go to. Starting with this one."

Raquelle laughed.

"You got our getaway wheels ready?" he whispered. Sliding a hand down between her legs.

She closed her eyes. Sighed.

"Ready," she whispered, spreading her legs.

"I hate to teach a romance novelist her job," he said. "But baby. Pacing."

And he kissed her lips.

About the Author

M Jane Colette writes tragedy for people who like to laugh, comedy for the melancholy, and erotica for men and women who like their fantasies real. She believes rules and hearts were made to be broken; ditto the constraints of genres. The result? "A whole new sub-genre of her own... social realist erotica that's frenetic and complex and funny and very well observed."

Also, smoking hot. Which is still the most important thing in erotica, romance... and, life?

A poster child Gemini, she is, most of the time, at least two people. Her left-brain persona sold out long ago. She wears severely-cut suits of black, blue and only *that* shade of green ("No, not *that* shade—have you seen the colour of my hair and eyes? Please. Let's coordinate.") and spends a lot of time in board rooms, offices, and "war rooms" (what a name!) parsing lies. It's a living.

(But, oh, what a plethora of source material...)

Her right-brain persona longs to be an iconoclast and an artist. When nobody's looking, she writes poetry.

Twitter / Instagram / GoodReads / *sign up for* LOVE LETTERS

follow Facebook Profile + *like* Facebook Author Page

Let's exchange SECRETS TellMe @ mjanecolette.com

BLM

ANTHOLOGY

SHORT

Piper Rayne

Chapter One

Ande

A wall of humidity hits us when we step out of the airport, even though it's nine at night.

"Jesus, it's hot." Sophie waves her hand at her already red face. "I feel queasy." She hooks her arm through mine then stumbles. I right her before she falls flat on her face.

The person who should be half in the bag, stuttering and on the verge of throwing up, should be me. The shots on the plane should've been mine. But my best friend took it upon herself to start my girl's 'better off without him party' all by herself.

"Soph, you're such a lightweight," Brit says, her accusatory finger pointed. "We need to catch that bus to our resort, otherwise we'll be stuck here all night. One time when I came down with my brother…"

She continues to recount her story while walking in front of us like our designated tour guide. Sophie and I exchange the look. The one to say Brit's already starting. Hell, she started as soon as we reached the airport. Lecturing a half-asleep Sophie sliding into our Uber about what's going to happen when we arrive at the airport.

We all have our roles in our threesome. Brit is the planner, the organizer. In college, she bought our groceries, paid our bills, and would leave little notes on the dry-erase board to let us know what we owed.

Sophie is the neurotic one. Hence the drunk version of herself right now. Did you think I'd say she's the partier? Nope. She got drunk because she hates to fly. She obsesses

499

over every little thing outside her control. Which makes Brit the perfect friend for her. She plans so much, Sophie never has to worry about what-ifs with her around.

As for me? Well, I used to be the "head in the clouds daydreaming" kind of gal until my college boyfriend broke my heart six months ago. Now my mantra is that romance sucks and every man is only out to use you for as long as he needs/wants you. Not a healthy attitude by any means, but you should've heard me during my anger phase.

"Let's go Candy Ande, we're not going to make it!" Brit yells.

"Well, I'm lugging about one hundred and twenty pounds!" I yell out, earning glares from the other people waiting for buses to take them to their hotels in this mecca of transportation vehicles. "Come on, Soph, you gotta walk."

"I'm tired. I never should've taken my anxiety medicine and drank."

"You didn't. Oh, Soph." I stare down at her since she's inches shorter than me unless she's wearing heels.

She nods and Brit runs back to us after handing her luggage to the van attendant to grab mine. "Just give me your suitcase."

"You could take Sophie," I suggest, but she's already back at the attendant, handing over my luggage. "Or not."

"She's so bossy, but I love her so much." Sophie rests her cheek on my upper arm, staring up at me like a little girl.

"Who knows what we would do if she wasn't here."

It's the truth. I rely on her in situations like this. She probably mapped our path virtually before we arrived—five times over.

"Hola Raul," Sophie says, rolling her r's because she was the president of the Spanish honor society in high school. She's supposed to be our interpreter on this trip.

"Hola," he says, and Sophie leans forward like she has a secret. Raul steps back.

"It's okay, I'm not one of these people." She spins and points to everyone around us. "I actually speak Spanish. I'm not the 'hola and gracias only' kind of person. We can hold a conversation."

Raul stares at her and widens his eyes at me and Brit.

"But maybe now is not the time for that." Brit tugs Sophie up the stairs and into a seat, proceeding to sit next to her, giving her the bottle of water she bought at the gift shop and the plastic bag it came in.

"Finally, I'm off the babysitting shift." I scour the large bus searching for a spot without a head popping up over the back of the seat in front of it, but the bus is packed full. I'd rather be near my friends, but I'll settle for any seat now.

"You can sit here," a deep voice says from behind me.

Brit peeks around me and her eyes widen.

Great. I can't read whether her expression is good or bad.

"You're a cutie," Sophie says. Apparently her usual shyness was drowned in mini bottles of vodka on the plane.

I slowly turn and he stretches his arm out, removing a backpack from the empty seat beside him.

"Thank you." I slide in with only a quick glance his way because Sophie has already embarrassed us enough.

"No problem," he says, his deep voice eliciting a shiver up my spine.

I sit and put my oversized purse I use when I travel in my lap. He fumbles with his phone between his legs, a text message screen up.

Other than noticing his strong dark-skinned hands, I don't catch much about him. Leaving me in the dark about Brit's look. He sighs and I instinctively glance over. His hands are kind of sexy. Hands don't usually get me going, but I do appreciate short trimmed nails and those veins that bulge just slightly out of the skin on the forearms. I mentally note no wedding ring. Not that I should care, I'm in no shape to have a man in my life, no matter how briefly.

"Excuse me," he says.

My eyes slide up the corded muscles in his forearms to his bulging biceps and over his broad shoulders to a set of stunning brown eyes. Looking deeper, there are small bags underneath them and his eyelids hang low as though he could fall asleep at any moment.

Other than looking like an exhausted mother of a newborn, he's all strong jaw, high cheekbones wrapped in a beautiful copper-bronze skin.

"Do you know?"

Shit, I was gawking and now I have no idea what he asked me.

"Yep, you're on the right one. We're going there too," Brit interjects, her head peering over the back of our seats.

He nods. "Thanks." I watch him hammer out a text to someone, his phone vibrating every millisecond after as his screen pings one text after another.

He sighs again and turns the screen off, ignoring the vibrating.

Busy man, I guess.

The two of us sit in silence. Sophie's groaning and Brit's lecturing her is the only conversation on the bus filled with travel-weary passengers.

"Okay guys, cool it," I whisper.

Sophie sighs and puts her head against the glass window, while Brit rolls her eyes. But at least they both quiet down.

"Have you been there before?" The deep timbre of his voice next to me undoes something inside of me that I can't explain.

"Where's that?" I ask.

He chuckles and I realize he's talking about the resort we're staying at.

"Oh, the resort?" I glance over and make eye contact. He truly is a beautiful man. He nods, a smile tipping the corner of his lips. I find myself waiting for his full lips to open completely but they don't. "No. But my friend Brit can probably rattle off any fact you'd like to know. She's like having your own personal travel guide."

He turns slightly in his seat and glances back to Brit. Following his vision, I find her scouring through papers. She looks up, sensing our eyes on her. "What?"

He laughs and he falls back into the seat. "Always a good thing to have a friend like that."

I nod. He's not wrong. It's nice never having to plan a thing when we're together. Although sometimes her stress ups my anxiety. "Once we get there, I'll force-feed her a few drinks and she'll relax."

"I'd love a bed, but I'm pretty sure my friends will force-feed me some drinks too." Just as he says it, his phone vibrates again.

"Guy's trip?"

"No. I'm here for a wedding. But all my tea—friends are here too, and it might turn more into a guy's trip if someone doesn't keep them in line." There's a fleeting look like he's holding something back. Not that I'm stellar at reading people, I couldn't even read when my jackass ex was coming home late from being out with another woman rather than working late at the office.

I nod.

"Is it just you three girls?" he asks.

"Yeah."

"Well, I will apologize for my… friends. They can get rowdy and loud. Let's just say you'll probably hear us before you see us."

As though he knew exactly what his friends would do, the bus pulls up to our resort and a bunch of guys are outside with drinks in their hands hooting and hollering 'Free Man' at the bus.

His head falls forward and he shakes it back and forth. "See what I mean?" he mumbles.

Everyone on the bus stares, Brit's head turns right next to me. "Holy shit," she whispers.

Brit won't say it, but Sophie would if she were awake. The guys standing outside the bus are all hot. Every single one has big muscles and a cocky arrogance that somehow makes them more appealing. I raise my eyebrows at Brit, and she hits me in the elbow and whispers, "Rebound material, Candy Ande."

She grabs her bag and coaxes Sophie up and out of her seat because she wants to be the first one to check-in. I see the competitiveness on her face.

Then the guy next to me stands and my gaze travels from his chest up to his rich brown eyes that hold a flirtatious glint mixed with embarrassment. "Sorry," he mumbles.

"No need," I say. "Tell me though, do you and your friends play beach volleyball?"

Brit cracks up, bending over and laughing, jolting a comatose Sophie.

"I'm not sure I understand the joke?" he says, starting down the row toward the exit.

"Oh, you shouldn't."

"Top Gun, big guy," Brit says, walking down the stairs and dragging Sophie toward the check-in desk.

"Ah… so you want to see me shirtless and sweaty?" We stop right outside the bus to retrieve our luggage.

My face heats. "Don't act like you don't have mirrors in your house."

The bellhop from the resort pulls our luggage out. He hands the stranger a large duffel bag, and he puts it sideways over his body. "Let me help with these," he says, taking Brit and Sophie's large suitcases.

"You travel light," I say.

"Can't say the same about you."

"Touché, but it takes a lot for us women to look good."

His crazy group of friends grows louder as we approach. He leans in, leaving the luggage right outside the doors to the resort. "Ah, don't pretend there aren't mirrors in *your* house." He winks and clicks his tongue against the roof of his mouth before his friends swallow him up.

"What the fuck, Jet? Why the hell would you take the bus to the resort?" one of the guys asks.

He ducks his head and looks back one more time before a girl surprises him by jumping into his arms. Then all of his friends, and the girl who could be his girlfriend, head toward the bar area.

Chapter Two

Ande

"You'd think he was a celebrity or something," Brit says from next to me, her gaze following mine to where the mystery bus guy is going. "Here, can you put her in the golf cart?" She hands Sophie over to the poor bellhop who's going to drive us to our room.

"Weird, right? I got the same vibe. He's here for a wedding, I guess."

"I can't even imagine planning a wedding here. The logistics of being so far away and just showing up and finding out whether the resort has put everything together properly? No way. Not for me." She climbs into the front seat of the golf cart, leaving me in the back with Sophie.

"I just want a bed," Sophie whines and lays her head on my shoulder.

"Almost." The guy presses too hard on the gas and we jolt. Sophie growls and I enjoy the night air blowing on me even if the air is so damn hot it feels like it's coming out of an oven.

A few minutes later we arrive at our small oceanfront villa. Brit called in a favor to her loaded stepdad who has friends in high places. Although they don't share blood, she's more like him than her mother.

"Isn't this gorgeous?" The tension leaves her shoulders with the view of the moon casting down over the water.

The employee brings our luggage in and Brit hands

him the tip money that she's left easily accessible in the side of her purse. Once the door clicks shut, she flips the lock and Sophie lays on the couch. The two of us take the opportunity to walk out on the balcony that overlooks the water.

"Thanks for this," I say, never feeling appreciative enough of everything Brit does for me.

"Oh, I needed the vacation, too. Let's just forget Jackass once and for all. That guy from the bus would make a great rebound." She waggles her eyebrows.

"Did you not see the girl plastered to him when we were walking away?"

"Okay, one of his friends then. They were all hot. I think there's more to it than just a wedding. Nobody *only* has friends who look like that."

"Yeah, he almost stuttered or changed what he was going to say like maybe he was hiding something."

"You don't need to know anything except for how big their dick is anyway," Sophie calls out, standing from the couch and stumbling down the hallway. "I'll see you all in the morning." She waves her hand in the air and a door shuts a moment later.

"I'm going to unpack," Brit says.

"Yeah, I'm beat too." I wheel my suitcase down the hall. We're extremely lucky to all have our own rooms on this vacation. I unpack my clothes, put my toiletries in the bathroom, willing myself to do my nighttime routine but lacking the energy to do so.

My phone vibrates in my purse and I scramble to pull it out, expecting it to be my mother making sure I made it here safely. And yep, it's her, unable to sleep until she knows I'm okay. I fire her off a text to let her know I arrived safe and sound but that I'm tired and I'll check in with her tomorrow. Then even though I took this week of vacation, I scroll through my work emails to keep tabs on what's going on. I pause at an email from my boss asking me to call her as soon as I get this. No other information. Our company took a hit last year and an entire branch was closed. I really hope they didn't decide to wait until I was on vacation to announce our closure because the thought of someone else cleaning out my desk might make me fly home tonight.

I grow more tired the longer I lay there and play the what-if game in my head about what I'd do if my branch closed and I got laid off. The guy from the bus flickers to my mind again. An image of his hands and what they would feel like on my skin. I haven't been with anyone since Jackass and only two people before him. I'm inexperienced in the casual sex department, but that man has my libido screaming. As much as I loved the jackass, toward the end of our relationship, our sex life turned redundant and predictable—like a bad community center play where we both knew our roles and acted them out without much effort or enthusiasm. A slow drum of arousal beats inside me as I wonder what it would feel like to be with a new guy. To be surprised about how he maneuvered my body.

I fall down into the posh pillow top mattress, sinking into the softness, wondering what the weight of his body would feel like on top of me.

***

The next morning, I'm the first one up. Since my boss won't be in the office for two more hours, I sneak out of our hotel room and head down to the private swimming pool. With Brit's connection to the private villa, we also get access to a private workout facility, spa, and swimming pool. There's no better way for me to clear my head before calling my boss than to swim a few laps. But when I jiggle the handle after using my swipe card, the door won't open. Scouring the area, I discover a sign that says it doesn't open for another hour.

My head falls back. "Damn it," I murmur.

One of the resort attendants walks by and stops. "May I help you?"

"I had wanted to do laps, but I see it's closed." I purposely try to keep the whine out of my tone.

"Yes, sorry. It will be open soon though." He walks away and I blow out a breath, pulling my phone out. I could go do cardio on the beach, but I hate everything it represents. I want the water to cocoon me. I want to feel myself powering through the soft wall of water on every muscle in my body. I look once more to the attendant that's already too far down the path to watch me. I peer over the fence and the pool feels like a carton of ice cream did after Jackass broke up with me. It's only being in that water that's going to make me feel better.

I throw my bag over the iron fence and do another double-take to see if anyone is close by. If someone says anything, I'll just say it was open and I didn't see the sign.

I climb the fence and I'm teetering on top, almost to the other side when a man's voice says, "Ma'am."

I lose my footing and somehow slide down the other side right into a bush.

"Ma'am!" It's that same attendant and he uses his magic key to get into the pool area. "Are you okay?"

I nod, standing to my feet and brushing off the leaves. These scrapes aren't going to feel so great for the rest of my trip. Karma really rained down on me just now.

"I'm good. Thank you." I pick up my bag and swing it over my shoulder.

"You really want to swim, yeah?" he asks.

I bite my lip and nod.

He sighs and glances around the area. I don't want to get him in trouble, but why are there rules about when I can and cannot swim?

"Okay. Go ahead."

"Are you sure?"

He nods and smiles.

"Thank you so much. I'm just going to do laps. I won't be terribly long."

He nods again and heads farther inside to where I believe the workout facility is.

I put my bag on a chair, fishing out my goggles and sink into the cool fresh water. Ever since I was a kid, chlorine was my favorite smell. It wraps me up and makes me feel like home. Once I finished high school and decided not to swim in college, I still only worked out in the water. Me and land workouts aren't so in sync. Hence the time I tripped on an elliptical and broke off half my front tooth. But for some reason, I'm coordinated in water.

After my warmup, I do a two-hundred-meter freestyle stroke to get going. And as soon as I'm done with fifty meters my mind clears and all those worries about my job and Jackass dissipate. But one thing that doesn't leave my mind is the guy from last night. Although I never saw his teeth, I imagine in my head how perfect they are when he's really happy. He was so quiet natured, and there was a hint of embarrassment when that girl jumped him. I wonder who she is to him? All of this shouldn't matter because no matter who he is, he's on vacation, and even if I did get with him, nothing would come of it. A fling does have a certain appeal. No attachments and just fun would be ideal in my life right now. Maybe Brit's right, maybe one of his friends can at least be some fun for me this week.

As I'm coming to the end of my second two-hundred-meter freestyle, a figure looms at the end of the lap pool. Shit, maybe it's a different resort employee and I'm in trouble. I stop and pull up my goggles, hoping to sweet-talk another resort attendant into letting me use the pool. But as my eyes move upward, they keep on moving until they graze over a perfectly chiseled chest and land on a familiar face.

Chapter Three

Ande

"I see you used those horrible looks of yours to score an early dip in the pool?" He chuckles.

I shake my head, pulling my goggles off completely. Thankfully, I'm in a cool pool so I don't overheat. My friend from the bus squats down so we're closer to eye level. Sweat drips down his delicious chest and six-pack of abs, glistening on his warm brown skin. He runs a towel over his face.

"You have no idea what I did to get in here early." Wow. Am I trying to flirt with this man?

He studies me for a second and glances up to the workout windows until he looks back down at me. "Why don't you tell me over breakfast?"

"Breakfast?"

"You do eat, right?" He rests all his body weight on the balls of his feet, his calves flexed as are his strong thighs.

"Yes, I eat, but..."

"Are you not finished? I thought maybe you might be since you've been out here for forty-five minutes." A smile tilts the corners of his kissable lips.

"Were you spying on me?" I look over my shoulder to that wall of windows from the inside workout area.

"Technically, I was running on a treadmill. Just when I was about to call it quits and enjoy my vacation, you came into view. Somehow watching you swim kept my interest. My body thanks you." He winks. Instinctively, my hand floats under the water to my belly to calm the flips of my stomach.

511

"Ah, how did I not think people in there would see me out here?" I grab the lane separator to stay afloat.

"Don't worry, it's me, you, and an elderly gentleman that's in better shape than both of us combined."

I smile.

"So… breakfast?"

"Don't you have wedding duties to attend to?"

He blanches. "Fuck no. Er… sorry, I mean, no. I'm not a groomsman."

"I thought maybe you were the groom after the greeting you got last night."

He falls to his ass on the cement and keeps his legs bent up to rest his forearms around. "Is that a no for breakfast?"

I tilt my head, not understanding.

"You keep asking me questions we could discuss over an omelet, French toast, fresh fruit…"

"One more question and then I'll give you my answer."

He raises his eyebrows. "My name? Cory. Cory Freeman."

I gathered the Freeman part last night from the chanting of his buddies.

I shake my head. "The girl from last night. Do you have a girlfriend, Cory Freeman?"

He squints like either the sun is in his eyes or he doesn't remember the girl who jumped in his arms and he carried away. "No." He laughs. "She's just a friend."

"Friend?" Now I raise my eyebrows at him and he laughs again.

"I'm single…" He waits for me to fill in my name, but I don't.

"Friend can have a lot of different meanings." I lean over the concrete edge of the pool and his gaze dips to my cleavage in my one-piece suit, but his vision bounces up quickly.

"None that would make us sharing a meal wrong."

I wait and stare blankly at him. I'm not about to be stuck in some love triangle. Did that six months ago and I don't care what side of the equation I'm on, I won't be a part of it.

He leans closer and lowers his voice. "I went to bed about twenty minutes after we arrived… alone."

I narrow my eyes as though I could tell whether Cory Freeman is a liar. But who am I kidding? I couldn't tell with Jackass, I'd never know with a stranger. Breakfast couldn't hurt though. He's flirtatious and his attention is spurring the part of me who's wanted to feel desired and attractive since my breakup.

Brit is right, I'm on vacation, time to live it up.

"Okay. Let's do breakfast." I pull myself up out of the pool so I'm standing on the edge. Cory stands as well, and it's only now that I realize how small and feminine his height and size make me feel.

His eyes widen and I realize that I could lose myself in those rich brown hues.

It's just breakfast, Ande. You're not looking for anything serious.

"I have one question though?" He raises his finger up in the air and the length and width of his finger causes me to clench my thighs together with the thought of it buried deep inside of me. "My mom would not approve if I had breakfast with a strange woman." I giggle and shake my head. "What's your name?"

"Ande," I say with a smile.

"Ande?" he asks and I know he's thinking Andy with a y.

"Like the small chocolate. A.N.D.E."

He sticks out his hand in front of me and licks his bottom lip. "Pleasure to meet you, Ande."

I shake his hand, and water drips off my skin onto the concrete. "Pleasure, Cory."

Chapter Four

Ande

Cory covers up his chest with the T-shirt that was tucked into the waistband of his shorts. Luckily, I have my swim cover-up in my bag.

"Buffet or sit down?" he asks when we approach the two restaurants open in the all-inclusive resort.

"Let's do buffet," I say. "More options."

"You like having options?" he asks, his large hand landing on the small of my back. "And you were worried *I* wasn't single."

I open my mouth to respond, but he leads me with the warmth of his hand to the buffet restaurant hostess stand.

"Two please," I say.

"Can we be on the patio facing the water under an umbrella, please?" Cory leans in for his request and since I'm positive he's not wearing cologne, it must be just his natural scent that has me leaning in closer.

The hostess' eyes light up and I watch her gaze fall down his body before popping back up. "Yes. For sure. Um… just give me a moment."

"Thanks," he says and we walk to the side by the waiting area for her to return.

"I have a feeling you always get what you want," I tease.

He shrugs. "Lately," he mumbles, without adding anything else.

The hostess returns moments later and grabs two

sleeves of silverware wrapped in napkins. "Follow me." She's probably close to my age, mid-twenties or younger. She's also shorter than me and more tanned than me and—I stop myself from making any more comparisons. It's a hard habit to break after Jackass ticked off the reasons his homewrecker was the perfect fit for him over me.

We follow her to the table and when we arrive, not once does Cory's gaze flicker to the hostess with any interest. He pulls out my chair and slides it back in after I'm seated. "Thank you," I say.

"Now you know three things about me. My name is Cory, I'm a gentleman and I'm…" He sits down, leaning in closer. "Single," he whispers and winks.

I lose myself momentarily in his flirtatious gaze. My core pleads with my brain to welcome this man into our orbit.

"Yet, all I know about you is that you like options, and you have two friends with you on this trip, and I'd certainly lose if I tried to swim against you."

I giggle and the busboy fills our water goblets. Then a waiter comes by to introduce himself and tell us to help ourselves to the buffet before I can respond.

Cory stands before me and we walk to the buffet area. I opt for a yogurt, granola, and fresh fruit.

I weave my way through the sparsely filled tables of the restaurant back to our table on the patio. It's early, so the few guests that are here remain quiet and subdued like they're not fully awake yet.

Cory joins me, placing two plates down in front of him. An omelet with egg whites and vegetables with a side of cantaloupe, grapes, and berries. The second plate has a big waffle with melted butter puddled into every crevice with a syrup cup overflowing on the side.

"Do you work out just to eat?" I ask, my eyes big as his waffle.

He chuckles, putting his napkin in his lap and pulling out his silverware. "I eat this." He points to the omelet and fruit. "So I can eat that," he says, pointing his fork at the waffle.

"And you work out?"

"Yeah." He nods, cutting his omelet with the side of his fork. "This is off—" He abruptly stops, just like he did on the bus. "I'm a growing boy," he says and pats his flat stomach while chewing a mouthful of egg and mushroom from what I can tell.

He's definitely a growing boy and my mind wanders to naughty thoughts about other parts of his body growing.

"So, Ande, tell me about yourself." He picks up his juice and gulps down half of it in one swallow.

"Not much. I live in Salt Lake City."

He pauses from eating when I don't say anything else. "And?"

"Do you want me to spout out some profile for a dating app?"

He leans back, laughing and wipes his mouth on his napkin as his tongue skates around his mouth. After I watch his Adam's apple bounce, he opens his mouth to speak but I beat him to the punch.

"I'm twenty-five. Like I said, I live in Salt Lake City. I'm a graphic designer for a large firm, but I'm the newbie so don't ask whether I've worked with anyone well-known. I haven't. And you met my two best friends—Sophie and Brit. We're here on a girl's trip."

He nods and from our conversation I'm reminded that I need to call my boss soon. Cory has provided a pleasant distraction from my upcoming call.

"Girl's trip? This an annual thing, or is there a specific reason?"

I choke on my coffee. "What?" I squeak out.

"Is it someone's birthday or something?"

"Oh." I take a deep breath. "No. Nothing like that."

He lowers his fork and stretches out in the seat like his long and wide body is feeling confined. "You're hiding something," he says.

"No." I sip my coffee, taking care not to choke this time.

"I can tell. You're dodging eye contact," he says, pointing to me.

My cheeks heat. Why do I care what this man thinks? There'd be no future for us even if we did hook up.

"It's a 'better off without him' trip," I say.

He nods as though he might have assumed that already.

"Your friend Sophie, the one who drank too much?"

I shake my head.

"The one who probably does spreadsheets for fun, Brit, right?"

"You have a good memory since I never introduced you," I say, spooning my yogurt.

"What can I say, that's another tidbit of information about myself. I'm observant."

"And yet you didn't know if you were on the right bus?" I look at him over the rim of my coffee mug.

"So it's yours." He finishes his juice and pushes the empty plate to the side, sliding the waffle in front of him.

"Mine what?"

"Your 'forget the asshole' trip."

A tinge of embarrassment colors my cheeks. "It's a 'better off without him' trip."

He cocks his head. "So give me the deets?"

I remain quiet, unsure how to answer.

"How long were you together? When did you break up?" He waves his hand like you get my drift, start talking.

"Why do you assume it's me?" I point to myself, probably doing a shit job of hiding the fact that he's right.

"You clearly didn't realize I asked you about the bus as an excuse to talk to you. Now I need to know what I'm up against."

Chapter Five

Ande

A huge shiver runs up my spine at his comment. While he continues to eat his waffle like he doesn't mind if I ruin our meal talking about my ex, my stomach clenches, not wanting to live in that bubble of scorned girlfriend. I want to get back to the girl I used to be. The one who believed in happily ever after's and destiny. For a moment, I was back to being her again while sitting at this table while a gorgeous man who could have his pick of any woman in this resort flirts with me.

"We met our senior year of college. We dated for almost four years until six months ago when I caught him with someone else." I get all the basic details out without sounding angry or tearing up. I deserve a pat on the back.

"Sorry." He shakes his head and swallows.

My gaze falls to the ocean, spotting a few couples walking hand-in-hand as the sun travels farther up into the sky, the waves rolling to a slow tumble by their ankles. A woman squeals when a man pretends to push her in.

"You miss him?" he asks, his voice low.

I shake my head. "No." An urge falls over me to tell him it's not Jackass I miss. It's me, the person I used to be. The one who thought people came into your life for a reason.

"Hmm…" He pushes his plate away and wipes his mouth before downing the entire bottle of water in front of him. "I'm not sure I believe you."

He waits as though he's aware I'm holding something back. How can a man I don't know see the fear gripping my insides? I open my mouth to tell him. He's a stranger and when we leave here, he'll quickly forget about the broken girl he flirted with over breakfast.

A crowd of men emerge and head in our direction with overfilled plates of food making a lot of noise.

"Freeman!" one of them says, taking a chair at the table before he even realizes I'm sitting here.

Cory pulls at his neck and catches my eye. "What's up, Tweetie," he says.

I scrunch my eyebrows at the name.

"Get away from Jet and his girl," another guy who looks a little older than the rest, smacks the guy who's already digging into his plate across the head.

"Thanks, Zeus," Cory says and the blond goddess nods and smiles at me.

The difference from last night is there aren't any girls with the group of four.

"I should go." I push my hands on the arms of the patio chair to stand.

"Wait," Cory says. "I'll walk you back." He stands himself. As we tuck our chairs back in, he pulls out a money clip and leaves a nice tip on the table. "Don't touch it, Tweetie," he says.

"No promises," he mumbles over a muffin while forking a piece of fruit. Once he swallows, his gaze fixates on me. "You have a nice day. I'll be at the pool later. I'll be the stud with all the ladies, but there's always room for one more."

"Fuck off," Cory says and shakes his head.

We're just about to step off the patio to the walkway leading to the villas when the Zeus guy calls out to Cory. "Jet, we've got volleyball in an hour. I grabbed your sorry ass, so you better be there and ready to win!"

Cory waves his hand and nods.

We pass the attendants adding towels to the lounge chairs and the bartender stocking up the swim bar. It's still so early, I have to wonder what kind of wedding trip this is that people get up this early.

"What's with the names, Jet?" I push my shoulder to his and he fumbles to catch his footing like he was lost in thought. He seems different since the guys interrupted us.

"Ah." He pulls at his neck again. "You know guys. You do one stupid thing and you're branded for life."

"I guess. I've never had a nickname." I shrug, stopping at the path to our villa.

"No? Pet name?"

"Not anything past babe or sweetie or some other cliché."

He taps his finger to his full lips and again the sight of his hand draws me in. What is it about them? Except this time I'm wondering what our hands would look like together, our fingers interlaced around one another. The contrast of his rich complexion and my fair skin. Now I'm imagining what our naked bodies would look like gliding and sliding along one another.

"I might have to change that for you."

His deep timbre draws me from my thoughts.

As if he was wondering the same thing as me, he reaches for my hand, his fingers grazing the edge of mine until I link one finger with his. I've never been with anyone as forward as Cory, and it's nice not to second guess what he's thinking. "I have a lot of obligations this weekend, but I want to see you. Will you and your friends come down to the beach today? I have the rehearsal dinner tonight and it's on a Catamaran, so I'm not sure when I'll be back, but…"

He's so forward but still wanting me to meet him halfway. It's perfect, really. I dig inside my bag and grab my phone, unlocking it and handing it over to him. "Add your number in there. Text me and we'll see."

Our fingers brush as he takes the phone from my hand, his thumbs making quick work of his task. "I'm not usually like this, but…" He steps closer, sliding my phone into the small slit of my bag. He raises his hand

and I watch his tongue slide out from between his lips and wet them while he stares down at my own lips, his eyelids heavy. "Is this too much too soon?"

I shake my head without even thinking. It's like my libido has short-circuited the pathway from my brain to my mouth and taken over control.

He smiles and his perfect teeth appear with the wideness of his grin. It's way too much for a girl like me to handle. His lips fall closer and I inhale one last breath and release it with the hope that by the time this is over, I'll be starved for oxygen.

His long fingers grip the back of my hair, positioning my head to the perfect angle for him to bend down to meet me.

"ANDE!" I squeeze my eyes shut at the sound of Brit's yelling.

Cory shakes his head and peers over my shoulder. He steps back, his hand sliding down my arm. "Hmm… tell your friend to put me on your to-do list today." He squeezes my hand once and walks back down the path. "Morning Brit." He waves.

I laugh and turn toward my fuming friend who just cockblocked me.

Chapter Six

Ande

"I've been worried about you. Answer your phone." Brit walks into the villa where a very hungover Sophie is flopped over the desk chair.

"How are we feeling?" I rub her back, ignoring Brit. She'll get over it.

"I'm starving and woke up with Brit screaming about your whereabouts."

I nod. "I went for a swim."

Brit comes back in wearing her bikini, tying it around her neck. "Actually you were about to suck face with the guy from the bus."

Sophie peers up at me with a smile like "give me details."

"Kiss, I wasn't going to suck face."

"That guy is seriously hot. Like magazine model hot," Sophie says.

"I'm surprised you remember," Brit says.

"I was drunk and sleepy, not blind. No one could forget a guy like that."

"I'm starved and I want a good spot on the loungers. With any luck, he has some available friends." Brit puts on her cover-up.

"I have to change my swimsuit. I'm in my one-piece. But I ate already."

Brit throws me an annoyed look. I'm pretty sure the itinerary she sent me had breakfast this morning on it.

"Would you say no to a breakfast invitation from

Cory?" I raise an eyebrow.

"Cory? You're on a first-name basis now." She smiles so I know she's over the fact that I went to breakfast without them. "We'll meet you down there after we eat then. Snag us a spot by the pool."

"I actually heard there might be a volleyball game with Cory and his friends on the beach."

Sophie perks up. "Tell me one of them looks like Slider from *Top Gun*?"

"Well, they're all well-built with chiseled jaws. There isn't an unattractive one in the bunch," I say.

She raises her hands. "Sign me up."

"You were half dead a second ago," Brit says, sliding her manicured feet into a pair of flip-flops.

"The Advil is kickin' in."

"I think it's more hormones than Advil." I chuckle.

Sophie rises off the chair, taking a moment to gain her equilibrium. "Let's eat and have a beach day."

"Ugh, I hate the sand." Brit sighs. "But…"

"Let's go," Sophie says, ushering her out the door.

I laugh as the door shuts behind my best friends. I pad down to my bedroom and change out of my one-piece into the bikini Sophie convinced me would grab some attention while we were here. I'm just about to pull my cover-up back on when I do a double-take on the clock.

Sara is at work or should be. I pick up my phone, seeing that Cory not only put his number in, he texted himself, so he'd have mine.

Cory: I need more details to come up with a proper nickname for you. I really hope to see you today or maybe later tonight.

I smile and move into my contacts, pulling up my work. Pressing call, I wait for her to answer or someone else in the office if she's not in, but it goes right to her voicemail which would mean no one is in the office.

I check the clock next to the bed again. Maybe they're all busy.

"Hey Sara, it's me. What's going on? I'll be in and out today but call me as soon as you get this message."

I hang up, not understanding what could possibly be happening. I hammer out a text message to my co-worker, Rachel, asking if the office is open.

Rachel: I'm running late. Damn coffee place messed up Jack's order and I would rather be late than wear his coffee when he throws it back at me again.
Me: Text me when you get there.
Rachel: Three blocks away.

I tuck my phone back into my bag. I'll check it once I'm in a chair on the beach.

Chapter Seven

Ande

Cory comes to my side as I'm talking with the attendant who handles the cabana rentals for the day.

"Is there a problem?" he asks.

The attendant looks at him and his eyes widen. Yeah, Cory is at least six-three.

"They're booked up and Brit thought one came with the villa." I look at the attendant. "It might not seem like it, but I'm saving you if you get me a cabana before my friend shows up."

Cory laughs at my side and mumbles, "Truth."

"JET!" Zeus screams, spinning a volleyball on his pointer finger over by the nets.

Cory holds up his finger to give us a minute and then digs something out of his string backpack. "Bill it to my room."

"No." I cover Cory's hand with my own. "You can't do that."

He slides his hand away from mine, turns around, and rests his back against the counter the employee is behind. "Maybe I have my own reasons for needing a cabana." He taps his keycard to his lips. Why is that so sexy?

"Like?"

"Truth?"

"Always."

"It might scare you." His gaze locks with mine and I can't look away.

"Try me."

Although I've never had one, between all the sexual energy on just a bus ride, a breakfast, and now this, I'm starting to understand one-night stands.

He leans forward, swiping the hair from my shoulder to my back and lowering his voice. "If your friends get distracted by my friends then we have the cabana all to ourselves."

My face heats even with the sun practically baking us.

"Damn girl, I love that look on you. I want to see that flush cover your entire body."

I close my eyes for a moment and breathe in deep. I should be turned off by this man I've known less than twenty-four hours but I'm ready to hide away in a cabana all day with him.

"So…" He walks around me until my back presses against his front and he slides his card across the ledge of the counter. "I cover the cabana."

Goosebumps erupt on every surface of my skin. His lips are so close to my ear I find myself arching. Just as I'm about to ask the attendant for that cabana right now, Brit and Sophie appear on the beach. Even with each of them having cover-ups on, Cory's friends' gazes follow their movements.

"Seriously, you two are always in a compromising position." Brit rolls her eyes, but her smile says she doesn't truly care.

"Another thing you should know about me—I'm a matchmaker extraordinaire." He leaves me, waving for Brit and Sophie to follow him.

I watch from afar as Cory introduces my friends to his.

Sophie and Brit shed their cover-ups and toss them by their bags. Brit starts bending and stretching. I guess she's playing volleyball. Sophie sits on a brick ledge, the Tweetie guy leaning his hip on the ledge with his arms crossed while he chats her up.

Cory walks through the sand back toward me and

the attendant tells me which cabana number we are. "It's all set. Do you want to play with us?"

We walk away from the attendant. "Volleyball?"

He chuckles. "We can't make our getaway just yet."

"Says who?"

He stops and his eyes widen. "Here I thought I'd have to convince you."

I lean forward, feeling braver than I have in years. "Convince me of what?"

"To play some tonsil hockey in the cabana."

My body reacts to his words like a drug addict to cocaine. Demanding and wanting whatever he'll give me.

"No convincing needed, but I'll play first," I say, tossing my bag next to my friends' and lifting the hem of my cover-up over my body.

"Shit," he murmurs.

"You look smokin'," Sophie calls over.

Although Tweetie doesn't say anything, his eyes are eating me up.

"Fuck, Tweetie, stop gawking," Cory yells.

He holds up his burly hands. "You can't be serious."

"As a fucking heartbeat. If your tongue doesn't get back inside your mouth, it's on."

Tweetie laughs. "You're full of shit." But Tweetie does return his focus to Sophie who tells him she's not really into guys who look at her friends with fuck-me eyes.

Fact: It's impossible to look sexy when you're walking through the sand, no matter what bikini you're wearing.

Cory's hands fall to my lower back and this time it's skin on skin and my insides heat. "I change my mind. Cabana it is."

I giggle. "You saw me in a swimsuit this morning."

He guffaws. "You're kidding, right? This has about eighty percent less fabric to it."

"I'm going to be honest, I'm not really sorry."

His gaze rolls over my body like warm honey and my nipples stiffen. He definitely notices. "Don't be. Not one bit."

I laugh and Zeus huddles everyone together, dividing

me and Brit off so there's one girl on each team. She gets to be on Cory's team and I'm on the other one with guys named Superstar and Train. Cory mumbles but doesn't argue. He's different with Zeus than Tweetie and since it's noticeable that Zeus is older than the rest of the group, I wonder if he's an older brother or something to someone.

On the first play, I jump to get the ball, but Superstar reaches it first, spiking it. The ball hits Cory, who's busy staring at me, and it bounces off his head.

"I'm going to call myself out right now. I just can't with her across from me." He raises his hand like we're in school and he's asking permission to be excused.

Then without another word, he dips under the net to my side and takes my hand. "We're going for a swim."

Chapter Eight

Ande

We're barely submerged in the water before Cory wraps his arm around my waist and bends down for me to straddle him in the water.

"Is this okay?" he asks, walking us out to the deep water.

I nod, biting my lip. The feel of his hard body against my soft curves is divine.

"I need you to know something before we go any further."

I stiffen. "You're not single?"

He laughs quietly. "No, I'm single. Man, that chump did a number, huh?"

"Okay, that's all I need to know. You don't owe me any other explanation. This is just a vacation fling. You don't have to bare your soul." I'm trying to keep things easy between us because I don't want to get all up in my head about this for fear that I won't go through with it and will regret it for years to come.

He studies me for long enough that I worry I said something wrong. "Right. Yeah."

I wrap my arms around his neck, the water cooling off my skin, but my insides are practically goo from having him so close. "Where were we then?"

He kisses the hollow of my neck. "Here?"

"That's a good start." I grind along his hard length. His *big* hard length from what I can tell.

"I'm not really into the public thing. Want to disappear to the cabana or can I entice you to my room?" His voice is gravelly.

This is moving faster than I thought, but I want this. I want to feel another man's weight bearing over me. I want to experience the rush of my libido rising and cresting as his hands travel the length of my body.

"Your room?"

"Thank fuck."

I dislodge from Cory and he fixes himself so that his bathing suit isn't tented with a huge hard-on as we emerge from the water.

We each grab our bags while Brit and Zeus are chest to chest arguing about a call. Sophie and Tweetie are busy at the bar getting drinks, so no one really notices us sneaking off.

"What a waste of money for the cabana," I say.

He shrugs, linking his hand with mine. "It's fine. I'd rather have you in my room anyway."

We walk past our villa and up the pathway leading to his room. We climb two floors and he pauses at his door with his keycard out. "You can change your mind. There's no rush."

I place my hand over his and swipe his keycard. The light goes from red to green.

He opens the door and I walk in to find a room that already holds his masculine scent. He faces the ocean just like us, but there's a king-sized bed, a small sitting area, and a balcony.

Walking the length of his room, I drop my bag on the couch and wrap my arms around myself. He comes up behind me, his arms around my waist, his hands clasped at my stomach. "You sure?"

I nod and turn around in his arms. "I know I said the whole thing about not having to tell each other anything, but you should know that I've never done this."

"You're a virgin?" He smirks.

I lightly smack his chest. "I've never had sex with someone I barely know."

He nods and rests his forehead to mine. "I've never done this either."

"Somehow I doubt that."

He blows out a breath. "I've never felt so connected to someone I barely know. Felt this pull. Like there's something here to be discovered."

"After only a day?"

He frowns, assuming I don't feel what he's describing. "I guess what I'm trying to say is..." His fingers run up and down my spine. "I'm a private person. I don't tend to let anyone in, not even just for one night. I'm guarded."

His honesty swims in his dark eyes and I almost choke up witnessing how he can just wear his feelings so openly.

"I know you've been hurt, and I've been burned a few times myself, but since you trust me enough to tell me you've never had a one-night stand before I want to tell you... my friends at the beach. Zeus, Tweetie and them..." He pauses and he splays his hand on my back, pulling me flush against him.

"Go on."

"They're my friends, that's true, but they're also my teammates. I play for the Florida Fury."

"Oh. Is that football?"

He chuckles and his fingers slide a stray hair behind my ear. "No. Professional hockey."

And all the nicknames make sense now. I don't know much about hockey or any of the players, but it explains the looks they get and the women hanging off them.

"I'm going to be honest, I wouldn't have known if you didn't say anything." I cringe.

"Well, I want you to know. It's why I'm guarded. Women use professional athletes, they trick us into trying to get pregnant. I'm one of the few Black hockey players in the professional level. I feel responsible to be a good role model for kids and to let the black kids out there know their dream is possible. So I guess this is my confession to you that I don't usually do this either."

I think there's so much more he has to tell me but as quickly as he opened that door, I can tell he's slamming it closed. I step closer to him so my breasts smash against his chest. "Your secret is safe with me." I take the risk, standing on my tiptoes to kiss him but his lips meet mine first and it doesn't take long for all the sexual energy to take control.

He circles us without breaking the kiss, the back of my knees hitting the bed. His fingers trail up my back and tug at the strings of my bikini. He watches the two triangles fall from my chest, revealing my breasts.

He sucks in a breath. "I've been dying to do that all morning and damn, it's lived up to every expectation I had."

"Can I see if my expectations have been met?" I glide one finger down his chiseled abs and cup his hard length in my hand. His dick feels as long and thick in my palm as it did when I rubbed against it in the water.

He slides his shorts down to his ankles, baring himself to me. "Well?"

I shove my swim bottoms down and crawl up the bed. "You'll do," I say, giggling as he tackles me to the mattress, sucking one of my breasts into his mouth.

He pins me to the plush hotel mattress, and after we're spent and enjoying a post-coital bliss, Cory gets a call from Zeus about the rehearsal and is told he needs to be in the lobby in five minutes. He tosses me the key. "I'll text you when we're on our way back and you can meet me here so we can do more of that again."

I fiddle with the keycard in my hand as he gives me a chaste kiss goodbye, and he's out the door. My phone dings in my bag a minute later.

I rise off the bed, assuming it's Brit or Sophie ready to give me hell for disappearing. I'll take their censure. It was worth it.

Cory: Figured out your new nickname… Hat Trick

Me: What?

Cory: Look it up and you'll understand.

PIPER RAYNE

Chapter Nine

Ande

I laugh after Googling "hat trick" and finding out it's when a player scores three goals in one game. Something that rarely happens in hockey.

I do as Cory requested, meeting him in his room that night after he returned from the rehearsal. He swindled a spot for me to join him at the wedding of his teammate but we left early for a walk on the beach which turned into beach sex, which turned into the two of us showering in his room afterward to remove about a million grains of sand from every square inch of our bodies.

He's heading back to Waterfall Springs, Florida now and I joined him in the lobby to say goodbye. It's hard to think we won't see each other again. I've told him so much about my dreams and fears over these past few days.

"Maybe we can meet up sometime. I start my season in a month. I could come to Salt Lake City?" he says.

We both know that it can't happen, having agreed last night that long-distance won't work. I haven't told Cory, but I think doing a casual thing when we meet up from time to time would be a bad idea for me. I want a boyfriend. The irony is that he's the one who made me see that.

He tucks my hair behind my ear. "You'll hear rumors. But trust me, okay?"

I swallow him in a hug that doesn't nearly cover half of his body and hold him so tight I fear tears are going to spill. He owes me nothing.

"Let's go, Jet," Zeus said as he passes. "See you around, Candy Ande." He winks and heads to his Uber where his teammates already are.

"Hey, how come you took the bus instead of a private car on the way here?"

"Don't you know me at all?" He flashes me his smile. I guess he wasn't one who wanted the fame and attention that comes with his profession. "Not to mention, if I had, I wouldn't have met you." He kisses me briefly, but it turns hot with his tongue sliding against mine. The hoots and hollers from his teammates rise out of the open windows of the Uber. "Think about coming to see me, okay?"

"Okay," I say, but we both know I won't.

"See you soon, Hat Trick," he says and shakes his head. "Damn, I need to come up with something better."

"Maybe next time," I say with a sad smile.

He nods. "Next time for sure."

I watch him walk to the Uber, Brit and Sophie linking their arms in each one of mine as though they fear I'll crumble. He takes one last look before disappearing into the large black SUV, the dark tint of the windows hiding his movements from me. Is he looking at me until he can't see me anymore, or is he already in full razz mode with his teammates? I'll never know.

"You good?" Brit asks.

"It was just a vacation fling, I'm awesome," I lie and all three of us turn around.

The woman behind the front desk flags us down and says they've been leaving messages for us. "Miss Ande—"

"That's me," I cut her off.

"Here you go." She hands me some handwritten messages. I go through them, all of them saying to call Sara ASAP.

"Shit!" I look to both my friends. "I never called my boss back. I guess I—"

"Spent every minute with Cory since you've gotten

535

here?" Sophie grins.

We rush back to the room and I dig through my bag until I find my phone. I press the button. "It's dead. How is it dead?"

"Um…" Sophie purses her lips like she wants to say something.

I run to the two chargers Brit plugged in when we got here. Tapping my toes, I wait impatiently, bringing my nails to my mouth. "If I'm not fired yet, I sure am now."

Finally, the phone starts booting up and I grab it, my thumb hovering over the home button to unlock. After what seems like a lifetime, I open it and scroll through missed calls, spotting a text from Cory first. Unable to resist, I open it. He snapped a picture of himself pouting. God, how can I already miss him?

I press the last voicemail and put it on speaker. It's Sara. "Where are you? I wanted to discuss this with you and not have to leave a voicemail, but I guess you really took this vacation thing to heart. I have news. The Salt Lake City office is closing but I've been transferred to Waterfall Springs, Florida. I'd love for you to come there with me. You have a lot of potential. I know it's short notice but…" I listen as my friends frown because if I take the job it means I'll be moving away from them.

Waterfall Springs is where Cory is. Is this some weird cosmic sign? Even if it is, all Cory and I discussed was casual meetups. He might be freaked out if he found out I was moving to his hometown.

**

Two months later…
Cory

After I leave practice, I pull up to the grocery store to buy something pre-made for dinner. Even though I can cook for myself, it puts a pit in my stomach every time I see all the leftovers when I attempt to cook for one.

My mind travels back to months earlier when I went to Superstar's wedding and Ande was waiting for me when I returned from the rehearsal dinner. She was not only naked in my bed, but she had room service deliver one of every dessert. Of course I skipped the cheesecake and went right to the pie—and not apple.

I wished we would have kept in contact. There are late nights in the hotel rooms after games that my thumb hovers over her name. I can't help but feel like our time was cut too short. That there was something between us and if we'd had the time to explore it, it could have really been something.

I grab a basket and walk toward the pre-made items, pushing Ande out of my head. If she'd wanted to reach out, she would've.

I pick up a rotisserie chicken and as I place it in my cart, my vision lands on a woman with a great ass ahead of me. The longer I stare, the more I struggle to tear my gaze away because the body looks familiar, like my hands have been on it before.

She places a bag of salad mix in her almost empty cart and she must sense me because she peers up right at me in that moment.

Ande.

I blink and shake my head.

She giggles. That same giggle that drew me to her at breakfast that morning. One I somehow know I'd love to wake up to every damn day.

I break the distance, weaving through the stands of produce until I'm right in front of her. "It's you, right?"

She giggles again and moves her finger to tuck a loose strand of hair behind her ear. I intercept and do it for her and earn a mega blush on her adorable cheeks.

"Are you here on vacation? You should have called."

She shakes her head and all I want is to hear her voice. "I moved here."

"What?" My shoulders deflate—why didn't she call me? Although that probably shouldn't be the first question to come to my mind.

She nods. "I got the call right after you left the resort offering me a position in a different branch. I didn't call because I didn't want to make it weird. It was a vacation fl—"

I place my finger on her lips and step forward, my basket free falling to the ground. Setting both my hands on her cheeks, I tilt her head up to look at me. "We were so much more than just a vacation fling."

"I know." She looks ashamed, but I don't fault her for not reaching out when she got here. She's here now and I'm not going to mess it up.

All I want to do is kiss her, but the one thing that I wished I could do with her all these months will come first, because I have to convince her she isn't just a vacation fling to me.

"Come home with me. I'll cook you dinner."

"Okay," she says and the way she doesn't play games makes me even more attracted to her.

We walk through the grocery store as I pick up items I'll need to prepare a meal for her. I grab some breakfast items too because hey, a man should always plan for the best possible outcome.

"It's so good to see you, honey pie."

She giggles at my attempt of another nickname and oh hell, I can't not kiss her right now. So I stop her in the meat section, weave my fingers through her long blonde hair and kiss the hell out of her.

IN THE LIGHT

Shannon Bruno

Chapter 1

The only sound as I walk down the hallway to the office of Roland Vester, Private Investigator, is my boots echoing off the wood floor; no other office is open yet, no lights behind the glass doors, waking them up to greet a new day.

Everyone in New York City has taken the week off, it seems; there is the World's Fair to attend and a second World War to fret about.

This year, 1939, has certainly been eventful thus far.

I stop in front of the frosted office door emblazoned with Vester's name and juggle everything. I'm holding; a stack of files, box of puff pastries, my handbag and attempting to unlock the door.

Well, I try.

The lock is old and the summer humidity has gotten to it, making it stick; it won't turn.

Blast it all.

Suddenly a voice, smooth and distinct with a British accent to my right says, "Please, Miss Coelho, allow me."

I try very hard not to be unladylike or rude and groan out loud; I like to get here ahead of everyone else and compose myself, open a window, catch my breath.

It isn't that I'm not pleased to see the man who has materialized next to me; quite the contrary.

Oscar Davies, Mr. Vester's associate, is one of the finest men I have ever known and everything that implies.

IN THE LIGHT

It's just that, although the walk between my shared apartment to the office is quite brief, a scant few blocks, by the time I reached the office this morning I was quite a mess; flustered, flushed, out of breath, my broadcloth dress and underclothes sticking to me, hair coming loose of it's chignon in an unbecoming way.

I feel most unappealing.

As the key surrenders under Mr. Davies touch and the door swings open to reveal the dark stuffy office, however, I'm so relieved that I meet his eyes and smile.

I wonder if he knows that seeing him is my favorite part of every day.

The day is busy and Mr. Vester is in a mood; I answer the calls that come through on the switchboard and deliver the messages to his desk when his head is turned.

I steal glances at Mr. Davies, dapper in his 3 piece suit, a gold pocket watch tucked into the vest pocket. He listens to the particulars of the case Mr. Vester is working on, a case of accidental death ruled as suicide as he puffs on his pipe with his forehead creasing in thought. The resulting nonpayment of life insurance has hit this family so hard- it is a pity.

Just looking at this man with his regal bearing and his dark eyes, his black skin flawless, save for the scar that runs from forehead to chin on one side of his face, makes my heart kick so hard I feel I might faint.

He is, simply, the most beautiful man I have ever seen.

"You see Oscar, I am at a dead end. Is there something I'm missing here?"

Mr. Davies leans forward and scans the documents splayed on the desktop quickly, then meets Mr. Vester's eyes and gives a subtle shake of his head.

"No Roland, not that I can see. But we're not done here."

Mr. Vester lets out a grunt of frustration and slams his hand down so hard on his desk that papers erupt like a cloud of dust and I startle.

Mr. Davies notices and gives me a nod, letting Mr. Vester indulge in his tirade so he can, simply, let it out.

Bottled frustration won't help him see clearly and he desperately wants to help this family, The Montgomery's, whose patriarch fell from pier 5 in Brooklyn Bridge Park while fishing and drowned.

The problem is proving that it was unintentional and not the bid of a desperate man facing financial ruin as Mr. Montgomery was when he met his unfortunate end.

When Mr. Vester finally runs out of words, his red hair a halo around his head, eyes watering from his own raised voice echoing in his head, Mr. Davies rests a hand on his shoulder and says, "Take the afternoon, Roland. Miss Coelho and I will go back over all the case files and see if there are any loose ends to be tied that have been overlooked."

Mr. Vester sighs heavily and I realize for the first time today how exhausted he looks; no wonder he is in such a state.

He hasn't slept sufficiently, maybe for several days.

"It's a lot of work, Oscar. How can I foist all of it onto you both?"

Mr. Davies weighs everything- the prospect of extra work, staying late, putting off his own case to help as though it's of no consequence and says, "I have no other plans today, Roland. Go rest. Miss Coelho and I will read through everything, make notes, and I will see her home safely after."

"If you're certain," Mr. Vester says but he is already donning his suit coat and hat.

He's already gone.

Day runs into night and Mr. Davies switches on lights, opens windows to air the stuffy room; he brings in dinner, Chinese takeout, which I can find no way to eat gracefully in front of this refined man so I decline, although I am famished.

"Please, Miss Coelho, I cannot bear the rudeness of eating while you are not. You've not eaten a thing today, please, indulge me."

IN THE LIGHT

I refrain from sighing out loud and nibble pieces of chicken although eating anything has made me hungrier.

Despite listening to Mr. Davies musical speaking voice and seeing his skin glow in the low light of the room, I begin wishing we could call a halt to the day.

Nonetheless, I enjoy this man's company, the way he puts everyone around him at ease, even when they don't want to be.

I hate the hours between work when I don't see him; and engineering a way to see him outside those hours feels an impossibility.

In the 9 months we've worked together for Mr. Vester, an opportunity to do so has never emerged.

I do so wish to know more about him and his life.

It is half past 9 when I feel myself yawning. We have been reading on the case for hours and nothing has become clearer- nothing new is standing out.

Mr. Davies puts his large hand over mine, pats gently.

"Miss Coelho," he says, his head tilting in sympathy, "it's late and I fear more questioning of those involved in the case is necessary before we move forward in a way that makes sense. Let's close up."

I look at his hand, which has remained over mine, the long elegant fingers and the clean, squared-off fingernails and without thinking I turn my hand face up, thread my fingers through his.

"Mr. Davies, I have a favor to ask of you."

He is looking down at our entwined fingers, his expression inscrutable, then he looks up at my face and smiles.

It is like the sun coming out from behind a cloud to warm you.

"What is it?"

"Would you call me Iris?"

He lets out a laugh that turns my insides to liquid and squeezes my hand before letting it go, standing.

"Absolutely. As long as you do me the favor of calling me Oscar."

Chapter 2

Roland Vester is ill.

He phones the party line that runs to my apartment late that night to inform me that he won't be in the next day and that, until he is, he expects a Friday afternoon summit in his home to keep abreast of the progression of the case.

He will inform Mr. Davies thusly.

As soon as I hang the phone back into its cradle, I finally let out my long pent-up low growl of annoyance.

I don't own a motor vehicle and getting to Mr. Vester's home in Brooklyn from Flushing will be an issue as the 1939 World's Fair in my neighborhood has street and subway traffic slowed to a halt.

It will be easier for Mr. Davies- Oscar, who resides in Brooklyn as well, so for that I'm grateful.

My roommate, a silly girl by the name of Dottie Jo, emerges from her room with her sheer floral robe floating around her, a cigarette smoldering in her hand, the stink of which finds my nose right away.

"Who was that, doll? That wasn't for me, was it?"

She is quite exasperating, to be sure, and quite fond of herself and the sound of her own voice, as well.

Thank goodness she is moving out at the end of the month when she weds her fiancé, William, a fine man of means who doesn't see her clearly.

She is lucky that way; her beauty is a gift that hides her glaring character flaws.

"Did I call you into the room and say that the telephone was for you?" I ask, hearing the testiness of my own voice and not bothering to hide it.

She isn't the man who signs my paychecks or the one who so often has my undivided attention, so I am through marshaling my tone for the day.

Not for the likes of her.

"Geez, doll, it was just a question. You know what might improve your mood?"

I hold my hand up to silence her which, thankfully, works like a top.

"Spare me your vulgarity, Dorothy Jo. I am off to bed. *Goodnight.*"

"It's Dottie," she snaps and whirls into her room, slamming the door behind herself.

The woman has no grace.

Much luck to her future husband.

I am awake, groomed, and dressed by 6:45 the next morning; I pause to eat a breakfast of toast with orange marmalade, brought to me as a gift by our landlady, Miss Hawthorne, and sip a cup of tea before I leave for Mr. Vester's office.

The sun has just begun to lighten the sky in the distance as I step onto the sidewalk, pulling the heavy door securely behind myself.

"Iris," a voice behind me says, causing me a start, "good morning."

I turn to see Oscar behind me, smoke encircling his head from his pipe; he is wearing my favorite of his suits, a three-piece grey pinstripe that makes him look even more elegant than usual. As he steps closer I note that he smells of a popular cologne water- lime, greenery, and pipe smoke; that is the scent I have come to identify with Oscar Davies.

"Good morning, Oscar," I say recovering myself, hopefully before he notices how taken aback I am to see him, or the flush I fear is creeping up my neck to color my face an embarrassing pink.

No such luck.

"I'm sorry to have startled you. May I walk with you to work?"

I smile at him, at how genteel his manners, and nod my head ever so slightly.

"I would like that, thank you."

He smiles back and positions himself between me and the street, then offers me his arm; I take it, the contact thrilling me to my toes.

We walk in silence until we are in the final approach of the building that houses Mr. Vester's office; as we climb the stairs Oscar says with a backward glance, "I am going to Manhattan later this morning to question Mr. Greene again. I need a few details clarified and as he is the only person aside from Mr. Montgomery who was present when the accident occurred he is the only man who can provide that for this investigation."

"I see," I respond with a nod of my head, "that is sensible."

At the office door, he extends his hand for the keys.

"Allow me. This lock gives you no end of trouble."

I bite back a smile and a moment later, we are greeted by the ringing phone in the office and a blast of heat from the confined space.

"It's another day," Oscar says as he begins opening windows.

We work in relative silence all morning until it's time for him to make the trek to Manhattan to question Hollis Greene.

The man is touchy as he is the prime suspect should the police decide that Harold Montgomery didn't leap into the Hudson River and die intentionally.

He likes Oscar, however; the odds of him refusing to answer his questions are slim.

"I shall return in several hours. Wish me luck."

I look up from the report I'm transcribing from Mr. Vester's notes and smile at him, standing in the doorway grinning at me.

"Much luck, Oscar. I shall see you shortly."

"You shall. And Miss Coelho?"

"Yes?"

"I'm afraid we shall need to work late again this evening. I do hope this isn't an imposition."

I am soaring on the inside, but I manage a calm tilt of my head.

"If we must, we must. I shall rearrange my calendar."

Oscar returns several hours later with a few bits of new information; Hollis Greene remembered a detail he didn't reveal to the police, a detail regarding how much Mr. Montgomery had to drink that day.

He claims that, because the empty bottle of Jack Daniels tumbled into the water with the man, he forgot to tell the police during questioning.

As I listen to Oscar's account, I find myself scowling.

"You don't believe him," Oscar says, sitting on the edge of my desk and giving me his undivided attention, as he often does.

He has no idea the way that my notions and thoughts being of value to him makes me feel; his faith in my opinions makes me feel quite powerful indeed.

I'm not just a clerical worker to Oscar Davies; I am an intelligent, educated woman whose thoughts are worth consideration.

"It just seems an odd detail to withhold from the police. It doesn't make Mr. Greene appear guiltier, so why not provide it to the police? Not doing so is what makes him appear guilty of something."

"My thoughts exactly. We need to shift our focus to the relationship between Mr. Greene and Mr. Montgomery; determine what it is we're being made to miss."

I nod, knowing this means that we've reached every possible conclusion without more research and with a sinking heart begin tidying the office so we can go home; straightening papers and clearing my desk of the remains of the sandwiches Oscar brought in for dinner.

As I do so, Oscar makes notes of who to talk to and what to look into further the next day- as he does, however, I feel him watching me.

I turn and see that I'm right; he has put his pen down and is leaning back in his chair, his hands interlaced over his chest, his face thoughtful.

"Oscar?" I say softly, holding back from taking a full step toward him.

I cannot describe the feeling welling inside me but in my just over two decades of life I have never felt a thing like it.

"I was thinking how splendid it would be to take you out to a proper dinner and to walk you home after, make more plans to see each other again. I was thinking how I would love to kiss you goodnight at your door."

Now I can feel the blush crawling up my neck, my breath quickening- I do not care like I usually would.

"That does sound splendid," I say, my voice huskier than I intend; I clear my throat and try again.

"It pains me that it is not possible here, to do those things out in the open, in the light. I wish we lived in a world where doing so isn't even a consideration."

I nod in agreement, but I am very taken with the idea that Oscar is clearly as preoccupied with me as I am with him.

"It would be a lovely thing to take for granted," I say and now I do step toward him, "but I must say Oscar, if I may be so bold, that we have had dinner two nights in a row. You shall walk me home shortly, as you're a gentleman."

"This is true," he says, standing, "but I would like your next words to be very clear Iris. Please. I need them to be."

"My front door is not the only place suitable for a goodnight kiss. And I would very much like to share one with you now." I say and step into his arms.

Chapter 3

It is the first of many kisses we share over the following weeks; stolen kisses in the shadows of the office at night, Oscar pressing me to the wall and snaking his knee between my legs, stealing my breath.

I become preoccupied with the idea of what would come after that breathlessness if we allowed such a thing.

In the meantime, Roland Vester isn't recovering from whatever ails him.

We make the pilgrimage to his apartment in Brooklyn for the second week in a row to find him groomed but convalescing in his blue pajama set and silk robe; his color isn't at all encouraging and he has dropped an alarming amount of weight since the week before.

The deep rumbling cough from his chest has Oscar pulling me to stand across the room from him; when Mr. Vester turns his head to get papers from his files Oscar discreetly hands me the clean hanky from his pocket.

"Place this over your mouth and nose, Iris," he says quietly, "I do not wish for you to catch what ails Roland."

"What about you?" I say softly, looking up at him.

He produces a second handkerchief from his other pocket and gives me a nod.

When Mr. Vester recovers, red-faced, from his coughing fit Oscar says, "Before we begin, Roland, I have a question."

Mr. Vester looks up from the sheaf of papers in his hands, his gaze behind his glasses one of intense annoyance.

"Yes?"

"Have you seen a physician? This illness is hanging on

longer than one would expect."

Mr. Vester whips his glasses from his face onto the desk in front of him.

"Yes, Oscar, I have seen my family doctor. He assures me that this will pass in time. Now, if you're quite finished being a mother hen to me, I would like for you to question Hollis Greene more about the work he did at Mr. Montgomery's accounting firm. Go. The infirm need their rest after all."

I clear my throat and say, "Mr. Vester, is there anything I can do for you before we go? Anything you need?"

He looks at me a long moment before he dismisses me with a wave of his hand, "No, darling girl, you may be on your way. I fear I am beyond any sort of help at the moment."

When we step back out onto the street, I look up at Oscar, whose face is one of sadness; so, I am not the only one who believes Mr. Vester is downplaying his illness.

"What do you think he has?" I ask as we make our way to the subway to descend into the station.

"It sounds suspiciously like consumption, I'm afraid. My Grandmother succumbed to it when I was a boy, and this looks very familiar. It's a terrible way to meet one's end."

I want to hold his hand- we could both use the comfort but as we wait for the subway car, I notice that other passengers awaiting their ride as well are staring at the two of us; some with curiosity, others with open contempt.

"Miss Coelho," Oscar says primly with a tip of his hat, as he takes a large step backward, "I shall meet you back at the office. Be safe."

And with that, he turns on his heel and ascends the stairs to the street.

Because the other passengers continue to stare, I

deliberately do not board the train; I, simply, wait for the next one in order to ride in peace.

It takes nearly an hour to make the return trip to Flushing; I am hot and annoyed as I navigate the World's Fair crowd on the platform and even more-so after climbing the stairs.

I fear all the meals Oscar is buying me are making me heavier than I want to be, although I don't look any different and my garments still fit.

Perhaps the heat is, simply, beginning to get to me.

I enter the building that houses Vester, PI and climb the short flight of stairs to the hallway; there is a calm quiet that I suddenly don't care for.

It's not the sound of peace; it is the sound of before.

Before a storm, before an automobile accident, before an explosion or a catastrophe.

The hair on the back of my neck stands at attention as I approach the door to the office, which is standing ajar- I push it open, the door forcing the hinges to squeak in a blood-chilling way and gasp.

The office has been ransacked and Oscar, standing in the midst of it, bleeding from a wound on his head is holding a gun on me.

Chapter 4

I should be cautious but the instant we make eye contact Oscar's arm drops to his side and I rush toward him.

"You're bleeding," I cry out, inspecting the wound on his head, but he bats my hands away.

"I'm fine," he snaps and then staggers on his feet so drastically I fear he shall hit the floor; he is too big a man for me to even attempt to catch him, as well.

"You're not," I say firmly, and guide him to his seat, "you're hurt, and you will not push me away. Sit down, please."

"I said I'm fine," he says, closing the door and locking it, "I don't need you to be my nurse maid."

I have been absorbing weekly tirades and verbal upbraiding from Roland Vester since I took this job nearly a year before, have taken the abuse silently and still shown up for work every day, on time and only left when I was given permission; I will not allow this man, a man who kisses me so sweetly, who talks to me over dinner about the what-ifs of our newfound relationship, and who sees to my well-being to talk to me this way.

I won't have it, not now, not ever.

"I apologize. I somehow gave you the impression that I was making a request. I wasn't. Sit down before you fall so I may see to your wound, sir."

He pins me with a surprised and annoyed look, but he does as I ask.

I pour whiskey from under Mr. Vester's desk onto the hanky Oscar gave me just a few hours before and begin cleaning the wound on his head; he lets out a hiss as I touch the alcohol to his injury.

"I'm sorry," I say softly, as my fingers travel over his scalp, parting his soft hair, until I find what I'm looking for; a large knot that is getting bigger by the second and is purplish in color.

"Am I going to live?" he asks as I sit down in my desk chair and begin rummaging through the desk drawer for the tiny Eveready flashlight I keep on hand in the event of a power outage.

"It is likely," I say as I power it on and shine it in one eye, then the other, "but you have one whopper of a concussion. Somebody hit you?"

He nods, "As I was unlocking the office door, yes. I didn't get a look at them, only their shoes as they ran around the office doing, well, this." He gestures around at the melee of paper strewn about.

"Did they say anything to you?" I ask as I survey the mess; it will take hours to restore the order properly, of this I'm sure, wanting to cry at the sight of my meticulously kept records reduced to so much confetti.

This is not the priority, however; seeing to Oscar's care is.

"Come," I say and switch off the flashlight, then stand, "we have more important things to do at the moment. This will keep."

"Where are we going?" he asks, looking up at me; the trust on his face tells me that he will listen and give me the respect of doing as I ask.

Good.

"Just come, I will see to your head in a place where you may better rest."

I send him 100 paces ahead of me to the back door of my building, let myself in the front, and then open the building to him; he follows me to the third floor where my apartment waits, blessedly empty of sound and of Dottie Jo.

She moved out one week early after we nearly came to blows over a remark she made about Oscar.

She stumbled in from a night out with William as I was meeting Oscar on the sidewalk to walk to the office together; when I got home that evening she sidled out of her room and began questioning me.

Who was that man?

How did I know him?

Did he actually *work* with my boss?

"What is it, Dottie Jo?" I asked finally, tiring of the inquisition when in the last two years she had said no more than 6 words at a time to me.

"Nothing," she said, holding her hands up in mock surrender, "I would just find him very distracting to work with. He is quite handsome for-"

I turned with the knife in my hand I was using to slice a tomato for my dinner and pointed it at her, "For a what? Finish the sentence. Do it."

Her eyes narrowed to slits and she said, "Never mind. This doesn't surprise me, though. Not one bit."

"Go back to your room, trash." I said and went back to my cooking, "I've no interest in further conversation with you. Go, now. Go."

The next morning, she was gone and so were all her possessions.

Thank heavens.

Had I but known, I would have gotten cross with her sooner.

Oscar surveys the living room now and I wonder how he sees it; there is minimal furnishings and little to no art, but it is clean and the smell of smoke has almost dissipated after repeated scrubbings and a continuously running box fan in the living room and Dottie Jo's former quarters.

Does it seem sad to him?

Do I seem a woman who is failing to get my life on the expected track of a husband and children of my own?

I am unsure.

Oscar Davies is incredibly hard to read.

IN THE LIGHT

"This is very cozy," he says, hat in hand, "it suits you."

"Thank you," I say and take his hat and suit jacket to hang on my coat rack by the door, a parting gift from the former tenants.

He takes a seat on the stiff, antique couch in front of the working fireplace and watches as I gather what I need to treat him; aspirin tablets, an ice bag from the freezer, one of the chilled bottles of Coca-Cola that Dottie Jo left behind.

I hand him the pills and the cola, then set the ice in front of him on the coffee table; he continues to watch as I draw the blinds and move about the room, making busy.

Chapter 5

It is Monday morning, just at sunrise, when we leave the confines of my apartment, doing a reverse of the dance we did on Friday; Oscar leaving quietly through the back door, me throwing the bolt, then exiting the front.

We meet on the sidewalk in front of the building.

Oscar looks at ease as always, but I feel timid in the light of day- for in the confines of my home we became quite comfortable touching each other and the night before we slept in my bed curled against each other.

I woke just before my alarm to my body quaking under Oscar's fingers, his hands roaming skillfully over my breasts, his lips on my neck, trailing kisses and heat from behind my ear to my collarbone.

"Give yourself over to me, beautiful Iris," he whispered as I held back my sounds of pleasure, "you need not be shy."

I gripped him to me and felt myself shatter into a thousand tiny pieces, a strained cry bursting from somewhere deep in me that had never been reached before as Oscar muffled the sound with a kiss, long and deep.

Now, as we walk to the office, it is hard to fathom that it was a scant hour ago that we were clinging to each other in my bed- I never wanted to leave that moment, that space with him.

There are other people on the street so when Oscar addresses me it is formally, which feels strange after the last two days of letting down our guard.

IN THE LIGHT

"Miss Coelho, as there has been the rather insidious incident of last week at the office I ask that you not enter or exit the building without me; and I shall ask, also, that you escort me to the investigation inquiries that Roland asked me to see to this week."

I look up at him and nod, keeping my face neutral even as the fear kicks my heart into high gear.

"You do not think it safe," I say as we ascend the stairs, Oscar holding the door for me.

"I'm afraid not." He replies, leading the way down the hallway to the office door.

I am quite surprised to find it not kicked off its hinges or the glass shattered; it looks undisturbed despite the disarray I know very well is waiting behind it.

We step inside and I begin gathering up sheaves of papers; it is disheartening to imagine the work involved in reorganizing this amount of information but as I work to clear the floor Oscar pats my shoulder and says, "Give it no thought. They disturbed only the archived filing cabinet it seems. We are lucky that way."

I want to cringe imagining leaving it in disarray, even if there are other, more pressing, matters to see to before making sense of this.

Archived cases are at completion; the information might become necessary at some point in the future, but it's unlikely.

"Well, that is a relief, then."

It is cleaned up and stashed in the closet within the space of a few minutes- as Oscar closes the door he says, setting his bowler hat back on his head, "Shall we?"

"Yes," I say, retrieving my handbag, "we shall."

Hollis Greene is a squirrelly man that I take an immediate dislike to; his eyes roam over my body and assesses me clearly.

Good for recreational usage and not much else if the sneer is anything to go by.

"Mr. Greene," Oscar says as the man leans against the brick wall of the alley where he has been unloading a truck of paper goods for a grocer, "the last time we spoke you told

557

me that Mrs. Montgomery didn't remember if her husband was drinking before he left the house and that you met him at the pier to fish. Was he intoxicated when you met him?"

Hollis Greene is busy staring at me in a way that is causing the hair on the back of my neck to stand at attention- his upper lip curls before he turns his eyes back to Oscar.

"What? When we met on the street in front of his building, Josephine was busy . . . I apologize; Mrs. Montgomery was busy. Forgive me. When we met at the bridge he was half in the bag, yes. Why? I told you all this before. Maybe you should write things down."

He's lying and I know Oscar sees it, too.

"If there is nothing else I can help the two of you with, it's my coffee break and I don't care to spend it with you. Well," he says looking back over at me, "unless the lady wants to help me occupy my time."

I have to work not to shudder visibly, and Oscar steps between us and says, "As you said- Miss Coelho is a lady. So, we shall leave you to your devices and trust that you can idle that time away on your own. Good day, Mr. Greene."

We're halfway down the block from his workplace when I look up at Oscar and say,

"What is next?"

Oscar looks troubled.

"We need to check in with Roland. I have some questions for him about the research we've done thus far. Come along now."

Chapter 6

Oscar descends into the train station 20 paces ahead of me and we wait for the train separately, not making conversation or eye contact.

We sit where we can see one another but that is the extent of our interaction; Oscar doesn't so much as glance at me until we have ascended the stairs at our train stop.

We begin the walk down the street, but I slow when I see a floral shop.

"Miss Coelho?" Oscar says a look of concern on his face.

"I shall meet you at Mr. Vester's apartment. Perhaps flowers would cheer him. I will be there shortly."

Oscar smiles and offers a gracious half bow, then sets off down the street, straightening his hat as he does so.

I duck into the shop and select a bouquet of daisies, plump and perfect, misted with dew, and set off for Mr. Vester's apartment building.

The day is lovely, bright and temperate; September is so much more enjoyable than the depths of August when it is stifling and there is no relief.

After we check in with Mr. Vester, I decide, I shall invite Oscar for a proper dinner, a meal I put thought and effort into, something special.

I realize as I climb the stairs into the building that I am quite happy- I wonder when the last moment of striking happiness I felt was.

Maybe when my Mother had Christopher.

I decide not to dwell as I climb the stairs to the second floor where Mr. Vester's apartment is located, am on the verge of humming a tune when a pair of arms snatches me out of the main hallway and into the shadows, clapping a hand over my mouth to hush me.

The arms are like a vise around me and I am lifted off my feet- I struggle and fight, pounding my fists onto the strong firearms locked around me until I recognize the voice in my ear.

The elegant British accent belongs to only one person I know.

"Iris, be still, and be quiet. Please." He whispers and I do as I am asked instantly.

"I'm going to take my hand off your mouth, but you must remain silent. For both our sakes." Oscar whispers and I do so.

In the next instant I hear floorboards squealing under shoes as the roost steps recede into the distance- Oscar sets me to my feet and says softly, "Stay here. Do not move until I return for you."

I am mute with fright so I simply nod as he slinks quietly into the hallway and goes up the staircase to the third floor quickly.

He returns a moment later, his face ashen, "We need to leave, immediately. We shall go to my home and I will explain everything there, when I know we're safe."

I look up at him and nod my agreement, allowing myself to be led down the stairs, over to the back door and into the alleyway.

Oscar's home is a small, impeccably clean one room apartment only 6 blocks away from Roland Vester's place.

Unlike in my building where I must sneak Oscar in, there is no need for such treachery here; Oscar and I enter through the front door, he tips his hat at the superintendent who is sweeping the hallway, and leads me up the stairs.

We only climb to the second floor and he leads the way to his apartment, letting us both inside; he pulls a chair out for me and then takes the seat next to mine.

"When I entered the building I heard a gunshot from the second floor; when I ascended the stairs I saw Roland's front door standing open. On a hunch, I hid until you entered the hallway, where I grabbed you to get you out of sight."

I look down at the bouquet of daisies, still gripped so tightly my knuckles are white; despite that, I still managed to forget I was holding them at all.

"When we heard the footsteps, I went up to the third floor to look down to street level and see if I could see the killer as he fled the building."

I blanch at the word and say, "Well, did you? Killer?!"

He takes my hands in his and says, "Yes. I did. It was Hollis Greene running from the building; he must have taken a taxicab and beat us to Roland's home. But, Iris? You must understand this; Roland is dead. Shot."

The blood drains from my face and I feel myself sag; I fear I might faint.

"Oscar," I say weakly, and he pulls me close, holding me for a moment before he stands and fusses in the kitchen, setting the kettle to boil.

I lay my head onto my arm on the table top and allow myself to reel from the idea that vibrant, obnoxious Roland Vester is no longer.

It doesn't feel real.

The kettle whistles and Oscar returns a moment later with a steaming mug of tea in his hand; he sets it in front of me and asks if I would like some honey.

I blink up at him for a long moment and finally say, "Have you any brandy?"

He tilts his head in surprise and despite the circumstances a smile quirks his mouth.

"I have. One moment."

He returns with a very fine-looking crystal decanter and splashes what can only be described as a baby amount of the sweet liquor into my tea.

"Just to steady you. There is more I think we should discuss and you need your whits about you."

I take a bracing sip of tea; it burns all the way down but

it breaks my haze, another sip clears my shock and my cobwebs.

"You think we aren't safe," I say, sparing him the effort, "you believe that Hollis Greene is coming for us both next."

He nods.

"I do. We need to discuss what we're going to do."

We're about to do that very thing when a heavy knock sounds on the door- and before we have a chance to answer, the knob jiggles.

Then heavy banging ensues, so loud the neighbors will surely complain- so loud that with each echoing strike I jump further and further out of my skin.

Oscar tenses and says, "On second thought, it seems the time for talk is behind us. Iris hide in the bathroom. Do not come out until I say it's safe."

Chapter 7

I hear the front door creak open and the vibrato of deep voices talking, but nothing else for a long moment.

When the voices begin again they are a bit more agitated and strained; I hear Hollis Greene demand Oscar tell him where the woman is, where I am.

They are moving closer to where I am hiding behind the shower curtain in his porcelain bathtub.

"Where Miss Coelho is remains nothing of your concern, Mr. Greene. Your business, it seems, is with me so maintain your focus sir."

"Perhaps I have business with her as well, Mr. Davies. And I don't do the bidding of anybody who is beneath me, which you surely are. You're not walking out of here, anyway, so you might as well give me what I want."

"I will never tell you where Miss Coelho is. Put the pistol down and let's discuss what you need. I fear you have found yourself in quite the pickle this morning."

"Pickle? That's putting it mildly. Whatever you wish to call it, I can't leave you alive. You know too much of my personal affairs, as did Roland Vester. He discovered beyond a shadow of a doubt that I killed Harold Montgomery and called my home to tell me that he would destroy the evidence he came across if I paid him."

My ears perk up at that; it sounds like nonsense but I am reminded of a client months earlier who once stormed into Mr. Vester's office raving about what an extortionist he was before slapping a check on his desk.

As the man left, he turned back and said, "Roland Vester, if we cross paths again you had better move to the other side of the street to avoid me. Otherwise, your head may end up taxidermized and hung in my clubhouse along with the other animals I've taken for sport. You, sir, are a maggot."

Hollis Greene is a murderous bastard, but I have no doubt that he is telling the truth; Roland Vester was a villain in his own right and his pompousness got him killed.

It might do the same for Oscar and me before the day is through.

"How much did he ask you to pay for his silence?" Oscar says softly.

"10,000 dollars. I don't have that kind of money; when I told him, he said to come up with it and that tales of my poor financial planning were not his concern."

Now I know he is telling the truth; Mr. Vester blamed me on many occasions for things out of my control, telling me that my failure was of little concern to   him.
Roland Vester was a monster.

"Why did you kill Harold Montgomery?" Oscar asks, "You're going to do away with me, anyway, so you might as well tell me. I have been unable to figure out why you would do such a thing."

"Why? Because Harold Montgomery was a crook who was embezzling money from his clients and running a side business laundering money for the mob and when the FBI started sniffing around he told them I was the CPA responsible for those accounts. He expected me to take the fall."

"Why would he do such a thing?"

I think of the way Mr. Greene referred to Harold Montgomery's wife by her first name, as Josephine, and I know before he says it.

"Because I have been carrying on with his wife for months, since before he decided to set me up to be his patsy."

"He wanted you out of the way."

IN THE LIGHT

There is silence, then the distinct sound of sobbing.

"I have always done everything that is expected of me, Mr. Davies. Now look what I have become."

There is suddenly the sound of a struggle and Oscar saying, "No!"

Then a gun blast so loud that I cower down further into the bathtub.

Tears begin to trickle from my eyes, then stream.

If Oscar is gone, what shall I do?

It is the barest of moments before the bathroom door handle jiggles and Oscar says my name.

"Open the door, love."

I do so and a second later I am swept into his arms.

All I can manage for a moment is to cling to him; he is warm, alive, and uninjured.

"You're alright," I breathe, my hands twisting into his suit jacket.

"I am alright, my Darling, as are you. But we must go. Come along."

Chapter 8

Oscar grabs a prepacked suitcase from the closet and ushers me out of the apartment, ignoring Hollis Greene's lifeless figure crumpled on the kitchen floor.

He stops in the hallway for a hushed conversation with his super, whose name is Hal, and tells him he won't be returning to the apartment and that he shall wire the remaining rent to him when we reach our destination.

Hal seems remarkably unfazed by this development and looks over Oscar's shoulder at my pale, tear streaked face.

"Is the lady alright?"

"She is, thankfully. We need to be on our way to gather her belongings."

Hal nods and then digs in his pocket for a set of keys, "Use my motor vehicle, post haste.

Leave it in the back alley behind the building when you're finished, keys on the visor, please."

Oscar nods and says, "You will let the authorities know about the body upstairs?"

Hal nods again, "I will handle it. Be on your way. Ma'am."

I breathe out a thank you as Oscar takes my arm and leads me out of the building to Hal's automobile in the alley behind the building.

We are quiet for a few moments before Oscar says, "Are you alright, Iris?"

I breathe in, then out, and consider before answering.

"I am unsure." I say, my hand fluttering to my chest, then finding his shoulder, "Are you?"

His expression is grim.

"I am fine. I tried to stop him from pulling that trigger. I really did. He was determined."

So, that is what occurred; Hollis Greene, unwilling to add to his current body count or be held accountable for his actions had chosen to leave this life instead.

He is not only a murderer but a coward as well.

"There was nothing you could have done," I say, patting his shoulder, watching his expression begin to melt into something else, something sadder.

He shakes his head and says, "No. Not without risking getting myself shot in the process and you were not safe with Hollis Greene."

Thinking of the way Mr. Greene gazed upon me; with such lascivious intentions in his eyes, I know Oscar is correct.

I try not to shake from fear.

It is not yet 10am- I fear what evening will look like.

We arrive at my building and Oscar says plainly, "You're not entering without me; your lease conditions are of little consequence now."

I nod because I knew we were fleeing; I am hoping Oscar has some idea of where to go, what to do next.

My landlady is in the hallway, polishing the front windows with newspaper soaked in vinegar; she claps her gaze onto Oscar, then me, and frowns.

"Miss Coelho," she starts, her tone a reprimand, but Oscar holds his hand up to silence her, which works instantly.

"Madame, there is no time. Miss Coelho is leaving, and the apartment shall be vacant and ready for other renters in a matter of minutes. Please. Your chastising is unnecessary."

She blinks rapidly but says nothing else; she simply shoots a glare at me over his shoulder, then returns to her task.

My apartment is a mess.

The door has been jimmied open and my things are

overturned, drawers open, the refrigerator door ajar and a Coca-Cola bottle, half empty, pooling condensation on the dining table.

I frown at the rings underneath it but leave it where it is; I do not wish to touch anything that my intruder touched or drank from.

"Stay by the door," Oscar says, and enters to sweep the rooms, ensuring that the intruder is no longer in my dwelling.

"There is no one else here," he says, as he enters the doorway of my bedroom, "please come pack only what you need."

I look over my shoulder into the hallways and do as he asks.

It takes me less than 20 minutes to pack my suitcase with my clothing and necessities, and all the letters my father has sent me, as well as pictures of my family.

Some things are, simply, too precious to leave in my wake.

He drops my apartment keys into Mrs. Hawthorne's silently outstretched hand as we exit the building and load my suitcase into the motor vehicle.

Within moments, we are on the move and my spare, practical and sufficient apartment is a thing of the past.

Chapter 9

By the time we have parked Hal's vehicle behind Oscar's apartment building and stashed the keys over the visor in the driver's seat, there is fatigue and hunger sweeping through my whole body.

I desperately require a moment to catch my breath and fear there will be none.

It is as we are walking down the street that I finally look at Oscar and speak, "Oscar, where shall we go?"

He looks down at me and sees my exhaustion, my fear.

"Oh, Miss Coelho, of course. My apologies. Let us sit for a moment."

He steers me to a nearby bus bench, blessedly empty of people, and allows me to rest for a brief spell.

"A dear friend of mine, Fergus McGinty, captains a cargo ship that makes frequent trips between Southampton, England and New York City. He sends me a letter every time he is coming and I meet him for lunch on the day he leaves to make the return voyage home. He has been telling me for the past 5 years that, should I decide to do so, there is a room for me on the ship to take me home to my family."

I look up at him and nod.

"He is here now, I surmise?"

"He is. He leaves today. I suggest we take him up on his offer and take that ride. What say you?"

I am not a rash woman; I am deliberate in everything I choose to do, and everything I decide isn't worth my finite time, but as I look up at this man, I find there is no hesitation.

Where Oscar lives is where I want to be.

"I say yes. I agree."

"Very well," he says, helping me to my feet, and picking up my suitcase and his own.

"Then let's be off."

We catch a train from Brooklyn to Hell's Kitchen in Manhattan, where the Port Authority Ship terminal is located; this time Oscar sits directly across from me and we work to ignore the stares of other passengers whether curious or aggressive- neither of us is willing to risk being separated in the interest of escaping the rudeness of others.

We are at a sprint crossing the Port Authority; it is 1pm when we locate the ship, the Mary Louise- frighteningly, a young, dark haired worker is walking down the gangplank to begin untying the ship in preparation for departure.

They are about to pull up anchor and leave.

Oscar raises his hand and waves to him, catching the young man's eye.

"Morris! Hello, lad!"

Morris lights up and calls, "Hello, Oscar! You're finally joining us!"

The men shake hands and Oscar introduces me to Morris who smiles at me with genuine fondness on his face, "Hello, mademoiselle. Welcome. Does my brother know you're coming, Oscar?"

Oscar shakes his head, "No. Is he in the cockpit?"

"Aye," he says, "the two of you go on up, and I will catch up with you later. It's good to see you, my friend."

I follow Oscar breathlessly up to the cockpit of the ship where a man who looks like an older, more wizened version of Morris is readying the ship for departure.

It takes a moment for the man to notice us but when he does, he barks out a laugh and rushes to hug Oscar, thumping his back roughly when he does.

"I thought you broke our tradition, but I see that our tradition is about to change anyway. You're coming home, finally?"

"That I am, and I have brought along someone very

special. Fergus McGinty, meet Iris Coelho."

He smiles at me and bows, kisses my hand.

"It's a pleasure to meet you, Iris."

I smile in return and thank him, tell him the pleasure is mine but I am, suddenly, swaying on my feet.

The day, only half over, is beginning to get the best of me.

Fergus guides me to a seat and shoots a questioning look at Oscar, who says tersely,

"Today has been a pip so far. Iris is merely feeling it's effects."

Fergus nods knowingly and says, "Iris, let me get this beauty moving and then I will see the two of you to your quarters."

I nod and lean back in my seat, and a moment later, I am sound asleep.

Chapter 10

When I wake, I am in a room with low lamplight; the sky out of the porthole is a navy blue that suggests dusk.

I am ravenous with hunger.

Oscar is sitting in a chair reading; his bow tie is off, collar loosened; I have never seen a finer man.

We are alright; we are together.

I am suddenly overcome with emotion.

"Oscar," I say and as he rises from the chair, I throw myself into his arms; his mouth finds mine and in an instant those magical hands are traveling over me, leaving fire in their wake.

It is as I am under him and he is beginning to disrobe me that he stops.

"Iris, before we do anything of this nature, I need you to know that I have nothing but the purest intentions with you. I wish for us to be wed; I want you to be my wife and the mother of my children. I would never toy with your virtue if my intentions weren't above board."

My breathing is shallow and fast; even Oscar's words set me ablaze in a way I never dreamed possible before I knew him and what he is made of.

"Then disrobe me, my husband," I say, unbuttoning his shirt, "everything that is of me is yours for the taking, Oscar."

With a soft groan his mouth finds mine as he fumbles with the many buttons of my garments; despite the cumbersome nature of our clothing, it is no time at all when we are disrobed.

IN THE LIGHT

I gaze up at him, at the beauty of him, and tell him how his scar reminds me of kintsugi, a Japanese art of healing cracks and fissures in pottery with gold dust to honor what left its mark, what tried so hard to break it completely and failed.

How it makes what could be fractured and left in pieces or discarded altogether even more compelling and beautiful-the way he is.

The way he makes me feel that *I* am because he deems me worthy of his attention and his love, despite the very humanness of me.

And it is there, in that bed, as I admire how Oscar's beautiful brown skin goes gold in the low light that he takes me, on a gasp of surprise from me, and a sigh of satisfaction from him.

I watch him move above me, inside me, and the feeling that only Oscar can create in me begins to build and build; and it is too soon that I go flying, Oscar following a moment later, muffling my pleasure with the sweetest of kisses my breath and his breath forever entwined.

We are sleeping, curled together, when Fergus knocks on the door a bit later; he has brought us two sack lunches and bottles of milk.

Dinner.

"Come up on the upper decks for meals starting tomorrow. I imagined Iris might be in the mood for rest this evening."

Oscar thanks him and Fergus says, "Absolutely, Oscar. I shall see you in the morning."

We dine at the small desk in the room, and as soon as we are done, Oscar suggests we go up the deck above for fresh air.

Nothing has ever sounded better.

It is late, so I do not bother with pinning my hair up or washing my face, I simply dress, Don my shoes, and follow my beloved as he leads the way.

There is nobody else on the deck as he pulls me to the railing and wraps me in his arms and his suit jacket, his warmth enveloping me.

This man is my home; I never dreamed a love like this could ever be for me.

"Marriage between us will be accepted in England?" I ask, leaning my head against his shoulder, looking up at his stunningly handsome profile.

"It is legal. Accepted? Perhaps not unilaterally. But I can handle whatever stares or comments anyone should choose to offer until acceptance is as practiced as the lack of it is.

Can you?"

I consider what the days and nights in our future will look like and I know that I can, as well; I will take all the ostracism and gawking in the world for just one of Oscar's precious I love yous.

"I can. You are my everything. You are everything Oscar, and nothing will stop me from being your wife aside from an act of God."

He kisses my forehead and squeezes me, the two of us, wound together for all the world to see.

"When shall we be wed, then?" I ask, curling my fingers over his.

"I was thinking about that. I do not wish to wait; when we cross into British waters, we shall ask the ship clergy to perform the ceremony."

I tilt my head up to the sky and sigh, my happiness coursing through me, and wish on the brightest star in the sky to one day live in the world Oscar spoke of the first night we went to dinner.

I wish for a world where all love is honored, all love between people who feel it for one another a thing of beauty and not a means of control.

I wish for all love to be allowed to thrive as this one shall; flourishing beautifully in the light.

About the Author

Shannon Bruno

Shannon Bruno is a coffee, book, and DIY addict and the author of The Blooming Falls and 'Til I Break series'. She got her first library card at age 7 because she already read books too fast to buy everyone she wanted to read. She lives in Arkansas with her husband, daughter, and 3 stinky dogs.

You can follow her on Amazon at:
https://www.amazon.com/Shannon-Bruno/e/B07XM4TGX9?ref_=dbs_p_ebk_r00_abau_00_0000

ABOVE THE RIM

(Color Theory: For the Love of Color)

By
Sierra Hill

Chapter One

Olivia

"Look at me...I am going to be mistaken for a prostitute," I grumble, stamping my foot on the bedroom floor in a hissy fit. "I am not going if I have to wear this piece of thread you call a costume!"

Marissa's hands land on her curvy hips, her usual wild dark hair tamed into two long braids, hanging over her voluptuous breasts. I hold her glare that's pinned on me in frustration before she gestures to the floor, littered with all the other costume choices that have been carelessly tossed around in a heap in my attempt at finding something to wear.

"We've already committed to going to this party at Alpha Sig. You have several other selections you could choose from, but I think this one suits you perfectly. You're a super badass in my book."

Rolling my eyes hard, I mirror her stance to prove my seriousness. "Marissa, I can't do this. It's unreasonable to expect me to wear this tiny costume. While I'm all for the superhero, ass-kicking Wonder Woman idea, this is too revealing. It will only serve to draw all eyes to my boobs and my ass."

To prove my claim, I wave a hand over my attire – or lack thereof – and point behind me at my very healthy booty.

Marissa scans my outfit and gives me a nod of approval. "You look perfect as Diana, the warrior princess of the Amazons. And those frat boys are gonna drop to their knees for you."

I stamp my foot again. "Which is exactly what I don't want."

She steps in front of me and places her hands, one on each shoulder, squeezing gently. Maybe it's her way of placating and shutting me up in the hopes I'll just acquiesce.

"You need to have some fun. You've had a horrendous year and all you ever do is study. Enjoy yourself just one night."

Her eyes plead with me and hold a solemn oath of friendship and love. Marissa has been my rock this year and she's right. I've been through the ringer with the death of my mom and my dad remarrying almost immediately afterwards. It's been a lot to handle.

As if she reads my mind, Marissa continues. "You're banging gorgeous. You're in college. We're going to a frat party. Just go with it for one night. Plus, you never know. You just might meet a masked crusader of your own."

Waggling her dark eyebrows, she steps back, adjusting her crown and then the corset of her medieval queen costume with a regal flourish.

With a heavy sigh, I fiddle with the headband and groan. "Fine. We'll go but then I'm coming home to work on my paper for lit."

She laughs and claps her hands with a squeal of enthusiastic glee. "Of course. Just a few hours and then we'll come right home before we both turn into pumpkins."

***

The stench of stale beer, overly-perfumed-girls, and the sweat leaking from the pores of ambitious dancers in the crowded living room of the Alpha Sig house, along with the strobe light flashes and loud thumping music has already given me a headache.

We've been here just under an hour and I'm ready to book it back home. Somewhere in the span of five minutes into our arrival, I lost sight of Marissa, who went off immediately with a guy from her Stats class to find the keg, winking at me over her shoulder. I watched as the pair weaved through the crowd, him easier to pick out due to his Green Lantern costume. Not exactly the superhero I was looking for, but she seemed enamored with his attention.

That left me sipping my bottled beer I'd snuck from an open cooler in the back and hanging out by the stairwell, watching partiers get wilder and lose their inhibitions. After being jostled and run into by the third sloshed girl looking for the bathroom, and a few inebriated guys who tried starting conversations with me, I finally decide to go in search of a bathroom and then find Marissa.

Peering down the staircase, I see a line has already formed for the small washroom in the basement. So I make the ascent up to the next floor, finding that door already locked and grunting noises coming from inside that can only be one thing.

I roll my eyes at the couple going at it inside and continue working my way up to the third floor of the house. When I reach the landing, I'm relieved to see that it's relatively empty and I'm left with a long hallway with six doors to choose from.

Starting with the first door on the right, I tap lightly against the scuffed wood door, jiggling the handle for good measure.

"Occupied," someone says with a sickly groan. And then I hear retching and the sound of someone puking in what I hope is the toilet bowl.

I shudder squeamishly at the grotesque noise and proceed on. Trying two more doors, I finally stumble on an unlocked door. Pushing it open, I realize instantly I've hit the jackpot.

"Hey, anyone in here?" My question is met with silence, so I take my chances and step into the room, noticing the small door at the far end of the room. It's open and is indeed a bathroom.

Thankful to have found a bathroom and privacy, I

close the door behind me and realize it's going to take some creative wiggling to get out of this damn costume. What I wouldn't give for the simplicity of crotch snaps right now, as I hastily unzip the side zipper, and work up a sweat as I shimmy the tight suit over my hips and past the knee-high boots.

Feeling oddly exposed, I cross my arm over my naked breasts, and glance around the bathroom as I relieve myself. Every surface looks tidy, clean and spotless. If I had to leave a Yelp review, I'd give it a 5-star rating.

I snicker to myself as I wash and dry my hands before slipping back into the costume. But as I work to wiggle the tight material back over my hips, I hear the sickening sound of ripping material.

"Oh my God," I say aloud, trying to peer around to my backside to see what kind of damage I've done. "No…no, no, no."

In order to inspect the damage more closely, I slip the cheap spandex material off again and hold it up in front of my face.

Sure enough, the entire bottom half has come apart at the seams, leaving me standing here naked except for a pair of panties. Knowing my fake Wonder Woman powers can't transport me out of here or offer a new outfit from thin air, I decide I'll go in search of a T-shirt in the bedroom bureaus before escaping here without being noticed.

I'm about to open the door when there's a heavy handed knock on the door.

"Yo, you're in my bathroom without permission."

Oh shit.

Chapter Two

Tra'Von

After the grueling pre-season workout today and back-to-back scrimmages this week, busting my ass out on the court and in the weight room in preparation of our first season game next week, I'm ready to bounce and hit the sack. All I want to do is sleep in tomorrow morning before another practice.

I did my formal duty and hung out for an hour while I watched my boys play beer bong, let a hot girl take a body shot off my abs in the kitchen, and then chatted up some costumed ladies in the living room before I took the stairs two-by-two up to my third floor bedroom.

I let out a loud sigh of relief when I find my room is exactly as I left it, even though I forgot to lock it. Shrugging it off, I head to the bathroom to take a piss, and realize my private bathroom door is closed. And I always keep it open.

Taking a second glance around the room, I confirm no one else is here. But as I turn the doorknob for the bathroom, I hear what sounds like a female whimper.

"Yo, you're in my bathroom without permission. This is a private room and y'all are trespassing."

I stand back, crossing my arms over my chest, waiting for a response and hoping whoever is in there isn't getting it on and leaving any of their skank behind.

But the voice I hear from the other side isn't a horny dude whose sex life has been interrupted, but a soft, apologetic female voice. "Um, I'm so sorry…but I need

582

some help in here."

Alarm bells go off in my head. Is she hurt? Did someone do something to her without her consent? Motherfucker, if some fucking drunk asshole tried anything…my big brother instincts kick in and I'm about ready to kick down the door to help.

"Hey, you okay? Can I come in?"

I jiggle the handle and a hand slams on the other side. "No!" she cries out in a panic. "Don't come in, I'm not fully clothed."

My eyebrows dart skyward. "You're naked? In my bathroom?"

Now, don't get me wrong. I've had naked girls in my bedroom and bathroom before. But not usually when I'm not around so her announcement has me a bit intrigued.

My attention is drawn to some shuffling and grunts of displeasure on the other side. I lean my ear in to listen closer, but everything is drowned out by the Drake song being blasted downstairs on the sound system.

The sound of a snick and the latch unlocking has me taking another step back, watching as the door opens just a crack. Through the small strip of space, I see startled but brilliant green eyes blinking up at me along with a bare shoulder, covered by wild, curly blonde hair.

"Oh, hi. Um, I've unfortunately had a bit of a wardrobe malfunction and could really use a T-shirt or something to cover up so I can get out of your hair."

Relief washes over me to learn this isn't anything like I thought it was. Hiding the grin that's trying to break free over the situation, I suck in my bottom lip. "Huh. Wardrobe malfunction. I see. Is that why you're hiding in my bathroom?"

The door opens a bit more so I can now see the top of her head and the smooth skin of her neck. Reddish-blonde hair with big, bouncy curls flows down in a cascade over the front of her chests and I notice some headband across the crown of her head.

"Yeah, sorry. Both incidents were purely accidental. I'm so sorry for using your room without prior approval," she says with sincerity. "But please, there is no way of salvaging my dignity if I have to trek down three flights of stairs into the middle of a party practically naked."

While I may have been mildly inconvenienced by this interruption at first, I'm kind of digging on being this girl's savior. The picture she paints is rather amusing and it's kind of hot to know there's a half-naked girl standing in my bathroom. One I haven't gotten naked on purpose.

"I see," I muse. "On a scale of one to five, just how naked are we talkin? Five being naked as the day you were born."

Her eyes grow wide and I hear her mutter under her breath. "*Dickhead.*"

I cover my mouth to muffle my amused laughter.

"Really, dude? My costume was barely there to begin with and now it's a shredded mess. Can I just get something to cover up with so I can leave?"

Although I'd love to continue this fun cat-and-mouse game, I also don't want her to feel uncomfortable or intimidated, so I head over to the dresser and yank out the first T-shirt I find. It's one of my maroon Arizona Sun Devils basketball warm-up shirts and I know she's going to drown in it.

Heading back to the door, I tap on the wood and she opens it again. Dangling the material in front of the slit, I say, "I'll give it to you on one condition."

She huffs out an aggravated breath. "What?"

"You have to tell me your name."

There's a pregnant pause and then a soft, exasperated exhale. "Olivia. Liv for short."

"See? That wasn't so hard." The T-shirt disappears as she snaps it quickly from my fingers as if it was a piece of bread given to a starving prisoner.

"Thanks," she says, latching the door again.

"My name's Tra, by the way," I say, my tone ripe with sarcasm. "In case you're interested."

I wait a beat to see if there's a reaction or Liv

recognizes my name.

Although I transferred from Kentucky last year, I'd ended the year as the leading scorer on the team and become very recognizable on campus. But the mention of my name doesn't seem to trigger any waves of recognition. Liv finally – with a little trepidation - opens the door with eyes cast downward. I move closer to the bed to give her enough room and stare at the beautiful girl in front of me.

She drowns in the shirt, which is made to fit my six-foot-six frame, and I only see her knees and legs. When she lifts her eyes, I just smirk and wiggle my fingers in greeting.

"Hey there, Liv. Nice to meet you." I say with a smile, hopefully encouraging her to smile back. But instead she stares at me with a slack jaw and a surprised expression. Her eyes narrowing and then widening in surprise.

"*You*...you're..."

I shrug figuring she's starstruck over my presence. "Yeah, I'm Tra'Von Matthews."

She shakes her head, looking bewildered and confused by this, her eyes brows cinching together.

Liv points a finger at my chest, and I look down to see what has gained her attention. Maybe I dropped some cheese dip on the shirt when I was eating chips downstairs earlier. But when she responds, it's not what I expect at all.

"No," she laughs. "You're Superman."

And then she doubles over in belly-clenching laughter.

Chapter Three

Olivia

What are the freaking odds I'd find myself in Superman's bedroom?

Tra'Von stares at me like I'm a crazed lunatic, which could very well be the case. I was pretty wigged out being caught naked in his bathroom. But I can't contain the hysterical giggles escaping my lungs over the sheer fact that my hero is dressed as a superhero.

A super-human hero of epic proportions.

I've never seen a man so tall as Tra up close and personal before. And I'm not short for a girl at five foot seven inches, but he gives new meaning to 'tall as a tree.'

A freaking gorgeous male tree that I wouldn't mind climbing or maybe lassoing with my Wonder Woman powers. I snort out another giggle at this thought, garnering another amused smile and a gaze that says he's questioning my sanity.

But it's Tra'Von's smile that shuts me up. He'd put even the most gleaming toothpaste campaign models to shame. Offset by his dark complexion, and he has the most sparkling set of teeth I've ever seen.

And nothing makes me melt faster than a beautiful smile on a guy.

I continue to take in his features, his eyes shining a lighter shade of brown, contrasted by a deep-grooved scar at the corner of his eyelid, and two diamond studs in both ears. His hair is perfectly styled alá Odell

Beckham, with a Mohawk twist, shaved short with a fade on the sides, accentuated by a tuft of springy curls bleached blond on the top.

Tra continues to stare at me, and judging from his comically raised eyebrows, he's second guessing my sanity. "What's so funny?"

I gesture to his Superman emblem on his shirt. "It's your costume. I was dressed as a superhero too, before this happened."

Holding the tattered piece of costume up for him to get a good look at it, he tips his head to investigate and then grabs it in his hand. When he does, his fingers graze my knuckles and an honest-to-god spark of electricity sizzles between us.

"That *was* my Wonder Woman costume before"—I gesture behind me to his bathroom— "And the funny part is my roommate joked earlier about me hooking up with Superman tonight."

I can't believe I just said that. Slapping a hand over my mouth, I can feel the blush creeping over my neck and over my cheeks. I sometimes say the stupidest things when I'm nervous. And after all the anxiety in the bathroom, and then being confronted by this giant, I'm a little tongue tied and now I'm worried he thinks I just want to hook-up with him.

But Tra seems to take it all in stride and nods. "We'd make a great team. But truth, I think this has lost all its power."

He returns it to me, and I shove it under my arm, uncomfortable now with what to do now that I'm standing in Tra'Von's room in only a T-shirt and panties.

Awkward.

Feeling apprehensive standing so close to him, I turn and check out the framed photos on his desk, leaning over to get a better look, realizing too late that in doing so, the T-shirt hem rises and bares my ass.

Tra clears his throat and steps in next to me as I pick up the first photo.

It's of him standing proud in his yellow graduation gown flanked on both sides by a woman and three younger girls – all much shorter than Tra. I glance sideways up at him, inviting him to share. He points a finger at the older of the four women.

"That's my mama and my sisters, Tamar, Tresha, and Tracee."

I smile because his voice softens with brotherly love as he says their names.

"They all look like they adore you."

He shrugs, a smug smirk edging at the corner of his mouth. "What's not to adore?"

I elbow him playfully in the ribs, carefully replacing the photo before turning my attention to the other one. This one is clearly his basketball team all geared up in blue and white uniforms, and five older men in suits. I don't follow sports much, but I do recognize the university and it's not ASU colors.

"That was my freshman year at UK." His arm brushes mine as he reaches over and points to a kid standing in the row in front of Tra. "That's my best friend Sean. He drafted into the NBA right at the same time I decided to transfer."

I turn and gaze up at him, having to tip my head back so far my hair brushes the top of the desk behind me.

"Why'd you transfer instead of staying there or drafting, too?"

The question appears to bring discomfort because instead of answering it, he asks, "Hey, you thirsty? Want something to drink?"

"Oh, I um…I've had my fill of beer tonight."

Tra grins over his shoulder, bending on knee to open a small fridge and pulling out two Mexican coke bottles, opening the tops with his teeth, spitting them in the trash can and handing me a bottle.

He tips the glass edge toward me and we clink our glasses.

"Here's to random meetings of superheroes," he toasts, and I laugh at the randomness of tonight.

"How about you? Give me the run-down on you." His eyebrow shoots up inquisitively inviting me to share.

"Well, let's see. I'm Liv Peterson. Junior and an engineering major. I grew up near Chicago. Came down to Arizona because I wanted sunshine in the winter and to get as far away from my dad and his new wife as I could get."

He nods with empathy, his own voice low and laced with bitterness. "I hear ya. My dad left us when I was twelve and I have a stepmother of my own. My mom never even dated again. How about yours?"

I stagger a little, catching myself with my hand against the desk behind me. Tra's hand snaps out and slings around my waist, steadying me with his arm securely wrapped around my body.

"Whoa there. You okay?"

We both look down at where our bodies meet, a moment passing between us that I thought only existed in the movies. The skin underneath his touch actually burns from the heat radiating there. My nipples pebble tightly under the weight of his deep penetrating stare, my breath caught in the hollow of my throat.

I don't know what's happening between us but as awareness streaks through my spine, all I want is for him to lean down and kiss me.

There's movement as his soft, warm hand gently brushes down the curve of my lower back, lingers at the top of my ass, and then slips further below where his fingers toy with the hem of the T-shirt.

His thumb slides underneath and strokes over that dip between my legs and my ass, and then in a heart-stopping move, he jerks my body into his rock hard chest. He positions a powerful thigh between mine nudging my legs open to offer him room.

He places his already empty bottle on the desk and takes mine from my hand, joining my bottle with his.

My hands take up residence over the ridged muscles of his chest, which can't be hidden with the shirt he wears, and I coast over his stomach, my panties going wet with need.

When I look back up at him, his eyes have closed, semi-hooded with desire and I can feel his erection heavy and pulsing against my center.

"If you tell me no, I'll stop," he says with a ragged voice. "Otherwise, I'm gonna kiss you."

"Yes," I sputter out, my lips remaining open as I lift myself to my tip-toes and open for him.

His mouth crashes into mine in an urgent kiss. Wet, hungry and exploratory. Eager to taste and feel.

We both moan into each other's tastes, his tongue slipping through the seam of my parted lips and sucking mine into his own mouth.

And that's when the lights go out.

I gasp in shock and he grunts out a "Oh, fuck, not again."

"What's happening?" I shriek, going as still as a doe in the field surrounded by hunters.

There's nothing but pitch darkness and everything has gone eerily quiet in the house, the music having shut off and throwing us into deafening silence.

"We must've overloaded the circuits with too much demand. I need to go downstairs to see if I can fix it. I know none of those drunk motherfuckers will have a clue."

I swallow, the sound echoing between us. His warm hand skimming my back reassuringly. "It's okay. I'll be right back. Just don't leave."

My body shivers and shifts, my mind racing about what happens if I stay. I like the gentle strength of his grip. He smells so good too. Like an earthy pine aftershave mixed with a smoky wood scent. Like he's just come from the outdoors after splitting wood all day.

Tra leans down and kisses my forehead before dropping his arm from my waist.

He takes a step back, but the intensity is still there between us. "I'm not finished with you yet. Please stay."

Oh, when he asks me like that, how can I say anything but yes?

But then I think about the ramifications and what

would happen when he returns. I'm not ready for anything with him tonight and I don't want to set false expectations.

I smile and shrug noncommittally. "We'll see. Now, go be a hero and save the party."

Chapter Four

Tra'Von

What a cluster.

It takes me at least five minutes to make my way down to the basement as I work my way through the clusters of people huddled around in the dark.

When I finally make it to the basement and locate the electrical box, three of my frat brothers are already trying to remedy the situation, which is a hilarious rendition of the "Who's on first" skit because none of these boys know anything about electrical components.

"Move your asses and let the expert take a look," I order, pushing through their barricade to their disgruntled drunken arguments. "My dad's an electrician so I know what to do."

Jarrod Klein gladly steps away with a sweeping palm. "Have at it, bro. I'm going back upstairs for another beer and to reclaim Shayla Cummings."

Denny Potter and Milo Kishner, two of the newer brothers in the house this year, both remain behind, oddly fascinated by my skills in the electrical field. It shouldn't surprise them that I'm studying electrical engineering. But my focus of study is mostly in renewable energy.

It takes me no more than a few minutes to identify the problem, and then another ten minutes to jury-rig a few wires and clips in the circuit breaker, redistributing the electrical flow. The circuits will need to be fixed by a real electrician this coming week, but in the meantime, it would make do.

With the lights back on and the music blaring once again, I hear a hoop of celebration from upstairs, which is where I'm eager to get back to see where things lead with Liv. Things were just getting good when the lights went out.

Patting Danny on the shoulder, I say, "I'm out of here. Just holla at me if there's any more problems. Otherwise, don't touch shit."

I point at them both, giving them each a menacing glare. They both raise their hands innocently in the air.

"Won't touch a thing."

I take the stairs two at a time now that I can easily see where I'm going and push through my bedroom door, excited to pick things up where we left them.

Unfortunately, when I step inside, I'm met with an empty room. And nothing of her left behind except a scrap of red, white and blue material.

"Well, shit. That blows."

***

Monday's are pretty easy class days for me, designed that way on purpose. With the upcoming basketball season set to start in a few weeks, games are regularly played on Saturdays, travel days on Sundays and therefore, I want to sleep in on Monday mornings. That's why my first class, my English lit elective, doesn't start until ten a.m.

Being a college ball player affords me some advantages when it comes to classes and studying, but my parents taught me never to rest on my laurels. I'm not here just to get a passing grade. Basketball may have been what got me into ASU, but it doesn't mean it'll let me slide out of it.

I take my college education seriously. Sure, there are a few courses where I get a little extra help using the tutors provided to us by the school. And when it comes to lit, I'm a numbers guy, not a nouns, if you know what I mean. It takes every ounce of my concentration to figure out what the hell some of these English novelists and poets are saying. But I work hard at it because I'm not a slacker.

Which is exactly the reason why I've never noticed the curly-haired blonde with glasses sitting in the second row to the front. Until now.

I'm already in my back row seat when I see her walk in, bookbag over her shoulder and her head down moving into her seat.

Jumping out of my chair, I nearly plow another student in my rush into the aisle.

"Excuse me," I apologize, clomping down the lecture theater stairs, angling my way through several sleepy-eyed and aggravated students. "Sorry. 'Scuse me."

Working my way down I see an open spot in front of Liv, who is clearly oblivious to my presence, even though I've caused quite the commotion getting there. I take a seat in her direct line of sight but she still hasn't noticed me.

A few whispers fill the auditorium, students leaning in conspiratorially to chat with their seatmates about the six-foot-six basketball player making an appearance at the front of the class. I don't blame them. I typically stay in the back to avoid the attention. But I pay them no mind. The only thing I'm interested in getting right now is Liv's attention.

Clearing my throat, I turn around and casually drape my arm across the back of the seat, noticing now the reason she's not noticed me yet. Liv's head is buried in her phone, earpods in both ears, reading something on her screen.

"Hey there, beautiful."

I say it loud enough that the girls behind Liv snicker and giggle, but Liv still doesn't respond. Doing my best not to gain the entire amphitheater's attention, I lift my hand and wave it in front of her face.

Her reaction is almost comical as she screams — loudly, I might add — as if it was straight from a scene in a scary movie where the main character sees the monster for the first time – and practically bolts upright in her seat. The entire room is now staring at us due to her outburst.

"Christ on a cracker, you scared me!"

Liv's eyes are stunned wide and then her forehead pinches in confusion. "What are you doing here, Tra?"

I give her a toothy grin, plucking my backpack from the floor at my feet and tugging it over the chair along with me as I climb over the row. My knees knock against the back of the seat as I settle in the open seat beside her.

Hooking my thumb behind me to try to offer an answer, I lean in toward her, getting a good whiff of her sweet scent. Shit, she smells so delicious. "I've been in this class the entire semester but I'm usually in the back row."

"Huh," she says blandly, neither pleased or displeased.

I add on a little more charm, waggling my eyebrows at her. "I have to admit, this class finally got interesting now that I know you're in it."

"I heard that, Mr. Matthews," Professor Laurie calls out from her lecture spot in front where she must've come in during my seat move. "And I'll remember that when I'm grading your paper on twentieth-century modernism next week."

The class laughs and I chuckle along at my expense.

It doesn't bother me like it normally would because in my opinion, this week has just granted me a pretty great start in the form of the beautiful girl who slipped out of my room like Cinderella.

And I have her glass slipper.

Chapter Five

Olivia

He's been in this class this whole time?

That's all I could think about the entire class, my mind on the hot jock sitting next to me instead of on today's lecture.

A wave of guilt crashed through my belly as I sat there wondering what he thought about me ditching him on Saturday night, after he'd specifically asked me to stay. I did plan on staying at first. But the longer he was gone, the more I thought about what we would do when he returned. Maybe some girls would've been ecstatic to bag a college basketball player, but that's not me. I don't go in search of hook-ups with athletes and then share it with all my friends afterwards.

But Tra doesn't seem too bent out of shape. When the hour hand hits eleven a.m., Professor Laurie gives us her final direction on our assignments and then dismisses the class.

Having not said anything to me the entire hour, I pack up my laptop and bag and realize Tra hasn't moved and is sitting in the chair just waiting for me. When I peer through my peripheral vision at him, he's slunk down in his chair, arms crossed over his broad chest, biceps making a brilliant display of his athleticism, and he wears a smug smirk fixed across his mouth.

His perfectly kissable mouth.

The one I dreamed of kissing the entire remainder of the weekend.

"What?" I say with as much cavalier attitude as I can muster.

I move to stand but he doesn't budge. And let's face it, unless I plan on crawling over the back of the row of seats in front of me, there's no way I'm getting over him unless he moves.

He rubs his chin, tilting it to the side. "I'm trying to decide if you're a coffee or tea kind of girl."

"What? Why?"

Tra stands and blocks out the world in front of me with his physique and tall frame. This guy is built like the Empire State building. Tall, imposing and immovable.

Without even a word, he slips my backpack off my shoulder with a quick tug and slings it around his shoulder. The bag is weighted down with three textbooks and a laptop, along with all my personal belongings, yet he makes it seem as light as a feather, whereas I might need a three-day massage from carrying that bag of bricks.

I watch in amazement as he strides casually down the aisle, pausing at the end to look over his shoulder at me.

"Because I'm going to take you out right now and want to know your preference."

Although it sends ribbons of excitement through my blood vessels and veins, pumping a flood of thrill to my heart, I pretend to be offended.

Scoffing, I scoot by him, getting a whiff of his freshly showered, spicy scent, and begin my ascent up the stairs.

"That's pretty presumptive of you. What if I have another class right now?"

Reaching the top, I turn to find he's bounded up effortlessly and stands inches from me. I hold out my palm to request my bag, but instead, he grabs my hand and folds it in his.

"Do you?" Tra asks, gazing down at me, his dark eyes hopeful and a bit puppy-dog sweet.

Sweet enough that I can't lie. "No, not until one. But—"

Tra leaves no room for opposition and gives my hand a quick tug, our arms flinging back and forth with the force of his momentum.

And that's how I end up going on my first date with Tra'Von Matthews.

***

"You transferred here last year from Kentucky?" I ask Tra over the delicious caramel macchiato he bought me at the student union coffee shop. It's a mecca for every student on campus who bustles through on the way to and from one building or another. And it's a nonstop turnstile of greetings and calls for Tra'Von, who has to return the *"Hey man"* and *"Yo, Tra"* acknowledgements from every two or three passerby's.

For a quiet moment, Tra takes a gulp of the Red Bull infused drink he ordered, knocking it back as I watch his Adam's apple bob up and down in his throat, an oddly sexy movement. I've never thought a guy's throat was sexy before now.

"Yeah, when I started at Kentucky my freshman year, I was so full of myself. All swagger and shit. But my expectation of how much game play I should expect was vastly different from the coaching staff at UK. I realized pretty quick that I wasn't the player I thought I was and there wasn't a spot for me in the rotation."

I watch with interest as Tra's eyes wander off toward the large bank of windows before tracking back to meet mine. Knowing very little about basketball, I don't quite see the problem, but this was obviously a sticking point for him.

"Okay," I hedge, unsure whether to ask the question or not. "But why not stick around, develop your skills and wait your turn?"

Tra lifts a brow skeptically and chuckles. "The arrogance of youth demanded I get what I deserved. Right now, ya feel me? In my mind, I was worth getting all the playing time immediately or I'd leave."

He shrugs apologetically and laughs in a self-deprecating manner. "It was a hard decision to make, but I'd been in contact with Coach Welby, who initially offered me a spot here before I took UK, and we'd exchanged some texts over the last part of the year. I guess I just clicked with him more than the UK coaching staff. The easy part was transferring and starting here last year. The hard part was leaving my Mama and sisters."

I nod. "I'm sure they miss you too but know it's the right thing. Has it worked out like you'd hoped?"

To this Tra chuckles good naturedly. "*In this world there are only two tragedies. One is not getting what one wants, and the other is getting it.*"

My mouth gapes open at his response. "Did you honestly just quote Oscar Wilde?"

Tra laughs, the sound making something twist in my chest with longing, stealing my breath. Giving me the feeling of being wrapped up in a warm fluffy comforter straight from the dryer.

He shakes his head in dismay. "I'm not some *himbo* like some of my teammates. I pay attention in class, regardless of what Professor Laurie thinks."

I'm about to ask him what the hell 'himbo' means when our attention is diverted to a rowdy group of students arriving through the double-doors, chattering loudly and swarming the tables. They go around from table to table, passing out fliers to everyone in the vicinity.

A pretty girl turns our way, her long braids swaying as she does and she saunters up to our table, her wide smile turning from cute to coy when she realizes it's Tra'Von.

"Hey, Tra'Von. You're looking good, baby doll. Nice to see you again." Her tone rather implies an intimacy that strikes my jealous meter.

Tra returns the smile but it doesn't quite meet his eyes, suggesting he knows her but isn't interested in what she's offering.

Good.

"Hey, Leila. Thanks. What's going on?" He nods his chin over toward the group scattering across the open atrium and café.

Leila, completely ignoring me, hands Tra'Von a leaflet, which he accepts and scans briefly before sliding it over to me on the table.

"We're holding a rally and Black Lives Matter protest tomorrow out in the quad. You should come. We can really use the support of one of our black brothers on campus."

Her head then whips to me, eyes blazing over the whiteness of my Nordic features and curly blonde hair, swiftly disregarding me with a flick of her chin. It's in this moment where I feel my white privilege like an open sore, ugly and festering because I've done little to nothing to fix it.

Shame eats at my insides and I swipe the pamphlet from the table, quickly perusing the time and details of the event.

"I'd like to go," I announce to the surprise and shock of both Tra and the girl. "I only have a lab in the morning and would really like to be there."

Peering up at Leila I see a reaction I wasn't expecting. Appreciation, camaraderie and solidarity. And then she bends over and embraces me in a hug.

"Thank you. I'd like that. We have all the frats and sororities involved – or at least some of them," she pulls back and trails off with a scoff. "And a handful from each athletic team and the heads of each academic department."

Tra doesn't look at all that interested but nods. "That's cool. Yeah, I guess if Liv is going, I'll be there too."

This doesn't go over too well with Leila based on her sneering eye roll. Then she pokes him in the arm with a finely manicured nail in bright orange nail polish and glitter.

"As a black brother, you best show up for yourself and *all* your black brothers and sisters. It's your duty and responsibility. They look up to you, Tra. This is our time in a long history of oppression and injustice, and you need to stand up and represent."

Someone calls from the opposite side of the hall and Leila's head snaps over her shoulder giving them a brief wave.

"I gotta bolt. I'll see you both there tomorrow."

We watch as she runs gracefully toward the remaining group members and then I turn my attention back to Tra'Von, who now looks a little queasy.

"Hey, did I say something I shouldn't? Do you not want me to go?"

I'm worried I've overstepped my bounds for some reason, even though it's an all-student rally and not just for certain races or skin colors unlike mine.

He shakes his head and stands, an indicator that he's ready to leave. I take a cue and do the same, gathering my things and throwing away my trash in the garbage next to the door.

We make our way outside the union doors and stop, each ready to go our separate ways when he reaches for my hand, threading his fingers through mine.

"Listen, it's not that I don't want to stand up for social injustice, Liv. I love the fact that you want to act on it, too. But I grew up in a small town in the south where a black man who protests can get the shit kicked out of him. Or even worse."

My lips part, forehead wrinkling at the picture he paints. A view I didn't realize still existed in this country we live in today.

Making a promise I shouldn't, I reach up on my tiptoes and wrap a free hand around the back of his neck, tugging him closer.

"It's not like that here, Tra. I promise. And that's exactly why we *need* to protest, so that those hateful acts don't continue, and we show the world what love and tolerance is all about."

My eager lips graze over his, nipping and playing, my tongue slipping past my parted lips and into his mouth. Tra's groan is wild and needy, his tongue swiping over mine and then invading my mouth as his hands glide over my hips, gripping them and pulling me closer.

Everything else around us fades away. There are no students or class schedules. No world full of hate and racism.

It's just the two of us, our mouths and bodies becoming reacquainted with one another and building on a promise for more.

Chapter Six

Tra'Von

I can't stop thinking about that kiss.

Even after playing an exhausting scrimmage game this morning, followed by strength training with the team trainers, my focus and obsession over Liv hasn't diminished a bit.

While I'll admit that I am very concerned over the possibility this student rally might turn into a riot instead of a peaceful protest, there is nowhere else I'd rather be than by Liv's side in support of the BLM movement. The fact that she cares enough about it and me to support it, and wants to see positive change is just another reason I like her so much.

As I sit waiting in the spot we agreed to meet by the library, I can see her bounding toward me carrying two homemade signs that say #BLM and Silence = Violence.

When she sees me, she gives me a bright, heart-stopping smile. "Hi."

Instead of answering, I wrap my arms around her and sweep her off her feet, her whoop of laughter ringing in the air between us.

"I missed you." I whisper in her ear, her cherry-licious scent going straight to my crotch. Placing a kiss along her neck, I nuzzle into her soft skin.

"You just saw me less than 24 hours ago."

Moving my lips up her jawline my mouth brushes over her face with open-mouth kisses until I get to her mouth. Her lips part in invitation and I slip my tongue inside, feeling her entire body go slack in my arms, my cock growing painfully aware that this isn't going to go any farther any time soon.

When I draw back and look her over, Liv's face is flushed with a soft cotton-candy pink warmth and her eyes glaze over. I mentally kick myself for starting something I can't follow through on because this girl makes it difficult to stop.

"We gonna finish this later, a'ight?" I announce, letting her slide down the front of my jeans, knowing exactly when she feels the bulge in my pants based on the gasp she lets out. "In my room."

Liv nods with a smile quirking at the corner of her lips as I take a poster from her hand and clutch her free hand in mine, as we head toward the rally point.

Nearing the grassy common area, we see the growing crowd of protestors milling about, signs held above their heads, all facing the podium on the stage. I look down at my phone to see the time, indicating we have a few minutes before the speakers will take the stage.

Liv leads the way, pulling me through the breaks in the crowd until we're off to the right of the stage about fifty people back. A few speakers take the stage to a roaring cheer from the audience. The first one is a young black student leader from one of the student groups on campus, who steps up to the microphone and in a soft, yet compelling voice, speaks.

"This oppression must end for our fellow Black Americans. Black lives have always mattered and we've always been important to this country. Now is the time and freedom is not ours until things change. We must do that now!"

The crowd roars and chants a resounding chorus of agreement. "Black Lives Matter!"and "Freedom for our people" are shouted through the space, a rally cry and outpouring of frustration mixed with grievance.

Within a matter of minutes, movement in the crowd has us being shifted, pushed and shoved from all sides,

Liv getting the brunt of it since she's a much smaller target. Ahead of us is a group of young white guys, who look to be stirring the pot, even though I can't hear what they're saying. I look to my right, toward the building and I see a group of security guards and officers have assembled, standing and waiting to ensure peace.

But sure enough, that peaceful protest doesn't last long, as there's suddenly a fight that breaks out a few feet in front of us, fists flying and the sounds of flesh being beaten.

I see everything happen in slow motion, as a big dude in front of us is hit and then teeters backwards, his elbow flying back and slamming directly into Liv's unsuspecting face.

I do what comes naturally, stepping in front to shield her from any further encounters, my brain only thinking of protection. I shove the guy in the back for him to give us room so he's not right on top of us. Unfortunately, he takes this the wrong way, spinning on his heels and using his barrel chest in a move of aggression, shoving back into us, this time knocking Liv to the ground.

The growl that escapes my lungs is feral and vicious. "Motherfucker. Get off her!"

As I swing down to assist Liv up to her feet, my legs are suddenly kicked out from under me and I'm flying face first toward the ground next to her. Landing with my face smooshed up against the dirt, my arms are violently pulled behind me and I feel a knee crunching into the middle of my back.

An authoritative voice booms over me, as I register that it comes from the man who holds me down. "Resist and you'll give me a reason to use my taser. You're under arrest."

***

With my body pinned to the ground so I'm unable to move, all I can see is feet and legs of people gathered around us.

But I hear the panic in Liv's clipped voice as she stands near me.

"Officer, what are you doing? Please, this wasn't his

605

fault!"

There's a grunt and the pressure in my back is relieved when I'm yanked up to my feet, my body jerking forward and back like a pendulum before I'm righted and standing, my hands bound with some type of plastic tie.

"That's not what we saw, miss. He instigated the physical assault."

My eyes meet hers, which have transitioned from shock to fear to anger, crystalizing with unshed tears. I shake my head, resigned to the fact that there's no way out of this. The officers only saw what they wanted to see.

She reaches out to touch my chest, but even with my arms tied behind my back, I'm able to twist away so her attempt meets air. "Don't Liv. It'll be okay."

Her tears flow fast and furious now, righteous indignation coloring her cheeks on my behalf.

"Goddamn it, this is wrong! Let him go!"

The officer jerks me toward him as I'm lead, bound and humiliated, toward a parked squad car. Although it's only campus security, and I know I won't be carted off to jail, it will still be witnessed by hundreds and could affect my basketball career.

I knew this would be a bad idea. I just had a feeling something would go wrong. I've strived my entire life to be better than everyone else. To keep my head down and my nose clean, to practice hard and study harder, and to earn my reputation as a good man and good ball player.

And yet it all boils down to this one moment and the spin that it will be given once the media gets involved.

With videos being recorded and people calling out in confirmation that *"Tra'Von Matthews is being arrested,"* I realize I'm just another causality in the lives of black men everywhere.

I've turned into another statistic.

SIERRA HILL

Chapter Seven

Olivia

The minute the car door slams shut with Tra in the backseat like some rap-sheet criminal, I'm on the phone trying to figure out what to do to get him out of this situation.

A situation I helped create.

Why didn't I listen to him? I saw the concern written all over his face, yet I wanted so badly to prove that I supported black and brown students that his well-being was put in jeopardy.

Dialing the number listed in my contacts, it rings a few times when I hear the well-known voice on the other end of the line.

"Olivia. To what do I owe this pleasure?"

"Hi Dad. I need your help. It's urgent."

My dad is an attorney back in Chicago where I grew up. And while we had a falling out last year over my decision to attend ASU and not his alma mater Northwestern, along with the way he was so quickly remarried three months after my mom's death last year, I'd say our relationship has suffered over the long haul.

"Are you hurt? Are you pregnant?"

I huff out an exacerbated breath. "No, none of that. My friend was just arrested, I think. I need to know what to do."

A deafening silence across the line, as if he's preparing his little father-daughter speech. But he ever-so-calmly asks, "What happened? Tell me everything."

SIERRA HILL

And I do, as quickly and succinctly as possible, not wasting a breath on anything related to the fact that I might just be dating the guy who got arrested.

My dad calmly and with the practiced voice of a lawyer, gives me the details on what to do and who to contact. I let out the breath I didn't know I'd been holding, and thank him before hanging up, promising to call him later.

Sprinting over to the campus security building, I open the door to find a madhouse of activity. There are at least a dozen people in the entrance, talking loudly and spewing about their rights under the First Amendment. I avoid getting sidetracked by all the commotion and wait my turn at the window where a uniformed officer is handling the inquiries.

Finally making my way to the head of the line, I lean into the cubby and make my position clear.

"I'm here for Tra'Von Matthews who was brought in about thirty minutes ago."

The officer's eyes grow wide as saucers. "*The* Tra'Von Matthews?"

I shrug. "If you mean the student and basketball player, then yes. He was arrested and brought here for something he didn't do. And if he's not released and charges are filed, I will call the ACLU, followed by his attorney."

This is exactly what my dad told me to say, and as the officer types the info in her computer, the room suddenly grows silent, as a hush descends over the crowd. When the officer lifts her head, her gaze slides to something, or someone, behind me.

"No need for any of that. I'm ready to go."

Whipping around, I don't wait for an invitation but jump into Tra'Von's arms, crashing into him with my entire body, holding on for dear life.

"Tra, I'm so sorry."

The tears gush from my eyes, falling like apologetic diamonds down my face and onto his T-shirt.

Instead of soothing him, he's the one who comforts me, his hand petting my hair, whispering shushing sounds into my ear.

"Liv, it's okay. Let's just get out of here."

My tears have dried up by the time we walk the three blocks to Tra's frat house. Word has already circulated around campus and as we approach the porch, two of his frat brothers come rushing up to him.

"Dude, you okay?"

"Hey man, heard you were arrested. What'd you do?"

I give them both evil glares, pissed off that they'd assume the worst of their very own frat brother, but Tra takes it all in stride and answers with humor.

"Can you believe I finally got caught for writing papers for money? Crime doesn't pay, bro."

They all laugh, but there's a note of anger in his chuckle. We make our way up to his third-floor bedroom, the place we met only last weekend, and he shuts the door behind us before flopping down on the edge of the bed, head buried in his hands. Silent and grieving.

I rush to his side, kneeling in front of him, hoping he'll look at me.

"I'm sorry Tra. I had no idea. I'm so angry on your behalf. It's not right and it wasn't fair for you to be singled out like that."

He lets his hands drop and then cups my jaw, staring at me with his warm brown eyes. They're filled with sorrow, conflict and hurt.

"Liv, you gotta understand something. That wasn't the first time and it probably won't be the last in my lifetime. You're going to have to get used to that type of harassment if you want to hang with me."

And then sorrow fills his eyes, his shoulders rolling back in a defensive posture. "But I'd understand if you didn't."

Clamoring to get up onto his lap, I slide my hands behind his neck, peppering him with kisses. A kiss to wash away all the pain and misery he's ever been caused today and in his lifetime.

"I want to be with you, Tra. So much."

Without consideration to anything else – all of that behind us for now – I slip my T-shirt over my head letting it drop to the floor behind us with a soft *whoosh*. I watch as Tra's eyes turn from golden brown to a blazing inferno of heat as he curls his arms around my back, curving over me so our bodies are pressed to one another.

I reach around and unsnap my bra, letting it fall to my lap and with the reflexes of a ninja, Tra flips me over onto my back and a smile plays across his mouth.

A gasp is torn free when he flicks my tightened nipple with the flat of his tongue and I arch into him when he sucks it into his mouth.

It's been so long since I've been with a guy. An entire year, in fact. But I don't believe my body is responding this wildly or turbulently because of my sex draught. No, I think that has everything to do with Tra'Von.

He makes quick work of removing his shirt and then with a savage snarl, unbuttons his shorts and unzips, shucking them off so he's just left in his boxers. Nearly his entire body is exposed to me and my mouth waters with need to pleasure and be pleasured by him.

I run a hand down his impeccably taut abs, thrilled by the shudder he makes as my fingernails trail down past his belly button, over the ridges of the V along the path leading down to his underwear.

My fingers playfully creep along the elastic until he lets out a loud grunt and yanks them down to expose his full enlarged cock.

When I wrap my hand around him, he lets out a sound of contentment, as I stroke roughly, his dick thickening in my grip. My body reacts with eagerness and mini-zaps of excitement when he slips a hand between us and up my skirt.

I know when he reaches my panties, he'll find me hot, wet and responsive.

Chapter Eight

Tra'Von

"Tra'Von...can you tell us what was going through your mind when you were detained at the protest? Do you consider yourself a hero or a martyr?"

Cameras, flashbulbs and microphones suffocate me as I sit up at the press conference table surrounded by Coach Welby, Coach Parker and the team's publicist, who set this thing up. They wanted to set the record straight on the team's position and what happened at the rally and to ensure I was cleared in the media of any wrongdoing.

I clear my throat, swallowing thickly and taking a small sip of water from the bottle on the table. This type of attention is not my wheelhouse. I like to showboat out on the court, but not in front of an audience where I'm on stage with all eyes on me.

My mind reels back to the other day – all the good, the bad and the ugly that transpired. It all feels like a distant memory, the only thing that mattered was the time spent in bed with Liv. Kissing her, being inside her and making her come was the highlight of that day and the only thing worth remembering. And the only thing I want to continue doing as an outcome of that brutal experience.

I lean in close to speak in the microphones. "I'm not going to sugarcoat what happened."

I turn to the coaches and they nod their agreements. "I was unfairly targeted for what I believe was simply the color of my skin. I had every right to be at that rally and protest what is wrong in our country and rally against the social injustice in our black and brown communities. My only statement is this: I am not your spokesperson or caped crusader for this movement."

I search the audience to find Liv and give her a nod to our inside superhero joke and continue. "All I want is for this school, my team, our communities and our country to remember that we are all in this together. Change will only happen if we speak up when we see injustice and do something about it. Do not allow violence or hate to interfere with the truth. The truth that everyone can be a hero in this world if we speak up when we see injustice and no longer tolerate acts of hatred and discrimination. Thank you."

More questions are posed from the press, but I've said my piece and only have eyes on one person.

The minute the cameras are off and I'm free to go, Liv rushes up to me and I lift her in my arms.

"You'll always be my superhero."

PEACE

By Willow Aster

If you haven't read my Kingdoms of Sin *series, there are just a few things you should know. It is set in the present where there are monarchies in a world that doesn't operate quite like ours. There are no dragons or fairies, but there is lust, greed, pride, and wrath…something that exists in any world and has since the beginning of time.*

Chapter 1

Brienne

I look out over the water of Niaps and think about home with its snowcapped mountains. I feel a pang of longing for the cooler weather as I wipe my forehead. It's a scorcher today and it's not even noon.

I set my sword aside, done with my fencing exercises for the day, and jump into the nearby pool, clothes and all. I swim until even my muscles are waterlogged and climb out, the weight of my wet clothes hugging my tired body.

I never know what to do with a day off; they are so few and far between. Eden, Queen of Niaps, my friend and the one I serve and protect, has a date with her husband Luka, and they both insisted that I enjoy the day. I didn't need the break—too much time on my hands makes me wish for things I don't have. *I'm happy here in Niaps*, I remind myself. Really happy. Serving Eden has been the best time of my life, and while I sometimes miss Farrow, the ocean has filled a place in me that almost feels like home.

Everyone around me is marrying off. Even Ava, the youngest sister of Eden, is married, which is good. It gives me less to worry about, knowing they're taken care of, but I can't help but feel unsettled. Jadon bit the bullet too, the oldest brother and last of the Safrins to marry. The family I have protected for years are having babies of their own and most of the time, my heart is full.

But when it's quiet, when I stop being on guard for even a few hours…

Well, it's no use thinking about what I don't have.

I step into the Catano mansion, suddenly conscious of my wet clothes making a mess. I look around. No one is here. All but Harmi are out watching the king and queen, and I know for a fact that Harmi is putting a new alternator in one of the cars. I drag my shirt over my head and fling it onto the marble while I wrestle with removing my pants. I groan as my foot gets caught in the leg and jump around until it finally comes free, nearly falling over in the process.

"I've always thought the queen's guard was the most graceful creature," a deep voice says from behind me.

I whip around, hurriedly grabbing my shirt from the floor and holding it over my chest.

A tall—and I do mean tall because I am the tallest woman in this country and this man still stands inches taller than me—man with skin as dark as I am light stares at me with an amused expression.

"I've surprised you. You didn't hear I was arriving today?"

I fix him with my deadly gaze—I can be frightening when I need to be.

"I'm no creature," I practically snarl, even though I do feel a little flutter in my chest that this man could find me graceful.

"You are the queen's guard, though…am I right?"

"State your name and your purpose for being here or I will kill you within the next ten seconds. I might do it anyway, just for fun."

He laughs and his smile does amazing things to his face. His eyes light from the inside and his seductive mouth makes me want to step closer for a better look. I swallow hard and force my eyes to stay on him. It's hard. He's spellbinding and I need to look away or I fear I will be swallowed whole.

"I'm Silas Pega of the Sea of Caninsula. King Luka has recently hired me to be on his counsel. When I informed him I was a little early to arrive, he told me to make myself at home. As I'm sure you're aware, he's on a date with his wife." He then holds up his phone and shows me a text exchange between him and Luka. It confirms that Harmi would let him inside the mansion and he could make himself at home. Silas smirks and I can tell whatever he's about to say will get me riled up. He just has that look of mischief. "He probably didn't imagine you doing a striptease as soon as they were out of the house."

I take a deep breath and hold out my hand in as dignified a way as I can being half-naked. "Show me your papers."

He reaches into the tailored vest pocket and I admire the way his arms flex with the movement. He holds up his papers, and I grab them, studying carefully to make sure they're in order. I hand them back reluctantly.

"Luka's had a lot on his mind. I'm sure you weren't significant enough to warrant a discussion."

His eyebrow lifts as he presses his lips together. "Come on now," his voice becomes a coaxing whisper and I feel it in every part of me, "let's not start off on the wrong foot." His smile breaks through and I just know he's imagining me jumping around trying to get out of my pants again.

I roll my eyes and push past him, wishing I'd worn cuter underwear this morning. I really should go shopping one of these days.

I hear him take a deep breath as I walk past and when he exhales, his breath skitters across my skin, causing me to shiver. He chuckles again and I walk faster, turning the corner where I'm out of sight. I don't stop until I reach my room and when I close the door behind me, I lean against it and stare at myself in the mirror. My skin is flushed, and I look like a drowned rat.

Graceful, he said.

I wonder when and where he saw me before—I would certainly remember if I'd ever seen him. My cheeks darken again, and I shake my head, walking to the bathroom and turning on the shower. I don't know who Silas is or what he's really doing here, but I can't let him get under my skin. The last time I felt anything similar to this agitation was with

Elias Lancaster, Luka's right hand, and it was a prime example of why I should never pursue relationships. He was too hung up on Mara, Luka's sister. Now we're all friends and I know they belong with each other, but for a brief moment, there was a flirtation and I had hoped…

And that's just it, I'm not someone who should ever hope. I have one job—to guard the queen—and nothing can stand in the way of that.

I love my job.

I'm *content* with my job.

End of story.

Chapter 2

Brienne

My day off is ruined, wondering what trouble Silas might be getting into with everyone away. If Harmi let him in, he should be the one looking out for him, but Harmi has been in a mood lately. He's snapped at everyone besides the royal family, which means there are a lot of us who are steering clear of him. I should probably be concerned about him, but he's always been the moody sort.

I read for a while and listen for any sounds coming from outside my room. In the afternoon, I hear someone playing the piano and I open my door just enough to hear better. It shouldn't surprise me that Silas is so skilled—he looks like he excels at everything he touches.

My cheeks flush again when he stops playing and I hurriedly shut the door. It's silly. I'm across the castle and there's no way he can tell I'm listening. I open the door again, embarrassed with how ridiculous I'm being. I can't hide in here forever. I'm hungry after all. I can't avoid eating all day just because I don't want to see this man. If he's going to be around, I should make a little effort to get to know him.

I venture down the hall, bypassing Silas and heading straight for the kitchen. Our new chef, Ceney, is nowhere to be found. I open the refrigerator, scanning for something easy to reheat. A tap, tap from behind startles me and I turn around, feeling even more off my game.

"I preferred your other look." Silas has to duck to enter the kitchen and the spacious room instantly feels smaller with him in it. His smirk sends heat straight to my cheeks and various places throughout my body. His eyes take a leisurely roam as if he's remembering my bare skin fondly.

I scowl at him and he chuckles.

"Are you always so easily agitated or is it me?"

I turn back to the refrigerator and pull out the ingredients for a pianlas.

"It's definitely you," I say as I pass him.

"Oh, that looks good. I'll take some too, please." His eyes brighten when I pull out a loaf of bread and I level him with a look. "That I will prepare myself," he adds.

I hold out the bread once I've gotten two slices out of the bag and he smiles tentatively as he takes it from me.

"Thank you."

My heart picks up a few beats. How does he manage to make every word sound like seduction? And why does everything he says annoy me so much?

I pile shaved slices of Niaps' specialty fluman on the bread and I can tell Silas is assessing my work. He takes a few more slices and puts them on his bread too. Next comes the spicy cheese. Once I've cut a few slices of tomato and lettuce and piled them on my pianlas, he takes what is left and puts them on his. I sprinkle salt and pepper over the lettuce and tomato and press my lips together when he copies me again. At the last second, I pour drops of hot sauce over everything and then pat my hands together, dusting off the crumbs. He does the same.

By the time we place the bread on top, we have sky-high pianlases. I carefully cut mine in half, going diagonally across. When he does the same, I finally turn to face him.

"Have you ever made yourself a pianlas?"

He shrugs. "Never."

"Why—is someone always eager to do your

bidding?" I can just picture a beautiful woman lovingly preparing his meals so he doesn't have to lift a finger.

I don't enjoy the image.

"It's possible that someone would make me one if I asked, but—" He grins and I move my hand, trying to get him to say the rest.

"But what?"

"What did you call this?" He points at the food. "We don't have these in Caninsula."

"You're kidding." My mouth drops open. "Pianlas? I thought they were universal! We have them in Farrow too."

"We eat mostly fresh fish, vegetables, and fruit. Not much of this." He holds up the loaf of bread. "And ours is a much different texture...not so thick."

A low growl from his stomach interrupts us and I laugh in spite of wanting to keep my barriers up where he's concerned. I pick up one half and maneuver my mouth around the massive pianlas. I take a huge bite and close my eyes. *So good.* For a moment, I forget myself and enjoy the flavors. When I open my eyes, he's staring at me, his mouth parted.

His Adam's apple bobs up and down and he leans in just a bit, reaching out to wipe a little bit of sauce from the corner of my mouth. The contact of his thumb by my mouth is enough to send my heart thundering out of the room.

He smiles and puts his thumb in his mouth, slowly savoring the taste while I stare at him transfixed.

"I can't wait to try it," he whispers.

I gulp and pick up my plate, practically running to the nearest barstool. I sit down and watch as he picks up his Pianlas and takes a huge bite.

"Ohhhh," he groans.

I grin in spite of myself.

He closes his eyes and shakes his head. "How have I never tasted this before?"

"Do you not travel much?"

"I haven't been out of Caninsula much, no. My twin...she has two boys and has had to raise them on her own, so I've tried to help where I could. She recently remarried though, and it seemed like a good time for me to let them bond…I needed to get out of the way a little bit." He sighs and takes another bite and I study him while he's distracted. His whole demeanor seems heavier now.

"You'll miss them." It seems trite to say it out loud, but he nods like I've said something profound.

"With every breath. But I'll go visit often. I've…well, I've given my life for them, in many ways, and I'd do it all over again, but…it's okay if I live a little for myself too. Right?" He turns to look at me then and I feel like I'm looking into my own heart. His eyes are raw and vulnerable.

I reach out, placing my hand on top of his. "It's absolutely okay," I whisper.

He looks down at my hand and I yank it back, alarmed that I let myself go there. I don't even know him. I don't touch the people I'm close to, much less complete strangers. Flustered, I focus on my food.

I pick up my plate and stand up, scooting the stool back. "If you're still hungry, help yourself. Our chef usually has a variety of sweets over there." I point to the corner where a few cakes sit on various glass-covered stands.

He stands too. "Where are we going?"

"Uh..." I look around the room frantically. "I was going to take this—"

"What if we take it to the beach and eat it out there?" he asks. He grabs a bottle of wine and tucks it under his arm, the stems of the wineglasses between his fingers.

"Oh. Well." I stare at him and have to make a decision. Should I say no to ward off the butterflies this man gives me or do I show the hospitality of the Catano household to our guest? I know my king and queen consider me part of the family and trust that I will always represent them well. It's only considerate to take care of their guest until they return. "That sounds lovely," I say with a smile and when he smiles back at me, I nearly take it back because I very nearly swoon like a lovesick child falling for the very first time.

He is dangerous, very dangerous. But I'm Brienne, guard of my queen. I can handle anything. Right?

Chapter 3

Brienne

"Do you miss Farrow?" he asks, as we watch the waves.

We're both stretched out on the sand, stomachs satisfied, and my veins are running hot between the wine, the sun, and the close proximity to Silas.

"Yes. But this has become more of a home to me than I expected. Do you think you will miss Caninsula?"

"I'll miss seeing my nephews every day, but I have a short trip planned to go back in three weeks. If it weren't for them, no, I wouldn't miss anything about home." He stares out at the water and from the clenching of his jaw, I know there are memories there he's trying to wipe out. He looks at me and smiles, the heaviness vanishing with one blink. "I studied up on you before I said yes to this position."

"Me? Why?" My voice comes out in an embarrassing squeak and I put my hand to my throat, as if that will help.

"I've always wanted to know what makes you tick. I first saw you when you accompanied the queen and her brother, King Jadon, to the Sea of Caninsula. All eyes were on them…except for mine."

My mouth drops and I turn back toward the water, willing my excitement to taper down. I swallow hard and try to force nonchalance into my voice.

"And—what did you find out?"

PEACE

He leans over until our shoulders are touching and says so softly, "I found out I needed to come here and experience you firsthand, in the flesh..."

I press my lips together and ignore the thrill his words give me. "Sounds like you're setting yourself up for a disappointment."

He chuckles and I feel it in my bones. "Quite the opposite. I can see I am going to love it here."

I take a deep breath. What is even happening right now? This was supposed to be a day alone for once and I'm being sweet-talked by a man I've never seen before today?

"Here's what I've assessed so far," he continues. "Yes, you're beautiful—that goes without saying. Anyone can see that. But you are also selfless, brave, and stubborn."

I wrinkle my nose and look at him again. His smile widens, almost as if he's goading me to argue with him.

"And how did you assess all of this in, what—pictures? Royalty magazines?" I wave my hand. "First of all, I'm not covered in those articles, my queen is. And if I were, you think they'd get it right?" I laugh and shake my head. "You know nothing, Silas Pega."

I sneak another glance at him and he's smirking, his eyes flashing with humor and a confidence I'd love to possess.

We stare each other down and he eventually shrugs.

"Very well then. Prove me wrong." He leans in and I find myself pulled toward him like a magnet. His next words are whispered. "I dare you."

I take a sip of wine to distract myself from his mesmerizing lips and eyes and then he gives the back of his shirt a tug and it goes over his head. I turn away completely so he won't hear the gasp that comes out of my mouth. Mother of all that is holy and perfect. I'm going to have to work around this? These are impossible conditions. His rich brown skin is intoxicating, perfectly smooth and glistening in the sunlight. It takes everything in me to not take another look.

It's a good thing Eden keeps me busy. I don't know how I'll survive being around him. One day and it's like I've lost all sense. This all started because I'm on a rare day off and was feeling sorry for myself. Tomorrow I'll be back to normal.

I stand up and walk toward the water with my wine. I feel him move behind me and I tense when his shoulders brush against mine. I shift away and take a few more sips before turning to look at him.

"I hope you'll like it here," I tell him. "I really mean that. I can tell you're ready for a new start and the Catanos are a dream to work with. I'm still surprised I didn't know you were coming, but if Luka trusts you, I will too. But whatever this little angle between you and me you're trying to work, I'll just remind you that you don't know me at all, and also…I have no time for…any kind of—" I let the words hang and hope he will fill in the rest.

He doesn't say anything, just grins and nods slowly. "I hear all you're saying and all you are not." He lifts his glass and clinks it to my nearly empty one. "To getting to know you…and all the angles." He laughs when my eyes widen and tilts his glass to his mouth, emptying it.

I don't bother trying to recover from that one. I stalk away, hearing his laugh follow me all the way to the house. I want to ask him who the hell he thinks he is, but I'm too afraid he'll manage to sweet talk me even more. I hustle into the house and hear him whistling behind me, a jaunty little tune that doesn't sound one bit apologetic for running me off. I wash my glass and he washes his after me, and I'm on my way to hide in my room again when he touches my arm.

"I apologize if I came on too strong. I've been looking forward to meeting you for such a long time, I tried to say too much too soon." He smiles and takes a step back, holding out his arm to let me pass. "It will be an honor to work with you. I hope in time you can see me as a worthy comrade and, who knows, maybe this fire that is between us after just one day will simmer down to a low roar and we will be able to ignore it." His grin drops and I feel every ounce of that fire with the way his gaze takes me in. "I, for one, am up for the challenge of finding out."

I bolt from the kitchen and make it to my room in seconds, closing the door behind me with a firm and final slam. I lean against the door, trying to catch my breath.

Hours later, I still feel the burn.

***

I hear Luka and Eden come in late that night and pull my pillow closer. I've been in bed for at least an hour and normally I'd be waiting for their arrival, making sure Eden has everything she needs and to check on tomorrow's schedule. But I remember how much they both said they wanted me to really rest today and I close my eyes, embracing the sleep. I'll be more myself tomorrow. Silas won't be so forward with everyone in the house and I won't have time to notice him.

My one day of heart flutters and palpitations can exist as a sweet memory that I remember when I'm old and alone.

All words and no substance, I'm sure that's all it was today with Silas anyway. Maybe he hoped I'd be an easy sell and he could have some fun before his new position begins.

Little does he know, if I haven't given it up to anyone before now, well into my twenties, the chances of him winning me over are slim to none. I sigh into my pillow, fluffing it one more time before I close my eyes and dream of chiseled abs and skin as smooth as the sea rocks.

Chapter 4

Brienne

I wake up frowning and already agitated. I toss my covers aside and shower quickly, scowling at myself in the steamy mirror. My shoulders sag and I suddenly see myself as a teenager. Kathryn, the Queen Mother, took me in after my mom passed. She'd helped with her medical expenses and when nothing could save her, she invited me to the Farrow estate to work for her household. Because of my height and capability with a sword and gun, I was hired to follow Eden when she left for the university. We were close in age and our relationship quickly eased into a comfortable friendship. It was a fairly easy transition to move to Niaps when she married Luka because they both do their best to make me feel like family. I know they love me, but I also recognize that I will never be one of them.

Most of the time, it doesn't bother me.

I love my job and the family that I serve, especially now that our kingdoms are running peacefully, unlike the beginning of Luka and Eden's marriage. And it's not like I suffer from lack of friendships or male attention. Harmi tries to get me to go on a date with him after work almost every week and I insist we cannot ruin our friendship.

I guess I'm just starting to realize if I don't settle for someone like Harmi, I won't have any chances left. It's not like I can go out and meet new people and explore the possibilities.

Silas comes to mind and I pause in applying the tiny bit of mascara I use every day. No…he probably has a different woman wherever he goes. I've seen men like him before—too self-assured for their own good—come through the Catano mansion more times than I can count.

I shake myself out of my stare and finish getting ready. When my hair is pulled into a messy bun, I take one last look in the mirror and leave before I get distracted again. I'm the first one in the dining room and Cheney comes in to set out the basket of pastries just as I'm pouring my coffee. Eden walks in next with Luka tailing her.

"How was your day off?" Eden asks.

"Nice. Some unexpected surprises." I smile back at her.

"Oh yeah? Good or bad surprises?"

"Let's hope I'm a good surprise." Silas walks into the room and it can't be possible, but he actually looks better than he did yesterday.

Luka jumps up and they go through a series of hand bumps and shakes and elbow rubs that have Eden and me staring in shock and then laughing when they finish with a small synchronized jump.

"What was that?" Eden says, her voice cracking when she starts laughing again.

Luka shrugs. "We go way back."

Silas and Eden hug like they're old friends and I wonder when she's had a chance to get to know him without me around. I'm her shadow ninety-nine percent of the time.

Eden points between the two of us. "You guys met in Caninsula, right?"

"Uh, no," I say, just as Silas answers, "Yes, briefly."

"What?" I turn to Silas. "No, we haven't—"

He smirks. "You were a bit preoccupied."

He lifts an eyebrow and I feel myself flushing so furiously that I want to go back to bed and restart this day. Apparently, the night's sleep didn't cure me of his charm. It doesn't seem possible that I could ever forget his face and that smile, but when I am Eden's main security—especially when we're traveling to other kingdoms—I have to be hyperfocused on her surroundings. It's possible if Silas was closer to me than Eden and didn't pose any sort of threat to her, I would have only given him a passing glance. If that. Still. Staring at him now, it's incomprehensible that anything could tear my eyes away from him. And I'm embarrassed that he didn't say anything yesterday about us meeting once already.

Eden giggles next to him and when I glance at her, her eyebrows are raised to the sky and she's pressing her lips together to keep from laughing harder. If she wasn't my queen and best friend, I'd pinch her so hard right now. She wiggles her eyebrows as Silas stares at me, and I have to walk away to keep from laughing and/or killing her.

"It's what I admired about you most," he says behind me.

I focus on piling my plate high with eggs and fruit.

"What, her exquisite beauty?" Eden asks.

I really am going to have to kill her now. She knows I love her, but *could she be any more obvious right now?*

Silas steps next to me and his shoulders brush mine as he fills his plate. "Well, that's a given, yes." He leans closer and every nerve in my body stands at attention. "I've never seen anyone as beautiful," he says under his breath and I shiver, his words causing my heart to pound out of my skin. Louder, he adds, "Her beauty is exquisite, I agree, but her unflinching dedication to keeping you safe is truly legendary. I don't know of another guardian in all of the kingdoms who is thought of as highly as she is."

Is this what it's like when people talk about feeling weak in the knees? I need to sit down. But he keeps talking and I can't take my eyes off of him.

"It was a hostile time when you came, if you'll remember, and she watched you like a hawk. No one would have dared cross Lady Brienne to get to you."

I look up at him and my voice is weak when I respond. "It is my honor to protect my queen."

PEACE

Several beats pass as we stare at one another, only jumping apart when Luka clears his throat. Silas and I turn around and Luka and Eden are watching us like two proud parents.

"This is going even better than I expected," Luka says, rubbing his hands together and winking at Silas.

Out of the corner of my eye, I see Silas shake his head.

"What?" I frown.

Eden puts her hand on Luka's arm and they sit down to eat. I'm not sure what's going on here, but it feels like whatever it is, I'm the last to know.

Chapter 5

Silas

Luka flashes me an apologetic look and I avoid looking at him as I walk to the table and pull out the chair next to Brienne. I didn't come all this way to meet this woman, to the extent of moving to another kingdom and getting a job with Luka, just to have him blow it by ruining my cover with Brienne. Not that my job is a cover—I really will be working with Luka, but my intentions are not exactly pure.

I want to get to know Brienne Jarvis, find out if the way I can barely see straight when she's near means anything.

I've never been struck so hard by anyone. Ever. I don't believe in love at first sight. Lust, maybe. But when I watched the way she tended to Eden while they were in my country and then on the videos I watched over and over—anything of her I could get my hands on—I felt like her kindness practically reached out and gripped my heart through the screen.

I know it sounds crazy. And I'm not a crazy man. Or at least I didn't think I was…but she renders me senseless.

I finally decided to do something about it when thoughts of her invaded every date I tried to go on, every hookup I tried to get through without thinking of her…

Okay, yeah, I've lost my damn mind.

When I called Luka almost a year ago, asking about

his wife's guard, he gave me a hard time, teasing me relentlessly about my mad crush over a woman I didn't even have the nerve to introduce myself to when I had the chance. Luka and I have had a weird friendship over the years—we met at a science camp both of our parents forced us to attend when we were just fourteen and became fast friends, despite him being the future king and me working as a protégé under King Otto in the Sea of Caninsula. We stayed in touch after that and it's always been easy between us.

I've asked about Brienne every time we see each other or talk on the phone and a couple of months ago, he'd finally had enough.

"If you don't get over here and see for yourself if you're meant to be together, I'm gonna send the two of you to a deserted island to find out for myself," he said. "How about you make it easier on me and come work with me here like I've been asking you to do for a couple of years now? You've made huge strides in protecting our oceans. I've implemented what you've done in Caninsula here in Niaps, but I know we could do so much better if you were here to see what needs to be done in person."

"What if she doesn't feel the same?" I asked and he laughed so hard, he didn't talk for what felt like five minutes.
Asshole.

"Man, do you hear yourself? You used to be *the shit*. A nerd, but you owned it and had your own special kind of swagger." He snorted. "What the fuck has happened to you?" He laughed again and I wanted to reach through the phone and throttle him. "You've got it so bad and you haven't even talked to her. I have to tell you—she's even better than you think. I mean—obviously—I trust her to keep my wife safe at all times and that's saying a lot, given what we've been through together. Brienne is one of the best people I know, and I happen to like you pretty well. You're all right, I guess."

I remember groaning into the phone and letting him tease me for at least another twenty minutes before I finally gave him an answer.

"I'll do it. I'll come. See for myself if this is all in my

head or the real thing."

"Get everything in order there and I'll have my plane ready for you whenever you say the word. But listen, before you get here, you better resurrect those missing balls. Brienne deserves a real fucking man."

"Shut up." I hung up on the king of Niaps and felt pretty damn good about it too.

And now, here I am, in the same house as Brienne—it's a huge castle when it comes down to it, and we could probably go days without seeing one another if we tried, but it's like we're magnetically charged to find one another.

Luka clears his throat as he picks up his fork. He points it at Brienne and creases his brow like he's just come up with an idea at the spur of the moment. I can see through his bullshit and I wonder if she can too.

"Silas is the leading environmentalist of all of our kingdoms put together. We're really fortunate to have him in Niaps to evaluate our practices and get us in shape."

She looks at me and nods. "That's great. I didn't realize you were doing something so—"

She leaves her sentence trailing and I press my lips together to keep from laughing. "What, you thought I was just some new muscle sent to help keep an eye on things?"

She gives me a look and I feel the heat flickering between us. She flushes, like she's taken a look at this body and likes what she sees. *Okay, girl. I can work with this.* The look I return sends her eyes fluttering down to her plate, her cheeks lifting slowly as her smile builds.

"Maybe," she finally says.

I lean into her ear and hear her quick gasp. "There's a brain behind all this, pretty girl," I whisper. "Just like I think there's a flame about to explode behind that calm exterior of yours."

When she dares to glance at me again, her eyes are playful. "Well, let's see how long you stick around.

PEACE

You'll have to prove there's a brain in there for me to believe it."

The whole table laughs and yes, I'm the loudest. I am so fucking turned on right now and we haven't even touched.

"Game on," I tell her.

I clink my coffee mug to hers and she grins.

Oh, it is so on.

Chapter 6

Brienne

My skin prickles with awareness the rest of the week. It's like my entire being knows Silas Pega is in the vicinity and it's screaming out for me to take note. I try to pretend everything is normal and that I'm unaffected by our new houseguest—or occupant might be the better word since it sounds like he's here to stay for a while. But every time Silas and I around each other, Eden finds reasons to leave me alone with him and has an amused smirk as she quickly exits the room. It's driving me crazy.

And Silas is wearing me down way too quickly with his charm. The guy could convince an alligator to become an herbivore. Easy on the eyes and a smooth talker. I know better than to be swept away, but he just has this spark about him that I'm drawn to.

When Eden and I come back from a charity luncheon, she once again gives me the side-eye smirk as Luka and Silas walk around from the back of the house.

"Oh, Luka," she calls, "can I see you for a second in the house?"

I grab her arm and stop us both, our long skirts rustling with the sudden turn.

"Are you aware that you are blatantly throwing us together every chance you get?" I ask under my breath.

They're still far enough away that they can't hear us, but she lets out a dreamy sigh as she watches them over my shoulder.

"I am one hundred percent aware." She grins so wide I wish a bug would get caught in her teeth. "And I am *loving* all this sexual tension between you and Silas. I'm here to give you the nudge. In fact, take the rest of the day and the weekend off, and if you do not have sex with Silas by Sunday night, I will force you to take another week off." She says the last part between gritted teeth, still smiling all the while.

"You have officially lost your mind."

She lifts a shoulder and laughs like I've said something hilarious while my eyes narrow on her.

Luka and Silas step beside us and Silas puts his hands in his pockets while he nods at me and then Eden. Luka gives Eden a kiss and takes her by the elbow as they go off to tend to whatever made-up excuse she's giving him for leaving me alone with Silas.

Right before they step inside, she turns and yells over her shoulder. "You should show Silas the cliffs tonight. Take supper out there and watch the supermoon. It's supposed to be bigger than ever tonight."

"I'd love to see that." The genuine excitement in Silas's voice is endearing and I glance at him, appreciating how open he seems to be. He puts his hand on my arm. "Would you like to have dinner with me tonight?"

"Are you and Eden in on this together?" I put my hand on my hip and his eyes trail down my body before lazily working their way back up.

"Is it working?" he asks quietly.

"Maybe." I can't help the laugh that comes out and his hand moves from my arm to my waist. I love the way it wraps around my side and makes me feel secure, while also sending my emotions into overdrive.

"How about you let me take care of everything and I'll pick you up at seven?" His thumb rubs back and forth against my waist and I think I could agree to anything he asked right now.

"You say it like we're not both living in the same place."

"Okay, I'll stop by your room at seven and we can go together? That better?"

637

I grin. "Yes."

"It's a date," he says.

Harmi walks by us and I hold my breath, hoping he won't be rude about this. He huffs. "It's about time. The two of you have been playing cat and mouse all week." He waves his arm. "Put us all out of our misery and seal the deal already."

"Harmi!" I snap.

But Silas just laughs and Harmi gives him a high five as he walks past.

"How have you managed to even win Harmi over?"

"Simple. I've told everyone but you how I came to Niaps just to win your heart."

"What?" I reach out and put my hand on his chest, needing to steady myself.

"You heard me." He takes a step closer, so close that if I take a deep breath, my chest touches his.

I take a deep breath to test it out and feel a rush of adrenaline.

He reaches out and moves a strand of hair out of my eye and then leaves his hand on my cheek.

"This can go however you want it to go, Brienne. I can be patient and take my time proving myself to you and getting to know you, or I can cut to the chase and we can learn as we go, but either way, I am going to woo the shit out of you."

A laugh sputters out of me and dies just as fast when I see how serious he is. His eyes are sparkling like shiny brown marble and his lips part as the air between us shifts. He smells like the sun and leather and mint. I want to inhale him. I lean forward just the tiniest bit and he meets me the rest of the way. When our lips connect, it's like heaven has finally opened up and welcomed me home. I feel weak and alive all at once. His lips and tongue dominate, and yet he groans like he's the one who is captive to my touch.

I never want it to end.

When we finally break apart, chests rising rapidly,

PEACE

I stare at him like I'm seeing him for the first time.

"What do you say?" he asks.

"Kiss me like that and I'm willing to be wooed."

His eyes light up and he pulls me closer, giving me a huge hug as he laughs. I like the way laughs are easy and frequent with him, the way he seems to think I'm funny even when I'm not trying to be, the way he makes everyone smile when he's around.

And most of all, the way his arms wrap around me as he holds me close—I like everything about the way I feel when he touches me.

I lean back, studying his face. "Why me?"

He brings my hand to his face and leans his cheek against it. "You have a gentleness about you that calms me. But you also have a light in you that sets ripples across my heart like fireworks going off every few seconds."

"That sounds exhausting."

"It's exhilarating. I felt it the first time I saw you and I've wanted that high ever since. Kissing you just further cements it for me."

"Cements what?"

"We're meant to be together." He doesn't even hesitate. His words are assured and determined.

I blink at him for a few seconds and look around, wondering if someone is going to jump out and tell me this has all been a joke. I work for the royal family; I'm the one who stays out of the action, not the lead in a love story.

"H-hold on," I stutter and take a deep breath so I can try that again. "We haven't even had a date yet. Moving a little fast, don't you think?"

"So you're voting for the taking-our-time version of this romance?" He kisses my hand and my heart flutters.

"What would it look like if we didn't take our time?" I don't really think we shouldn't take our time because—this is crazy!—but I'm curious about his answer.

"We get married tonight under the supermoon."

My eyes widen and I step back, dropping my hand out of his.

He holds both hands up. "Sorry. I mean, I'm *not* sorry,

I *meant* that, but I know I'm pushing my luck..."

I can't think straight. Every reasonable, practical thought I usually possess seems to have dissolved as soon as he kissed me. In fact, it pretty much went missing the day I met him, half-naked.

I should've known by that little episode that my sensibility was doomed around him. And my libido.

He stands waiting, his broad shoulders distracting me with how good they'd feel if I took that shirt off and ran my hands across every sinewy muscle. I swallow hard and force myself to look in his eyes.

"Seven o'clock," I whisper. "A date under the supermoon."

He nods, his shoulders relaxing in relief. "Seven."

Chapter 7

Brienne

I take extra time with my hair and put on a little more makeup than usual—anything to keep my mind preoccupied about this date I'm going on. When he knocks promptly at seven, I open up the door and am taken aback by how gorgeous he is. The dark richness of his skin is offset by a white linen shirt and he looks so unbelievably sexy I don't know how I'll keep my hands to myself.

He stares at me with the same wonder and I flush under his scrutiny, wishing now that my sleeveless dress covered a little more skin. He holds his hand out and I reach toward him tentatively, breath catching in my throat when he clasps it in his. That simple act of our hands being entwined makes my heart gallop way faster than it should.

"I am really nervous to be alone with you tonight," I confess.

The words spill out of my mouth before I can stop them and I look up at him, horrified. I know better than to show an opponent when I've lost my cool, and this is kind of the same thing. Right? I don't really know. I'm on guard all the time. It feels like I should be on guard with my heart more than anything else.

He smiles and something in my chest evens out. A calm thread wraps around my veins, centering me. He lifts our hands to his chest with my hand closest to his heart.

"Feel how you make my heart pound? I'm nervous too, and *nobody* makes me nervous. That's how I first knew to

641

pay attention to you." He leans over and kisses me softly. It's too quick. One second, two, before he pulls back. "There. I feel better already. But it didn't slow my heart down a bit. Have you *seen* the way you look tonight?"

My face hurts from trying to hold back my smile and I finally give in to it.

We start walking toward the back of the house and when we get near the kitchen, I think we're going to stop by to pick up our food, but he surprises me by walking past. We walk outside and wind around the pool and the gardens. Instead of taking the steps down toward the beach, we walk up the path of the mountain with the best views.

It's not a long walk, but he tends to me along the way, making sure that I'm steady on my feet and not running into any of the overhanging branches as we make our way to the top. It's sweet, his attentiveness. I'm used to providing it, not receiving it, and for a second, I let his words about marrying him tonight flood my mind before I shush the madness.

When we reach the top, there's a table set up with candles and I look around to see who's left this magical setting. No one is in sight and when I stare at Silas in shock, he looks both proud and shy.

"You did all this?"

There are covered plates on the table, flowers, and next to the table is a pile of pillows and blankets.

For watching the sky.

Definitely not for anything but that.

My face heats as I imagine us consumed by each other right here under the stars and on top of the world.

"This is beautiful. You keep surprising me."

"In a good way, I hope?" he asks.

"In the best way."

He leads me to my seat and fills our wine glasses. When he sits down and looks at me, the quiet surrounding us soothes out the rough edges of the day.

PEACE

The stillness I feel inside, the calm, in the midst of the havoc Silas is creating in my heart, seems it should be at odds with one another, but it's anything but.

"What are you thinking right now?" he asks.

"I'm thinking you have cast a spell on me, Silas Pega, and I am one hundred percent here for it."

His face lights up and I have the thought once again that marrying him doesn't seem like a bad idea at all.

Chapter 8

Silas

Six months later…

My sister touches my Caninsula wedding stones intricately stitched on the left side of my suit before kissing my cheek.

"I'm so excited for you, Silas. If someone had told me I'd feel this way about you marrying someone from another kingdom, I wouldn't have believed them, but that was before I met Brienne…before I saw how perfect you are together. You know I've never believed in insta-love, but you knew the moment you saw her, didn't you?"

"I did. It wasn't something I imagined happening before her. But I've never doubted this for a second. If I could have married her six months ago, I would've in a heartbeat."

Nila laughs and steps back, her hand dropping from my cheek. "It didn't take you very long to convince her, in my opinion. You've left a trail of broken hearts back home though."

"They'll recover." I laugh.

"It's time. Are you ready?"

"Long past," I say, grinning at her.

We walk outside and up to the spot where Brienne and I watched the night sky on our first date, where I could see her walls chipping away, and she gave me the hope I needed to keep pursuing here. Hope that I'd be standing in front of her today, marrying her.

A few weeks after that, I claimed her body up here too and swore I'd never leave her side if she'd have me. It's powerful simply when we're in the same room together, but when I'm driving into her as deep as I can go and she's panting my name, pulsing around me like she'll never get enough, it's another level of explosive. Something that will keep me coming back for more every day of my life.

Luka, Elias, King Jadon from Farrow, and my brother-in-law, Josiah, are standing near the floral archway we set up for this day. My family arrived earlier in the week—it's felt more like a wedding week than a wedding day—and they're mingling with our friends, looking like they've all known each other forever.

I get in place and wait eagerly to catch sight of Brienne. I never thought I'd be the kind of man who wanted to seal the deal with *marriage*, but so help me, she does that to me. My breath catches in my throat when I see her walk around the corner, her blond curls cascading down her back and her smile radiant. Her long blue gown matches her eyes and the sea, and she's a goddess, pure and simple. The fact that she loves me is something that will never cease to astound me.

When she reaches me, I take her hand. "Are you really marrying me?" I whisper, grinning.

"With all my heart," she whispers back.

Luka, dressed in his custom Niapsian finery, greets our guests before addressing Brienne and me.

"I still remember the call I received from Silas the day he saw Brienne. He sounded like someone who had been beat up but more excited than I'd ever heard him. And then, one look at Brienne after he arrived, and I knew if anyone could wrangle the heart of our dear Brienne, it would be Silas."

Our guests laugh and Luka steps aside to let King Jadon perform an ancient Farrow wedding tradition. It involves two cords and I follow Brienne's lead with the movements, unable to stop staring at her.

Jadon's words are simple, yet profound. "Honor and

respect one another, believe the best in one another, but above all, *love* one another. God grant you an abiding love." He kisses Brienne on either cheek, their adoration for each other apparent, and he does the final twists with the cords, making the elaborate work come apart with one tug…only now it's one cord instead of two.

My eyes blur with tears as I look at her, but my words are low and steady.

"Our love knows no bounds. Our differences are one more thing to love about each other, from the tones in our skin as we're lying side by side, to all the foods we're discovering from each other, and even at times, the ways we have had to learn to communicate if we don't understand something about the way one of us has been raised. You accept me and I accept you, completely. And because of this, the ways we come together to find out how we're the same are all the more beautiful. You're unlike anyone I've ever known, Brienne, and I want every today, every tomorrow—all of forever—with you."

She smiles and a tear drops down her cheek. She squeezes my hand and I can't tell which of us is trembling.

"I didn't know how much I was missing until I met you," she says. And that's when a tear makes its way down my cheek. "You make everything more beautiful, more fun—more meaningful—with your love of life and your love for me. I love everything about you." I reach out to wipe her cheek and she leans into my hand. "Marrying you sounds like the best life I could possibly live and I am *so ready*."

I can't help myself—I wrap my arms around her and kiss her.

Our guests clap and cheer as Luka announces, "Silas and Brienne Pega, everyone!"

I get lost in her and she's the one to pull away, her eyes sparkling and lips swollen.

"We'll revisit that later," she says.

PEACE

"Promise?"

She leans into my side and we lift our hands in the air, turning to our friends and family.

"I promise!" she yells happily.

Brienne

A few hours later...

"You. Feel. So. Good," he says with every thrust.

My head thrashes against the pillow. I'm so close and he's loving dragging out this tormenting pleasure. "Silas," I whisper, unable to be more coherent than that. In the next breath, I'm shattering around him and he swallows my groans with a searing kiss.

Then his head falls back and he follows me into oblivion. I will never get tired of this. Since our very first time six months ago, it's been like this—an earth-shattering connection. I can't imagine that it can get any better, but each time it does.

Later, we're wrapped around each other, the only sounds our breathing and the waves beating against the sand.

He turns toward me and his fingers feather across my chest. "How do you feel?"

"Completely blissed out. I can't believe my life." I trace across eyebrows and down his nose to his plush lips.

"I don't want a day to go by without making you feel this way."

"Game on," I repeat his words back to him from early in our relationship and he laughs, remembering.

"Oh, it is so on."

About the Author

Willow Aster is a USA Today bestselling author and lover of everything book-related. Although an introvert, this lifelong writer is convinced that the best part of this career is meeting and connecting with readers and authors.

She lives in St. Paul, MN, with her husband, kids, and rescue dog.

Website: www.willowaster.com

Facebook Author Page: https://www.facebook.com/willowasterauthor/

Instagram: https://www.instagram.com/willowaster/

Bookbub: https://www.bookbub.com/authors/willow-aster

Amazon: https://www.amazon.com/Willow-Aster/e/B00E4N2MIC

Goodreads: https://www.goodreads.com/author/show/6863360.Willow_Aster

Made in the USA
Monee, IL
19 February 2021

59621820R00367